If They Knew

Sophie Flynn is a Cotswolds based psychological thriller author with an MA in Creative Writing from Oxford Brookes. Alongside writing, Sophie is the Head of Marketing at Jericho Writers.

Also by Sophie Flynn

All My Lies
Keep Them Close
If They Knew

if they knew

SOPHIE FLYNN

hera

First published in the United Kingdom in 2022 by

Hera Books
Unit 9 (Canelo), 5th Floor
Cargo Works, 1–2 Hatfields
London SE1 9PG
United Kingdom

A CIP catalogue record for this book is available from the British Library.

Print ISBN 978 1 80436 085 9
Ebook ISBN 978 1 80436 080 4

Cover design by Rose Cooper

Look for more great books at www.herabooks.com

Printed and bound in Great Britain by Clays Ltd, Elcograf S.p.A.

1

To all the parents-in-waiting

Chapter One

Now

Hannah

All of the couples in the waiting room look just like us: scared, shell-shocked, hopeful. The man opposite us jigs his foot relentlessly, one leg folded at the knee taking up all the space between him and his wife. She is dwarfed in comparison, her body so curled in on itself it's amazing she takes up any room at all. Her eyes flit between the clock and his foot, as if it's his obsessive movement that's powering the tick of its hands.

Charlie squeezes my hand and I sit back in my seat. His legs are pressed together at the knee, straight, solid. Still. His feet don't tap, his eyes don't roam the room; he simply stares at the door. Waiting for it to open, waiting for our names to be called.

It's not that this day doesn't mean as much to Charlie as it does to all other nervous couples in here – it probably means more – this is just the way my husband is. Unflappable, his mum often calls him. Cool in a crisis. And that's been helpful these last few years when we have raced from one crisis to another and I have simply let myself be blown away with it all while he stands stock still, blocking as much of the impact from me as he can. Sometimes, I've wished he would show some more emotion

– I've screamed that at him more than a few times – but I've learned to recognise the signs of feelings in him now that have nothing to do with crying or screaming or falling apart. Where I flail around in our losses, Charlie goes stiff. Right now, he is more rigid than ever.

'Charlie and Hannah Wilson?'

The smiling receptionist appears from behind the door and calls us through. We've been here often enough for her to welcome us like old friends and I feel the eyes of the other couple boring into our backs. There will be all sorts here; couples on their first appointment, slightly misty-eyed about it all still, through to couples who've already got their little miracle safe at home and are simply here for a check-in. It's strange to think that Charlie and I are right in the middle; the doe-eyed magic of it all long lost in the mountain of paperwork, but not yet secure enough to be strolling through this door completely happily. I cross my fingers and shove them in my pocket, embarrassed at my own childish rituals, still with me after all these years.

'Take a seat, Andrea will be with you in just a moment. Can I get you anything to drink? Tea? Coffee? Water?' It's been a few weeks since we've been here and I'd forgotten the rapid pace at which the receptionist speaks. I rack my brain for her name as Charlie replies.

'No thanks, Emily, we're fine.' He smiles. Of course Charlie remembers her name. Charlie remembers everything.

She exits and leaves us in silence, both too nervous to speak or even acknowledge each other. Within a few moments, Andrea walks in and I feel Charlie grow even stiffer beside me. This woman holds our hope in her hands.

'Hannah, Charlie. How are you both?' She pulls out her chair and slips into it, smiling brightly as we garble our replies. A mixture of 'good, nervous, fine,' between us.

'Good. Good. Now, I know you're both probably incredibly anxious so I'm going to cut to the chase—'

My heart bangs in a haphazard rhythm, the space between her words feeling gigantic, like we could both get lost in it. The next words Andrea says will either be the start of something or the end. Suddenly, I'm desperate to stay in the 'between' moment forever. I flick a glance at Charlie who stares resolutely forward at Andrea, his square jawline hard.

'I'm delighted to tell you that your application for Issy has been approved by the panel.'

Charlie breaks then. His hand flies to his mouth to contain the sob that starts to erupt; I'm so taken aback by it that I can't fully take in the news for a second, instead transfixed by my strong, silent husband finally letting his emotions get the better of him, if only for a moment. As if aware of my shock, he clears his throat, coughing away the sob and takes a deep breath, steadying himself. He grips my hand, a controlled smile stretching across his face as he wipes away the rogue tear he wasn't quite quick enough to contain.

'We did it,' he says to me, his voice now steady. 'We finally did it.'

–

We calm down after a few minutes of 'I can't believe it's finally happening' and other meaningless exclamations, aware that Andrea still very much has a job to do and that

3

the couples outside may not wish to have our joy rubbed in their faces. It's a tough line to tread, wanting to share success stories with hopeful parents without overstepping and parading it around. I have spent many nights enviously scrolling through strangers' Facebook profiles after they've shared their happy news on the adoption group. *We've finally been approved! Meet our new daughter.* These posts would make me hopeful and hateful at the same time. So happy that it really could happen to people just like us yet seething with jealousy that it was happening for a couple just like us, but not actually us. But now it is. Now we are the lucky couple. And isn't that what we deserve after years of being 'that poor couple who can't have babies'; after living with hundreds of 'I just don't know how you cope' statements thrown around without care? We deserve this. That's what everyone would say. Yet the old feelings of nagging guilt start tugging at me.

I shift in my seat and feel Charlie's warm hands on the dip in my back, a reassuring heaviness against my spine. There's no space here to start debating again whether I've made enough reparations for my past to deserve something good. Even if I don't, Charlie does. Charlie always has.

'So obviously we're not quite over the line just yet,' Andrea says, bringing me back to reality with a jolt.

'No,' Charlie says. 'There's still the meet-up with Isabella's foster parents before we meet her but then that's it – isn't it? – before the final home visit where you bring Isabella to ours?'

Andrea nods and Charlie looks at me. This is the part he's been preparing for. The part I've not dared to dream could really happen. It's the reason he's spent every night after work for the past two weeks retiling the kitchen and

4

bathroom, painting the bannisters, clearing the garage. As if the only thing standing in his way of becoming a dad is a less than perfect home. I wish I'd helped him more, now. But I couldn't let myself make plans for something I couldn't believe would ever happen and wasn't sure I even deserved. For Charlie it was more simple, and he was right to hope.

'When will that all start to happen?' he asks, already poised with his phone in his hand, the calendar app open.

'Well, as you well know, in this process there is usually a bit of a wait but…'

Charlie nods, he's prepared himself for this too. Throughout this entire process, right from when we started trying, totally unaware of what was to come, to now, five years on, he's marked every significant date in his calendar – both for when he knows things are happening (highlighted green) and for those he expects to happen (orange). It kept me vaguely sane throughout the IVF process, when all the other women I knew through the fertility forums would complain how in the dark they felt about the process, and how out of the loop their husbands were. I had my own hand-crafted calendar detailing how everything should run, predicted by Charlie, based on diligent research. *The NHS says you can be referred for fertility investigations after twelve months of trying if you're under thirty-five*, he told me after a few months of trying when we were thirty. *But if you think you might have an underlying health issue, they'll investigate sooner. Fancy making up an STI?* It's funny thinking about how it started, when fertility still felt like a given – something that would come to us if we just tried hard enough, wanted it bad enough.

'The stars have aligned for you two this time as we can arrange the meeting with the foster parents this

Wednesday, followed by a meeting with Issy the next day.' Andrea takes a breath. 'And then the final visit – where I'll come to the house with Issy and do the handover – will be Monday twenty-seventh at' – she checks her computer – '2pm.'

'Of September?' I ask, my heart in my throat.

'Yes, is that okay?'

I laugh. 'Yes, that's brilliant, I—'

'We thought it would take longer,' Charlie helpfully adds. 'I know that it can take a month or so but this is brilliant. That's one week today.'

'Yep.' Andrea smiles. 'I managed to pull some strings for my favourite couple.'

Tears brim and then swiftly fall down my cheeks. Charlie puts his arm around me and squeezes my shoulder. He leans in and whispers in my ear, 'I told you everything would be okay.'

'Shall I give you a moment?' Andrea asks and Charlie quickly pulls back, sits upright and shakes his head.

'No, no. We're all good, let's fill in the next forms, please.' Always the practical one.

I watch as he and Andrea go over more forms, nodding where I need to and signing the appropriate boxes but I know Charlie has this all under control, like he always does, so I let my mind wander. I picture Issy's beautiful face; her big round hazel eyes and sweet cherub curls, the dimple in her chubby cheeks and her curled up left hand, the right one not visible in the photo. I know that image of our prospective daughter so well, every inch of her painted on my memory. Will she look the same when we finally see her in real life? The photo must be six months old now, taken when she first got brought into care. When her short life changed irrevocably. They tell

6

you it's important to acknowledge to yourself, and one day to your adopted child, where they came from and the circumstances of their childhood, but I haven't quite come around to it yet. Overdose. That's how Issy's birth mother died. Only nineteen, barely out of childhood herself. Her eighteen-month-old daughter left screaming in her cot for over twenty-four hours before any of the neighbours bothered to call the police. She wasn't the sort of woman people care about all that much.

Charlie fell in love the second Issy's name came up on the adoption portal.

'Isabella,' he said one morning when I was racing around the kitchen before work. 'Don't you love that name? Isabella. Isabella Wilson.'

I stopped what I was doing and turned to face him. He was sitting at the breakfast bar, his eyes glued to his phone. We'd been doing this for long enough that I didn't have to ask him what he meant.

'When was she added?' I asked, grabbing the phone from his hands.

'Two minutes ago—'

'Put a request in!' I shouted. 'Now!'

Charlie laughed then rested his hand on my shoulder, fixing me with those big, calm brown eyes, and told me he already had.

You don't understand what it's like before you've gone through the process. The way that you have to make a decision based on nothing but a name, gender, age and a few thrown-together facts. *Isabelle loves feeding the ducks and eating strawberry-flavoured yoghurts.* So often it's about speed. They tell you it's not, the adoption services; that everyone's applications get reviewed equally but we learned early on that if you didn't get your name down for a child within the first twenty minutes of them becoming available on the site, it's very likely your application would never see the light of day. Luckily for us, Charlie works from home on his computer all day and set up a special alert to notify us as soon as any updates were made to the site. Part of me wondered if this was unfair, if we'd get bad karma for using Charlie's professional tech skills to give us the upper hand, but after a few months of getting absolutely nowhere with our applications, I realised none of this is fair to begin with so why not use all the tools at our disposal?

'So, nothing to do between now and then. Just focus on keeping yourselves calm and happy. This period can get quite stressful because it's the final hurdle,' Andrea tells us with a small smile and knowing eyes. She was born to do this job. She's been our adoption representative since day one and I'm so grateful we have her. She's around our age and has two little girls herself – naturally, I believe, though I've not been bold enough to ask.

'We'll try and keep calm,' I say. 'In between cleaning and repainting half the house...' I look at Charlie and laugh.

'Honestly, every couple I have in here tells me the same at this stage. It's perfectly natural, your own kind of "nesting period". Enjoy it, you're almost there.'

Andrea sees us out of the office, back into the room of hopeful faces. I avoid the other couple's eyes as Charlie basically skips through the room. I feel the envy radiating from them.

'I'm just going to pop to the bathroom, Charlie,' I tell him, tugging his jumper, hoping instinctively he'll understand he needs to stop flaunting our good fortune.

'I'll go bring the car around,' he tells me, grinning from ear to ear. Despite feeling like all eyes are on us, happiness trickles through me and I return his goofy smile. Once he's skipped through the doors, I turn towards the bathroom down the corridor on the left. You pass another waiting room this way; it's bigger and quite often full of children coming in with their adoptive parents for catch-ups with the resident psychologist.

As I pass through the room, I notice the eyes of almost everyone are glued to the television on the wall. I stop and look up to see what they're all watching.

'Breaking News' from the BBC flashes on the screen, the red ticker tape scrolling too fast for me to make out at first. Terrorist attack, I think immediately. London, probably. But no.

It's not a large-scale tragedy.

Not in the scheme of things.

To most people, this is barely a tragedy at all. And yet I feel the ground shake beneath me as my eyes take it in.

> Infamous pop star Jesse Carter, 38, found dead at elite Oxfordshire members' club. More information to come.

'Are you okay?' Suddenly, a stranger is in front of me, her eyes wide. 'Do you need to sit down?'

I swallow, then breathe in, unaware I was holding my breath. The whole room is staring at me and I feel sweat trickling down my back. My whole body is on fire.

Jesse is dead.

I run from the room down the hallway to the bathroom where I throw up every last morsel from my stomach.

Chapter Two

ONE WEEK UNTIL ISSY COMES HOME

Now

Hannah

'Are you sure you're okay?' Charlie asks me again as we pull onto the main road.

'I'm fine, I've said I'm fine—'

'You're shaking, Han.' He takes one hand off the steering wheel and rests it on my knee. 'Talk to me.'

How can I possibly begin to explain this to him? Jesse's face blurs as I try to remember him as he once was and not the infamous pop star he'll now be forever known as. But no, I don't want to think of him. I can't bear to have him occupy any space where Charlie is; it feels like a whole other betrayal.

'I know it's a lot to take in, believe me, I'm nervous too,' Charlie carries on. 'But this is what we wanted; it's what we've dreamed of for years. I promise you everything will be okay.' He squeezes my knee then puts his hands back on the steering wheel, taking up his ten-and-two position once again.

I let a tear drip down my cheek as guilt washes over me. I shouldn't be thinking about anything right now except for Issy; this moment should be one of the happiest in our lives. It's the equivalent of seeing two pink lines on the pregnancy test; knowing that you've taken the first big step towards becoming a real family and praying to God that the luck doesn't run out before someone official can make it real.

'I'm sorry,' I say through the tears. 'It's just... I want her so much, Charlie. I almost can't bear it.'

'I know, darling. I know.'

I close my eyes and rest my forehead against the window for the rest of the drive home, telling myself that Jesse's death has nothing to do with me. I don't have a right to grieve, or feel anything at all. But I do – deep down, if I let myself admit it, I feel more than just grief: I feel relief. Because surely now he's gone, there's one less person alive who knows the truth about me? If I keep telling myself these things, over and over, perhaps I'll start to believe it.

—

Charlie reluctantly drops me back at the office before heading home. I assured him I was perfectly fine to go back to work; that I'd much rather have something to focus on and keep me busy than spend the afternoon worrying at home. He didn't look at all happy about this but relented in the end. We have quite different outlooks on work, Charlie and I. For him, it's something he has to endure to get the things he wants – a nice home, no worries about bills, holidays with me. For me, work is much more than that. My job gives me a purpose, it always has.

As soon as I walk through the doors to the office, Kate appears with a coffee in hand. 'How did it go?' She ushers me into the meeting room before anyone else has a chance to even notice I'm here. 'Here, have this. I made it for me but you look like you need it.'

I gulp the too-strong coffee before I let myself reply. Kate eyes me eagerly and I wish more than anything I could confide in her, but I know that's not an option.

'We got approved—'

'Oh my god!' She screams, making me spill my coffee down the front of my shirt. 'Shit, sorry. But fucking hell, Hannah! That's amazing!' She pulls me in for a tight hug and I smell the scent of her sickly sweet perfume; such a contrast with the harsh exterior she presents to the world. 'I bet you can't believe it,' she says, pushing me back so she can look at me again.

'Not really, no.'

'Have you told Diane?' she asks, referring to Charlie's mum.

'Charlie will tell her today,' I say, though I didn't check this with Charlie.

'God, she's going to be so excited. And what about your parents?'

I sigh. 'I haven't yet. I will.' I try to imagine phoning my dad with the news and hearing his reaction but the truth is I can't add any more stress to my plate and interactions with them always end that way. We barely speak now since I moved here and they brought on various 'lodgers' to stay in our falling-down Devonshire house to help pay the electricity bills. It's got worse in recent years; they never approved of IVF, finding it unbelievable that I could want to be a mother that badly, as if it made me some sort of 1950s housewife.

'I'm sure they'll be thrilled, Han. Don't worry.' Kate squeezes my hand, well aware of my difficult relationship with my parents. Her kindness threatens to topple me.

'Oh Han, don't cry. What's wrong? Was there something else? What's happened?'

I wipe my face with the back of my hand as Kate rummages in my handbag for a tissue. 'Nothing. It's just… hard to believe, you know? We've wanted this for so long and it feels so close now, but still like anyone could come and take it away from us.' The last bit is said through such a sob that I wonder if Kate can even make out the words.

'Han, you said it yourself that once you were approved all the other visits and meetings are just to make you and Issy more comfortable, right?'

I nod. 'We have to meet the foster parents on Wednesday, then there's the group meet-up with all of us, and finally the home visit and handover this time next week.'

Kate smiles broadly. 'So this is the best bit, right? Stop thinking of them as stages you have to "pass" and enjoy them. You get to finally meet Issy in real life and, Jesus, if you think for a second that anyone would come to your home and find it not fit for a child then you're bonkers.'

'But it's not just the house they'll be judging… it's us.'

'What, the two people so bloody perfect to be parents it's an absolute crime that the universe has made it so hard for them? Come on, darling, you know that you and Charlie will make amazing parents. What do you think they could possibly find out about either of you that would put them off?'

I can't look at her then, my kind, trusting friend who has absolutely no idea of the things I've done. Instead, I hug her again and tell her I love her.

It's a funny relationship really, mine and Kate's. Technically, I'm her manager, which means that breaking down crying on her shoulder and telling her I love her should be wildly inappropriate. But we've known each other, and worked together, for six years now and I think any barriers between us are long dead. Charlie finds it all rather baffling, coming from a corporate background where his team members are no more his friends than the guy who delivers our post, but at WomenGoFree, it's a family environment. When the owner of the charity relocated from London to a small village for a quieter life, she set up the head office here in the Cotswolds and I came with her. I was only the communications assistant back then, renting a cheap, cramped room from an elderly couple in Little Tew, the village next to where we live now. Despite the less than luxurious lodgings, I knew from day one that I'd found my place here. Now, I'm on the leadership team running the communications department and more sure than ever that this is the best place for me. Somewhere I can help women rebuild their lives after abuse from behind the scenes; a way to right the wrongs of the past. Kate joined just before our infertility struggles began, and has since become one of the most important people in my life.

'I guess you haven't even seen the news,' Kate says when we're back at our desks, which are opposite each other in a large, open-plan room. The rest of my small team have their heads down, typing away fiercely as if their lives depend on it. 'About Jesse Carter?'

A stab of pain registers in my stomach at his name but I'm more worried about the heat that's taken over my body, my face and neck no doubt flushing, alerting the office to my discomfort. 'Oh, yeah, I did—'

'Good riddance,' Kate says. 'That's what I say.'

Carleigh, one of the youngest members of the team, joins in then. 'My mate tried to go to the gym there this morning and they wouldn't let her in—'

'Wouldn't have pegged you as mixing with The Farm lot!' Kate replies.

Carleigh shrugs but her cheeks glow slightly pink. 'Well, just a school friend. Family thing, you know?'

Kate rolls her eyes at me and I know she expects me to join in with this bashing of the elite private members' club that's just up the road like I usually would, but I can't, not today.

'Does she know what happened?' I ask.

Carleigh shakes her head. 'No, she just said the security up there is crazy. Like, even more so than usual. Loads of the members were kicking up a fuss apparently, super pissed off that they couldn't get in for their workout.' This time it's Carleigh who rolls her eyes and Kate laughs.

'Poor little rich folk, so inconvenient when a dead body ruins your day.'

'Kate—' I say.

'What? Come on, Han. That guy was a parasite.'

'Yeah, he really was,' Carleigh adds. 'My friend didn't see him while he's been staying there but her mate did and apparently he was a total letch to the younger girls. Like, buying them shots, hands all over one of them. It's gross. He's like forty.'

'I bet it'll all come out now,' Kate says, knowingly. 'It always does once they die.'

'What will?' My question comes out sounding more desperate than I intended and they both look at me in shock, but I need to know what they know. 'What will come out?'

'Oh you must have heard the rumours,' Carleigh says, a small smile on her plump pink lips, too young to be marked with wrinkles. 'They've been going around for years. You know, the usual Hollywood men bullshit—'

'I wish we were able to publicly say something about him,' Kate interrupts, her voice clear and determined as my stomach churns.

'What?'

'What, like you wouldn't want to?' She scoffs. 'Imagine how much more powerful our work would be if we could stand up and call out men like Jesse Carter. Abusers get away with this shit their whole lives and then they die and people act like they were some sort of hero – but he wasn't. Everyone knows he wasn't. The only reason he's got away with it for so long is because people have been scared—'

'He's never been charged with anything,' I cut in.

Carleigh shakes her head. 'No 'cause he's got that slimy PR guy on his side. You know the one, looks like a rat.'

Owen's too-long face fills my mind and I squeeze my eyes shut to be rid of him.

'Yeah! These men always have someone doing their dirty work. Seriously, Han, I know we can't say anything about him specifically but is there anything we can do that would reference it subtly?'

'Like a subtweet!' Carleigh chips in and I tilt my head, unsure of the reference but Kate jumps on it.

'Exactly! We're supposed to stand for not allowing men to get away with it and we hardly ever speak up when something like this happens—'

'This has nothing to do with us,' I say, trying to keep my voice stable while my whole world is imploding. 'We're not going to tarnish the name of a dead man just—'

'Tarnish his name? Are you joking? Jesse Carter's abuse of women is one of the most well-known secrets in the music business!' Kate's eyes burn with fury as she looks at me like I'm a stranger. I close my eyes, both to block out her anger and to stop the memories of Jesse playing in my head. The flashes of that night; his face against mine as he pulls me from the floor. *Get up*, I hear his gruff voice say, *Hannah, you have to get up.*

'Hannah!' Kate's voice breaks my thoughts and I flick open my eyes. She's still glaring at me but now there's some concern behind her frown.

We are always on the same side; this is unknown territory for us. Usually, I back Kate's anger enough to get us the goal she wants, even if I can't back the delivery. Kate has more righteous anger than I ever could; she knows without a doubt that she is on the right side of things. For me, it's a little blurrier. So I can't be as bold, I won't push as hard as Kate, and she doesn't always know when to back down. It's why we're such a good team, but right now I wish she would just shut up.

'None of us know anything about Jesse Carter,' I say, loud and clear. 'And it certainly has nothing to do with our work – which is the actual reason we're all here.'

The rest of the team is staring at us now, open-mouthed at my blatant show of hierarchy, something I never do, especially with Kate. She stares at me with her lips pursed for a second before standing up.

'Wow, really? So a known scumbag has died up the road from us and yet we're all just going to pretend it has nothing at all to do with our work here? Jesse Carter abused women. Everyone knows it. And if you won't stand up for silent victims even in the safety of this office, then I don't even know what you're doing here.'

With that, she turns and walks out of the office, leaving me alone to face the disappointed looks from every woman on my team, my eyes swimming with tears, my mind full of Jesse's face. The face I promised myself I'd let go.

Chapter Three

Then

New York

I can't actually believe that I'm in a bunk bed. A bunk bed?! I'm nineteen years old so it should feel totally embarrassing and awful, but it's not just any bunk bed. It's a bunk bed in *New York*!!!

Even writing it down sends a fizz of excitement through my stomach. I can't believe I'm actually here. Right from the moment I got the letter telling me that I'd been accepted for the scholarship to study music here, I imagined someone was going to come and tell me it was a joke, or they'd made a mistake. I never believed I'd really get here. But I am. I'm at college in New York.

Okay, so it's not *exactly* like I'd imagined.

There are three of us in the dorm room. As if a bunk bed wasn't saving enough space on its own, the college has also managed to squeeze another single bed opposite us against the far wall. Apparently they over-accepted on housing applications this semester so we all have to share. Which is fine! It's fine. Who needs loads of space when you're in New York City?

There is a slight sting when I think about the cost of the room, though. When I asked my roommates about whether us sharing one room between three instead of two meant we would get a reduction in our room rent they looked at me like I'd spoken another language.

'Erm, maybe? You'd have to ask at student services,' Ari said, twiddling her long curls around her fingers.

'Maybe I will,' I said, unsure of myself. I added with a laugh, 'I mean, we pay $12,000 between the three of us for this room for the semester? That's mental!'

They both just looked at me and shrugged and I realised then that the reason they weren't concerned by our situation was that they literally had no idea what it cost. Their rent money certainly wasn't coming from their own bank accounts. As soon as I brought it up, I regretted it. Moaning about the room made me sound like a total brat, but I suppose it's easy not to care about being ripped off when it isn't your money.

Ari and Zia won't get that, obviously.

But I'm not going to let this one tiny thing ruin my mood. I am in New York, studying music. I am living my dream!

And okay, yeah, I didn't imagine living my dream would involve sleeping in bunk beds but I can make do. The college isn't really like I imagined at all, to be honest; it's not like you see on films. I re-watched the Harvard years of *Gilmore Girls* before I came and got totally obsessed with Rory and Paris' little apartment in it; they had a living room and everything. We've got one oblong brightly lit room with one set of drawers each and a bed, and we share the bathroom with the other twenty-four girls on our floor. Dad says I must be exaggerating; 'You're at the most exclusive, expensive college in New York, how could it be that bad?' He laughed when I told him but he's got no idea. He saw my uni halls in first year and admitted they were a bit grimy but at least we had a kitchen, our own bedroom and a bathroom.

But anyway, I need to stop focusing on all the downsides, be more positive.

This is where my life begins.

No more Mum and Dad draining the life out of me whenever I go home for a visit, seeing their shrunken forms diminishing every few weeks. No more Exeter open mic nights with middle-aged men manning the mics. No more shy, sad, lonely Hannah.

I'm going to be a totally different person here.

I'm going to be the confident, funny, British singer-songwriter who rocks up to open mics on her own, guitar strapped on her back, and takes to the stage without a moment's hesitation.

I can do this.

Here, I can do anything.

Chapter Four

Now

Hannah

I already know it's Kate from the way she knocks on the door. *Knock. Knock-knock.* She always does it like that, like she starts patiently enough but within seconds grows tired of waiting and has to hit the door twice in a row to show her frustration.

'Come in,' I eventually say when I've left her hanging just long enough to let her know that all is not quite yet forgiven.

Kate walks through the door and gives me a sad, almost apologetic smile but there's still a hint of defiance in her green eyes. This isn't going to be an easy conversation.

'Look,' she says, taking the seat opposite me. 'I'm sorry for flaring up like that. I know it wasn't appropriate in front of the others—'

'Erm, it wasn't nice either way, Kate, not just because there were juniors around.'

'Well, no, but you know what I mean. That made it worse.'

I nod. We're in one of the private rooms in the office. Our HR team likes to call it a 'break-out space' but really it's a small meeting room with a station to work at if you need to get away from prying ears or noisy mouths.

'But surely… surely you understand where I'm coming from?' Her eyes plead with me across the desk and I grit my teeth. 'Oh come on, Hannah. What's going on with you? Is it Issy?'

'Is what Issy?'

She flings her hands up and scoffs. 'This!' She gestures towards me as if my mere presence is a source of great disappointment. 'The way you're reacting to that prick's death. You're usually just as on them as I am.'

I shake my head. 'You don't know anything about him.'

'When do we ever know anything about celebrities?' She narrows her eyes but her look of fury has been replaced with total and utter confusion. 'Look, I get that you've got a lot on right now, and the next week is going to be super stressful. I spoke to Marcy just now—'

'What? Why?'

'Because I'm worried about you.'

'So you went behind my back to HR?'

She rolls her eyes and shakes her head. 'You know it's not like that. She caught me in the kitchen and asked how you were coping with everything.'

I let out a choked laugh. 'Great, very professional to be discussing private details of your employees—'

'She knows I know! Of course she knows. And she heard our argument, Han. Everyone did.' Her cheeks flash with embarrassment and she looks away. 'Why won't you tell me how you feel? What's wrong?'

'Nothing,' I say, quickly followed by, 'everything.'

'See, this is what I mean, Han.' Kate flops back in her chair, exasperated. 'You've got so much on outside of work and I think you need to take a step back. I know you think you can do everything – be the superwoman you always are – but Marcy and I were just wondering if—'

'If what?'

Kate rolls her eyes. 'Han, stop with the attitude. You're acting like I've gone behind your back here, I haven't – Marcy just caught me while I was making tea. But this isn't about you, or me, this is about the charity.'

I grind my teeth as tears prick at my eyes. How has Jesse got into every aspect of my life so quickly? I've kept him hidden for fifteen years and yet here he is now, ruining everything even from beyond the grave.

'I need to call Charlie,' I say, getting up from the table. Kate reaches into her bag and shoves a file into my hand.

'Fine, but please can you at least read these?'

'What are they?'

'It's about Jesse Carter. Stories from women that someone online has been collecting. Han, so many people are already speaking up about his death, to make sure he doesn't go down in history as a glorious rock star. It's unlikely that this won't become a media story soon; we should be prepared.'

I stalk out of the room, the papers gripped in my sweaty hand.

Kate doesn't follow as I make my way out of the office onto the lane outside. It's a bright, brisk September day, the sort that Charlie loves, and I wish I'd brought my jacket. That's the problem with storming out of places; you're never quite prepared. I walk down the lane into the village, it's only five minutes or so but we're basically down a farm track so every step is a hopscotch between potholes to avoid a broken ankle. By the time I reach the village, I've calmed down somewhat and am vaguely embarrassed by my outburst. Kate will think I've totally lost it. I should have never let myself get publicly worked up about Jesse. It's not like men in power dying, leaving behind a trail of abuse, is something we've not dealt with before. But we never make statements; that's not who we are as a charity. We focus on helping women rebuild their lives by finding them housing, providing coaching for job interviews and anything else they need. We don't go after the 'bad guys' and now is no different.

The village is quiet – it often is in the week, the tourists not yet set free – but particularly at two thirty on a Monday afternoon. I have around thirty minutes before the mothers of the village descend; I always avoid school times wherever I go now. We both do, Charlie and I. It became too painful eventually, to see everyone around us get everything we wanted as if it was easy. But I don't have that luxury today; I need to be out of the office, and I need somewhere to read the reports about Jesse without a million eyes on me.

The café is quiet as I walk in, there are a few dog walkers and tourists enjoying coffee and cakes but I can't see anyone from the village who'll want to chat which is a relief.

'Afternoon, Hannah!'

'Hi.' I force a smile at Roger, the cafe owner, then stare at the menu behind his head. I know it by heart, but I can't get into a conversation with him today, and Roger really does love to chat.

'How are you today? Busy at the office?' he asks while I stare.

'Mmm,' I murmur. 'Always busy. Could I get a decaf flat white with oat milk, please?'

Roger nods before I even finish the sentence, my standard hipster order suiting the vibe of his Instagram-worthy café perfectly.

'Actually,' I say, 'regular flat white today, please.'

He raises his eyebrows. 'Absolutely. Coming right up.'

I thank him and walk to the table in the corner where I can see out to the street but you can't see in. After a moment, he brings over the coffee and I look at it in wonder. Caffeine. Proper milk. I gave up both years and years ago after reading about the negative impacts on both for fertility. Even though we accepted over eighteen months ago that no matter how many rounds of IVF we did, I'd never carry a child, the habit stuck. Deep down, perhaps I hadn't quite given up on the hope of my body sorting itself out. That's the problem when after years of tests and investigations, you're left only with the non-diagnosis of 'unexplained infertility'. Letting go of the hope that the mystery of your body might one day magic-ally fix itself is hard. Near impossible. But today, I don't need to hold onto that last glimmer of hope any more. Today, Issy is all the hope I need. I take a mouthful of the coffee and instantly feel the buzz of caffeine swimming in my veins. I smile and close my eyes. Soon I won't need to avoid this place at three p.m. either. Soon, perhaps I can be just like the other mothers who sit here proudly, knowing without a shred of doubt that they belong.

But first… First, I have to deal with Jesse.

–

Half an hour later, I feel like I might throw up again. Whether it's the effect of caffeine and whole milk after years of abstaining or because of everything I've read, who

26

knows. But I can feel the sticky veil of sweat across my top lip and the familiar thud of panic in my chest. I spread the papers across my small table, reading the headlines afresh.

> Poster Boy for 'Getting Away With It' Murdered in Hotel Room

> Jesse Carter: Another one bites the dust. Revenge murder? We can only hope...

> I've known men like Jesse Carter and I'm glad he's dead

Murdered? The word sticks in my throat. That's not what the news said earlier – that's not what I thought... Oh my god. This is worse than I could have ever imagined. I assumed there would be reports of an overdose; a party gone too far, possibly a horrible accident. But murder? This changes everything.

I flit my eyes across the headlines again, desperate to see something that tells me I've read it wrong – that the world isn't shouting out for everyone to hear that Jesse's death is something cold and calculated. Kate has obviously been scouring the depths of the internet for these reports. It's not the coverage the rest of the world will be reading today; instead she's looked in places that most people never think to. Opinion pieces in female-run journals, press releases from some of the more controversial women's aid centres, and of course, Twitter. I open BBC News on my phone which provides momentary relief.

> Beloved Pop Star Found Dead at Elite Cotswold Members' Club

Beloved. But no mention of murder.

Where's the truth? To some, Jesse is a monster who deserves his fate, but to many today's news will be a tragedy. I know enough about reporting restrictions to know that reputable organisations won't call it murder until the police release that, but small journals and blogs will have no problem hedging their bets based on rumours alone. And the thing I've learned about rumours is that they usually turn out to be true.

'Hannah!' I hear my name being called in a happy sing-song voice across the cafe and inwardly groan. It's Olivia, the wife of one of Charlie's friends from the village. It's not that I don't like Olivia, it's just that—

'How exciting, we never see you in here during the week, do we, Pops?' Olivia has made her way over to me with one-year-old Poppy in tow – quite literally the prettiest baby you have ever seen. Her big hazel eyes stare up at me in wonder as she pulls at the hem of her Cath Kidston patterned dress.

'I was just heading off, actually...'

'Oh my gosh, no please, stay!'

'I'm working, I just popped out for—'

'We won't be long, ten minutes; surely they can spare you for that long?'

Before I have a chance to refuse, Olivia's plonked Poppy on my lap and gone to the counter to order, presumably for us both. Poppy continues to stare at me and I can't help but smile at her gorgeous little face, her inno-cence so alien in amongst my current thoughts. She looks so much like Olivia, with her cherubic jawline, perfect blonde ringlets and red rosy lips. Despite everything else on my mind, a familiar grief washes over me; I will never see my reflection like this. No one will ever comment on how much my daughter looks like me. I bite my lip and think of Issy; gorgeous, perfect little Issy. She may not have my genes, but she already feels so much like my daughter. That's got to be enough. It's somewhat repugnant of me to wish for more.

'Here you go, hun.' Olivia sits opposite me and pushes a cup of coffee across the table. 'I got you another flat white, that's what Roger said you were drinking.'

I thank her, thinking of my already jittering hands from the shock reintroduction of caffeine into my system.

'Mamma!' Poppy suddenly cries as she wriggles out of my grip towards Olivia who reaches for her and props her up on one knee. My arms feel empty without her so I reach for the coffee, caffeine shakes be damned.

'She's so clingy lately,' Olivia says, smiling adoringly at her daughter. 'I was warned she might be worse once Florence went off to pre-school and she certainly is. Honestly, I thought I'd have more me-time with one of them in school but it turns out not so much…' She rolls her eyes so I smile and laugh back, as if I understand the burden of being so very wanted. 'And I hear you'll soon be joining the no-sleep brigade yourself?'

Olivia gazes at me with questioning eyes and a smile curled on her lips, pleased to see the shock that must be written on my face at how fast our news has travelled. Is there also a glimmer of a challenge in her question? Does she really think I'll be just like them, the normal mums? The mums who decided to get pregnant at twenty-eight, just before their thirties hit and their fertility started to plummet, and were yummy mummies by twenty-nine? The mums who never had to think about AMH levels or DNA fragmentation tests; whose only trips to the hospital have been for joyous baby scans; who know without a doubt that they are meant to be mothers? Can I ever really be like them?

'Yes,' I say, taking another sip of my coffee. 'Well, if it all goes through—'

She waves her hand dismissively. 'Of course it will, darling. Honestly, we're all just so thrilled for you. It's such a wonderful thing you're doing, after everything you've been through.' She leans across the table and gives my hand a patronising squeeze.

I don't bother to ask her how she knows about Issy; our village is like a school yard. Nothing stays secret for long. Charlie plays football with Olivia's husband, Tim, every other Sunday morning on the green. He must have mentioned that we were in the final approval process to the team yesterday; perhaps he was nervous about today and wanted someone other than me to talk to about it. It's very like Olivia to assume that this morning's meeting went well; everything in her life does. But I can't be annoyed anymore at things like this; I realised years ago that infertility puts you into this strange category of people where your most private moments become ripe for public consumption. When your body won't do what it's supposed to, everyone feels like they're entitled to give you their opinion.

Just relax! It always happens when you least expect it.

You just need a break. My friend/sister/aunty/cousin did IVF for five years and as soon as they stopped, got pregnant with twins!

You need to go organic and vegan. Dairy is responsible for SO many health problems, you wouldn't believe it!

Of course, none of their tips worked. Nothing worked. We went from being told, 'You're young, don't worry you have ages!' to, 'You're still the right side of thirty-five' to finally, 'Given your age and lack of response so far, it might be time to start looking at other options'. So now instead, we endure the stories of adoption. Stories of families bringing home perfect babies only to discover years later they'd suffered abuse and were so traumatised by it they wrecked the family home. Stories of biological mothers turning up years later, clean and sober and ready to take back their children. Stories of failing to bond, of never fitting in with the biological siblings no matter what the parents did.

We've heard it all.

I don't know why people tell us these stories. I'm quite certain half of them are not even true, but it seems like people feel the need to do a public service announcement when they hear we are trying to adopt. As if they don't relay these urban myths of when it all went wrong, then we might befall the same fate. As if we have walked into this whole thing completely blindly. As if we haven't had to endure more paperwork than you'd ever think possible; information videos, instructional classes, informal interviews, formal interviews. There is nothing we have not done and do not know to prepare for adoption. And yet...

'You'll have to bring her to the toddler music class in the village,' Olivia says in her sing-song voice. 'She'll love it!'

I murmur some sort of agreement, too terrified of things going wrong to be able to make such flippant plans. But Olivia doesn't know that; Olivia has no idea what it's like to feel such a tentative hold on your future. In one week, we could be parents of a toddler. Or, we could fail the final processes and be nothing. Just the two of us. Only time will tell.

'I really have to get back to work,' I say, eyeing the door where a crowd of mothers and school children have begun to gather. I gather up my things and shove the articles about Jesse into my bag, but I'm too slow and Olivia catches sight of one of them.

'Oh, god! I read about that this morning. They're saying he was murdered now, you know. Can you believe it? Just up the road.' Her eyes go wide and she shakes her head in mock horror but it's glee that shines in her eyes. 'You would never think it could happen there! It's so safe; their security really is excellent. We were there on Saturday morning for a coffee, and, well, I shouldn't say but you know, now he's dead it's hardly like the privacy rules have to be followed...'

My heart thuds in my chest as I wait for Olivia to continue her gossip. She bites on her lower lip and looks around the now full cafe before leaning in, conspiratorially, to talk in a hushed whisper.

'He looked terrible—'

'Who?'

She rolls her eyes and tuts, annoyed at me breaking her flow. 'Jesse Carter! Who do you think?'

'You saw him?' Blood rushes to my cheeks but Olivia doesn't notice, too caught up at being able to put herself at the centre of a scandal.

'Yep, he was having breakfast right next to us. I said to Tim at the time, he isn't half as good-looking in person. He looked like he'd not slept in weeks; so much older than you see on his Instagram! But I suppose that's filters for you.' She sits back and chuckles to herself at that last part and I resist the urge to grab her and beg her to tell me more. 'Something was off with him, though. He was sitting with another man, about the same age but not anyone, you know… he wasn't famous. They were arguing.' Her eyes light up with this latest fact. 'I'm sure I'll be called in to give a statement to the police, you know, as a witness. I could very well have been one of the last people to see him alive.'

My mouth is dry as I try to unpick the flurry of emotions that flow through me. For so long, Jesse has felt so removed from any part of real life that I could pretend to myself that he wasn't a person at all; that he was just a character that would pop up in gossip magazines or late-night chat shows that I would be quick to turn over from. But hearing Olivia so casually refer to him as a real person, a person who sat right next to her a few miles from where we are right now, it's almost unreal.

'I just wonder why he was here, you know? I know everyone loves The Farm, but he didn't look like he was here for a getaway. And that's really why everyone goes. Why else would you come all the way from America to a village in the middle of nowhere?' Olivia shrugs and shakes her head. 'Still, I'm sure we'll all find out soon.'

'What do you mean?'

'Well, the police will be asking all those questions, won't they? It's going to become a murder investigation! They'll find out everything there is to know about Jesse Carter.'

I slam my chair back in a panic, causing all eyes in the cafe to turn to me. Olivia's mouth forms a perfect O as she stares up at me but I can't even bring myself to apologise and instead grab my bag and run from the cafe into the cold afternoon air.

Breathe. Just breathe.

Everything is going to be fine.

Chapter Five

Then

New York

Hmmm. So, maybe things aren't working out exactly as I'd hoped. It's been over a week and I still don't feel like I've got any real friends. It's making me feel like I'm back in high school! I thought I would be different now – that I'd meet people who I could actually get on with, and find some proper mates. I thought that I'd left the weird awkward shy girl back in the UK, but turns out she was always there, just waiting for a chance to come out.

The classes are harder than I thought they would be, too. Everyone here is grossly talented. But then, most of them are the kids of musicians and actors and writers so it's hardly like they wouldn't be. Dad would remind me that I'm also the child of two artists but it's not quite the same, is it? My parents spend all their time drinking five-quid bottles of wine from Asda while massaging each other's egos and bemoaning the loss of the old days, not having sold a painting in decades, whereas the kids here have parents whose names you see on billboards. I've only spoken to Dad twice since I got here, and last time Mum was in the background shouting down at him to get off the phone because the bill would be huge for an overseas call. Neither of them have even emailed me since and I can't help but think they've already forgotten about me. But isn't that what I wanted? To be far enough away that I didn't have to think about anyone but myself?

I just wish I could fit in better. I don't feel like the other kids here at all.

Argh. '*Kids!*' See? I *am* changing! Everyone here says *kids*, like we're twelve. It's so weird. I asked Ari about it the other night and she said they are kids until they're twenty-one. *Twenty-one?* I laughed: you stop being a kid years before that. But she just shrugged like I was being dramatic. Back at home, I know we're still young but at least we have some sense of being adults. Here, they don't have to do anything. The college provides all our meals in the dining hall, so there's no arguing about the washing up, or making the weekly shopping trip to fill the fridge with a combo of hangover treats and enough pasta and tomato sauce to keep us alive. We don't even use money on campus! We have these college cards which we have to top up online and everything is paid for with that. It's so weird but I guess a lot of the 'kids' here have their parents topping them up from home. I haven't bothered giving Mum and Dad the details of mine; it's not like they'd remember to do it even if they did have some spare cash.

Back at home, I'm the exceptional one. I know I sound like a total egomaniac, but it's true. I'm not surrounded by friends or boyfriends or anything like that but I am thought of as the talented one. I always have been – that's basically ninety per cent of my personality. But here... here *everyone* is talented and so I'm nothing special. I should have realised it would be like this. The process to get this scholarship was mad – hours of Skype interviews and three separate audition tapes before they'd even consider me! Everyone else here will have done that too. Everyone here is the very best of their class. The difference is, they already come from elite New York and LA classes and I am the best of… Exeter.

I think the other big difference between here and home though is that I'm so bloody lonely. The problem with being an exchange student is that they stick you in halls (or as they call them here, *dorms*) as if you're brand new to uni life. But I'm too old to be properly friends with the eighteen-year-old first-years they've roomed me with and I'm not cool enough to be friends with the fourth years who look at me like I'm a fresher.

I'm just stuck in the middle, appealing to no one, just like the old days.

But at least I have my music. Even if it no longer makes me exceptional. I've been practising loads since I got here; the upside of not really having any mates is that I've got hours and hours to rehearse. I've looked up some open mics in the city too, but not had the nerve to venture out to any just yet. And yeah, maybe my confidence is a bit knocked at realising how mediocre I might be, compared to NY musicians.

But to be honest, I've barely been into the city at all. Campus is big enough to wander around and give myself the illusion that I'm living in New York without worrying about anything like being mugged, or cat-called, or getting lost – you know, the real bits of New York. I did go for a wander the other night; a few girls from my class said they were going for a coffee after class and I managed to get myself sort of invited (and by that I mean I was standing so near them when they were arranging it that to not invite me would have been insanely rude, so they did). One of the girls in the group, Sadie, actually lives in New York. Her parents have an apartment a few blocks from campus – Astor Place, it's called – so she took us to a coffee shop she knows. She lives on campus too despite being so near home. Isn't that mad? Imagine having an apartment that close to campus and still paying the insane college rental rates. I guess a lot of the kids here have more money than sense.

Even though none of them really spoke to me much and I felt very much like a hanger-on, I loved that night. We walked through the busy streets as the dusk settled and I felt like I was in a movie. Men in business suits stormed the pavements, phones pressed to their ears, barking instructions. Women in yoga gear power-walked in pairs, their hair brushed off their faces in tight bands, their mouths moving a hundred miles an hour as they talked. An older woman rode past us on a scooter. A scooter! I had one like it when I was a kid and laughter bubbled up through my throat as she rode by, winking at me.

I love this place. I'm not sure it loves me yet, but one day I think it might.

Before we got to the coffee shop, Sadie stopped at this big cube statue in the middle of the street and told me to push it. I thought she was joking, trying to make me look stupid, show that I wasn't a New Yorker like her, so I laughed it off, but then she rolled her eyes and walked up to the statue – calling me over again. I leant my weight against it, copying her, and felt the cold flat surface against my back. It didn't move an inch and I stood back up, feeling stupid, but she kept pushing and then, like magic, the statue moved. All the other girls laughed and cheered and a few tourists stopped to watch her. She told us there's a point at which if you put your weight behind it, it moves. Tourists love trying it, but they never make it move.

I hope in a few weeks I won't feel like a tourist any more.

I want to feel at home here. I want to be someone else. I want the city to swallow me whole.

Chapter Six

Now

Hannah

I pull up to the house and see Charlie in the kitchen. The window's starting to steam from whatever he's cooking and in the reflection I see a look of concentration on his face as he stands over the hob, stirring. The evening is still light, the night not yet drawing in and for a moment I forget the awfulness of Jesse's death and just watch my husband, knowing in a few moments I'll be wrapped in his arms as he asks me how my day has been. He'll want to talk about Issy, probably over a glass of wine. His day will have been different to mine, of course. He is not dealing with earth-shattering news and long-carried guilt; today for him will have been pure joy. Perhaps he told his colleagues the news about Issy as soon as he got back online, sending those silly GIFs they all seem to communicate with instead of actual words. It suits him, working like that, away from people day to day yet connected through silly messages when he needs a boost. I smile at the thought of his celebrations and try to keep up the positivity as I walk through the door. Nothing is wrong, I tell myself, everything is normal.

'Hi,' I say, walking into the kitchen and placing my bag down on the floor. Charlie doesn't turn around and for a second I panic; does he know about Jesse? But then I see the black headphones embedded in his ears and roll my eyes. I tap him on the shoulder and he jumps.

'Fucking hell!' he shouts, and I take a step back, thrown by his anger. 'You scared me. I didn't know you were there—'

'I could have been anyone! You shouldn't cook with headphones in!'

He shakes his head and batters away my concerns. 'The door was locked, Han. I'm not an idiot.' He turns back to the pan and pulls it off the heat, the rising steam bringing sweat to my forehead. I wait for a moment, expecting him to say something else, to apologise for the shouting but he brushes past me to get salad stuff from the fridge, saying nothing.

'I saw Olivia earlier,' I say as he chops the lettuce head.

'Did you?' he asks but it's clear he isn't interested.

'Yes, we had a coffee.'

This stops his chopping and he wrinkles his nose. 'Why?'

I shrug as I pass him the cucumber, knowing this will be the next item to chop. 'She came in with Poppy while I was in there. We chatted. I don't know. She asked me to come to the music toddler group at the village hall—'

He scoffs. 'Seriously?'

'What?'

'Bit presumptive, that's all. But then that's Olivia all over.'

I bite my lip. Despite having had the same initial reaction to Olivia's invite myself earlier, I hoped that mention of this would bring Charlie out of whatever has put him in this funk. 'I think she was just trying to be nice, to make me feel like a mum.'

His eyes soften then and he nods slowly before putting down his chopping knife and bringing me towards him. He buries his face in my hair as I'm pulled into his warm chest. I breathe in his familiar smell mixed with the scent of buttered onions from the risotto on the hob and close my eyes.

'Go sit down,' Charlie says, letting go of me. 'This will be ready in about ten minutes; I'll bring it through.' He kisses me on top of my head and I do as I'm told.

-

We're trying to get out of the habit of eating on our laps in front of the TV. It's one of the many things that we started doing as a form of comfort over the last few years that we've never really been able to shake. Setting the table and sitting at a hard surface began to feel, like a lot of things in our lives, pointless and faintly ridiculous. Why drag your body from the warm sofa when it's just the two of you? Why bother with set meal times at all? We could do anything, no one would know. Or care. I would say this to Charlie sometimes. 'Isn't it crazy that we just keep getting up and going to work and making dinner and washing up like nothing is wrong? Like we're totally normal?' He'd sigh and tell me that we *were* totally normal and things wouldn't be like this forever, but I never really believed him. Life didn't stop when we realised we'd never create it. But it became duller; heavier somehow.

But tonight, I set the table. I pull the placemats out of the cabinet, lay knives and forks beside them and place coasters at a forty-five-degree angle. This is what a family does. We need to get back into good habits for Issy; I have to believe that Issy really is coming home soon. Otherwise... what then? A swell of panic skitters across my

41

skin as I imagine a future without her. Without anyone. The relentless, endless days that will come for us… but I breathe through it and come back to the room. I place the salt and pepper in the middle of the table as Charlie walks through the door.

'Oh, wow, are we eating in here?' He looks at the table as if I've laid out multiple knives and forks and folded napkins fit for fine-dining.

'Yes,' I say. 'We need to stop eating on the sofa. It's not good.'

'No,' he says, still eyeing the table suspiciously. 'It's not. I'll bring stuff in.'

He brings the hot plates and places them on the mats then leaves and returns again with the bowl of salad and takes a seat opposite me.

'Look okay?' he asks, nodding at the steaming risotto. I glance down at my plate and my stomach rumbles in anticipation.

'Looks lovely, thank you. Shall I put some music on?'

'I'll do it.'

He runs into the kitchen and back to bring in his speaker. We never use the dining room and it feels cold and uninviting with just the two of us sitting here tonight. I try to imagine Issy in here, a highchair at the end of the table, her giggles filling the empty room. Suddenly the silence feels overwhelming and I bark at Charlie to just put anything on.

'Sorry,' I say as he sits back down, music now playing through the speaker.

'You should be, I've just clicked the first playlist that came up,' he smirks.

'Which was?'

'Pop hits,' he laughs, and I smile back.

We don't speak for a few minutes as we eat. Charlie's made one of my favourites, goat's cheese and beetroot risotto. Beetroot is a hangover from my IVF days; I read somewhere that beetroot was good for fertility and it became one of the staples in our fridge. Along with spinach, cashew nuts, Maca powder, Brazil nuts, pomegranate juice, and even bee pollen at one point. I lived on Maca and bee pollen smoothies for a month during our third cycle, in one of my most desperate measures, as if the cure to my infertility was to be found in ground-up powders whizzed together with oat milk in a Nutribullet.

But tonight's risotto is not a fertility recipe. I've no doubt Charlie cooked the rice with wine, another formerly banned substance, and lashings of butter. The goat's cheese has been drizzled with honey and placed under the hot grill before being dolloped on top of the gooey rice, the dish's decadence undercut by a crisp lettuce and cucumber salad with sliced apple.

'Do you think Issy will eat beetroot?' I ask, slicing the bright pink vegetable on my plate.

Charlie tilts his head, thinking. He never answers a question straight away, even if it's as simple as whether he'd like a glass of water. Everything is considered.

'Probably not, no. But that's okay. I'll make her something else.' He smiles and looks back down at his plate.

'Are you okay?'

He looks up and smiles brightly but worry is creasing his brow. 'Yeah, I'm fine. It's just a lot, isn't it? The hope.'

I swallow and nod.

'We're so close now,' he adds. 'It almost feels too good to be true, like something will come up and take her away from us.' He looks down and I'm gripped by a stabbing of

43

guilt so painful that it makes me tilt forward to catch my breath.

'Hey, hey.' Charlie's up and around the table suddenly at my side. 'I'm sorry, Han. I didn't mean that, don't worry. We're going to be fine.' He rubs my back and I close my eyes, unable to look at him in the eye. We're silent for a moment as he rubs my back and I try to collect myself, then I hear him.

Jesse.

Jesse's gravelly voice coming through the speakers.

Before I know what I'm doing I jump up and switch off the speaker. Charlie opens his mouth and closes it again.

'I hate that song,' he says.

'Me too.'

He walks back to his side of the table and gathers up the plates, scraping what's left of my risotto onto his plate and piling the leftover salad on top. 'Did you hear he died?' Charlie says and I do everything in my power to stop my body from tensing.

'Who?' I ask.

'Jesse Carter. The pop star. It was on the news today. He died up the road, at The Farm.'

I tuck my hair behind my ear and mumble that I had heard; Kate was talking about it at work, then take out my phone and begin to scroll Instagram, not seeing a single post. Charlie walks past me to take out the plates but stops to kiss me on the head.

'Everything is going to be all right, Han. I promise.'

Chapter Seven

Then

New York

Oh my god. Something exciting has happened. Like, really, really exciting. Even thinking about it makes my ears hot.

Okay. It's probably not that exciting. I'm just being dramatic (as usual, Dad would say). God, but thinking about what *could* happen makes me actually want to scream with excitement. And I need it! It's been two weeks now and nothing has happened at all, I'm so *bored*. Bored in New York City? Ha. But that's exactly what I am. I didn't think it was going to be like this, I really didn't.

The classes are *so* hard and they actually give you home-work. Every. Single. Night. Part of me feels too old to be here, like I'm not in school any more so why do they treat us like that? But then the other part feels like a stupid kid who grew up in a shitty house in the countryside and knows nothing about the real world so maybe I'm just finding it super hard because I'm actually way out of my depth as a musician and need this to take me to the next level.

I've started to go out more now, at least. I take my guitar and find places with open mics. The first time I went I was so scared I thought I was going to be sick right there on the pavement outside the shabby-looking cafe. But it was good. Well, it was okay. Every open mic has been 'okay' so far and I've done three now. The audiences always love my accent but that's probably the only thing they really love about me. My music maybe just doesn't translate to the US? I don't know. Laura Marling manages it okay.

But Laura Marling is why I'm in this insanely excited state in the first place!

I should explain.

I bought tickets to see her playing at Webster Hall before I came out here. I tried to play it all cool like I was totally fine to go to a gig on my own, but really I thought by the time it came around I'd have loads of friends and would just go along with them. Ha. But it's been almost three weeks now, the gig is next week and I still have no one to go with. So today, I'm sitting in music theory class (absolutely the worst one, just a load of complicated maths which to me has absolutely nothing to do with music – oh and so far, I'm failing the class, so there's that) trying to not show the utter panic that's ripping through me as the professor draws yet more illegible symbols on the board when I hear them chatting at the back. The cool group.

There's about six of them. They're all impossibly good-looking in that elusive New Yorker way that I can't quite explain, and they sit at the back of every class pissing about and yet still getting As on every test. They're not the textbook cool group that you see on films about campus life, though, they're a bit grungy – but I guess being cool at a liberal arts college is not being a cheerleader. I don't think we even have cheerleaders here – or a football team, come to think of it.

But anyway, they're chatting away about what they're doing next weekend and then one of them says about going to see Laura Marling at Webster Hall. Some of the others groan *Really? She's so boring!* and I can't help but turn around at this point to stare at them, open-mouthed. Laura Marling, boring? They're off their tits. I catch his eye then, the guy who always seems to be in the centre of their group. Jesse. And he smiles at me.

'You're British, right?' he says, his New York accent smooth like butter.

'Yeah,' I reply, trying to sound nonchalant.

'You know Laura Marling?'

I nod.

'Whaddya think, boring?'

I laugh then, letting out the tiniest and most embarrassing of snorts. 'She's so far from boring I don't even want to dignify that with an answer.'

Jesse tips his head back and laughs so loud that the professor tells us both to get out if we can't keep it down. I turn back round, cheeks red, all too aware that a scholarship student can't be seen misbehaving.

At the end of class, I pack up my things quickly and head for the door but he catches me in the corridor. Up close, it's possible he's even hotter than I imagined – though actually not as tall which is weird, because he definitely *seems* tall, if that makes sense?

'You know she's playing Webster Hall next Friday, right?'

I nod. 'I've got tickets.'

'You do?' he says, smiling. 'Me too.'

'Cool.'

'Very cool.' He bites his bottom lip and just stares at me then, my whole body warm and tingling. 'I guess I'll see you there, Hannah.' He nods and walks off and every part of me is on fire. Jesus Christ. He's just wearing the same black hoody he usually wears to class and tight black jeans with rips in the knee (very cool-but-totally-not-bothered New Yorker) but honestly, the way being close to him is making me feel, you'd think we were naked.

Do *not* think of him naked.

Why is my body reacting like that to this total stranger? I didn't come here for boys. I came here for music.

But god, Jesse is just… I don't know what he is. I've never had that kind of feeling before just from someone talking to me.

But it doesn't mean anything. I'm just lonely. That's all.

I'll see him at the concert next week and he'll probably not even acknowledge me.

Then I can stop obsessing over him, over the way my name sounded on his plump lips.

Oh god. This is going to be trouble.

Chapter Eight

SIX DAYS UNTIL ISSY COMES HOME

Now

Hannah

I wake up thinking about the spare room. Should we decorate now, ready for Issy's arrival, or is that tempting fate? If we don't do anything though, surely that won't show Issy that we're ready for her when they bring her for the home inspection and handover. *Home visit and handover*, I hear Andrea correct me, *you are not under inspection*. But we are, aren't we? We have been ever since we started this process. Over the years, I've managed to convince myself that my past is so totally unconnected to my life now in every way that it could never hurt me. It's this conviction that pushed me through the adoption process despite the intensity with which they assess your life.

'Morning.' Charlie walks into the bedroom with a cup of something and I smile. 'Chai tea,' he says as he places it on my bedside table. He switches on the radio and Harry Styles' latest song fills the room.

'I'm drinking coffee now,' I say.

'Are you? Do you want that instead?'

I shake my head. 'No, I was just saying. There's no reason not to, right?'

He shrugs and says he supposes not, then goes back downstairs. He starts work a lot earlier than me; he prefers early mornings whereas I prefer sleep. And, if I'm honest, I'm finding it harder and harder to remain interested in work lately. It's not that I don't care, of course I do, but my thoughts have become so consumed with Issy that nothing else seems to fit. I remember being like this with our first round of IVF, so sure it was going to work I let everything else in my life slip. And then when we got that first negative, it was like the world would fall apart. But it didn't. Because if there's one thing I've learned over the last few years it's that you just keep going, no matter what happens. We just keep going.

Harry Styles fades out and the seven-thirty news bulletin replaces it. I need to get up; I should be dressed by now.

'Police continue investigations into the murder of popstar Jesse Carter after his body was found at The Farm, a private members' club in the Cotswolds. Police have today confirmed that Carter was stabbed—'

I jump from the bed and switch off the radio. Stabbed. Jesse was stabbed. The image makes my skin feel too tight, like my body is clamouring to be released.

'I'm heading into town this morning,' Charlie says, popping his head around the door. I didn't notice before that he was dressed in outdoor clothes, as we call them, the only thing defining them from our indoor clothes being their lack of elastic waistbands and oversized nature.

'What for?' I reply, smoothing down my hair in an effort to look less erratic.

Charlie waves his hand and tells me he has to meet a new hire to his team, then gives me a kiss on my sweaty forehead and leaves. Charlie hardly ever works outside of the house and I wonder why he didn't mention this to me before, but perhaps he did. I've hardly been attentive lately.

I pull off my pyjamas and shove them on top of the over-spilling laundry basket. I need to get a hold of the house stuff. We can't fix the whole house this weekend; we need to be prepared before that. One thing at a time, I tell myself. First, pee. Brush your teeth. Shower. I walk into the bathroom chanting it like a mantra. Pee. Brush teeth. Shower.

On the toilet, I see I'm bleeding. I sit and stare at the pink stains on the tissue for a moment, waiting for the grief that has, for years, accompanied this sight. But nothing comes. I throw the tissue into the toilet bowl and watch as the blood mixes with the water and disappears. I've done this so many times, watching my failure flush down the toilet along with the waste. Like that's what I deserve. Each period, each month, marking another round of loss. Another two weeks of wasted hope that, despite all the pain before it, let us believe for a moment that perhaps this would be our month. This would be the time I got to run out of the bathroom, piss-soaked stick in hand and scream at my husband, *I'm pregnant!* How many times have I sat here in tears over a blood-stained tissue? Too many to count. You stop counting, eventually. You have to. But you always know. Your life becomes a before and after. Before you realise you are not one of the lucky people whose bodies play fairly; and after.

But today, I don't feel grief. I'll never run out of the bathroom like someone on a film; that's not how I'll become a mother. And that's okay.

I tell myself Issy is my daughter; beautiful, small, scared little Issy who right now will be waking up in her foster home in a bed countless children have slept in before, waiting for us to bring her home. All of the hope and waiting and wishing and the grief and the pain will be worth it for Issy. She is what we have always been waiting for. Each month of crushing grief was our gestation period; our wait until the world could bring us to her. Brushing my teeth, I start to cry. A pathetic sight looks back from the mirror at me; tears mixed in with tooth-paste. We are so close to getting everything we want, and yet my body can't let go of the fear it's held for years as I hear the newsreader's voice in my head telling me Jesse has been murdered.

As if on cue, my mobile rings and when I answer, I'm not even surprised when they say it's the police.

–

I've never been in a police station before, though I know where our nearest is, two towns over. We don't have one in our village, though there is a derelict building where it used to stand. An old-fashioned blue and white sign still hangs above the doorway, the word 'police' now just an O and a C amongst the peeling wood. There have been various plans from the council to buy it and turn it into something else over the years, but nothing has happened and so the empty, sad building remains, haunting the otherwise perfect village.

This building is not like that. It's brand new, purpose-built. You can't imagine anything else ever happening in the brightly lit corridors and magnolia-painted walls. This is not a place of joy. Of course, it's quiet this morning. Though this station will likely serve as the central point for many of the nearby towns, we're still so far from a city that I don't imagine it sees much action. How must the police have reacted to the news of Jesse's death? I can't help but picture the scene from *Hot Fuzz* where their daily call-out involves a menacing swan. What were the officers doing in the moment before they realised they were now going to have to investigate an actual murder?

The word sends prickles over my skin and I lace my fingers in front of me on the cheap MDF desk. This is not a film. This is real. I am really here for an interview about Jesse Carter's murder.

'Thanks so much for coming in, Mrs Wilson.'

'It's Hannah, please.'

The young officer smiles and nods. He can't be more than thirty, perhaps even less, and I find this reassuring. If they really thought this involved me at all, they would send someone more senior, surely? They're probably interviewing everyone from the village.

'Well, as I said on the phone, we're very grateful for you coming in today.' As if on cue, another officer walks in at the moment he says 'we'. As he sits opposite us, my stomach drops. This is the man I pictured when my phone rang this morning. Older, thick square shoulders, eyebrows so dark they look like they've been painted on. This is the sort of man who investigates a murder. My body radiates heat from beneath my carefully chosen grey jumper. A jumper that should say, *I am not usually in police stations; I do not belong here; I am not a criminal* but right now feels like it's screaming *please sir, don't arrest me.*

'Morning,' the new officer says, pulling out the seat opposite me. 'I'm DC Harvey.'

'And I'm PC Dales.'

'Had you not got to introductions yet?' DC Harvey says and I detect an Irish lilt to his words. PC Dales opens his mouth to continue but DC Harvey tuts his tongue against the roof of his mouth, quietening him as they both turn to me.

'Do you know why we've asked you to come in today, Mrs Wilson?'

'It's Hannah.'

'Do you know why you're here today, *Hannah*?' He raises his eyebrows at me and sits back in his chair. My jaw clenches.

'Your colleague said on the phone… He said it was about the murder at The Farm.'

DC Harvey nods solemnly. 'Right you are, Hannah. And the victim, Jesse Carter, did you know him?'

Both their eyes are on me now, boring into my body, making my heart beat faster. Did I know Jesse Carter? I knew a boy called Jesse once; halfway between a boy and a man, he wasn't yet Jesse Carter. He was just Jesse.

'A long time ago,' I settle on. 'I don't know him now.' I stumble over the words, worrying about the tense. I don't know him now? I didn't know him now? How do you refer to your relationship with a dead man? My throat is dry and I reach for the plastic cup of water PC Dales gave me on the way in.

DC Harvey watches me with interest, waiting for me to finish my sip before carrying on. He sits forward in his seat, bringing his face closer to mine at the table and I instinctively move back. He smiles, and his whole face softens.

54

'Hannah, you aren't in any trouble here, okay? Don't you be worrying. We've just got to establish the facts. You know?' He says it so softly, like we're just chatting in the pub, no mind. But the unspoken question here, the one I can't bear to ask, is: how do they even know about me?

All these years I've fooled myself into believing my history with Jesse was so buried that no one would ever connect us. But I was wrong. Less than twenty-four hours after the news of his death broke, here I am. In the police station. Being questioned over his murder.

–

When Charlie and I started the process of trying for a child – and I mean really trying, not the fun bit where it's just the two of you lying in bed having sex then dreaming about babies. I mean the bit that most couples never have to see, the bit that involves NHS funding, and doctors, and tests and approval – they send you out forms. They need to get approval from your local commissioning group to fund the treatment. They're enormous, these forms. The nurse had warned us, *don't be alarmed by the amount of paperwork on its way, it's mostly the same questions over and over.* But we *were* alarmed when the fat pack finally landed on the doorstep. That's when we stopped believing that what we'd been doing in our bedroom would ever result in a family and accepted that our lives would be different now. Clinical.

The forms ask if you're fit to be a parent. They ask about history of abuse; mental illness; physical illness. They ask if you've ever been arrested for a crime.

I hovered over that one for so long.

It was as if they knew, from day one, that there was something wrong with me.

But when I circled 'no', firmly with thick black pen, I wasn't lying. I have never been arrested for a crime.

What they should have asked is if I'd ever committed one.

—

'Mrs Wilson?' PC Dales interrupts my thoughts.

'Sorry, what was the question?'

The officers look between themselves as if tossing up who will handle me before DC Harvey clears his throat and carries on.

'You were going to tell us how you know Jesse Carter.'

'Yes,' I say. 'Of course.'

I reposition myself in my chair, feeling the throb of a cramp in my pelvis as I wince.

'Are you okay?' PC Dales asks.

'Period pains,' I mumble and to his credit, he just nods without a hint of embarrassment. 'I met Jesse when I was a student in New York, around fifteen years ago.'

PC Dales writes this down as DC Harvey says, 'New York? Nice place. What were you doing there?'

'I got a scholarship to study music. I was in my second year of university at Exeter and they did an exchange with a school over there.'

'So you're a musician?'

I shake my head firmly. 'No. I don't play any more.'

PC Dales writes this down too and I wonder how long he's been an officer. He has the shiny eyes of someone brand new, who can't yet tell what is important and what's not so will run himself ragged trying to capture every detail so as not to miss anything. Is the music important? I suppose it is – to us, at least. Back then it was the most important thing. But now it feels like another world. I would barely recognise the girl who turned up in New York with a guitar on her back, traipsing from bar to bar for open mics, so sure that at any moment someone would hear her songs and change her life. Of course, that did happen. Jesse did change everything. But not in the way I wanted; not in a way that anyone would ever want.

We talk a little more about New York, PC Dales gets the details of my school and firms up the years I was there and I tell them I met Jesse through my music class.

'You were friends?' DC Harvey asks.

I scrunch up my nose, heart pounding as I battle with how truthful to be. How much truth can I get away with? 'Not really,' I say. 'We chatted a bit, the way you do with everyone when you're young.' It just slips out before I even really know I'm going to do it. The lie is out there now and there's nothing I can do it to take it back.

PC Dales looks expectantly at DC Harvey, who eyes me across the table.

'Can you explain then, Hannah, why Jesse might have been contacting you about being in the UK?'

'Jesse didn't contact me! I haven't heard from him since I left New York. We've not spoken. Why do you think—' I stop myself, hearing the panic in my words as they spill out in a rush.

'So you've not spoken to Jesse at all since you left New York fifteen years ago?' DC Harvey says calmly, sitting back slightly in his seat.

I shake my head. 'No. Not once.'

The room fills with a silence that I will myself not to break. PC Dales looks down at his notepad while DC Harvey looks at me curiously. There's nothing threatening about his stare; it's almost like that of a cat watching you across the room while it licks itself clean. The tick of the plastic wall clock grows louder as each second passes.

'Have you ever used the Telegram app, Hannah?'

It's such a random question that I don't answer immediately, racking my brain as to what that app even does. Then, I remember.

'No, I've not. I've heard of it.'

'What have you heard?'

'It's like WhatsApp, isn't it? But it's supposed to be more secure.'

DC Harvey nods slowly. 'That's right. Makes it very tricky for anyone to get any message history. Jesse Carter used it.' His eyes bore into me but I've nothing to say to that so I just nod back, like this means nothing to me. 'But you don't use it?'

'No,' I repeat. 'You can check my phone. I've never used it.'

DC Harvey smiles and tells me that won't be necessary. I let out a barely perceptible sigh of relief until he says, 'We haven't been able to find Jesse's phone, but we found an email he sent that we're interested in...'

PC Dales stops taking notes and looks between me and the other officer, as if waiting for one of us to slip and break the silence.

'It was sent to you,' DC Harvey eventually states.

'To me?'

The officers both nod.

'Did you speak to Jesse Carter about his stay in the UK at all?'

'No, I've told you, I haven't spoken to Jesse in over fifteen years. I had no idea he was staying here.'

'This email, the one sent to you that you say you've not seen, was asking to see you.'

'Jesse was asking to see me?' Heat creeps up my neck and lands on my cheeks, no doubt colouring them beneath my carefully applied foundation. 'I never got that email. We never spoke. I've no idea why he would contact me now.' I should ask to see the email, I know I should, but the idea of it saying something incriminating stops me. If I don't know what it says, I've no need to defend it.

A couple of seconds pass where DC Harvey taps his pen against his pad and looks away; I watch the clock. Ten thirty a.m. I've told the office I've got a doctor's appointment but Kate will be wondering where I am and I have no idea how I'll explain this to her. Sweat trickles down my back as the clock keeps ticking, then the silence is suddenly broken.

'Okay, Hannah. That's all we need from you today. Thank you so much for answering these questions for us, we certainly appreciate your time.' He stands up, pushing the chair out beneath him noisily, and smiles. I start to follow his lead and gather up my bag and coat just as he says, 'Oh, one last thing before you go. Can you tell us where you were on the evening of Saturday eighteenth September between the hours of six p.m. and one thirty a.m.?'

I stand, holding my bag in one hand and my coat in the other. 'I was at home.'

'And can anyone confirm that?'

'My husband. Charlie. He was with me all night.'

'Great. Lovely, I'll get PC Dales to take his details from you now please, just in case we need to confirm that with him.' DC Harvey holds out his hand and I awkwardly shimmy my coat up my arm to hold out my own hand to meet his. My palm is clammy against his cold, strong grip and I turn away as he smiles, my cheeks red; my lies burning in my throat.

Chapter Nine

Then

New York

I actually feel sick. Not like run-to-the-bathroom-or-you'll-throw-up-in-your-mouth type sick but like gut-twisting tummy-swirling is-this-really-my-life type sick. And it won't go away!

So, Friday night came around and I was all ready to go see Laura Marling on my own. Honestly, part of me didn't even care at that point that I hadn't made any friends to go with because I just kept thinking, *I'm in New York City and I'm going to see my favourite musician in the entire world.* But when I got there, I felt so embarrassingly alone I actually started to turn to leave, bashing straight into his chest.

'Woah, where are you going?'

Jesse was there. A smile spread across his ridiculously handsome face as he eyed me.

'Nowhere, I was just…'

'Not leaving?'

I shrugged, as if turning away from Laura Marling was no big deal.

'Come on,' he said, his American accent cajoling. 'Surely you can't have a better plan for this evening?'

I laughed because I didn't and he knew it. I noticed then a bored-looking girl by his side, eyeing me. 'I'll meet you inside,' he told her and she stalked off, giving me evils. 'Come on, we're going in.' He linked my arm and led me through the door to Webster Hall like there was nowhere else in the entire world we were meant to be.

I don't know where the girl went. He certainly didn't meet her inside; he spent the whole night standing behind me, his groin pressed into my bum as the crowds surrounded us, pushing us further forward until I was pressed up against the crowd control bar at the front, his breath hot on my neck as he sang along to 'Rambling Man'.

By the end of the night, all I wanted was to turn around, brush his floppy chestnut fringe from his face and kiss him.

But I didn't. When the music finished, the crowd quickly died down and his body came unstuck from mine. He smiled when I turned around, his eyes roaming my body as if we'd just engaged in some sort of passionate dance. I suppose in a way, we had.

'See you later,' he said, turning to leave before I'd even caught my breath.

I've seen him three times since then and each time we've had a conversation longer than the last. Each time I've begged the universe to make him kiss me, but each time he's kept just far enough away to make me wonder if this connection I feel between us is real or totally in my head.

Arghhh.

I knew Jesse was going to be trouble. When I read back my last entry I just can't believe how quickly it's all changed. Jesse isn't just some hot stranger in my music class any more, Jesse is… Jesse is everything.

God, that's ridiculous. He's not everything. I barely know him.

I need to write some songs about this feeling before I lose my mind.

As if I haven't already.

I thought I'd really feel like someone else by now. I thought I'd have stories of my own, friends that liked me. I thought I'd be wandering around the streets of New York with my guitar on my back and gigs under my belt. But all I have is this new obsession with Jesse.

Does he even notice me like that? Sometimes I think he must. Why else would he have abandoned his beautiful, bored-looking date and spent the whole gig pressed up against me? But I just don't know. I'm not the type of girl boys like him fall in love with. Despite being here, I'm still the same on-the-edge weirdo I've always felt like. I don't know if I'll ever escape being the weird kid that lived in the big house on the hill in my local village. Too posh for the estate kids and too obviously cash-poor for the rich ones. I've never fit anywhere, not at school, and definitely not at home with my self-indulgent, mostly drunk disaster parents. But then I found music; I got this scholarship; I'm living in New York City! Surely that means I'm different now? Special enough for Jesse to notice me.

Sometimes I have to remind myself why I came in the first place. The first few weeks I'd slope into the dining hall each night, feeling like I was in an actual scene from a teen film, anxiously looking around the hall for a place to sit that wasn't too near anyone but not too far either, to make it less obvious that I was completely alone. Occasionally, people would talk to me – mostly to get me to say words in my 'adorable' accent, but my novelty value would soon wear off and I'd be alone again. Those nights, I'd stick my headphones in and listen to my favourite songs on loop, imagining myself on stage plucking my guitar under the spotlight and looking back on these days with nostalgia. Where it all began.

Music.

That's what I'm here for. There's nowhere better in the whole world to make it than New York, right? And the thing is, as much as I tell myself I'm not here to have some film-worthy fling, I can't even separate Jesse from the music and say he's going to be a distraction because more than anything, Jesse can help me get where I want to be in ways that no one else ever could – he's told me he plays gigs all around the city and knows everyone in the industry. He's even offered to help me book some gigs – real, paying gigs, not the crappy open mics I've been playing at. Imagine, my name on a gig poster in New York City! Oh and in case that wasn't enough his dad's only *Anthony bloody Carter*. Actual pop-producing legend. Imagine the doors that could open!

Plus, Jesse is totally gorgeous. And funny. And maybe he likes me? Maybe he could really, really like me.

Chapter Ten

Now

Hannah

I need to speak to Charlie. What if the police phone him before I get home, asking him about Saturday night? What would happen then? I pull out my phone to call him but stop myself. There's no way I can tell him this over the phone and something tells me that texting that I need him to lie to give me an alibi would be a very bad choice. The police won't phone him immediately, will they? They seemed happy with my answers. I'm just a random woman that Jesse knew years ago. Nothing more exciting for them to look into. I hope.

I drive back from the station in a battle with my foot not to accelerate too much. The last thing I need is to be caught on camera going above the speed limit. That sort of thing would only further point towards my guilt. Why am I thinking like this already? Like one day there will be a trial and evidence will stack up against me. The thought turns my stomach. As I pull into our drive, my phone rings. Withheld number. Is it them? Did they speak to Charlie already? Is everything already ruined?

'Hello?' I answer.

'Oh good morning, is that Hannah Wilson speaking?'

'Yes?'

'Lovely, it's Jane calling from Oxfordshire County Council. How are you doing today?'

'I'm fine, what's wrong? Is it Issy?'

'It is indeed about Isabella but not to worry, nothing's wrong!' She chuckles down the phone. 'You're in that awful waiting period aren't you now, my love? I know what it's like, I adopted myself. Every phone call sends chills down your spine, doesn't it? But don't worry, it'll be over soon and hopefully you'll have a lovely little girl to show for it.'

I close my eyes and rub the spot that's beginning to pound in the middle of my forehead.

'I'm just calling to confirm our appointment time for the home visit and handover. I've got two p.m. on Monday twenty-seventh, is that all right?'

'Yes,' I say, opening my eyes to see Charlie standing at the front door, eyeing me curiously. I give him a little wave. 'Yes, that's great.'

'Perfect,' Jane says. She gives me some more information about the visit and I try hard to listen, knowing this is important, but my mind is whirring. In six days, Issy will be coming home. It's only six days. As long as Jesse doesn't get in the way. I'll do everything to make sure he doesn't.

—

In the house, Charlie is full of questions about the phone call.

'Did they tell you anything else we should be doing?'

I tell him no, again, that they just rang to confirm the date and time.

'Did you ask them if everything else was going through okay?'

'No, Charlie, there's no need. There's nothing else to do except wait now. You know that.'

Charlie nods and busies himself at the coffee machine. 'I'll follow up with them on email later, just in case.'

I sit at the kitchen table and flick through our post. There's nothing of interest, just junk mail that I throw into the recycling container on the side. Charlie puts a coffee in front of me then appears to notice that I'm here.

'Why are you home?' he asks, brows furrowed as he looks at the clock as if to confirm it is the middle of the day.

I sip the coffee as I debate how to start this conversation. Jane's phone call has thrown me, pushing Issy back into the front of my mind. But maybe that's what I need; a reminder of what's at stake if I mess this up.

'I've had a weird morning, will you sit down?'

Charlie pulls out a chair opposite me and sits. 'What's wrong?'

'Nothing,' I lie. 'I got a phone call from the police this morning...'

His face creases into confusion and I look away, unable to bear seeing the stress this will cause him.

'What? Why?'

Outside, the birds sing merrily and I turn to look out at them. The day has brightened and it feels wrong to be sitting inside.

'Han?'

'Sorry,' I say, pulling my attention back to the task at hand. 'It's about that murder... At The Farm. They're interviewing everyone who's a member there.' I meet his eye then, the lie sitting thick in my throat. He frowns.

'But you're not a member?'

I wave my hand as if this is no big deal. 'We have corporate membership through work. They give them to all the local businesses—'

'You've literally never told me that.' His voice is hard and his eyes narrow.

I try to laugh. 'Why? Would you have wanted to go if you could?'

Charlie hates The Farm and everything it stands for. We both do. You can't live in this village without it being a talking point so it's something we've discussed often over the years. Or more like, made fun of. One of our favourite Sunday activities is playing 'spot a Farmer' as we sit in the local cafe for breakfast and watch them walk by dressed in Barbour and Hunters which have never seen a muddy puddle. It's not often you'll see the celebrities that fly from all corners of the world to The Farm, though; they tend to stay confined to their Cotswold playground inside the grounds where the normal people can't touch them and the only 'farm' animals allowed are piglets and chickens, kept in perfectly clean pens. But the plain-old-rich do come out to play; to observe the 'countryside' and shop in our local, extortionate lifestyle shops, prices hiked to accommodate them.

I'm not lying. We do have a membership through work. The Farm gave them out a few years ago as a sweetener when they wanted to get approval to expand their grounds to include another outdoor heated swimming pool, like the council was ever going to say no to them.

'Why did the police question you, though? There must be thousands of members.'

This is where I'm going to have to tell some of the truth. Charlie isn't an idiot; he'll know that there's no way a random local woman would be top of the police's call sheet this morning just because we share a membership to the murder location.

I grip my coffee cup and look up at Charlie. His face is so tense but I resist the urge to go to him and stroke away the harsh lines. This is going to hurt and there needs to be some distance between us to get the words out.

'I knew Jesse Carter, a long time ago…'

I expect Charlie to look shocked, to say '*What?*' the second the words are out of my mouth but he doesn't say anything; he just opens his mouth slightly and stares at me, then out of the window before quietly asking, 'How?'

'He was in my music class at school in New York.'

Charlie looks down and I know then that I've truly hurt him, and yet this is not even a revelation. But we're honest with each other. We know everything about each other. That's what Charlie thinks; it's what we've always promised each other. No secrets. No lies. Not even stupid ones, the silly lies that couples tell that feel meaningless, like 'but I did leave work on time I promise, I just got stuck in traffic,' or, 'I didn't see that the bins needing taking out or I'd have done it.' We promised to never become that sort of couple. But here we are.

'Oh,' Charlie eventually says, then gets up from the table and walks to the sink. He looks out of the window onto the garden and I watch him as the room hums with various noises of the house, so familiar, yet this feels like unknown territory for us.

'It's fine,' I tell him. 'They just wanted to ask if I'd been in touch with him recently—'

'And have you?' Charlie spins around and I'm shocked to see anger flaring in his eyes.

'What? No! Of course I haven't. Don't you think I'd have mentioned that to you?'

He comes and sits back at the table and rubs his forehead. 'I don't know, Han. I'd have thought you'd have mentioned before that you were once friends with a pop star—'

'Not friends,' I cut in. 'We were in the same class. That's all.' My cheeks burn under the lie but I hold my husband's gaze, desperate for him to believe me. 'I never thought to mention it, I'm sorry. It's not like we spend a lot of time talking about Jesse Carter...' When I say his name like this, I almost believe myself. Jesse Carter is a world-famous pop star; someone everyone knows and loves or loathes. He's the guy you see on perfume ads or adorning the front pages of gossip magazines, falling out of bars with twenty-year-olds. I don't know that Jesse Carter. That man is a mystery to me.

I knew Jesse. Before all of that.

'What did the police say?' Charlie asks.

'Just that, really. I confirmed that I've not heard from Jesse Carter since leaving New York and that was all they wanted. It seems like they've really no idea what happened at The Farm.'

'Right,' Charlie says. His gaze is unfocused now and I wonder what he's thinking. 'Do you think they'll tell the council?'

My jaw twitches. 'No.' I shake my head firmly. 'I don't think so. Why would they?'

'Well, being involved in a murder investigation is somewhat of a red flag in adoption, I imagine...'

'I'm not involved! They asked me some questions and that was it.'

'Did they say they'd follow things up?'

I shake my head, then stop. 'Well, only with you—'

'What?' Charlie says. 'Why with me?'

I can't look at him for this next bit; Charlie hates things like this. He hates confrontation, it's not his way. 'They asked me where I was on the night of the murder—'

'Jesus Christ, Hannah!'

'It's fine, it's fine. They'll ask everyone that.'

'What, you know that, do you?' Charlie scoffs.

I ignore that remark because he's right, I've no idea what happens in a murder investigation but if I start to let questions like that burrow in my head then they'll never get out.

'It was Saturday night,' I say. 'I told them I was at home, which I was, as you know. But they asked…'

'What? What did they ask?'

'They asked if anyone could confirm that and… and I said you. I said you could.'

I look up and Charlie stares at me from across the table, his eyes furrowed in anger or confusion, I can't tell which, but it's not a look I've seen from my calm, stable husband before.

'Right…' he says eventually.

'I'm sorry, I'm sorry to ask you to lie. But I could hardly say I was here alone after we'd had a massive argument, could I?'

Charlie shakes his head and looks away, probably not wanting to remember how Saturday night ended for us.

We don't argue often, really hardly at all now. We did sometimes in the beginning, when we were young and more fiery-tempered, but now there seems little point.

Charlie is the best husband; he does his fair share around the house and I don't have to nag him to do basic tasks like so many of my friends do. He barely drinks and would rather stay in on a Saturday night with me and a takeaway than spend it down the pub or at the football with his mates. Our marriage is easy. It's cliché to say, but he's my best friend. When I search for reasons that we can't have children that don't wholly blame me, I think it might be because we've got everything else so good together. I know so many couples whose marriages are constant battles, but our marriage is the opposite. Comforting. Warm. Dependable. All the things I was so desperate for when I first met him.

But sometimes I do things that even calm Charlie can't let go.

The fight was about the adoption. I say we never argue, and mostly we don't. Even after years of gut-wrenching IVF, when so many marriages fold in on themselves until they're unrecognisable, we stood firm. But the adoption has been different. We stopped physically doing something together at that point, and I know that it sounds strange because IVF is so medical, but there was always that moment when they told us that my eggs had fertilised and when they put that little embryo back inside me; a special sense that Charlie and I had made something, just the two of us, that I was now responsible for carrying. Those eleven days – when you're carrying the precious embryo that the two of you made, desperately hoping it will make your body home – were the only times we ever really got that feeling of being parents. I loved and hated those eleven days. The high when they began, the hope I held onto each day throughout, followed by the crushing

72

disappointment at the end when that embryo, that almost living thing, was just *gone*.

When we finally admitted – or, more accurately, were forced to accept by our doctors – that this process would probably never work for us, I do think something in us broke. Not irrevocably, perhaps just a splinter fracture. One I hoped would mend with adoption. Most days it feels like it has, but there are just some parts of the process that Charlie and I are so far apart on.

Like Issy's birth mother.

You're told very little at first about the birth mother of your potential adopted child, enough to give you a background and understand what you're taking on, but not so much that personal details are sacrificed. The moment I heard about Issy's, I became obsessed. A nineteen-year-old girl who overdosed when Issy was eighteen months old. Issy was found screaming in their one-bed flat, an entire day after her mother's death, by a neighbour. The moment our case-worker, Andrea, told us these details one Tuesday afternoon in her too-stuffy office, my life changed. I knew that Issy was destined to be ours. This was my chance to make up for everything. I could do this thing; I was too late to save Issy's mother... but I could save her.

Charlie has never understood my need to know about Issy's birth mum – Sian, her name was. At first, it felt like self-preservation – to be prepared for what might come up. Though Andrea assured us, rather coldly, that Sian had no family in the picture as she had been brought up in the foster system, and Issy's father was unknown – not recorded on the birth certificate, nor had members of Sian's community offered any names. I wanted to cry for this poor, alone teenage mum who had lived such a short life in what sounded like such bleak circumstances, but I have to admit that her tragic story was somewhat of a relief. I'd read horror stories on online adoption forums of families loving their adopted children for years only for their birth mothers to come back into their lives years later, reformed, and claim them back. I was terrified of that happening, but we were assured that with Issy it never would. Sian was not cared about – not by anyone, it seemed – and so neither was Issy.

I just wanted to make sure of that myself. So yes, I searched for everything I could find about Sian. And on Saturday night, Charlie caught me doing it again. He was furious. He'd caught me before, the day we learned about Sian, and I had promised him never to do it again. He felt it was jinxing it somehow, that because Andrea had told us not to go looking for information on Sian's family or friends, by doing so I was somehow risking the whole thing. I reasoned with myself that there was no way anyone would ever know about my research, but that wasn't enough for Charlie, and on Saturday night, after finding me hunched over my laptop, scrolling years back to photos of Sian at her school leavers' prom, he went ballistic and stormed out. Charlie never storms out. We're not that sort of couple.

'Please, Charlie,' I say now, reaching to touch his hand. 'The police probably won't check, I'm sure of it. But if they do, can you just say you were here?'

He looks at me with a mix of disgust and distress before covering it with a small smile. 'Yeah, of course I will.' My stomach unknots just the slightest bit as Charlie looks away. 'I can't believe this is happening. I just can't believe it.'

Chapter Eleven

Now

Hannah

I had to get away from Charlie. The way his innocent eyes looked up at me as I lied broke my heart. How have I let it get to this? How will I ever explain things to him now? I should have told him about Jesse when we met. That would have been the right thing to do; we could have started the relationship with a clean slate from the beginning. Or more likely, not at all. Charlie is good. The kind of man that stops in the street and saves worms in the middle of the pavement, not caring how ridiculous he looks or how inconvenient his stopping is to anyone who has to route around him. *They can't look after themselves*, he always says when I roll my eyes at another rescue mission: *we have to do it for them*. Charlie would never have understood what happened in New York. What I did. There've been moments over the years when I've thought about confessing, of course there have, but each time I let Charlie see another side to myself that's less than lovable I pull back even more. I saw how he looked at me this morning after learning I am the sort of person who can lie to the police. A little bit of love fell away, a little bit of uncertainty crept into his eyes. I left before I could see any more love draining away, desperate for him to keep his view of me intact.

So now I'm sitting in my car with no idea where to go. I can't go back into the office; Kate will be all over me with questions about where I've been this morning, checking I'm okay, asking if there's anything she needs to know and worry about. After our argument yesterday, I spoke to Marcy and agreed that I'd take a step back this week; to both give me time to go to the many adoption meetings and allow Kate the reigns ready for next week when I'll, hopefully, be off. The feeling of not being needed, not necessary is one I'm not used to, but I should be grateful I have the time and space to think.

I pull out of our drive, still unsure where to go but aware that Charlie will be waiting for the sound of my tyres against the gravel to signal that I've gone. After a few minutes, the village comes into view. A group of young, attractive couples stroll through the high street hand in hand, wearing matching Barbour jackets. One of the women has a Holland Cooper hat on with a pheasant feather sticking out. I grimace. Those hats are vile and yet Londoners seem to adore them, as if they don't represent the old boys they claim to be so against on Twitter, out hunting on a Sunday morning, dragging back their dead birds in triumph. They'll be staying at The Farm, these couples. They always are. We have a few Airbnbs now in the village, much to the annoyance of the locals, but they're generally used by families who come with Labradors, buggies, and well-worn wellies. Not the London set. They never stay anywhere else.

What is it like at The Farm right now? Are the police still there, searching for evidence? It's been a few days since Jesse's body was found and I'm sure the management will have been eager to get them off the premises. It's hardly the height of luxury to see the police sniffing around. I pull my car into the one remaining spot outside the coffee shop and decide to wait it out a few hours here before returning home to Charlie. I just need some peace and quiet to think.

'Han?' A tap at my window followed by my name jolts me from my seat.

Shit.

I wind the window down. 'Hi, Kate…'

She smiles in the midday sun but then her brow creases. 'What are you doing here?'

If I tell her the truth, she'll want to come inside with me and I can't bear the idea of talking all afternoon, not even with Kate. 'Picking up a prescription,' I lie, pointing to the chemist across the road.

'Oh,' she says. 'I'll come with you, then you can give me a lift back to the office.' Of course Kate wants to come in with me; we're those sorts of friends. She knows every inch of my medical history and I know hers. The year before last I held her hand through a heart-breaking abortion and she's held me up in the office toilets after my period has turned up yet again. We're on two different tracks completely and I do wonder if that's why our friendship has become stronger when so many of my other friends have disappeared over the years. Kate doesn't want a baby. Not now; not ever. When she fell pregnant after a short-lived fling, part of me hated her – in the way I've on some level hated every pregnant woman I've known in the last few years. The injustice of it, the unfairness killed me.

When she told me she wasn't going to keep it, I felt a mixture of repulsion and relief. But we talked openly –

in a way that I can't with anyone else in my life except Charlie, and I became her biggest supporter. We even had one wild conversation about her giving the baby to me but it quickly fizzled out in the light of day when my sanity overcame my desperation and we agreed it was madness. I love Kate like a sister, or like I imagine you would love a sister, given I'm an only child, but our friendship wouldn't have survived me raising her child nor could it survive the truth about Jesse. She knows me as a woman who values honesty and integrity; who spends every day fighting to help women rebuild their lives after abuse and trauma; who does the right thing, even if it's not the easy one. She'd never look at me the same again.

But now, she smiles and takes a sip from her takeaway coffee cup, unaware of the thoughts racing through my head. 'I just came out to get some fresh air. A word of warning, it's hectic as fuck today—'

'I'm not coming back today,' I blurt out, desperate to get away from her and the conversation before she realises something is wrong.

'Oh! Are you really not well?'

'No...' I say and she waits for more information. Even before her abortion, we had very few barriers between us. Once someone knows your egg reserve and husband's sperm motility, there tends to be little else to keep from them. But today, I need my walls firmly up and finally Kate senses it.

After a couple of seconds of awkward silence, she gives in. 'Okay, well, I hope you feel better. Before you go though, I've got to tell you what I've just heard in there.' She motions towards the coffee shop and I spot Olivia and the other mums gathered in the window seat, chatting away. 'Apparently, Anthony Carter is up at The Farm.'

Her eyes widen and I catch my breath, covering it with a cough. 'Making an absolute scene, Olivia says. The police aren't even there any more but he's been going around questioning all the staff like he's some sort of detective.' Kate snorts and rolls her eyes. 'Olivia got quite excited telling us this, of course,' Kate smirks and I imagine how Olivia will have spun this to be a personal drama that happened to her.

Despite living in Oxford, Kate is well versed in the dramas of village life, both through me and her regular appearances at the coffee shop which forms the hub of all activity. Over the years she's come to know Olivia through pure fascination that such a stereotypical 'Cotswold mum' can exist and we often share stories of Olivia's ridiculousness in the office. But now, I don't want to hear about Olivia. I don't want to hear about anything to do with The Farm, or Jesse, or anything at all.

'But yeah, keep a look out for him in the village!' Kate says, wide-eyed like this is all a bit of fun. 'Reporters are already sniffing around, too. There's been about six in there just while I was getting a coffee.'

I follow her eye-line and try and spot which of the bodies inside the coffee shop could belong to the journalists but everyone is packed in so tightly that I can barely make out their individual forms.

'They're asking everyone if we met Jesse.'

Ice runs down my spine and suddenly I know I need to be away from the village, away from reporters, away from Kate and Olivia and Charlie.

I make my excuses with Kate and drive off, leaving her shouting about my prescription but I ignore her until I'm far enough away that I can't hear her any more.

Anthony Carter is here. The elusive Anthony. I only met Jesse's father once, but it was enough to make a lasting impression on me. Not the way I imagined; he was the most well-known record producer at the time, a proper household name, and I thought meeting him would be akin to meeting God. It wasn't. Instead, he was the one person that was able to diminish Jesse's swagger with nothing more than a stern look. What will he be doing at The Farm? Storming around, screaming at the young women on the staff, I imagine. There'll be no reporters up there; they'd never let them in.

Suddenly, I realise it's the perfect place for me to go. I've never used my corporate pass before, but I could. I could find out what's going on, perhaps overhear some waitresses talking about the investigation, try and understand how much the police know. My heart thumps in my chest as the idea takes hold and I find myself driving in the right direction, up the long private driveway lined by Scotch pine trees, blocking the view from the road. It must be at least a mile before I reach the entrance gates, my stomach gurgling suddenly as I realise I've not eaten a thing yet today.

My car crawls towards an oak cabin where a pretty young woman is sitting behind glass.

'Good afternoon,' she says, smiling to reveal perfectly white, straight teeth. She's the kind of youthful pretty that makes me feel old under the layer of foundation covering my dark eye circles.

'Hi,' I say, 'I have a corporate pass?'

She nods. 'Lovely, do you have the card with you?'

'Oh, no. No, I don't, I—'

'Don't worry!' She smiles wider in the face of my obvious panic. 'I'm sure we can find you online. What's the name of the company, please?'

I tell her as she taps it into her iPad. 'Perfect, and if you could confirm the first line of the address, please?' I do. 'And your name?'

'My name?'

She nods and waits. Why hadn't I thought they'd need this? This was such a stupid idea. Now they'll have a record of me visiting, straight after my police interview. God this is stupid. Unless... Before I know what I'm doing, I've opened my mouth and said, 'Kate, I'm Kate Lawrence.'

—

As I park my car, a ten-year-old Fiesta that's completely out of place among the Range Rovers and Aston Martins, I tell myself that using Kate's name really isn't that bad. She'll never know and no one will ever think anything of seeing her name on a list; she is in no way connected to Jesse. Not like me. I follow the hand-painted wooden signs showing me the way to the grounds. A family walks past me, the four young children so near identical I do a double-take. They look so perfect and ethereal; each child shockingly blonde next to the other, all dressed to match. Two boys and two girls. They giggle and chatter amongst themselves, totally oblivious to the rest of the world as their parents glide behind them, holding hands and takeaway coffees. What must it be like to be them? Four children. There was a time when that was our dream, then when the IVF began we pared it down – perhaps four would be too many. Then after a year or so, we decided we'd be happy with two. As long as they had siblings. Two years in, we realised that the life we'd seen for ourselves, a house full of giggling, happy children, was not ever going to be. One child, we told ourselves. That's all we need.

It's got to the point where I believe that, too. One child is enough. It's not what we dreamed, but then what in life is? Issy is enough. The thought of her sends a volt of excitement through me, swiftly followed by dread. We are so close to getting everything we want, but I know all of it could be taken away if Jesse's murder continues to impede on my life. I have to work out what's going on so that I can make sure I'm well away from it.

As I reach the main grounds I stop for a moment and take it all in. So, this is how the other half live. There's a large lake where a flock of fat fuzzy ducklings, not quite yet full grown, swim happily around and a wooden open cabin where pastel mint-green bikes are stored. No locks. You don't need to stop people here from stealing, I assume. *Take a bike and enjoy the grounds*, another hand-painted sign urges. A huge glass building with a flat top covered in a living flower wall stands in front of me, the light gleaming off the glass making me feel somehow unclean. I look around and marvel that anything bad can ever have happened here – let alone a murder, before walking through the door.

'Good afternoon.' I'm greeted by a shockingly handsome dark-haired man in a crisp white shirt. 'Will you be needing a table in our restaurant, bar, or coffee shop today?'

'Oh, um, yes please.'

'Lovely, and which would you like to sit in? Bar? Restaurant?'

'Just a coffee, please.'

'No problem at all. Have you been with us before?'

I shake my head.

'Do you have your membership card?'

I reach into my jacket pocket for the shiny new black card that the young woman in the cabin produced for me earlier and hand it to the man. He scans it then smiles.

'Follow me, Kate.'

Guilt gnaws at me again as I imagine Kate finding out what I've done, taking her name like this, but I concentrate on following the man through the building, my eyes widening at every corner. The high ceilings and floor-to-ceiling windows flood every area with light and there is a sense of being cocooned in another world here, where you can see the outside world but don't have to worry about interacting with it. Is this how celebrities feel every day? Safely stored behind glass walls where normal people simply cannot pass? The man shows me to a round table and I take a seat.

'You'll need to swipe your card when your waitress arrives,' he tells me, dropping some of the veneer now that he's sure I'm no celebrity. 'If it's connected to your company account, we'll charge it there.'

'Oh, no. No, it's not. I don't want my work to be charged—'

'That's okay,' he says, eyebrows raised at the sight of my alarm. 'I'll tell them to send over a bill later, no problem. Have a great day and shout if you want anything at all.' He winks before strolling away and I take a second to let my heart rate return to normal. I'll have to pay by cash, I can't risk using my own card and leaving evidence I was here.

Once he's gone, I busy myself looking at the thick cut, embossed menu, rubbing the paper between my fingers. I think of the print order Kate had to make recently for a campaign to raise funds for one of our domestic violence shelters. She complained about the flimsiness of the paper, how you could basically see through it when held up to the light. But the next spec up was over our pitiful budget. How much did these menus cost? How often do they replace them when a guest spills coffee over the front page? Every day? It doesn't bear to think about, the money that is wasted here. It's a different world.

Another waiter arrives and I order a flat white mindlessly. Outside, a group of young women float aimlessly in an infinity pool that leads onto a natural lake. I say natural, but one look at it tells me they've sucked all of the unpleasant things such as mud, fish, and reeds from the water to give guests an 'authentic' experience without having to worry about any of the realities of outdoor swimming. The women bob merrily beside each other, two with a colourful cocktail in hand, as they tip their heads back, laughing at something the other one said. Who are these women? What do they do that allows their Tuesday afternoons to be spent like this? The way this place is written about, the papers would have you believe it is wall-to-wall celebrities, that David Beckham and his troupe of shockingly good-looking children are simply wandering around all day, every day, but as I look around, I fail to spot a single celebrity.

I wonder what Jesse did while he was here. Would he have been relaxing in the pool with the beautiful young women, supplying them with drinks? Or hunched over his laptop like the man across from me, face full of worry as if the world is about to end? I imagine the former. Jesse was never a worrier, to a fault. But perhaps he changed. Perhaps he became weighed down by the horror of what happened, eventually. The waitress brings over my coffee and I take a sip, dwelling on that last thought. Did Jesse ever feel guilt over it? Everything I've ever seen about him in the years since New York led me to believe not. He appeared to party relentlessly with a string of gorgeous, ever younger girlfriends. Never married. Never had kids. It was as if he stayed the twenty-something boy I met forever.

I wish I'd seen him as he was now. The thought hits me suddenly and cruelly. It's been brewing in my mind since Olivia described him to me. It feels grossly unfair that she, a stranger, knows what he looked like in person before his death and I never will. I've seen pictures, too many of them to count, but it's not the same. I want to know if his left eyebrow still had the tiny patch of missing hair in the middle where he knocked his forehead against a table when he was a toddler, or if his chestnut hair still flopped to one side when he laughed. I want to know if he still chewed gum relentlessly, leaving a scent of peppermint wherever he went.

I don't know why these things matter to me; I thought they no longer did. I thought any connection between Jesse and me had long been severed irreparably.

Yet he emailed me, apparently. Why would Jesse do that? And why would I not have received it if he did? The way the police questioned me this morning, it was like they knew something I didn't. You see it on TV, when the detective questions the suspect. They're never asking things they want to know about; they're asking things they already know to see how you react. Was my reaction what they expected? I can barely remember how I answered, other than telling them I'd not heard from Jesse since New York. But the more I think about it, the more I'm sure that the younger detective frowned at that, as if he knew I was lying. Or at least, he thought I was.

I open my phone and scan Jesse's socials. Nothing has been put up since before his death, not even a post by his management team to confirm his passing. I open one of the rare photos of him taken in day-to-day life rather than on stage. He's wearing a plain black hoodie with the hood up, looking into the camera with a smile that suggests someone caught him mid laugh. Olivia was talking crap; he was still handsome. Older, more tired, less perfectly untouched than he once was but that smile, the dark eyes and floppy hair… You can't deny it.

'It's so sad, isn't it?' A waitress appears by my side to remove my empty coffee cup and nods at the screen. 'I still can't believe it.' Her cheeks shine pink as if she knows she shouldn't be discussing this with a guest, but there's something in her eyes that tells me she can't stop herself.

'Yes, it really is. Did you meet him while he was here?'

She nods and her eyes grow wide. 'He came in here every day. Always ordered the same thing. A babycino.' She giggles and I can't help but smile at the idea of this middle-aged pop star ordering hot frothy milk each day.

'That's not what you'd expect,' I laugh back.

'No,' she says. 'It really wasn't. Anyway, I shouldn't be talking about this.' She smiles tightly and flicks a glance over her shoulder to check no one has already caught her. I sense I'm about to lose her if I can't find a way to keep her talking.

'It's okay,' I blurt. 'I'm an old friend.'

Her eyes widen. 'Oh gosh, really? That's awful… I'm so sorry.'

I smile. 'Thank you. It's been a shock,' I say. 'I just wanted to try and work out what happened, you know?

The police won't tell us anything. All I really want to know is if he was okay. Before, you know?'

The girl bites her lip and I see then just how young she is. Barely out of school, I'd guess.

She takes another glance around us and when she sees no one of note nearby, lowers her voice. 'He did seem quite bothered by something, if I'm honest,' she confides.

'What do you mean?'

She frowns. 'He was always on his phone in here, not talking but sending messages. He'd mumble under his breath a lot, so much that other guests would ask to be moved if we sat them nearby.'

'Do you know what was bothering him?' I ask.

She shakes her head. 'No, but I got the impression he was trying to get hold of someone and they weren't getting back to him. I heard him once when I brought over his drink, he said—'

'Florence?' The good-looking man from before appears behind us with a tone that suggests he knows exactly what Florence has been discussing, and he is not happy. 'Can I grab you for a second?' Florence's cheeks turn bright red as she finishes taking my coffee cup before turning around to leave. The man nods at me then turns sharply on his heels and the two of them click away across the coffee shop, leaving me alone.

I try to ignore the rising sense of panic that flows through me as I imagine Jesse sitting here just a few days before me, angrily mumbling into his phone trying to get hold of someone. What if that someone was me? What if he came here to find me, to finally confront what we did all those years ago?

I open my phone again and search diligently through all my social media accounts. There are no messages from

Jesse, nothing at all. But then, there couldn't be, could there? My privacy settings are completely locked down. Even if he'd wanted to contact me he'd have hit a dead end on social media. Charlie and I both locked our accounts when the adoption process began, too scared that some drunken post from our twenties would somehow derail everything. Is that why Jesse emailed instead? I slam the phone back on the table. If he emailed, I would have got it. The police must be lying. And yet that makes no sense, because everyone knows the police don't lie. The police are the good guys. Only people like me lie.

Chapter Twelve

I'm writing this from Grand Central. It sounds romantic, doesn't it? If I'd pictured myself writing in my diary sitting on the floor of Grand Central Station a few months ago, I would have been so excited. I couldn't imagine being in New York City six weeks ago, let alone being in the middle of the most famous train station in the world, guitar beside me. But now that I'm here, it's not quite as glam as I imagined. It stinks, for a start. I don't even know why I'm here. It's ten thirty p.m. and it's not like I can just get on a train and go somewhere else. Except I could, couldn't I? No one would notice I was gone. The big black sign on the wall of the station gives me plenty of options. White Plains. Westchester. Connecticut.

My roommate is from there. Ariana. I've asked her what it's like but she's never really told me; she just shrugs like it's not important or interesting enough to give any thought to, or if it is, I'm not worth sharing it with.

I played a gig tonight. I was so excited about it. I'm embarrassed I was that excited. It was in Brooklyn so I had to work out how to get there on my own which sounded kind of easy but ended up being a complete nightmare and involved changing trains three times (one of which was a complete mistake and added forty minutes onto my journey). I should have known then that the whole thing was going to be complete disaster. But no, that would have been sensible and apparently I'm a fucking idiot. So, I got off the subway at Williamsburg and it was already getting a bit dark, but I managed to find the place okay. Pete's Candy Bar. That was the name of the bar. It sounded so cool! I'd looked it up online and it seemed like the sort of place you see on TV, covered in fairy lights, filled with cool, good-looking people. And it was. For once, the reality lived up to expectation and I walked in with my guitar on my back feeling like it was going to be a great night.

It was. Until I got up on stage.

I say stage, let's be honest here; it was a tiny platform in an even smaller room. I'd had to wait for five people to get called up before me and I felt quite confident because, though they were all right, they hadn't been amazing and still people had listened and cheered in all the right places. But when I played, it was like someone had told the entire bar not to pay any attention to me. I watched their faces turn away as I strummed the chords to the new song I've just written that sounded so great in my dorm room. At one point, a whole group got up from their seats and repositioned themselves at the bar, whooping at each other as they downed shots with the guitarist who'd been on before me. That's when I realised, everyone here knows each other. Everyone except me.

I finished my set to a barely audible applause, my cheeks burning with shame as my throat closed up. I've never felt more alone as I did in that moment. So alone and so stupid.

And now I don't want to go back to my horrible, cramped dorm room with the roommates who stop talking the moment I walk in. I don't want to be on campus where everyone knows everyone as they bundle down to the dining hall, arms wrapped around each other as they laugh. I don't want to go to the bar and desperately start looking for Jesse like I do every time he might be near. So I'm just going to stay here, just for a bit, where I can watch people rush from train to train, or meet in the middle of the station underneath the painted constellations and hug and cry like they've been separated by war. It doesn't matter that I'm alone here; everyone is too busy to notice.

Oh my god.

He's here.

He's actually here.

This must be actual fate.

It's him. It's Jesse!

Chapter Thirteen

Now

Hannah

I just needed some fresh air, and a sense of perspective. I've come to walk around the grounds now; sitting inside was making me feel like I couldn't breathe. Outside, the air is fresh and somehow devoid of the usual countryside smells. Though The Farm is very much in the middle of farmland, they appear to have scrubbed the air of the putrid earthy odour that lingers everywhere else this time of year as the farmers come to the end of muck spreading season. I suppose the people who come here only want *some* of the countryside experience. Through the court-yard, there are more tables and chairs with a painted pastel-green horse-box serving as an outdoors bar. There are more people out here than indoors and I scan the faces around me, recognising in the middle of a group of young men a TV presenter from Channel 4, I think. The group are all dressed alike in large black puffa coats, despite the warm autumn day, black jeans and bright white trainers. They're engrossed in their phones and don't look up as I walk past.

Further from the bar area, everything becomes quieter. I follow the Cotswold-gold stone paths and end up the other side of a large lake, the water glistening as if it too has been cleansed of anything less than perfect. There are buildings across the field; they look like individual lodges and I assume this is where the guests stay. Which one was Jesse in? I hold my hand up to my face to block the glare of the midday sun and study them, looking for the tell-tale police tape like I'm in a movie, but find no evidence of any sort of crime here. I don't imagine the management were keen to keep any trace of tragedy around.

My mind flicks back to the look on the officer's face when they asked me about Jesse contacting me. They also asked me about that app, the one which hides your communication. Telegraph? No, Telegram. I get out my phone and check that I've never installed it. I remember Charlie did once after a friend told him about it at a party, though I'm pretty sure like most fads, he never actually used it widely, just with that one friend. No, there's nothing on my phone. I come back to the same question: why did the police say Jesse emailed me if he didn't? He must have, I just never received it. Does that mean the person the waitress mentioned that Jesse was so anxious to hear from could have actually been me?

I try and work through it logically. I already know he wouldn't have been able to message me through social media. How else would you try and find someone? He could have googled me, I suppose. I get out my phone as I walk and type in 'Hannah James', my maiden name that Jesse knew. The first few results are useless but then my LinkedIn profile pops ups. Again, it's mostly closed down but you can see my small, professional headshot and my name 'Hannah Wilson (née James)' along with details of where I work. Next, I type 'Hannah Wilson' and 'WomenGoFree' and sure enough, there's my email on the bottom of a press release. For anyone to see and use.

Except what you wouldn't know is that emails from outside our server or not in our contacts list get rerouted to ICT – they don't come straight to us. It's something they had to put in place a few years ago when we became a target of men's rights groups. The *Daily Mail* featured us in a story where a prominent footballer was accused of domestic violence against his latest girlfriend and they believed she had been set up in a safe house by us. She eventually told the press that her allegations against him were false and was vilified everywhere since. I've no doubt whatsoever that she was telling the truth and was too terrified to keep to her story in the face of the relentless pressure from the media and the football fans. We did try and reach out to her to offer help, but she never stayed with us. Either way, we were flooded with hateful emails and threats. Words like I've never seen before. I thought I understood the level of hatred some men have for women, but I'd only scratched the surface of it until then.

Our ICT manager put in a system to protect us from having to read the torrent of abuse after that and so now any emails that aren't pre-approved by us land straight into another inbox, which we affectionately refer to as 'the bad place'. The approach is perhaps slightly over-zealous, but it saves us from starting our days reading about all the ways men will rape us.

If we want to retrieve an email from the bad place, it's simple enough; we just need to phone ICT and ask them to find it. I tap my fingers against my phone, debating whether Jesse's email could really be lost in the bad place and if it is, whether I really want to know. If I read it, I can hardly deny its existence from the police any longer.

'Ducks! Ducks!' a small voice shouts to my side and I drop my phone in surprise.

'Oh gosh, sorry!' A young woman appears and picks it up for me. 'I'm so sorry. Darling, say sorry to this nice lady. You made her drop her phone!'

The little girl runs out from behind the bench and smiles at me before pointing to the water and shouting 'Ducks!' again. The young woman, who I assume is her mother, rolls her eyes.

'Sorry,' she tells me again. 'She hasn't quite mastered volume control.' She roots around in her pockets then brings out a white scrunched up paper bag with The Farm logo on it and hands it to the little girl.

'Don't worry. She's gorgeous. How old?'

'Just turned three,' the woman replies. 'Do you mind?' She takes a seat on the bench next to me and I shake my head as her floral perfume wafts my way. She looks too young to have a three-year-old and jealousy fizzes in my stomach. She must have started early, like I should have. We both watch as the little girl reaches into the bag and pulls out pellets of duck food before chucking them into the lake. A fat brown duck swims our way followed by five or six chubby ducklings almost on their way to being full grown. The girl squeals in delight. 'Do you have any?' the woman turns to ask me and for the first time in my life, I don't squirm at the question but find myself smiling.

'Yes, well...' I say. 'We're about to adopt.'

Her eyes light up and she tells me congratulations.

'She's just turned two. Her name's Isabella.'

'That's a gorgeous name. Congratulations. If you're in need of a nanny, do let me know!' She reaches into her bag for her purse and hands me a card. I flip it over to read.

'She's not yours?' I say, nodding towards the child.

She laughs. 'God, no! Not yet. I have her two days a week and I've a day or so spare at the moment since my other family went back to Dubai.' She smiles again and I notice the total lack of wrinkles on her face. She must be in her early twenties at the most. I don't tell her that we could never afford a nanny, nor are we the sort of family who would have one because she would, rightly, wonder what the hell I'm doing at a place like this in that case. Instead, I thank her for the card and pretend for a second that I am just like the families here. After the girl runs out of duck food, they say their goodbyes and trot off down the path. I watch as they walk hand in hand, imagining Issy and myself in a few weeks doing the same. Perhaps I can bring her here. We could feed the ducks.

As soon as I think it, I shake my head. We're never coming here. This is not a good place.

My anxious brain throws out the line, *no, this is the bad place.* I need to phone ICT. I need to know if that email exists, tying me to Jesse. Pulling me away from Issy.

I dial the number and wait as the phone rings out.

-

The email is here. I've read it four times and yet it still feels unreal. A quick call to ICT got it unlocked and sent over within minutes and now it's here on my phone. I pull my jacket tighter around me as I read it again.

> Hannah,
>   I need to see you. Please. I've tried everything I can think of to get you to speak to me and nothing has worked. I'm coming to the UK. I'll be in your village. You have

to see me. I won't give up. This isn't going
to go away, Hannah. And nor am I.

Jesse.

–

The police must have read this. They must have. Will they
know that I've now read it, too? Heat pulses through my
body as I realise how stupid I've been. I should have left
it in the bad place. No one could have accused me of
knowing he was here, then. Now I'm implicated, aren't
I? I lurch forward as a wave of pain shoots through my
stomach. What have I done? I grab my phone and delete
the email, as if that will solve the problem.

Charlie would know what to do.

Charlie. The one person I can never, ever tell the truth
to.

What a mess.

I lift my head and see the little girl from before running
across the grass, her nanny chasing her. Their giggles float
across the lake and I scrunch my eyes closed as tears fall
down my cheeks. I've ruined everything. I'm going to lose
Isabella. I'm going to lose Charlie.

What can I do?

I need to be away from this place. I was stupid to come
here. How was this ever going to help me? There's nothing
to be found out here that will somehow stop me from
losing Isabella. Losing her before she's even had the chance
to become ours. My stomach twists as I pull myself up
from the bench and I feel the familiar ache of pain swelling
in my abdomen, reminding me that I am not fit to be a
mother. I'll go home. I'll tell Charlie I'm not feeling good
and hide away in the bedroom until I know what to say to

him. Anything is better than being here. I march across the lawn back towards the main building, avoiding eye contact with the well-dressed people I pass – not that they seem at all interested in speaking to me either.

As I reach the main entrance, I hear him. Jesse's dad has an unmistakeable voice. It cuts through the chatter of the groups drinking coffee in the courtyard, drowns out the relaxing background music. Crushes everything.

'If you don't know, why don't you find me someone who fucking does?' he screams at the young waitress who served me before. Tears pool in her eyes as she tells him she will then runs in the other direction, mortified.

I don't dare step closer as I watch him, though I'm quite sure he wouldn't recognise me. We only met once when I was in New York – me, a frightened teenager crying in her underwear, him red faced with fury and lust. We'd had a party in their apartment. It was absolute chaos when his dad arrived unexpectedly the next morning, half-naked bodies spilling from every sofa, sticky bottles lining every side, and the tell-tale smattering of snowy powder dusting the glass coffee table in the centre of the room. But still, his fury was something I'd not expected. I knew Jesse's dad. Everyone did. He was, and remains, one of the most famous music producers in the world. He was known back then for throwing the hugest Hollywood parties filled with women young enough to be called girls. Celebrities were always being spotted coming or going from their various houses across the US, often looking worse for wear as the paparazzi snapped them then splayed their pictures across the tabloids. I was never a big celebrity follower, but he was the kind of famous that you couldn't really avoid; you seemed to know his stories by osmosis, simply by existing in the same world as he did. So I guess

I thought he wouldn't care about the party that day: how could he when Jesse had been brought up surrounded by the chaos of his lifestyle? But he terrified me. I thought he might kill Jesse. He grabbed him by the scruff of the neck and hauled him off the sofa where we slept, slamming his body into the wall as he screamed at him. Jesse in turn screamed at me to get out but I was barely dressed and panicked; rooted to the spot. I wish I'd left. I wouldn't have had to watch it or feel the physical pain of seeing the person I loved hurt so badly.

I turn away from his dad now, scared at the feelings he's provoking, and dip my head to walk out the front door so he won't notice me. I manage to make it all the way without looking back but as I push the door open to freedom I can't resist one last look – it's then that I see him. A man worse than Jesse's dad; a man I hoped to never see again.

Owen.

He watches me from across the entrance hallway, his mouth twisted in a smile, eyes boring into me like they always did. *Rat faced*, that's what Carleigh called him earlier and it's true; I imagine him scuttling across the hall to reach me as I run out of the door, body on fire, but not before he lifts his hand and waves. Just like old friends do.

Chapter Fourteen

Then

New York

Oh my god. Last night was insane. I had to stop writing because Jesse came over and I didn't want to be that sad girl sitting in the station writing in her diary about how crap her life was. He was with a few mates but when he saw me, he left them and came straight over.

'Look who it is,' he said, a smile curling his lips. 'Are you going somewhere?'

I shook my head. 'No. Just...'

He laughed and moved my bag off the seat next to me to sit beside me. He smelled of cigarettes and peppermint and all I wanted to do was kiss him. His knee touched mine for a second and (because he never seems to wear jeans without rips in the knee) I felt his skin against my own.

'You're a weird girl, Hannah James.' He likes to full-name me, and every time he does it's like I've never heard that name before. On his lips, my name sounds magic.

His friends came over but he told them he'd see them later and waved them away. They looked disappointed and one of the girls at the back glared at me, but they followed his instructions and left us alone.

I still don't know what made me do it, but I told him about the gig. About the humiliation; the way that not a single person was interested in me or my songs, how I thought New York was going to be so amazing for my music but so far it was just a giant disappointment.

'Play me something,' he said, opening my guitar case.

I laughed and told him there was no way I was playing in the station in front of all these strangers, and then he did the most amazing thing. He pulled my guitar from my case and started playing. Then he opened his mouth and sang.

To me.

In front of the whole station.

His eyes locked on mine and he sang a song I'd never heard before about a boy falling in love with an English girl who barely knew he existed.

When he finished, there was a round of applause from the small group that had gathered around us. He barely noticed them though and looked at me to ask, 'Do you like it?' I laughed and told him it was amazing. 'Good, I'm glad. I wrote it for you.'

'What? You wrote that?'

He nodded, handing me the guitar. 'For you.'

I honestly thought I was going to die of happiness right then. I had no idea what to say so I did the only thing I could think of and I leaned forward and kissed him, fireworks exploding in my stomach. His hands cupped my face and then ran down my back, pulling my body closer to his. I have never wanted anything as much as I wanted Jesse right then. It was like the whole world faded around us as his hands explored my body, his tongue in my mouth. Eventually, he pulled away and everything came back into focus. My hands flew to my mouth, completely mortified that we'd just done that in the middle of the station and he laughed.

'I guess you do know I exist, after all, Hannah James. Come on then, let's get out of here.' He stood up and held out his hand for me, lifting me up off the cold, dirty station floor.

I knew right then that I would follow this boy absolutely anywhere.

Chapter Fifteen

Now

Charlie

Charlie hadn't been listening for the post the day he first discovered Hannah was lying to him four weeks ago, but even if he had, the sound of it clattering through the letterbox and landing on the hallway floor would have been unlikely to cause him to jump up and fetch it. Four weeks ago, things were different. The only thing on his mind was getting Issy and keeping Hannah positive. So the arrival of the letter was nothing to raise alarm, initially, just another letter addressed to his wife that he thought it would be okay to open. Instead, he was faced with something he had always feared but never put into words: Hannah had a whole other life that didn't involve him. The letter was short, to the point, clear in what was wanted. Charlie didn't know then that the 'Jesse' in the letter was the man that forced his way into the homes of millions every day with his obnoxious mix of pop and rock sung on the radio. He would have never believed that their lives would be entwined with a man like him.

Things have changed since then. Charlie knows far too much about Jesse Carter, and far too little about his wife. He's been stuck in a kind of fog these last few days, his movements slow, cautious. He wishes he was the sort of person who became manic in a crisis; rushing around doing everything at once, their words faster than their thoughts, their bodies propelled into action. But under this kind of stress, Charlie seems to stop. He has become weighed down with the indecision of it all.

But now, he knows he's going to have to do something.

He thought he'd planned everything perfectly. He thought he could somehow convince Jesse to stay away from his wife. Stop the affair, or whatever it was, before it had chance to take root and rip everything good away from him. He convinced himself Hannah had made a mistake but he could still put things right. It wasn't too late. Looking back, he wishes more than anything he'd simply confronted Hannah about the letter, like a normal man would have done. But he was so terrified of losing her that he couldn't even bear to ask. What if she admitted that yes, there was another man, that she loved him more than she'd ever loved Charlie? What then? Charlie couldn't face it. So instead he planned to quietly scare Jesse off before returning to his life as he knew it; like it never happened at all.

But instead he… Charlie can't even think about what happened instead. At least he'd been clever enough to hack into The Farm's CCTV ahead of that night and ensure only he saw what happened on site. Thank God he did.

He stares at the still captured from the CCTV on his screen again.

The quality is not great, the kind you see TV detectives poring over in frustration; *this could be anyone, we'll never convict with this.* And in some ways, he thinks this could be anyone, but deep in his gut he is sure that it's his wife.

The time stamp on the photo shows three minutes past nine p.m. on Saturday evening. He traces his fingers around the outline of his wife's body. Her face is turned away from the camera as she opens the door to the lodge. He doesn't need to see the name on the door to know the man it belongs to.

Broken.

That's how he feels. *Broken isn't a feeling, Charlie.* That's what the counsellor he and Hannah had to see before starting the adoption process had told him once. But had the counsellor ever been through IVF? No. So they couldn't possibly know what it felt like, how *broken* was the only way to describe it. It wasn't disappointed, or sad or hopeless like the counsellor had tried to supply instead. It was broken; when you are told it's unlikely you'll have a baby naturally, that's the first strike. But that one is okay after a while; you pick yourselves back up, you cuddle your wife as she cries over the blood in her underwear every single month, you talk about the future. You go to the doctors' offices, sit in the never-ending traffic through town as you rush to your nine a.m. appointment alongside all the angry commuters, and you sit patiently in the waiting room with no windows with the other desperate couples, but still, you feel okay. You feel like this will work. People are helping you now. But then it fails. Then, you start to really break. Small pieces of you each time. A chunk of you is torn off every time you have to tell your wife 'negative' again when you read the line on the pregnancy test. Just one line. Never two. You come to dream of two lines appearing so you can turn around and tell her, but they never come. And finally, the appointment where they tell you – despite up to that point promising that you just need to be patient, to keep positive, that it'll happen for you – that there's no more hope. That they don't know why, but they know this for sure: You have to stop. The two of you will never make a baby.

He heard Hannah listening to a Taylor Swift song once, one of her favourite artists who he'd previously thought was a bit vapid. But this song spoke about letting go of something you wanted so badly being like slowly dying from a thousand cuts and that's how he felt, he told the counsellor. The years of failure had broken him and Hannah down slowly, piece by piece, to the point where he didn't know how they'd look when he put them back together. The counsellor frowned. He knew the point of these sessions was to sign them off to start adoption and his job was to be the positive one, looking to the future, like Hannah never could. But he was stuck. It hurt too much. He thought it was the worst pain he'd ever feel, the most scared he could be. When they finally found Issy, he thought that part of his life was over – hope was here and he'd never have to be scared of the future again.

But looking at the photo of his wife entering the room of a man soon to be murdered, he realises he was wrong. Now, he is truly terrified. Because even though he's erased all evidence of his wife's visit to Jesse, the police have somehow connected the two of them, and worse yet, Hannah has lied to them. He can't let himself think about what this all means; Hannah is not the sort of person to lie like this. But it's Jesse Charlie blames for all of this, not Hannah.

Hannah doesn't deserve to be caught up in this – whatever this is. Neither of them do. For years, all they've heard is how cruel life is to them; '*It's so unfair this is happening to you, you'd make the best parents!*' and it's true, they would. No one will love Issy as much as Hannah and he will; he is so certain of that that he feels like screaming at the world for threatening to take it away from them yet again.

He closes his computer screen, relieved to be rid of the image of Hannah, then leaves the house. He isn't sure where he's going yet, but he knows he has to go somewhere; do something. Their journey cannot end like this. Hannah cannot be involved with Jesse Carter's death. They cannot lose everything they've been working for. Issy is waiting for them; they are waiting for Issy. Nothing can tear her away from them, he won't let it. Because he knows for sure this time, they simply would not survive it.

Chapter Sixteen

Now

Hannah

It takes all my effort not to run back to the car. My legs are desperate to; my whole body wants to flee, to get us away from this place as fast as it can but I know I can't do anything to make me look suspicious. The last thing that I need is to be memorable. So I walk calmly back across the gold-stoned path over the driveway which before looked so idyllic but now feels horribly artificial with my head down, checking over my shoulder every few steps to see if Owen is following me. As I finally reach my car, I let out a sigh of relief and slam the door closed behind me.

I should have known he would be here. He was always lurking in the shadows even back then before Jesse was really anybody. PR people are supposed to stay in the background and yet Owen has manoeuvred himself to be front and centre of Jesse's career – cultivating almost as much of a personality for the camera as Jesse himself. I've seen the two of them in various articles and TV shows over the years – though I try my best to avoid stories about Jesse, it's basically impossible. We were at friends' for New Year's Eve the year before last when Jesse appeared on their huge TV in the middle of the living room, sitting on the couch of a talk-show, laughing at whatever was being said. You'd think I'd have become immune to seeing him after so long and so much unwilling exposure, but I never have. Every time his face appears, my heart physically hurts. I've long given up trying to tell if the pain is heart-break or horror at the memories he brings. It's lucky that night that I was the only one sober; we were midway through what would end up being our last IVF cycle, holding onto the very last bit of hope that it might be the time my body decided to play ball. As if a glass of prosecco to toast the new year was going to be the thing that ruined our chances. Everyone was too drunk to notice how I fled the room while he was on, hiding in the kitchen until the interview was over.

Often, Owen is with him. He's changed a lot since I knew him. It's amazing what money and fame can do to a person's face. He's still ratty-looking, but you'd never know by looking at him what a truly ugly soul lives under-neath the tanned skin and toned chest. He's worked hard on transforming himself.

Shit.

He's followed me. I spot him across the car park long before he can work out which is my car and I turn on the engine and yank the car into gear, driving it the wrong way around the car park in the hope of avoiding his gaze. As I do, my phone rings.

'Hello?'

'Hi, Hannah? It's Annabelle.'

I keep an eye on Owen as I manoeuvre around the car park farther away from him. Can I get out if I keep going this way? Will the gates open for me without having to show my pass again?

'Hannah? Are you there?'

'Yes, sorry. Is everything okay?'

'Well, sort of. It's Tuesday and Charlie's not here? I've really got to leave?'

I sigh in frustration – as much at the annoying way Charlie's mum's carer goes up at the end of every sentence, as the fact that Charlie is for some reason not there.

'I'm sure he'll be there soon,' I reply, approaching the gate and praying it opens.

'He's already thirty minutes late and I can't get hold of him. Can you come instead, please? I really need to go? I've got plans?'

I speed through the gate, watching Owen get smaller in my windscreen mirror. Has he turned to face me? Does he know this is my car?

'Hannah? Hello?'

'Sorry, I'm driving. Let me call Charlie, I'll call you back.'

I drive down the stretch of the private lane which is now starting to get dark and tell Siri to dial Charlie. She does and the line rings out with no answer. Frustrated, I command it to dial again. Nothing. Where is he? Charlie is not the sort of man you have to chase about these sorts of things. He's the dependable one. He knows that Tuesday is Annabelle's evening off. Where is he?

My phone rings again but it's not Charlie.

'I can't get hold of him,' I tell an increasingly annoyed Annabelle. 'I'll come now. I won't be long.'

I indicate the opposite direction to our house and head towards Charlie's mum's, which is the other end of the village to ours. On the way, I try him again but now his phone is off. My mind starts whirring with possibilities of horrible things that would explain his silence. A car crash is first to mind but Charlie works from home and basically only drives to the local Tesco and back at most, so it seems unlikely. Could he have fallen down the stairs? Again, unlikely as he's a fit guy in his thirties, not an ageing frail man.

Then where is he?

I pull up to his mum's house and Annabelle rushes out with her coat on. Evidently, she's been waiting by the door for me to arrive. She's got a face like thunder as she comes down the path but rearranges it quickly as she meets my eye.

'Sorry about this,' I say, knowing the worst thing you can do is piss off the person who looks after your mother-in-law. 'I really don't know where he is.'

'Don't worry,' she says, moving past me. 'It wouldn't usually matter but I've actually got plans tonight? I'm meeting a guy off Tinder!' Her face beams as she tells me about him, suddenly unaware of her previous rush, and I nod and smile in all the right places, trying to remember what it's like to be twenty-two with the world full of possibilities, even on a Tuesday night in the middle of nowhere. Eventually, she waves goodbye after warning me Diane is quite upset that Charlie isn't here. Again, I look at my phone and feel a pang of worry.

I let myself into the cottage and instantly feel sweat forming on my top lip. Diane keeps the house at such a temperature I dread to think what her energy bills are like, but Charlie always tells me not to worry. He'd always rather his mum were warm, even if means us picking up some of the bill. I find her in the living room staring at the TV though it's not on.

'Oh, hello, love!' She smiles warmly as she sees me but her face falls when she realises I'm alone. 'Where's Charlie?'

I take a seat on the sofa next to her and take off my coat. 'I'm not sure, he's not answering his phone.'

She frowns and shakes her head. 'But Charlie always comes on a Tuesday. Where is he?'

'He's probably just got caught up at work or something,' I say, though I don't believe it. Nothing comes before Diane for Charlie, especially not work. 'Can I get you anything? Cup of tea?'

'Yes please, love.' Diane moves to get up but I tell her to stay where she is and go into the kitchen to boil the kettle, tutting as I notice the crumbs left on the side. As well as Annabelle, Charlie hired a cleaner to come in once a week to keep the cottage from getting too much for his mum to handle. They're booked in for a Tuesday morning so either they've done a crappy job this week, or the mess has been made after they left. I sweep up the crumbs and decide it's probably the latter and won't mention it to Charlie. We've enough to worry about without getting into a tiff with the cleaners.

'Here you go.' I place the weak tea on the table next to Diane's chair and she smiles at me, her eyes tired though it's not yet seven p.m.

'Where's Charlie?' she asks again and this time I tell her he's got caught up at work but should be here soon. Sometimes, it's easier to tell her what she wants to hear. It's been two years since we found out she had early onset dementia. Most of the time she's able to hold conversations just fine, and you'd never know there was anything wrong with her, but some days she's like this, can barely remember what you've just spoken about and prone to getting very upset and confused. It breaks my heart to see her in that state so I'll do everything I can to avoid it, even if it means a small white lie.

'How's our little girl?' she asks, taking a sip of her tea.

'She's great,' I say, unable to stop the smile that spreads across my face at the mention of Issy. Diane's referred to Issy like this ever since we first mentioned that we were looking at her details online. 'Our little girl', like she's always been part of the family. 'You'll be able to meet her soon.'

'I can't wait. She's going to get the biggest cuddle you can imagine.' Diane smiles at the thought and we sit for a moment in comfortable silence. 'I've got her a present,' Diane says, putting her tea down and going into the kitchen. She brings back a small brown bag I'd not noticed earlier and places it in my lap. 'Only small.'

'Oh, Diane, you shouldn't have. We don't even know…'

Diane tuts at me. 'She'll be coming home, don't you worry. Charlie said you're basically through all the—' Her face screws up into an angry frown as her mind grasps for the word. I'm desperate to supply it but know that it'll only make her cross so I wait it out, biting my lip as her eyes search around the room. 'You know, the things. The things you have to get through, the—'

'Checks,' I blurt.

She nods, firmly. 'Yes. That's what I was going to say. The checks. Is it cold in here, shall I turn the heating up?'

'No, it's boiling!' I laugh, wiping a bead of sweat from my top lip.

'Where's Charlie? He hasn't been to see me for such a long time.'

'He's on his way, he's stuck at work.'

'I never see him any more.'

'You saw him on Saturday, Di. That's just a few days ago.' After our fight on Saturday night, Charlie fled to his mum's house for a few hours. He's not the sort of man to get into a fight then disappear to the pub with his mates, so I wasn't surprised when he said he'd been here.

She frowns then glares at me. 'No I didn't.'

I sigh and try to distract Di by opening the present she's bought for Issy. It's a beautiful illustrated picture book about a polar bear that goes to live with a new family. Tears spring to my eyes as I turn the thick pages, thinking how lucky we are to have Diane in Issy's life, yet furious at the illness which is going to take away so much from her before Issy can ever really know her.

'This is beautiful, Di. She'll love it, thank you so much.'

'Charlie hasn't been here since last Tuesday,' she snaps back.

'Okay,' I say, putting the book down. 'Maybe I got it wrong.'

'You did,' she says. 'You're wrong. Charlie wasn't here.' She scowls at me, her face unrecognisable from the mother-in-law I've known and loved for over ten years. It's little things like this that seem to upset her so much and there's no point arguing with her, or trying to remind her that she's got a degenerative disease. This isn't the real Diane; the real Diane is the sort of mum who would say 'silly me, you must be right! I've got my days muddled' even if she was one hundred per cent certain you were wrong, because she'd hate to do anything that could upset you. I fight back tears as she continues to scowl at me, wishing more than anything that Diane could be here right now. I miss her. So does Charlie.

'I'll put *Corrie* on for you, Di, shall I?'

Her scowl slowly unfolds and she turns to face the TV as I switch it on, quickly absorbed by the unfolding drama on the screen. Despite only watching it when we're here,

Charlie and I have come to know the storylines almost as well as Di and I pull my knees up on the sofa and cuddle them to me as I watch, desperate for something to give my mind a moment's peace.

'There's been a murder, did you know?' Di says to me, her eyes still fixed on the screen.

'No,' I say. 'I must have missed that one. Who is it? Not Roy?'

She tuts. 'Roy left at Christmas. But I don't mean on here; there's been a murder up the road.' She turns to me then and points out of the window. 'Annabelle was telling me all about it. Been all over the news. Haven't you seen? Some pop star, apparently.'

'No. I haven't seen it.' The lie sits heavily in my throat and I'm glad for the first time ever that Diane is not wholly herself to spot the signs of my deceit. But how can I talk to her about this? How can I hold a conversation about the death of a man that once meant everything to me, as if he's nothing more than an idol to be gossiped about? As if by dying he hasn't potentially ruined everything I've built for myself since?

'I'm so sorry!' Charlie bursts through the door, shocking us both so much that Diane lets out a little shriek.

'Jesus, Charlie,' I say, hand on heart. 'What are you doing? You scared the crap out of us.'

He barrels into the small living room, minding his head on the beams, and goes straight to his mum, planting a soft kiss on her cheek. 'My phone died,' he says by way of explanation. 'I'm sorry I wasn't here.'

Diane shrugs as she beams at her son. 'That's okay, love. Hannah and I have been watching *Corrie*.' She turns back to the television, satisfied that Charlie is here and everything is right with the world. He slumps back into the sofa as if exhausted.

'Where have you been?'

'Bloody car broke down after getting petrol,' he says, his eyes mirroring his mum's, glued to the telly.

'Where, though? I didn't pass you on the way?'

He waves his hand as if this doesn't matter. 'I pulled off the road just after the petrol station when the warning light came on…'

I frown and tap him on the arm to get his attention. 'Why didn't you call? I was worried something had happened to you. Annabelle had to call me—'

'I know, you said on your text.' He finally turns to face me and I notice there are dark circles under his eyes. 'I'm sorry, I had no battery and I was stuck on the side of the bloody road.'

'What happened to the car?'

Charlie shrugs and tells me something to do with the spark plugs in an irritated tone. He hates cars. Despite being one of the most intelligent people I know, he can't work them out at all. When his dad was alive, he'd sort everything for us and despite dragging Charlie out into the cold on Sunday mornings to teach him how the engine works, how to change a tyre, and all of that, Charlie could never get the hang of it. It's a source of real irritation for him. I can tell he feels like it's the sort of thing a 'man' should be able to master and whenever we have car problems it sends him into a rage that we have to call the AA for the most minor issues.

'I had to borrow someone's phone to call them,' he tells me now. 'Luckily they were nearby and could come straight out. It's all fixed now.'

'Will it be expensive?' I ask. 'The last thing we need is a massive bill right now.'

He shakes his head and turns back to the TV. 'No, just the call out charge. I've paid it already, don't worry.' His hand finds mine and we sit for the rest of the episode in silence, watching the dramatic lives of the street's residents play out on screen.

When Diane gets up to go to the bathroom, I raise the issue of her forgetting his visit on Saturday night.

'I'm sure it's nothing,' I say when Charlie starts to scratch the back of his head anxiously. 'Don't worry about it. The doctor said short-term memory loss was normal. Still, it might be worth mentioning next time you see them—'

'She's fine, Hannah. You don't need to make a big deal out of this,' Charlie snaps with such venom that I don't know what to say. Charlie never snaps, not at me, at least, and pathetically I feel tears coming to my eyes. 'Shit. I'm sorry, Han. I'm being a dick.' He pulls me in for a hug but his body is tense against mine.

'Oh that little bugger,' Diane says, walking back into the room, breaking us apart. She points at the TV where a teenager is on screen arguing with his mum. 'He's a lying little toe rag, that one. Can't believe a word he says.'

Charlie smiles at me, but the air in the room has changed. We watch the rest of the show in silence, and all I can think about is what Diane would say if she knew the truth about me and what I've done. She'd never believe a word I said again, nor would Charlie.

Chapter Seventeen

FIVE DAYS UNTIL ISSY COMES HOME

Now

Hannah

'Have we got everything?' Charlie asks me for the tenth time the next morning as I lock my phone. I've been emailing back and forth with a local radio presenter all morning about finding someone to go on their show to drum up support for our latest funding drive, at the same time as fielding Charlie's worries about today. My phone dings again and I open a text from Kate. *Another one! Call me*, she writes, linking me to a Twitter thread with Jesse's name screaming out at me. I click it and quickly glance at the contents, relieved yet sickened to see it's another 'anon' account calling him an abuser – but nothing to do with me.

'Han?' Charlie says. 'Do we have everything?'

I jam my phone into my bag without replying to Kate, then turn to Charlie.

'Yes. I've got our whole folder in my bag but I've told you, we don't need to bring anything. Andrea said so. Stop worrying.' I give his arm a squeeze and try to take my own advice as I down half a glass of water then panic I'll need the loo as soon as we get there.

We're meeting Issy's foster parents today to talk about the handover process. Every time I say that phrase, handover process, it makes me wince. How can a child be handed over like a project at work? But I know it's important; the next few days are vital in making sure that Issy is stable and happy enough to make the final transfer next week. My hand idly caresses my flat stomach, thinking of all the times during IVF that a 'transfer' meant something else, something to be medically prepared for. But that's over now. This transfer is as real as any of the embryos we had – more real, in fact, because Issy is a little girl waiting to meet us, not merely the idea of one.

Well, she might be waiting to meet us. She's only two years old and will only be marginally aware of what's happening to her. She's been with her foster carers since her birth mum died when Issy was eighteen months old. In some ways, they're the only safe parents she's ever known. Elaine and Michael. We have met them before, briefly, at the suitability panel a few weeks ago. That's where Andrea, our case worker, presented us as a match for Issy to a panel of ten or so people in Child Protection Services to make a case for us as her adopters. Elaine and Michael weren't on the panel but they came to show their support, which meant a lot. They're the ones who've loved and cared for Issy like parents from the day she was found, so to have their support is huge though I must admit, under their watchful eyes I couldn't help but feel like Charlie and I could never match up.

My phone pings again and I scan my work emails quickly, aware that I've been stretching even Kate's good-will this week with my lack of presence at the office. There are a few marked 'Urgent' that I flick my eyes across and deem not to be urgent at all, but there are two that grip me. The first is a series of Tweets forwarded from Kate from a well-known feminist campaigner. I scan them, my eyes too frantic to take everything in but the gist is that they are collecting stories from women who say they've been abused by Jesse Carter. Kate has forwarded it with just one line: *I told you, the truth always comes out – let's talk.*

I close the email, unable to force myself to look at what this could mean and open the next one that's caught my eye. It's from ICT. I open it and read the short message telling me they've found a few more emails from the address I asked about yesterday and did I want to see them? My stomach churns. I'm going to have to tell the police. There's no way I can pretend that I don't know about the emails. I email back saying to forward the messages and switch my phone off.

'Come on, Han. We'll be late.' Charlie tugs at my sleeve like an impatient child and I glance at the kitchen clock.

We've left an hour and a half for a thirty-minute journey, so there's no way we'll be late but I understand Charlie's nervousness. In a process like this, you don't want a single thing to make you look anything less than perfect.

I grab my bag and finally leave the house, decisively walking to the car and slamming the door behind me. Charlie sits in the driver's seat for a second then gets back out of the car to double-check the front door is locked – something he always does when he's anxious – then gets back in.

'Okay?' he asks, his cheeks red from running in and out of the house.

'Yep. Let's go.' I give his hand a squeeze as he pushes the car into gear and bite my lip, waiting to hear for a sign that the car is playing up again, but we pull away smoothly and I let out a little sigh of relief. I did say we should take mine but he refused. I know why; he thinks my car would make us look unsuitable. It is a bit of an old banger, a slightly rusting Fiesta that I got second-hand five years ago and have never replaced, whereas Charlie has the sensible, grown-up car. He got it on finance when we started IVF, so sure that he'd soon need a big car with five doors and a massive boot to cart around our family. I could never even hate the car for its emptiness because I loved Charlie so much for his relentless hope in the face of all the crap.

After this, I'll call the police. I'll tell them about the emails. Perhaps they'll believe that I knew nothing about Jesse's visit; that we are not at all connected. I can't risk the alternative; that they think I'm lying to them and they tell the council I'm absolutely not a safe person to give Issy to. Even the idea of it brings my forehead out in a hot sweat.

'You okay?' Charlie says.

I nod, dabbing my hairline with the back of my hand. 'Just nervous,' I say.

We pull up outside the address we've been given but I tell Charlie to drive around the block a few times before we park the car. As he does, I study the estate. It's a 1980s or so new-build development, made for small families. We're on the outskirts of Banbury – the farther side from us, but it still feels too close. Andrea advised that the foster parents will not have contact with Issy for the first few months after we bring her home, to help her understand that the new transition is permanent and that we aren't simply minding her for a holiday. But what if we run into them during that time? I imagine the three of us strolling hand in hand through Banbury high street and spotting them, Issy perhaps shouting 'Momma! Dadda!' at the top of her voice and all the strangers on the street turning to stare at us like we're abductors.

'What's wrong?' Charlie says, pulling the car up.

'Nothing.'

'You're shaking your head?'

I tut, unaware of my movements. 'I was just thinking something stupid. Worrying about running into Elaine and Michael in Banbury after the adoption and—'

'We literally never go to Banbury. You hate it.'

'Yeah, I guess,' I say, remembering the one trip we made to the cinema here that was promptly abandoned mid-film when a group of teenage boys kept throwing popcorn at the screen. Charlie told them to pack it in and they flew out of their seats at him like feral animals, all gangly overgrown limbs and hair gel. Charlie found it mildly annoying but I was horrified and the cinema attendant, not much more than a teenager himself, had to kick the boys out. I spent the rest of the film worrying they'd be waiting for us outside when it finished, so much so that I begged Charlie to leave early to avoid them. He thought I was bonkers, kept telling me they were just kids, nothing to be scared of, but gave in eventually when I couldn't settle to the film. We've not been to Banbury since and so he's right; the chances of us bumping into Elaine and Michael here are slim.

'Ready?' Charlie asks. We both look at the house. It's a red-brick end of terrace with a small front garden and a paved path to the front door. There are ornaments in the garden; a small deer sits next to a cat with green gemstone eyes. I imagine the looks we'd get from our neighbours if we tried to put these outside our house – they'd be appalled, but really the ornaments are quite sweet. I imagine Issy squealing with delight at the cat and bite my lip at the thought of her not seeing it again.

Charlie leads me by the hand up the path and knocks on the door confidently. We wait on the step like school kids, watching through the flower-patterned glass of the front door. Two figures appear, blurred by the pattern, and I take in a deep breath. This is going to be okay. *Don't think of the emails, don't think of Jesse, don't think of the police.*

'Morning,' Michael says, opening the door with a smile. 'Come in, come in.'

We step into the small hallway and do an awkward shuffle as Michael steps back to guide us through to the living room. The smell of gravy and roast chicken permeates the house and I sneak a look into the kitchen as we pass, expecting to see a full roast on the sides but the small, square kitchen is empty.

'Hello!' a voice sings from the living room and I follow Charlie in. Elaine is sitting on the couch, dressed in a beige top and loose black trousers. 'I won't get up,' she says, pointing towards her hip, so Charlie strides across the room and energetically shakes her hand, bending over as his height dwarfs her.

I move to do the same but trip on the edge of an upturned rug and decide it's better to just take a seat as my cheeks colour. I hate introductions. I never know what to do with my hands; Charlie is a natural hand-shaker but for me it feels business-like and strange. He comes to sit next to me and places his hand on my knee, giving it a little squeeze as if to tell me to calm down, everything is all right.

As Michael and Charlie discuss a round of hot drinks for us all, I notice that the walls of the living room are lined with an array of framed photographs and take the time to study the children memorialised behind glass. There are so many. My heart aches as my eyes roam across their sweet smiling faces and try to spot which chunky baby from the many could be Issy.

'She's not on there,' Elaine says, and I blush, caught snooping.

'Sorry, I was just… there are so many.'

Elaine smiles. 'Thirty-six in total, that's how many we've fostered over eighteen years.'

My mouth drops open.

'Their pictures go up there once they've left. Something to remind us of their time with us.' She gazes at the wall adoringly and I search her face for sorrow, loss, perhaps even jealousy at the idea that these children she has loved so much have all left her, but find no evidence of those feelings.

'It must be so hard, what you do.'

She shakes her head, looking back to me. 'Best thing in the world. Getting those children, babies sometimes, and giving them whatever they need to start their lives over. Who wouldn't want to do that?'

Michael and Charlie return with the drinks and I'm glad for the interruption so that I don't have to tell Elaine I could never do what she does. How selfless she seems to me. What must she think of women like me who've put their body through hell for years trying to conceive before they even consider helping a child that is not naturally theirs?

'Bella will be up there soon,' Elaine adds, 'don't you worry.' She smiles at me as she sips her tea and I try not to wince at the name. Bella? She's Isabella, or Issy. That's how we've always referred to her, with no idea that we were wrong. I feel heat sweeping my cheeks at our mistake.

What else will we get wrong when this poor child has to leave the only loving home she's ever known and be placed with us, total strangers?

'We've been calling her Issy,' Charlie says. 'But Bella is lovely.'

Elaine waves her hand. 'Issy's nice, too. She'll be happy either way, love. Don't you worry.' She smiles at me and tears prick my eyes at her kindness.

'So, how are you both feeling?' she asks, and Charlie looks at me to respond but the words are stuck in my mouth.

I'm feeling like we're closer than ever to getting our family and yet I cannot imagine it happening. I'm feeling like any minute now the police are going to storm the door and demand I tell them everything I know about Jesse. I'm feeling like I've let down my husband in the worst possible way and he's going to suffer the most for the terrible decisions I made before I even met him.

'We're okay,' Charlie says, squeezing my hand. 'We're so close to the end now, aren't we?'

'It's just the beginning,' Elaine says, not unkindly but with a word of warning. 'The day she comes to live with you, your whole lives are going to change.'

Charlie nods enthusiastically. 'Oh, I know. Believe me, we know. We're doing everything we can to make the house ready for her. I've started painting her bedroom. I wanted to ask, actually, do you think she'd prefer a blue or yellow fairy castle on the walls?'

Elaine frowns and shakes her head. 'You don't need to worry about any of that, love. All Bella – all Issy – needs is a loving home with the both of you. She'd be happy sleeping in a plain white room if it meant there were two parents who loved her coming in to wake her up every day.'

Michael nods firmly at the end of Elaine's speech as if to mark the point, then sips his tea noisily.

'Of course,' Charlie says, his cheeks blushing. My heart aches for him. He just wants to do the right thing at every step but I already know we'll never be able to do that as parents.

'Blue,' Michael says eventually. 'She likes blue.'

Charlie smiles, his shoulders dropping slightly as he repeats 'blue' as if to confirm.

'Could we see her room here?' I ask, desperate to be up and doing something. 'I think it might help us make the transition for her if we know what she's been used to.'

–

Upstairs, the four of us stand shoulder to shoulder in Issy's bedroom. Despite Elaine's protestations that we don't need to do anything special, this is a lovely room. It's small, with barely enough room for her little toddler bed, a pine chest of drawers and a play table, but filled with cuddly toys that spill from the Ikea toy basket in the corner and it has a cosy feel that doesn't come from Instagram-worthy design but something else that I can't put my finger on.

'When we have the bigger ones, we swap that out for a single bed,' Michael says, pointing to Issy's bed. 'Bit tight, sometimes, but we make do.'

I imagine all the children who've claimed this room as home and hope wherever they are, they're happy and loved.

The room we've planned for Issy at home is much bigger than this; she'll be able to spread out on the floor once she's older and colour in or play games with friends, hidden upstairs. But already I see the vision we had of her room is based on Boden catalogues and Instagram; this is a real-life little girl's room, with chips on the furniture and crayon marks on the wall. It's lived in. Elaine is right; the colour we paint a castle on the wall isn't what will make Issy's room feel like hers. The only thing that will make it feel like that is Issy herself.

Elaine picks up a grey stuffed bear from the bed. Its ears are worn down like it's been nuzzled. 'She'll bring this with her. Clare Bear, she calls her.' Elaine gazes at the scruffy toy adoringly. I have to look away as tears fill her eyes. 'She can't sleep without her.' Elaine sniffs and Michael rubs her back, then takes Clare Bear from her hands and places her back on the little bed.

'Has Andrea talked to you about the book yet?' he says, getting back to business.

'Yes,' Charlie says. 'Yes, we've started it.'

'Good, good. That's the next step you know, giving Bella—'

'Issy,' Elaine corrects him.

'—giving Issy the book.'

Charlie nods and smiles at me, pleased that the process is playing out exactly as it's supposed to.

The book is something we read about online many times over the wait to find our match. Before your child can come and live with you, adopters are asked to put together a scrapbook of sorts, with pictures of you and your family and the child's new room, to help them become acquainted with you before you meet. We dreamed of making one for our own child one day and it doesn't feel quite real that we're at this stage even now. The book lies open in our living room, nothing yet stuck

127

down. It's been harder than we had thought. How do you choose which photos of your life to include? Every picture you have starts to look wrong – you're smiling too much so that it looks fake; you're looking off camera as if aloof; you're holding a glass of wine as if totally irresponsible.

'We should do the book tomorrow when we meet,' Elaine says. 'Give Issy the chance to look at it over the weekend.'

Charlie looks at me, momentarily horrified, like a child who's about to be found out for not doing his homework.

'Yes,' I say, saving him. 'That would be great. We have started it but…'

'Can't choose the perfect pictures?' Elaine offers with a smile.

I blush at our obvious quest for perfection. 'Yeah,' I say. 'We just keep finding problems with every photo.'

'All the couples say that. I promise you, Issy isn't going to be searching your faces for anything but love, and I can see you're both absolutely full of it, so don't you worry, my sweet. Don't you worry.' She rubs my arm and gives it a squeeze and once again I find myself biting my lip to avoid tears falling.

–

An hour or so later, we're back at the car.

'That was good,' Charlie says, opening the car door. 'Wasn't it?'

I nod and slide into my seat. 'Really good. They're so lovely, aren't they?'

Charlie starts the engine and we pull away from their street, Elaine and Michael waving us off from the doorstep. 'They are, we're very lucky.'

We've both read some horror stories about foster parents during the handover on various adoption forums. Experiences range from fosterers who don't care a jot for the children in their care who break the adoptive parents' hearts in their haste to hand over the child in a never-ending revolving door, to ones that hold on too tight and make the process so utterly heart-breaking for the child that the adoptive parents are seen as abductees.

'What if we can't be as good as them?' I ask.

Charlie sighs. 'We won't be the same for Issy, but we'll be good parents, Han. You know we will. We're going to love her so much and they've said, haven't they, that that's the most important part.'

I look out of the window and murmur agreement. 'But they're good, aren't they? Really good.'

Charlie shrugs, as if we have nothing to worry about, but I don't think he's hearing my words.

We drive for a few minutes in silence and then Charlie pulls into a petrol station.

'Want anything?' he asks, getting out of the car.

'Why are we stopping?'

He frowns. 'For petrol?' he says, as if I'm stupid.

'But you got petrol last night.'

'I didn't.'

'You said you broke down after you'd been to get petrol.'

He shakes his head, frowning. 'No. No, I didn't get petrol. I broke down on the way to get it. That's why I need it now, because I couldn't get it last night.'

He shuts the car door and walks around the back of the car to fill up. I watch him in the wing mirror, trying to ignore the voice in my head telling me that I'm not wrong – he definitely said he broke down after he got petrol. So why do we need it again? If he needed it so badly last night that he went before going to his mum's – in the opposite direction – how did we manage the journey to Elaine and Michael's without filling up? Charlie walks past the car door to the station to go and pay and I watch him in the queue. He doesn't look at me once, though I'm sure he knows I'm watching. He keeps his eyes trained on the floor, not even noticing when the queue moves.

I know one thing for certain: my husband is lying. But I have no idea why.

Chapter Eighteen

Now

Charlie

He's never been a good liar. When Hannah asks him about the petrol, he feels like his throat might close up. In the queue to pay, he tells himself to calm down and concentrates on counting the tiles on the floor in front of him. He's going to need to get a lot better at this if he's going to get her out of whatever it is she's involved in with Jesse.

Back in the car, he arranges his face into a smile and focuses his mind on what's important right now: Issy. They spend the rest of the journey talking about their few hours with Elaine and Michael, analysing every little thing they said and did, desperate to assure themselves they've met the fosterer's approval. By the time they arrive home, the petrol lie has almost been forgotten and they walk into the house hand in hand, just like you'd expect from a couple on the brink of getting everything they've ever wanted.

In the kitchen, Hannah switches on their coffee machine and fills it with water. He's glad to see her using it again; it's barely been touched in the last five years since they began trying for a baby. Even after they gave up on the IVF, Hannah kept up her strict rules: no caffeine; no alcohol; reduced sugar, red meat and processed food. He kept telling her she didn't need to do that any more;, that surely the one good part of closing the door on IVF was that she could finally let her hair down a bit, but now he realises it was the loss of control she feared. Years living under strict diets, routines and protocols have left a lasting impact on his wife, him too, but no matter what anyone says, he knows that the toll has been harder on her. How could it not be? It wasn't his body being subjected to weeks of hormones in relentless rounds, his skin wasn't being injected every few months, no one was piercing his ovaries multiple times to extract eggs. His only part to play was a sad act of masturbation in a too-white room where the sound of the nurses could be heard through the walls.

'Do you think we should start adding to the book?' Hannah says before flicking on the machine, the sound of the beans crunching preventing Charlie from replying instantly. He waits for the sound to stop.

'Yeah,' he says. 'They're right, it doesn't need to be perfect, does it?'

Hannah pours two cups of coffee and puts one down in front of him before leaving the room. She comes back a few seconds later, the book in hand, and spreads the photos they have chosen to include out across the table. Charlie sips his coffee and lets his eyes roam across them.

'Doesn't this feel like a million years ago?' Hannah picks up a photo of the two of them from when they first met. It had been at the local pub almost ten years ago now but the place looked much the same; the crazed collection of old beer mugs hanging from the dark wooden-beamed ceiling, the inglenook fireplace roaring behind a group of laughing locals.

Charlie has spent most Friday nights there since turning eighteen. There wasn't a lot to do in the village as a teenager – still isn't, but at least they had a decent pub and he had a good group of mates. Though they'd all gone off to university while he'd stayed at home, coding in his bedroom, a lot of them had come back to the village, to the surprise of all of them, for a few years after graduating. Friday nights in the pub were always the same: a few pints and bowls of chips between whoever was in the village that night, followed by drunken walks home through the pitch-black lanes, lit only by torchlight if one of them remembered theirs. Nothing exciting, but it was enough for Charlie.

But that Friday, everything changed. He was just leaving the bar, carrying four pints in one, when someone pushed him from behind. The pints went everywhere and the whole pub erupted in a childish 'Woooah!'.

'Oh my god, I'm so sorry!'

He looked up from the devastation of wasted beer on the floor, ready to tell whoever had knocked him where to go, but when he saw her, the words stuck in his mouth.

She was beautiful. To this day, he doesn't think he's ever seen someone as beautiful as Hannah looked to him that night. She wasn't dressed up or anything like that; she was wearing a baggy blue jumper and jeans, her shoulder-length brown hair tucked behind one ear, but to him she looked perfect.

'You're all right,' he managed to say eventually.

'I tripped,' she said, her cheeks colouring. 'I really didn't mean to, I'm so bloody clumsy.'

'No bother,' he added with a smile.

'Can I get you another round? Please, I feel terrible.' She did look like she felt terrible; her cheeks were blushed red and she bit her bottom lip like a school kid caught out. He didn't know what to do. Accepting her offer wasn't exactly chivalrous, was it? But if he didn't, he'd have to walk away and stop the conversation, and more than anything, he didn't want to walk away from this girl.

'All right,' he said, moving forward to the bar.

Before they'd even ordered, Caron behind the bar placed four pints in front of him and winked. 'This one's on me. What can I get for you, love?'

Hannah ordered a small white wine and while Caron disappeared to find a chilled bottle, they stood at the bar together awkwardly.

'I haven't seen you here before,' Charlie eventually said then winced at the clichéd line, but Hannah didn't seem to notice.

'I've just moved,' she said. 'Do you live here?'

He nodded. 'My whole life. Why would you move here?' he asked, genuinely interested. Unless you were born and bred or a very rich Londoner wanting a second home, you didn't tend to get new young people in the village.

Hannah laughed, seemingly aware of the unlikeliness of her being here. 'I keep asking that myself… My job relocated. I was in London but they moved here and I just thought… Why not? The countryside might be nice.'

'And is it?'

'What?'

'The countryside. Is it nice?'

She smiled then, so wide that she revealed nearly all her teeth. The two incisors at the front of her mouth were slightly wonky and Charlie didn't think he'd ever seen something so cute in his whole life. 'Some parts of it are, yeah.' She blushed even more then and looked down at her feet.

'Here you go, love. Five pounds fifty.'

'I'll get this,' Charlie said, pulling out his wallet as quickly as he could and handing over a scrunched up ten-pound note to Caron.

'Oh, but I was supposed to be getting your drinks!' Hannah looked genuinely horrified for a moment, but then Charlie smiled and handed her the wine and her mouth crept up in the corners to mirror his.

They spent the whole night talking after that. Charlie learned that Hannah had taken a job at the women's refuge charity that had recently opened an office in the village. He'd not heard of it but it sounded like a very grown up and worthy thing to do, and he told her how he'd skipped going to uni and instead taught himself everything there was to know about computers and had just been hired as a junior security analyst for a London tech company, and he got to do it from his bedroom. After that first night, they saw each other every Friday in the pub for weeks before Charlie finally got up the courage to ask her out properly. They've spent every Friday night together ever since and Charlie still can't quite believe that a guy like him has ended up with someone like Hannah.

'We should definitely put that one in,' he says now, taking the picture from her.

'But we're in the pub, does it look too—'

'No,' he stops her. 'Remember, we don't have to be perfect, Han. We just have to show Issy how much we're going to love her.'

Hannah bites her lip and looks down, nodding. Decisively, she grabs the Pritt Stick and glues the photo down onto the first page of the book. They stare down at it

135

together and Charlie marvels at the innocence in their faces, just ten years ago but another lifetime. Were they perfect, back then? Charlie's always thought that their lives only started to go wrong when the fertility stuff happened, but looking at this photo now, he wonders if Hannah was already carrying the darkest of secrets from the very first day they met. Is that why she settled for him?

He looks across at his wife, her tear-filled eyes glued to their photo, and a churning begins in his stomach.

'Come here,' he says, pulling her into him. Her body is tense against his at first but after a few seconds she begins to melt into him as he kisses the top of her head. 'It's going to be okay, Han. I promise.'

She sniffs and pulls away as her phone beeps. Cursing under her breath, she tells him Kate has texted from the office and asked what time she'll be in.

'You think she could give you a bit of a break for one day,' Charlie says.

Hannah sighs. 'She knows today is important and she wouldn't text if she didn't really need me. Something must have happened.' She types out a reply on her phone, tears gone as she swiftly switches into work mode. Charlie has always admired Hannah's work ethic, though he can't say he fully understands it. He's been lucky that he's been able to find work doing something he actually finds interesting, but he'd always rather be at home with Hannah than upstairs breaking systems to work out how to secure them. But Hannah loves her job. She always has. Even when they first met and she was essentially a glorified assistant, she never complained about being contacted on weekends or having to stay late. And it's not for the money. He feels guilty sometimes that he earns so much more than her, given that what he does is fairly inconsequential in the grand scheme of things, whereas she does something that really matters. But she never seems angry about it.

'I'll go in now and then we can finish this when I get home,' she tells him, already half out of the door. He gets up and gives her a kiss before she leaves.

For a moment after she's gone, he thinks about going upstairs and logging into work, distracting himself with an easier-to-solve problem, but the more he stares at the photo of them ten years before, the more he knows the only thing he needs to think about right now is saving his family.

Chapter Nineteen

Then

New York

I think I'm in love. God. That sounds stupid, doesn't it? But I am. I don't care how silly it sounds, or that it's only been a few weeks since I met him. Jesse is everything.

We spend nearly all of our time together now and I finally understand why everyone says New York is so magical. Before, it just felt like I was rattling around this big empty house. Outside, I could see all these people having fun but I didn't know how to reach them, but with Jesse it feels like being at the centre of a party all the time. I've never known anyone like him before. And it's not just because he's rich – because I've found out he is *very* rich – or that his dad's basically a super famous music producer who could make all my dreams come true (and Jesse promises he'll make sure he does). Jesse has just got this way about him that draws people to him. We can be literally anywhere, walking to class, in the middle of the city, in some cheap diner in the middle of the night, and people just stare at him, like they're transfixed. I get it! I used to do that too. I guess I probably still do, but now it's like he looks back at me like that, too. When we first started hanging out, I felt so plain and nothingy compared to him. How could I not? My clothes were old and dull, my hair a plain mousy-brown, everything about me screamed normal. But now I've started to see myself as he does; as someone interesting, funny, unique. Maybe even special. Buying new clothes has helped, but it's more than that. With him, I stand up straighter. I don't hide my face behind my hair. He makes me feel more like a whole person.

We've even started to have little couple's routines. On Sunday mornings, we walk for what feels like miles through the city down to Tompkins Square Park to get bagels. Jesse says they're the best bagels in the city and it's not like I've tried many, but I believe him. The lines outside are always huge, full of proper New Yorkers waiting for their breakfasts and when I'm stood there with him, side by side, I feel like I belong; like we belong. The walk back to school always passes by in a blur but I try and take in as much of the city as I can while we walk, each step feeling more like a movie.

Sunday mornings are definitely my favourite, though every day with Jesse is pretty special. He has a way of making the most normal moments feel magical and I can't quite believe my luck that this is happening to me.

Everything would literally be perfect, except for just one thing that is ruining it at the moment: Owen.

Eurgggggh. I can't stand Owen. He's Jesse's best mate but he gives me the creeps. He's always there, hanging out in the background, dying for Jesse to pick him. He doesn't even go to our school! He and Jesse have been friends since they were kids, apparently, though I can't imagine a world where the Carters hung out with Owen's parents. Even now, Owen doesn't have his own place – he crashes on the sofa in Jesse's dorm room! It must piss off his roommates

– imagine some ratty-faced guy sleeping in your dorm every night? But no one says anything to him because no one wants to piss off Jesse. I know Owen doesn't like me; he can't stand that I've come and taken Jesse's attention away from him but like, that's normal, right? I'm Jesse's girlfriend.

Ha! I don't think I've even written that here yet but yep, I am. We're official. He asked me to be his actual girlfriend – I thought New Yorkers were all about the 'dating' scene and we'd carry on like that for months, but THANK GOD Jesse wanted more. We were in Union Square when he asked. I'd dragged him to the big Forever 21 there to get a new outfit to wear to a gig I had the next day. Any other boy would have moaned and done the whole 'bloke at a clothes store' act but honestly, Jesse makes everything more fun. We raced up and down the escalator (the shop has four floors!) and then played hide and seek until one of the girls working there came and threatened to chuck us out. I found a cute pleated skirt and a little black off-the-shoulder jumper and a few other things to try and took them to the changing room, telling him to wait outside so I could show him before I bought anything, but as I was half changed, he appeared in my dressing room door, grinning from ear to ear.

'You can't be in here!' I squealed, but he pressed one hand gently over my mouth and the other to his lips, telling me to shush. He pushed me back against the changing room wall and oh my *god* it was hot. Like, ridiculously. He pushed my knickers to one side and we actually did it right there in the changing room! Like something out of a film. How can he do that? All the boys I've been with before are so clumsy about sex – okay, so there's only been three but still, it's enough of a sample to know that Jesse is really something special.

Afterwards, he grabbed all the clothes I was going to try and marched us to the tills.

'I can't get them all, Jesse,' I said when we reached the front of the queue and he piled everything I'd picked up onto the counter. I was thinking of the £275 I had in my account to get me through until the end of term, six weeks away.

'You're not getting anything, Hannah James,' he said with a smile as he handed over his card. The girl serving us couldn't help but smile and I blushed, thinking of what he'd just done to me in the changing rooms. All the clothes were bagged up and we basically skipped out of the shop.

'You didn't have to do that,' I told him as we walked out into the evening. Union Square was starting to settle down now the commuter rush was over and people were walking around in the dusk, chatting, all wrapped up in coats with coffees in hand.

'I know,' he said. 'But I wanted to.' We stopped to sit on a bench and he pulled my face towards his, his warm breath leaving clouds between us. 'I want to do everything for you, Han.' He kissed me again then pulled away suddenly and looked at me seriously. 'I want you to be my girlfriend.' The sound of the city hummed around us as I tried to understand what he'd just said.

'What? Why?'

He laughed and stroked my face with his cold hands. 'Because I like you. I like you a lot. Haven't I made that clear?' He tilted his head and raised his eyebrows and I blushed again, thinking of the changing rooms.

141

'Yeah, but, you know. You could have anyone you wanted so…'

'I don't want anyone. I just want you.'

Looking at him then, with the lights from Union Square behind us, his big brown eyes never leaving mine as people passed us by in a rush, I can honestly say I would have done anything for him. How is this my life? Things like this don't happen to me. Boys like me sometimes, sure. They like me enough to text me sometimes then forget. Or go for a drink, a quick snog, then say we're better as friends. Boys do not fall head over heels for me in a matter of weeks and ask me to be their girlfriends. Ever.

'So…' he said after a few seconds of me staring at him like a total idiot, speechless. 'What do you think? Do you want me to be your boyfriend?'

'Of course I bloody do!' I laughed and pulled him back to me, his lips meeting mine.

Even writing it again now makes me all warm inside. It really was perfect.

Until…

'Look who it is…' A voice broke us apart and I felt the weight of another person join us on the bench. Owen.

'Hey man!' Jesse said, apparently genuinely happy for our romantic moment to now include his ratty best friend. 'Wanna come celebrate with us?'

And that was that. I can't really complain; we did have a great night after that. Jesse took us to this bar in Hell's Kitchen where the drinks cost more than all of my clothes from Forever 21 combined and we stayed up until the early hours, drunkenly racing back through Times Square hours later — the lights so bright it felt like I was on acid. But Owen is just always there lately. Since then, he pops up all over the place. In a city so big, you'd think it would be near impossible to keep bumping into someone, wouldn't you? But he seems to find us every time.

Almost as if he's looking for us.

Chapter Twenty

Now

Hannah

I wasn't lying to Charlie; Kate did ask me to come into the office and I had every intention of going. But on the drive over, the news came on and once again all they were talking about was Jesse's murder. It's been confirmed now by the police. This time, the radio presenters had vox pops of people from around the village, people I knew.

'You'd never think it could happen around here,' Roger, the coffee shop owner, said. 'But it wouldn't be anything to do with the locals,' he added. 'Those celebrities treat this place like one big party. It's no wonder something happened up there.'

'I couldn't believe it when I heard!' Olivia squealed. I rolled my eyes. Of course she'd found a way to centre herself in this. 'But it's hardly surprising, is it, with his history? But no, I can't see how anyone from the village would have anything to do with it,' she said. 'I'm a member of The Farm, obviously, but most round here aren't. It's not for everyone.'

I imagined her smiling smugly at the journalist when she added that line, letting them know that although she lived in the village, she was more of a 'London elite' type, just like them. But eye-rolling aside, the interviews have really rattled me. I was so sure that any connection between Jesse and me would never be found, but if people are already asking about the locals, how long will it be before someone discovers that I was once at the same college in New York as him? That I've been interviewed by the police? I need to get ahead of this; I need to understand what 'this' even is, before it has chance to ruin everything and I can't keep denying that I'm involved.

Seeing Issy's foster parents today made everything so much more real. In a few days, that little girl is going to come and live with us. We're going to be responsible for her every moment of the day. She needs to know she can depend on us, no matter what happens. And right now I'm having trouble even getting myself through the day. I've got to sort this out before she comes home; everything is supposed to be perfect for her. How can I let her start another life in chaos?

That's what I tell myself as I pull into The Farm car park for the second day in a row. That this is all for her.

'Hello again, Ms Lawrence.' The girl from yesterday welcomes me as I show my pass to get through the gate. I smile and shield my face from the sunlight, partly hoping this will be enough to stop her from recognising me, though the idea is totally ridiculous. She's clearly not blind.

Even so, I put on my sunglasses and pull my coat up around my chin as I walk across the grounds to reach the main entrance. Once inside, I order a coffee and sit at the same table I had yesterday. I take out my laptop and pull up a blank Word document, then start typing mindlessly into it. My brain, for some reason, decides that typing lyrics to Adele's latest album is the best way to make me look professional and I keep it up for a few minutes until my coffee arrives.

'Here you go,' the waitress says. She seems pleasant enough but I was hoping for the chatty girl from yesterday who seemed so keen to gossip.

'Thank you,' I say, taking out my card automatically before putting it back, remembering again that I can't leave any digital trail. 'Is cash okay?'

'You don't want to put it on your account?'

I shake my head then begin to root around my bag for the spare change I usually keep in the inside pocket. Relief floods me as my fingers feel the shape of a few two-pound coins. Once I've placed the money on the table I make a show of checking my watch, then sigh loudly. 'Have you seen Owen Peters today?' I ask, trying to sound nonchalant.

The waitress opens her mouth to answer then looks around the room as if unsure.

'He's supposed to be meeting me here but he's fifteen minutes late. I'm worried perhaps he's gone to the other coffee shop?' I googled this place before I came. There are three coffee shops on site, and I hope this detail is enough to make the waitress think I'm genuinely concerned there's been a mix-up.

'I did see him earlier,' she says. 'You're best off trying Moonshine's, he's been there most days this week.'

I roll my eyes and fake a smile. 'Of course he has. Typical Owen.' The girl laughs and I slam my laptop shut.

'Shall I make that into takeaway for you?' she asks, nodding at my untouched cup of coffee.

'Oh if you could, that would be wonderful, thank you.'

She nods and takes it away. Is this what it's like to be rich? People bending over backwards to accommodate you? I imagine going into Nero and deciding to abandon my coffee half-way through; I doubt the staff would even notice let alone offer to go through the faff of transferring the hot liquid from a mug to a takeaway cup purely for my convenience.

Moments later, she's back with the coffee in a brown recyclable cup with The Farm's logo printed on the front. I thank her and head out towards the sunshine. Moonshine's is exactly what it sounds like; an exclusive bar set up to look like a 1930s speakeasy, only in the middle of a field and serving cocktails costing twenty-five pounds each, instead of bathtub gin. It takes me about five minutes from the coffee shop to reach the tall black doors of the bar, by which time I've drunk my coffee and can feel the caffeine buzzing in my veins. I push open the door and blink rapidly as my eyes adjust to the dark interior. Once they do, I'm greeted by another young, impossibly beautiful waitress dressed in a black waistcoat and crisp white shirt. Her auburn curls spill over her shoulders and even I can't help staring at her.

'Good afternoon,' she tells me in a softly spoken lilt.

'Hi,' I say. 'I was looking for Owen? He was supposed to meet me at the coffee shop but they said he's likely to be here.'

The girl nods and her face tenses just a tiny bit at the sound of his name. I wonder what it's like to be surrounded by men like Owen when you're so young and beautiful. Not all together pleasant, I imagine.

'No problem, I'll take you through.'

She moves across the bar and I panic. I can't waltz up to him with her in tow – god knows how he is going to react to seeing me.

'I just need the bathroom, actually—' I blurt, like a school child asking permission. She stops and turns.

'Oh, of course. Just through there.' She points to our left and I nod my thanks, hoping she'll go back to the front area. She does and I breathe a sigh of relief.

Once her back is turned, I head into the bar. It's busy, despite it being a midweek afternoon, but then I suppose the people that come here hardly have to worry about the nine-to-five in the way everyone else does. Despite the amount of bodies in the room, it's quiet. Most are glued to their phones. I spot a few faces I'm sure I recognise, perhaps from the TV or perhaps they just have those sort of sculpted Instagram faces that make all young women blend into one nowadays. Nerves make my legs wobble as I make my way across the room, scanning every table I pass, but not spotting Owen. I bite the inside of my cheek to stop myself from having a full meltdown as I approach the other side of the bar and sigh heavily. He's not here.

'Look who it is.'

His voice makes my heart leap into my throat as I turn to face him. Owen.

He looks me up and down and licks his lips – not appraisingly, more like a wolf would. Despite what photos have shown me over the years, he's still much the same. His body is more sculpted, he no longer stoops but carries himself like an athlete and I imagine he spends much of his life in the gym. His skin shows no sign of the acne scars it used to carry and as he smiles, I see that his sharp little rat teeth have been replaced with a Hollywood smile. But the essence of him is the same. I can't explain it.

'Owen,' I say, nodding.

'I thought I'd see you again.' He smiles again and puts out his hand to guide me to a booth in the corner where he must have been watching me from. Inside, it's intimate; black padded seats in a curved semi-circle with a low-hanging amber light. As Owen slides in beside me, I smell his pungent aftershave and wince. 'Drink?' he asks, pressing a button I hadn't noticed on the table. Before I have the chance to answer, the young girl from the front arrives.

'Same again for me,' Owen says, barely looking up at her.

'And for yourself?' she asks me.

I stumble, suddenly self-conscious. I can't drink alcohol – I need to keep my mind totally clear to have this conversation – but ordering a lemonade makes me feel about twelve in Owen's company. 'Diet Coke, please.' The waitress nods and disappears.

I turn back to Owen and his cat-like smile. He's sitting back in the booth, his eyes roaming over me like his prey.

'So...' he says.

'Jesse is dead,' I blurt.

He nods. 'That he is.'

I click my tongue against my teeth. 'You don't look very upset by that.'

Owen frowns and sits forward, bringing his face closer to mine. 'Jesse was my best friend. I'm truly sorry for the loss. It's a tragedy, don't you think?'

The waitress appears again and thankfully this causes Owen to sit back. I take the opportunity to move further away from him.

When we're alone again, I ask, 'What are you doing here?'

Owen smiles. 'I'm having a drink with an old friend. What are you doing here?'

'I don't mean today. I mean, why were you both here at all?'

Owen shrugs and sips his whisky. I wonder how many he's had today. 'England is a beautiful place.'

Annoyance colours my cheeks and I tap the table with my fingers. 'Come on, Owen. Did you know I lived here? Did Jesse know?'

He laughs then, a low guttural noise that repulses me. 'It's not all about you, Hannah.'

'You're drunk.'

He glares at me and knocks back what's left of his whisky. 'My best friend died this weekend. He was murdered. I think I'm allowed to be.' He slams the glass on the table and huffs and for a moment I think he's going to cry. He's right though; of course he's going to be a state. I may not have ever liked Owen, but he has been in Jesse's life for over thirty years. He's probably completely devastated by his death.

'Do the police have any idea what happened?' I ask, softer now.

He shakes his head and sniffs loudly. 'Not yet. I don't know, to be honest. They haven't told me very much. They keep turning up here and asking more questions. That's why I drink.' Owen nods over to the bar and holds his glass up to the waitress, ordering another one.

'What do you mean?'

'I don't know what else I can tell them,' he says, slurring slightly. 'So I keep drinking and that way when they come, it doesn't bother me as much to answer.' Owen suddenly seems very drunk, very fast. I wonder how many he's had before I arrived.

'Jesse was trying to get in touch with me,' I say, and wait for Owen to react.

'I know.'

'Did he tell you?'

'He didn't have to tell me,' Owen says as the waitress appears with another drink. He looks at me across the table as she sets it down and says, 'I know everything Jesse does. I always have. Haven't I? How else would I save him from his mistakes?'

A chill runs down my spine as I fight the unwanted memories away. Owen has always been too close to Jesse, breathing down his neck even before he was paid to do so. He positioned himself as Jesse's saviour that night and it seems like he held it over him for the rest of his life.

'If you know so much, Owen, why can't you tell me anything about his murder?'

He sneers and pushes his whisky glass around the table. 'Why are you so interested in playing Little Miss Detective, hey?'

'I'm not interested; I'm trying to stay as far away from this as I can. I've built a good life here, one that has absolutely nothing to do with what happened in New York with the two of you,' I spit. 'And I don't want to get dragged into anything to do with this. But why was he here, Owen? It can't be a coincidence that you two are camped up the road from my house when someone kills him. Can it?'

I want him to tell me I'm being paranoid. That they came here because they're another pair of idiot celebrities who thought it sounded 'adorable' on Instagram.

That this has absolutely nothing to do with me.

He leans forward and for the first time seems more aware of what's going on. The drunk haze has lifted from his eyes and his black pupils stare at me with a steady gaze. 'You think Jesse was killed because of what you two did?'

I suck in air too quickly and cough. 'I don't know... It just seems—'

'Because if you do, maybe I should tell them that. Give them a lead.' He nods behind me and I lean out of the booth to look.

Shit.

Two police officers are talking to the waitress at the front of the bar.

'Told you,' he says, smiling. 'They come here every day.' He downs the rest of his glass.

Tears spring to my eyes at my own stupidity. Why did I come here? How am I ever going to explain it to the police? I'm not supposed to be anything to do with Jesse, never mind sitting having a cosy drink with Owen.

'Don't worry,' Owen says, breaking the ringing in my ears. 'Go through that door.' He nods to the other side of our booth at a door I'd not noticed before. 'Brings you out by the lodges, just turn left when you get out. They'll never know you were here.' He smiles at me and I think of the mouth of a snake as his tongue licks his front teeth.

But I don't have time to question Owen's motives. In a few seconds, the officers will turn around and see us both. I have to get out before then. Grabbing my bag, I slip out through the door silently, as if I were never here at all.

I walk across the lawn instead of the path, cutting the time to the car park in half. My heart is still thudding in my chest but I try to steady it and by the time I reach the car, the adrenaline has started to wear off. Owen didn't seem to think this had anything to do with me, the location of Jesse's murder nothing more than a coincidence. And surely he's right. Celebrities come here all the time. Why couldn't Jesse just be one of them? A horrible thought crosses my mind that perhaps what happened in New York when we were young isn't even that big of a deal for Owen and Jesse. Perhaps that wasn't the only time... But no. I can't let myself think like that. Because if I do, it means I knew and did nothing to stop it happening to someone else.

As I drive out of the gates, I decide this will be the last time I come here. This whole crazy thing is over. It's nothing to do with me.

But then my phone lights up with an unknown number.

I ask Siri to read the text aloud and am horrified by the words her robotic voice announces.

Hannah, if you don't tell anyone what happened that night, nor will I. But if you do, I promise you'll end up worse than me. O.

Chapter Twenty-One

Now

Charlie

He doesn't know what's worse; knowing Hannah is lying about something so huge or that she's in so much trouble that it feels impossible to pull her out of it. He scans the text message again, but it doesn't bring him any more answers. But there it is, that sign-off again: O. Part of him feels guilty for spying on his wife like this. He's never done it before, but when she left her phone out last night, he couldn't stop himself from installing the app that would sync his iPhone to hers, allowing him to see every little thing she does. And he's glad he did, now that he sees this message. The threat. *Don't tell anyone.* He reads it with a thick taste of dread at the back of his throat. *You'll end up worse than me. O.*

O? He tries to think of anyone they know with this initial, who would sign off a message in that way. There's Oscar, one of the blokes in the village Charlie plays football with on a Sunday occasionally, but he's a semi-retired London banker who moved here a few years ago for the quiet life. Charlie can't imagine a world in which Hannah is caught up in anything with him. Olivia? Charlie frowns.

Hannah can't stand her, but he's pretty sure she's no criminal mastermind who'd plague his wife with threatening texts.

He types the number into his own phone to check it against his contacts. Nothing. A wave of relief floods through him at this; he couldn't bear for Hannah to have gone to someone else instead of him. This at least shows him that whatever has happened, whatever she's caught up in, it doesn't involve anyone they know.

Moving to his laptop, he opens up an untraceable browser window and types in 'Jesse Carter + O', hoping for the best. The search bar suggests 'Jesse Carter and Owen Peters'. He accepts the suggested search and his page is soon filled with news items about Jesse's death, with quotes from his 'long-term manager and best friend, Owen Peters'. Charlie flicks through the Google Image results of this man that has threatened his wife, his hands curling into fists as he scrolls. Owen looks around Charlie's age, a few years older than Hannah, and searching 'Owen Peters age' soon tells Charlie that he is. He tries a combination of typing 'Hannah James', his wife's maiden name, in with Owen's, but the search results don't bring anything up.

Charlie reads a short bio of Owen from one of the Hollywood news sites, his eyes narrowing as he sucks in the information. Owen has known Jesse since they were kids. Owen's mum was once Jesse's parents' cleaner and the boys became best friends, Owen even following him through college, the site tells him. Charlie sighs. This is how he must know Hannah. He keeps reading. Owen went on to become Jesse's manager after Jesse dropped out of his New York college, despite having no experience in the industry, Owen went on to be known as one of the most successful and ruthless music managers of his time. Is he wasting time reading about this? He has no idea. But the more he reads about this man, the more he wonders what the hell Hannah is caught up in.

When they first met, Charlie spent a lot of time worrying that Hannah was going to grow bored of the countryside, of him, and move back to London. She always told him she hated the city and had no intention of going back, but he never understood how swapping that life for his never felt too small for her. He was born and bred in the village and if he hadn't felt a responsibility to stay near his mum, he always said he'd have had a much bigger life. But now looking back, he wonders how true that ever was. He loves their life; the country walks, muddy wellies, Sunday roasts in the pub. Hannah loves it too, he tells himself; she's never shown any sign of settling for him, or for their lifestyle. But the more he reads about Jesse and Owen, the more he wonders whether her yearning for the quiet of the countryside was more about fear of what cities could hold than anything else.

He knew about New York, to a degree. You can't go through the adoption process and not learn every detail of your partner's life – at least that's what he thought at the time. They dig into every significant life event, which in Hannah's case included a four-month stint at an elite liberal arts college in New York. He thinks back to the questions Andrea asked her about that time, remembering how uncomfortable she looked when asked why she'd left New York earlier than planned. She'd told Andrea she was homesick, that it just hadn't felt like she'd expected it to. He'd gripped her hand – he remembers this now – and squeezed it. He'd thought she was ashamed that she'd failed to 'make it' as a musician; that she'd lost hope in New York City, of all places. When they first met, Hannah never mentioned that she was a musician. He found out when they first visited her parents – what a disaster that had been – in their tumbling down grand house in Exeter not long before it became overrun with lodgers. Her dad had been ranting about how Hannah had 'settled' for a 'predictable and boring' office job instead of becoming the musician she was meant to be. Charlie had looked around her parents' ramshackle house full of half-finished paintings and empty wine bottles and was grateful to be 'boring' if this was the life of a creative.

But it did make him sad that Hannah would never sing for him; that she wouldn't share that side of herself. Of course, he'd heard her voice plenty of times, not that she knew it. Over the years he'd realised she would sing when she thought no one could hear her and so began to put his headphones on when he cooked. Then, with nothing playing in his ears, he'd listen to the melodies of his wife's beautiful voice in the next room.

What else has Hannah kept from him?

His thoughts are interrupted as his phone lights up with a text message from Michael.

> Issy has made you and Hannah this. From Michael.

Charlie stares at the attached picture; it's a scribble of red pen that if he squints hard enough could look like three people holding hands. Tears well in his eyes as he thinks of this little girl full of hope for her new life, too young to understand how any of it is happening. He can't let anything get in the way of that.

He pulls up the map from Hannah's phone tracker again and looks at her last known location. The Farm. His stomach rolls; how did she even get in there during the day? It's the last place on earth he and Hannah would ever go before all of this; the snobby members' club up the road from their house is a source of constant amusement to them both. They spend Sundays celeb-spotting from the pub window, though Charlie is pretty useless, given the only actors he knows are the ones that appear in Marvel movies.

He needs to talk to Owen. But he can't go to The Farm, he has no way of getting in. Last time, he had had Jesse's help on that front (though of course Jesse didn't know that) and used the digital guest pass he'd been sent. As he'd already hacked into the security cameras, he was sure no one would ever know he was there.

Charlie can't risk going back to The Farm but he feels an overwhelming need to see Owen in person. If he'd been more proactive with Jesse, perhaps the man would never have ended up dead.

Charlie had toyed with the idea of meeting Jesse in person for weeks before he finally did it. He'd told himself it was a stupid idea at first, convinced himself he wasn't the sort of man who could do something like that, but then eventually the closer they got to bringing Issy home, the surer he became that he needed to put a stop to things once and for all. Now, he thinks if he hadn't dithered for those weeks, had trusted his gut the first time he had the idea, none of this would be happening.

Before he has time to consider it any further and risk making the same mistake with Owen, he opens an app on his phone that allows him to show a fake number instead of his own, then texts the man.

> I know what happened to Jesse. Meet me
> at the entrance to Wychford Woods at
> 4:30pm. Come alone. Don't tell anyone.

He presses send, feeling vaguely ridiculous. Reading it back, he worries that Owen won't show. Charlie wonders if he would, if he were in Owen's shoes. It sounds like a con, or like he'll get jumped. He shouldn't have picked the woods, what an idiot. But as he opens up Michael's message to reply to Issy's picture, Owen's number appears.

> I'll be there. O.

–

Charlie arrives at the woods at quarter past four wearing all black and feeling like some sort of cartoon villain. He is comfortable behind the screen of a computer; his work has led to him helping with many police investigations in the past, tracing phones of missing people, providing intel on suspects' hard drives, but never in real life. None of this feels quite real now that he's here, waiting for the man he suspects knows about a murder his wife has… his wife has what? Committed? Charlie bristles. Hannah could never do something like that, never. It must have been self-defence, if anything. But Owen won't care about that; no one will – not when Charlie's hacked into the CCTV and Hannah's lied to the police. Those are very much the actions of the guilty.

He takes a seat on the bench nearest the entrance to the woods. A few dog walkers pass him, muttering 'afternoon' as they go. He checks his watch. Almost time. The woods are busier than he expected. He and Hannah come here often on Sunday afternoons, before they go to the pub for a roast, sometimes with friends from the village, but more often than not, just the two of them. They have talked about getting a dog – people have often remarked how strange it is for them to do so much walking and not have one – but in truth, it is one of the many things that has been put on hold while they've waited to start their family. They've watched far too many dog rescue shows on Channel 4 to not realise that the combination of new child and dog can often end in heartbreak. So they walk just the two of them, hand in hand. He suddenly wishes he'd asked Owen to meet him somewhere else, somewhere with less meaning. Fewer good memories.

But it's too late for that. As he looks up, Charlie sees Owen approaching.

In comparison to Charlie, Owen has not dressed for a low-key woodland walk. Charlie frowns as he studies his choices; white trainers (clearly a city boy), skinny black jeans like a boy band would wear, and a thigh-length tailored cream coat. Charlie looks down at his own dark green wellies layered in mud.

As Owen gets closer, the two men lock eyes. There is no one else around now that the dog walkers have made their way into the trees, and Owen nods at Charlie as he takes a seat opposite him. Confidence oozes from the man and Charlie finds himself sitting up to his full height. For a second, neither man speaks. Charlie hadn't planned how to open and now he stumbles.

'Thank you for coming…' Fucking hell, he thinks. What is this, some kind of interview?

Owen raises one eyebrow but says nothing.

Charlie clears his throat and tries again. 'I think you know my wife—'

'Hannah.'

'How do you know that—'

Owen smiles, revealing his too-white teeth that look completely out of place in their rural surroundings. 'I know a lot of things, Charlie.'

Charlie sits back, the wind knocked out of him. He stupidly thought he was the one with the power here, that he could somehow convince Owen to tell him everything that was going on, but of course Owen is in charge. Owen, who lives in New York and travels the world and has the sort of money that makes Charlie's pay packet sound like pocket change. Fuck it. Playing the big man is never going to work here.

'Well, I don't,' Charlie confesses, placing his hands on the rotten picnic table between them, palm sides up. 'I don't have a fucking clue what's going on but I know Hannah is in trouble and I know it has something to do with you and what happened in New York when she was younger.'

Owen stares at him for a moment as Charlie feels colour rising in his cheeks.

'Please,' he continues. 'I know she saw you this morning, I just want to know what the hell is going on.'

Owen nods and places his own hands on the table, a slight tremor in them. 'She came to see me at The Farm,' he says, the transatlantic drawl making every word sound exotic. 'She told you?' The smell of whisky leaks from his mouth and Charlie realises that Owen is not entirely sober.

Charlie shakes his head. 'I tracked her phone.'

Owen raises his eyebrows again and a smile crosses his lips. 'Nice.'

'Why did she come to see you?'

'You know why, Charlie. Jesse is dead.'

Before he can reply, a group of children bound into the picnic area, school uniforms already flecked with mud, backpacks bouncing as they run. Owen doesn't turn around to watch them but Charlie can't take his eyes off them, because he knows who's going to appear around the corner any second.

Olivia.

She spots him the moment she enters and waves enthusiastically. 'Charlie! What on earth are you doing here?'

'Go into the woods,' Charlie hisses at Owen. 'Don't turn around. Please, go! I'll find you in a minute. Please, I need you to go.' His heart pounds as Olivia comes closer and he tries to imagine a world where he can explain Owen's appearance to her that won't blow everything up but there's no world like that, when suddenly, Owen does as he's asked and marches to the woods, his head down, back to Olivia, without a word.

'Who was that?' she asks, seconds later, as she reaches his bench.

'Oh, just a tourist asking for directions,' Charlie says, his brain suddenly kicking into gear.

Olivia frowns, bouncing Poppy on her hip. 'Hardly looked dressed for the woods?'

Charlie shrugs. 'They never are, are they? Londoner, I think.'

Olivia laughs, though she herself is from London (not that she'd admit that now; she's a local, apparently), but doesn't unknot her eyebrows as she watches the woods.

'What are you doing here, anyway, all on your own?'

'Just fancied a walk,' he says. 'Needed a break from the computer.'

With that, Olivia loses interest, as if Charlie might at any moment try and engage her with his world of computers that she has absolutely no desire to discuss.

'I saw Hannah yesterday,' she says, changing the subject. 'Such good news about your little girl, isn't it? I bet you're delighted. I said we'll have to have her over for a play date with Pops!'

Charlie smiles and says yes, he's sure they will soon. He's realised there's no point trying to explain to people like Olivia that even when Issy comes home, they aren't going to instantly become the perfect family of three, that it'll take time for her to adjust, for them to learn how to be a family. People like Olivia and her husband Tim live in a different world; a world where you leave London for the countryside the moment you decide to start a family and your first born arrives promptly at nine months after that decision, followed by number two eighteen to twenty-four months later, no questions asked.

Olivia whittles on for a little longer, planning dates for the girls that Charlie hopes he never has to attend in real life, until Poppy starts crying and the other women with the gang of unruly kids call Olivia back to them. He watches as she joins the group, taking a seat at the picnic table a few metres away. Once her back is turned, he takes his chance and enters the woods.

It doesn't take long to find Owen; he's not ventured in very far. Charlie almost laughs when he spots him. Despite everything, the sight of an immaculately dressed city boy like Owen desperately trying to avoid the mud always brings a smile to Charlie's face. As he reaches Owen and the two men walk side by side through the woods, he feels a power shift. Out here, Charlie isn't the local boy who's never left home, never lived in a city or learned much about the world. Out here, Charlie is confident, unafraid.

'Who was that?' Owen eventually asks.

'Just one of the village mums,' Charlie answers, walking through the middle of a big muddy patch that Owen tiptoes around. 'I didn't want her to see you, she'd probably recognise you. She's that sort.'

Owen doesn't say anything. He looks around and, realising they're alone, slows his pace then trips over a branch and rebalances himself unsteadily.

'Are you drunk?' Charlie asks, anger flickering at the idea that Owen has spent the afternoon drinking with his wife.

Owen shrugs. 'I've had a few. Your wife and I shared a drink—'

'Leave Hannah out of this,' Charlie snaps. 'She doesn't have to be involved; I need you to leave her alone. I've got the text you sent her; it sounds like you have as much to lose as she does.'

'I'm not sure I do.'

Charlie stops and turns to face Owen, anger ripping through him. 'Look, mate, I don't think you understand. There's nothing in this whole word that will stop me from protecting Hannah. I won't let you or anyone else take her away from me. Whatever she's done – Jesse must have deserved it.'

Owen raises his eyebrows, as if amused. 'You think Hannah killed Jesse?'

'Cut the bullshit, Owen. I know you know she was there that night.'

'Hannah was at The Farm?' Owen furrows his brows, looking suddenly sober, and Charlie panics. This looks like genuinely new information to the man. 'How do you know?'

Charlie is unable to speak for a moment. Can he back-track? It's too late, he realises. Owen knows something, even if it wasn't this.

'CCTV,' he mumbles, all sense of power long gone.

'They don't have CCTV of that night.'

Charlie shakes his head. 'No, but I do.'

'Show me.'

Charlie scoffs. 'Why the fuck would I do that?'

'Because,' Owen says, a snakelike look in his eyes, 'I'm probably the only person who wants to keep the reason behind Jesse's death a secret as much as you do.'

Charlie searches the man's eyes, his heart racing in his chest. Can he believe him? There's something not right about Owen – that much is obvious – but Charlie doesn't register him as a threat. They have a mutual interest, for whatever reason and, if Charlie's honest with himself, he literally has no other game plan right now.

He opens his phone and flicks to the still of Hannah from the CCTV. Owen takes it and studies the screen as if he's looking at it for the first time, a smile forming on his lips.

'You think this is Hannah?'

'It is; I know it is. I'd recognise her anywhere.' He says it like a point of pride, but his hands shake.

Owen shakes his head, a trickle of laughter leaving his lips. 'Charlie, this isn't Hannah. This is Haydee.'

Chapter Twenty-Two

Then

New York

Owen has met someone. I know I should be pleased 'cause it means there are four of us now, not that awkward triangle we were before. But it doesn't seem to stop him wanting to trail after Jesse wherever we bloody go. Only now, it's not just Owen I have to compete with for his attention, but her.

Haydee. That's her name. Weird, right? Makes me think of the underworld, which is quite fitting really 'cause she's a proper little creep. She's only eighteen though you'd never tell because she's been everywhere and done everything (and probably everyone). She's not from New York, though she won't tell me exactly where she is from, and her family don't live in the city. Owen met her on a night out with Jesse, one of the 'boys' nights' I was conveniently not invited to (which would be fine if they were actual boys' nights but they sound a lot like giant parties full of girls, so it's not like it's just the two of them hanging out).

I didn't like her from the moment I met her.

But Jesse does.

He think she's 'a fucking riot' as he keeps telling me. Owen is completely obsessed, of course. I think she's probably the first girl who's ever had eyes for him when Jesse has been around, though if you ask me the only reason she hangs around at all is 'cause of Jesse. It's pretty obvious; she's always trying to make Jesse laugh with the most insane stories of her wild nights out across the States. She has had a bit of a mental life, by all accounts. She's not in college, nor has any plan to be by the sounds of it, and just kind of floats around meeting people at parties. She says she's got this list of places she wants to visit and she just keeps going through it, staying until it's 'no fun' any more, then onto the next. Like she's in some sort of film. Eurgh, I can hear how pathetic I sound. I'm jealous. Okay? Very, very jealous. My life is so small and dull and nothingy compared to hers and I'm terrified Jesse will realise it soon. Why he hasn't already realised that I'm completely out of my league with him anyway is insane.

And it's not just that she's really funny and interesting and can act like 'one of the boys'.

She is absolutely bloody gorgeous, too. She kind of looks like a little cat with her huge pointed green eyes and freckled nose. She's thin like you wouldn't believe, probably anorexic, I said to Jesse the other day, but he told me to stop being such a bitch, so I haven't said it again. She's got the kind of tits that always make me rage with jealousy, they're so tiny that she never wears a bra and you can see her dark nipples poking through the material of her tops when we're out. Jesse looks, I've caught him so many times. I tried not wearing a bra under one of my own tops the other day, only in my dorm room, but the effect was not the same. Tits just don't stay up when you're over a C cup. I looked like a middle-aged mum too knackered to put on a bra.

Jesse says Haydee looks a bit like me. He said it in bed one night after we'd had sex, his semen still sticky between my legs as he stroked my face. I recoiled because I knew it meant he was thinking of her while he was inside me. Haydee: a younger, thinner, free-spirited version of me.

I've lost the sense of magic I used to feel around Jesse. The magic that spilled from him to me; that made me stand up straight, feel less plain, less utterly dull in every way. It's like all of that confidence and shine has transferred from me straight to her. I don't know what it is about her, she just draws you in. Even I find myself captivated by her stories. When she talks, all eyes are on her. I keep telling myself that there's nothing to be jealous of – she doesn't even particularly like music let alone play it, so I'm not competing with her on every front, but since she's been around Jesse has hardly wanted to play together any more and our gigs in the city have been almost totally replaced with mad parties that Haydee finds. I just feel like she's taking everything away from me.

But whatever. I sound totally pathetic. And anyway, hopefully I'll only have to tolerate her for a bit longer, then with any luck she'll piss off to the next place on her stupid list and she'll be out of my life forever.

Chapter Twenty-Three

Now

Charlie

'Who the fuck is Haydee?'

Owen stops and turns to Charlie but says nothing.

'What's going on?' Charlie snaps. 'Who is that? Who's Haydee?'

Owen signs and rubs his forehead. 'Has anyone else seen this footage? Is there more?'

'No and yes, but she's not in it. That's the only clear shot of Hannah—'

'Of Haydee,' Owen corrects him. 'Jesus Christ...'

'I don't understand. Who is Haydee? Tell me what the fuck is going on, now.' Charlie jabs Owen in the chest in a move that surprises them both.

The evening is drawing in and Charlie pulls his coat around him, suddenly freezing. A squirrel runs up a tree beside Owen, making him jump like a little kid as the animal's feet skitter across the bark. Hannah loves watching the squirrels; they've spent countless Sundays in these woods watching them fly between the branches, Hannah's face breaking into a smile as they land. What would she say if she could see him now? Charlie digs his hands into his pockets and shakes his head. This all feels so unreal.

'It's not Hannah,' Owen says again, looking at the picture on Charlie's screen. 'I can see why you'd think that, they kind of do look alike from the back; Jesse said they were alike back then but I never saw it.' Owen shakes his head slowly as he considers this. 'This woman,' he says, his tongue sliding across his upper teeth as he pauses. 'This is who killed Jesse.'

The relief in Charlie's chest threatens to floor him. It's not Hannah. Hannah didn't kill Jesse. He lets out an enormous sigh, his warm breath colouring the air in a *poof* of smoke. Of course it's not Hannah. How could he ever have thought that of her? He wants to run home, leave the darkening wood and this strange man behind, drag Hannah into his arms and never let her go. She isn't guilty. She didn't do this. But his relief is quickly replaced with unease. This isn't over; Hannah is still involved in this somehow.

'But who is she? And what has she got to do with Hannah?' Charlie asks.

'Can we walk?' Owen says before striding off. Charlie matches his step then overtakes, leading Owen through the lesser known track where they're unlikely to pass other walkers.

'Haydee's someone from a long time ago...' Owen says when they're deeper into the woods. 'We met her in New York.'

'We?'

Owen nods. 'Hannah, Jesse and me.' They reach a turn in the path and Owen looks to Charlie for guidance. He nods right and they keep going. 'I honestly thought we'd never see her again, but then she got back in contact...'

Owen stops walking suddenly and turns to him. 'Why do you have the CCTV?'

Charlie's neck prickles with unease; what can he say?

Owen narrows his eyes and then breaks into something approaching a smile. 'It was you, wasn't it? Jesse told me he was meeting Hannah that night, but it can't have been...'

Owen widens his eyes at Charlie but he keeps his head down, focusing on the muddy path in front of them.

'He was dead when I got there,' Charlie blurts, the words sticky in his mouth as he remembers discovering Jesse's body.

It had been like entering the scene of a movie. His eyes couldn't communicate with his brain properly, as if there was a blockage between the two. He's wondered often since that night why he didn't call out for help, run back out of the cabin into the night and bang on every door he passed until he found someone, why instead he simply stood there, staring at the scene in silence. Something came over him that night, something he never thought he had in him. A ruthlessness that he thought was reserved for a different kind of man. When he thinks about it, it's not like seeing a memory, more like watching himself as if on screen. He sees the way he stopped in the doorway, shutting it behind him but not stepping forward, avoiding the pools of red sticky liquid. He covered his hand with his coat before touching the door handle. How did he know to do that? How was his mind already thinking about the evidence? But he was. It was all he could think about. He imagined the police storming the room, collecting Jesse's phone and laptop, scouring through it, reading every single message sent and he knew then that he couldn't let that happen. He barely remembers how he managed to move Jesse's body enough to reach inside his jeans pocket. But he remembers the feeling of relief as he wrapped his hands around the phone, still sticky with blood. He remembers the way his heart hammered in his chest as he left the cabin, the night pitch-black and silent as he ran across the green back to his car, the sticky phone lodged in his hand. Fleeing the scene. Later, he drove to a nearby lake and plunged the phone into the dark waters, leaving no trace behind.

'If you knew Jesse was meeting Hannah, why haven't you told the police that?' he asks Owen now.

'Who says I haven't?' Owen smirks, his lip curling.

Charlie stops and grabs Owen by the lapel of his stupid fancy coat. 'Have you told the police Hannah is involved?'

Owen sniggers and shakes his head. Charlie lets go and Owen brushes his fingerprints from the coat like it's Charlie who's tainted.

'Why not?' Charlie asks.

Owen sighs then shrugs. 'I like to deal with my own business.'

Charlie nods, and they begin walking in step again. He doesn't know how to deal with men like Owen, so self-assured in that rich, nothing-can-touch-me way. There's an enraging arrogance about the man's face, as if it doesn't even matter that up close the veneer of handsomeness bestowed by well-cut clothes and an expensive gym habit slips away and reveals him for what he really is; distinctly average, possibly even ugly underneath all the money. Perhaps no one ever really gets close enough to notice.

'I didn't have anything to do with it,' Charlie says.

'Oh, I know that, don't worry.' Owen flashes him a smile. 'But it doesn't look great, does it? Husband of Jesse's ex-girlfriend turning up the night of his murder.'

'So they were together…'

Owen laughs. 'Yeah, man. Wow, you really don't know anything, do you?'

Anger curls through Charlie's chest but he squashes it down; he has to keep Owen talking and while smashing his fists into the man's face might feel good for a moment or two, it isn't going to help the situation.

'Why were you there, Charlie?' Owen asks as if genuinely curious.

Charlie sighs; he's already realised Owen is the type of man who will only give once he's taken. 'Jesse was messaging Hannah,' he says.

Owen lets out a little laugh. 'Bet that was a gut punch. A man like that having flirty little texts with your wife.'

'He wasn't,' Charlie says, anger fluttering in his chest again at the mere idea of Jesse with his wife. 'He just thought he was.'

Owen frowns for a moment then opens his mouth, as if understanding. 'So Jesse never spoke to Hannah? It was always you conning him?'

Charlie nods.

'Good for you, man.'

'I just wanted to know what was going on. Jesse sent a letter to the house, it was addressed to Hannah—'

'You like opening other people's mail, huh?'

Charlie shakes his head and scoffs. 'We're married; we always open each other's letters. Especially since—' Charlie stops, not wanting to share the most intimate part of his life with this man.

Opening Hannah's post was a habit Charlie had got into once the IVF started. Sometimes letters would be addressed to both of them about their treatment, but more often than not, they'd just name Hannah. She told him to do it – he wouldn't have invaded her privacy like that without her consent – because he was always at home and there were some points during treatment where they'd be desperately waiting on news and it made no sense for him to sit with an unopened letter, waiting for her to walk in the door at six p.m. before they knew what they were facing.

The habit had stuck and Hannah's post became their post. Most of their lives worked like this; they'd never been the sort of couple to have separate things. Perhaps that wasn't all that healthy, but it worked for them. They'd always rather be with each other; there was no need for secrets. Or at least, that's what Charlie had thought.

So reading that letter that day had totally floored him. He knew the moment he opened it that it wasn't something he should be seeing; it wasn't something that concerned them as a couple; it was solely for Hannah's eyes. But he didn't stop. He didn't put the handwritten letter back in its envelope and go back upstairs to his computer like he should have. He tore through the words hungrily, each line turning his wife into more of a mystery.

'Jesse was writing to her. The letter made out as if he'd tried to contact her before and this was a last attempt.' That had brought some level of relief when he read it; the idea that Hannah had ignored this man as much as she could. 'He said he was coming to the UK and if she wouldn't agree to see him, he'd turn up at the house.' Charlie shakes his head and balls his hands into fists in his coat pocket, the fury he felt when he first read the letter coming back to him. 'There was a number on the letter.'

'You got in touch with Jesse,' Owen says, understanding. 'Did you confront Hannah?'

174

Charlie shakes his head. 'I didn't need to. I had no idea who the bloke was but I could tell from his letter that Hannah didn't want anything to do with him anymore.'

'So why did you reach out to him? Why didn't you just ignore him too?'

'I wanted to! But what would have happened then? I couldn't have him show up at the house. He was threatening my wife. I thought if I played along, pretended to be Hannah and arranged to meet, I could turn up myself and scare him off.'

'So you had no idea who he was?'

Charlie shakes his head again.

'The whole time? Wow.' Owen laughs. 'Until you saw his body, I guess.'

'No, not even then. He was… It was too hard to see. The first time I realised that it was *that* Jesse Carter was the Monday after when the news reported the death.'

Owen whistles, the sound high-pitched and shrill amongst the silence of the woods. 'Jesus…' They walk in silence for a few minutes. Charlie keeps his head down. A weight has been lifted from his chest now that he's no longer the sole person who knows his story, but he knows the relief won't last. A trouble shared is not always a trouble halved, as his mum used to say, a reminder to keep your secrets to yourself.

Without realising, they've made their way back to the entrance of the woods. The picnic benches are now deserted as the dusk settles and Charlie realises he's running out of time and has so far got no information from Owen at all.

'Where is she now?' he asks. 'Haydee. Where is she?'

'Honestly, man, the less you know, the better. But her being back is nothing good. Not for any of us.'

A chill runs down his spine. 'You think she's dangerous?'

Owen scoffs. 'Are you serious? You saw what she did to Jesse, right?'

'What does she want?'

Owen clicks his car keys, briefly lighting up the car park area, his face a flash of orange in the dark. 'Revenge. She wants revenge.'

Chapter Twenty-Four

Then

New York

I don't know what I can do to get Jesse's interest back. Some days, I think it's all okay and he still loves me the way he did when we first met, but then other days, like today, I can feel him pulling away. I was so excited this morning because he finally agreed to come and hang out in the practice rooms with me. We haven't done that for ages, since Haydee came along really, 'cause he's always too hungover or on a comedown from the night before. But today we went together, guitars strapped on our backs and as we walked across the lawn to the music block, he took my hand and the sun came out and I honestly thought everything was going to be perfect.

It kind of was, too. That's the worst part. We had *such* a good day! The practice rooms here are way better than the ones at uni in Exeter; they're actually soundproof, for a start, and every single one has a working piano that's properly tuned. It made me kind of miss home in a funny way, walking into a perfectly white room where you just know everything is as it should be. There's something a bit unnerving about New York in that way, sometimes. As if there's no room for imperfection. But maybe that's the point? People who come here, people like me, know they're riddled with imperfections but they've dared to dream that they can make something better of themselves here; that's what New York is all about.

I'm talking rubbish as usual. What I really want to write about isn't even practice, though that was absolutely amazing; it's what happened after.

But I should mention practice too 'cause it makes everything even worse. So, Jesse was playing piano. We'd both brought our guitars but we hadn't even taken them out of the cases 'cause he was playing *so* beautifully, I didn't want to ruin it. He was playing and I was singing and god, it was so perfect. We work so well together and so I asked him if he'd come to the open mic at the pub that night with me and play what we'd just written and just like that, he stopped playing. All the air got sucked out of the room as he shut the piano lid and told me he had plans with Owen tonight.

'What sort of plans?' I asked.

He rolled his eyes. 'Just plans, don't be so needy.'

'I'm not being needy!' I said and yes, of course it was in a bit of a squeal that made me sound the very epitome of needy. 'I just thought it would be nice to play together.'

'We're playing together right now,' he said, a smile curling his lips and with that, I knew that I could breathe again. He pulled me towards him and I straddled either side of the piano stool.

'We can't, not here.'

He stroked the side of my face, then down my neck until he unzipped my hoody and traced a line around my breasts. 'Sure we can. That's the best thing about soundproofing.'

And yeah... that happened. Honestly, I don't even know how to explain it. Jesse just has this way of making me melt. Sometimes I don't even know who I am any more. The old me would have never had sex on campus, not in a million years! But I don't know, here with him, it's like I don't have any inhibitions.

But maybe I should have. Maybe blindly following whatever he wants all the time isn't the smartest thing. After we had sex, he said he had to go meet Owen and just like that, our day together was over. He didn't even wait for me to follow him out, just kissed me on the head and left while I was still putting my guitar on my back.

By the time I crossed campus on the way back to my room, it was already dark and groups of students were gathered, drinking from Evian bottles that disguised their tequila. It was Friday night, and on campus that means 'ragers' which are basically just shit parties where too many warm, desperate bodies pile into one dorm room heavy with weed and tequila until they pass out. I rolled my eyes as I watched two girls lying on the floor, smashed already. They're so embarrassing; I get that they're too young to go to the bars here and they haven't got someone like Jesse to get them into places, like I do, but seriously, they're in the greatest city in the entire world and they choose to spend their weekends so smashed they can't even see it?

Not that I can really talk. Usually, weekends are spent out with Jesse (and more recently, Owen and Haydee) but this weekend I have been royally ditched. I thought Jesse was going to stay on campus with me tonight but obviously he'd since made plans with Owen, which I was kind of okay about. A bit. I think I was anyway, but then I saw him across the lawn with Haydee.

Look, I know I'm going to sound insane now, but the way they were standing together instantly made my skin crawl. They were too close. Haydee was leaning against the wall with one leg up, wearing a tiny skirt that flapped open in the wind to reveal fishnet tights, and Jesse was leaning into her, his guitar hanging off one shoulder. Why was she even here? Just like Owen, she doesn't even go to this school. She shouldn't even be on campus.

But anyway, I wanted to know what they were doing and I didn't want them to see me, so I kind of crept up on them. Eurgh! I know I sound mad and pathetic, but he makes me feel that way! Like I've lost all sense of rational thought. They didn't see me 'cause they were so wrapped up in each other but I got close enough to hear their conversation.

'I told you, it's not really like that,' Jesse said, and Haydee smiled.

'I dunno, I think Hannah might disagree…'

My stomach curled at the mention of my name.

'Well, what Hannah doesn't know…'

Haydee threw her head back and laughed, the high-pitched cackle grating on my ears.

'Come on, it'll be fun. Just the two of us. You know you want to.'

She sighed as if deciding then said, 'Okay, sure,' as if it was nothing. Then the two of them walked off, arms linked, in the direction of the city.

I stood up then, watching them go and felt big fat pathetic tears rolling down my cheeks.

So now, I'm not playing the open mic, I'm not in the city hanging out with Jesse at a bar, I'm not even throwing my guts up on the lawn with the other desperate girls. I'm sitting in my bed, completely alone, bawling my eyes out like a total fucking idiot. While Jesse is off with Haydee doing god knows what.

I hate her.

I hate her. I hate her. I hate her.

Chapter Twenty-Five

Now

Hannah

The day we finally get to meet Issy has actually arrived. With all the insanity over Jesse, it's come around so much quicker than I expected. Should I be glad that something has taken my mind off the heart-wrenching wait to meet Issy and instead made time fly? But no, there's no way I can paint Jesse's murder as anything except what it is; absolutely horrific. But either way, today is finally here: the day we meet Issy. This day should be totally joyful, my mind should be wholly focused on Issy, but it can't be because there's something I have to do first. I have to phone the police. I have to tell them about Jesse's other emails to me.

I'm so anxious about everything I've barely slept, a fact that makes itself blindingly obvious when I step out of the shower and look into the mirror. My eyes are heavy-lidded and small – 'piggy eyes', my mum used to call them. It's not how I want to meet Issy. I want to be the best possible version of myself, so I pull open the basin unit drawers and look at my many lotions and potions, as Charlie would say. I'm not a massive one for make-up or expensive products, but have somehow over the years accumulated a drawer full of such things, usually gifts from Kate or, before she was too poorly, Charlie's mum after seeing some recommendation in the *Sunday Times* and thinking of me. I pull out a tube of eye cream promising to vanish 'dark circles, bags and puffiness' and dot it around my eyes, followed by a spritz of 'rose water hydrating facial spray' then inspect the results in the mirror. I can't say I look any different, but I leave the bathroom knowing I've done my best.

And that's what this phone call is about too. I've done nothing wrong – not recently, anyway – nothing they can pin on me and so surely it's better to tell the truth? Half of the truth, at least. I've gone over it in my head all night and concealing the truth feels too risky. Jesse must have deleted the earlier emails he sent me from his outbox before he died, that's why the police didn't mention them when they found his last. But what if they ask to look at my inbox? I can't just delete the ones I've received, our systems don't work like that, every email is stored in some 'cloud' somewhere by ICT. It's better to come clean now rather than be caught off-guard later.

Checking Charlie is still on the front drive messing with the car (making sure it has oil and water, probably, as he does before any journey he's anxious about, no matter how far) I pull out my phone and dial the number the officers gave me the other day.

'PC Dales.' He answers with a curt voice on the first ring.

'Oh, hello it's Hannah. Hannah Wilson?' There's a second of silence during which I hope he is racking his brains to place me. 'We spoke earlier in the week about Jesse Carter?'

'Oh, yes, Hannah. What can I do for you today?'

Relief floods me; he didn't recognise my name. That must be a good thing. 'It's about the emails, the ones you asked me about Jesse sending the other day?'

'Yes?'

'I said I hadn't received them and that was true,' I garble. 'Our work IT system catches any unknown addresses before they reach us to stop us… well, to stop us getting abuse.'

'Right…'

'So, the emails didn't come to me. But after we spoke, I thought maybe they'd got stuck with IT so I checked and they had. There were a few emails from Jesse to me but I hadn't read them. Not until I asked IT.'

'Okay, Hannah. We'll need to verify that with your IT team.'

'Of course,' I say, then give him the name and number of the best contact.

'And you still don't have any idea why Jesse would be contacting you so persistently?'

I watch Charlie from the bedroom window as he carefully pours water into the engine and my heart breaks a little bit all over again. How can he be down there making sure everything is perfectly safe and as it should be for today while I'm up here lying to the police?

'No, I'm sorry, I wish I did. It really doesn't make any sense to me either.'

PC Dales thanks me for the information and says he'll need a copy of the emails from our ICT department. I sit back on the bed and let my body sag with relief. That went well. He sounded like he believed me and why wouldn't he? There's no evidence of Jesse and I having anything to do with each other for fifteen years and the emails prove that. Jesse was smart enough to not say anything incriminating in them either, nothing I can't explain away should the police keep digging.

Though the relief feels tenuous, I force myself to believe that this could all really be over and not involve me any more. I need to concentrate on Issy. Owen will eventually slink off back to the US and the police will see this is nothing to do with me. Charlie never has to know what happened between Jesse and me; no one ever has to know.

Downstairs, Charlie has come inside, the car now presumably ready to go.

'Have you showered?' I call down to him, knowing he hasn't yet but not wanting to tell him to directly. There's no reply. I wrap my towel around myself and shout again. When he doesn't answer, I pad downstairs, the air prickling my skin. 'Charlie?' I say when I reach the living room and see him on the sofa, staring into space.

'What?' he snaps around. 'What's up?'

'Didn't you hear me calling?'

'No, sorry.' His eyes have a vacant look I've noticed more and more in the last few days and I bite my lip, a curl of worry in my stomach. I ask him again if he's showered yet and he says he'll go now, then brushes past me as he walks out of the room.

The adoption book sits squarely in the middle of the room on the coffee table. We finished it together last night, an activity I think we both imagined would feel quite different to how it really did. He ended up working late and after I got back from seeing Owen at The Farm, I was pretty much good for nothing so came home but spent the rest of the afternoon staring mindlessly at the television, desperate to take my mind off current events. So we ended up doing the book in a rush, me swearing under my breath repeatedly that I couldn't believe we were doing this so last minute, Charlie ignoring me as he mechanically stuck down photos of our lives as if on autopilot. But it's done. That's the main thing. It doesn't need to be perfect, just done.

-

An hour later, we're ready to go. Charlie is wearing my favourite shirt, a light blue Joules one I bought him last Christmas, black jeans and smart brown Chelsea boots. By all standards, he looks exactly like the type of man you'd expect a little girl to be spending the afternoon with in the park. He looks like a young dad. Butterflies tickle my stomach at the thought.

'What?' he says, checking himself for the cause of the laughter.

'Nothing, I was just thinking how lovely you look.'

Relief fills his face and he smiles. 'You too, Han.'

I give his hand a squeeze and then we walk out the door together to the car.

'We're an hour early,' Charlie says as he pushes the car into gear.

'I know... But it's better than late.'

Charlie murmurs agreement as we pull away but I start to feel a headache take hold. Since I've started back on caffeine, I've noticed if I miss my morning cup now, my head bangs. This morning, despite being so early, I didn't allow myself the time to get drinks, or breakfast, come to think of it.

'Let's stop for a coffee,' I say as we reach the village.

'Really?' Charlie looks anxiously at the dashboard clock. 'Do we have time?'

'I'll get takeaways. And something for breakfast. I've not eaten, have you?'

He shakes his head and tells me he's not hungry. Charlie can't eat when he's anxious. We pull up outside the café. The village is still relatively quiet this morning, tourists and walkers not yet up.

'I'll be quick,' I promise him before jumping out of the car.

Despite the quiet outside, the cafe is busy as ever with a mix of people in for their coffee before work and the school run, and friends meeting for breakfast. I join the back of the takeaway queue and study the menu, imagining what the three of us might get if we were to bring Issy here one day soon.

'Hannah!' I hear my name called and turn to see Olivia at the far table with another school mum whose name I've completely forgotten, and their kids. I wave but she beckons me over. I look forlornly at the front of the queue and reluctantly give up my place.

'Morning,' I say as I reach them.

'We don't usually see you in here at this time,' Olivia says.

'We're just on our way out. I was popping in to grab something to go actually—'

'Well, you'll soon be in here with us all!' Olivia places her hand on Poppy's head and smiles, then turns to her friend and says, 'Hannah is adopting a little girl. Two, isn't she?' She doesn't wait for my response. 'So I've said she'll have to join us on all our mummy dates soon.'

The woman smiles at me and tells me that's great, I must be so excited. Despite myself, I smile back and for the first time, I desperately want to be included in this mother-chat. 'We can't wait. We're actually going to see her for the first time today—'

'Oh my gosh!' Olivia claps her hands together. 'Oh darling, how fantastic.' She looks out the window and spots Charlie waiting in the car. She lifts her hand to wave but he's engrossed in his phone. 'I bet Charlie is thrilled.'

'Yeah,' I say, though as I watch my husband through the window, thrilled is the last word I'd use to describe him.

'I bet it's ever so stressful, though,' Olivia goes on. 'I saw poor Charlie yesterday out in the woods, I guess he needed to clear his head.' Her eyes widen as if she fully understands the impact of adoption on our marriage.

'In the woods?'

'Yes, with another man.'

'What?'

The other woman titters and Olivia laughs too. 'Oh gosh, darling. Not like that! They were just at the picnic bench by the entrance…'

'Who was it?'

Olivia shrugs and frowns, as if she wasn't expecting this reaction. 'I don't know, darling. He said it was just a tourist asking for directions but he was ever so well dressed for the woods.' She leans forward. 'Why, darling? Is something going on?'

I snap my stare back to her and plaster on a smile. 'No, don't be silly. It's fine…' Olivia frowns and I can just imagine this story of trouble in paradise being retold all over the village. 'I'd asked him to take some stuff up to

188

the tip and he said he had no time yesterday,' I laugh, 'but clearly he had time for a walk!'

Olivia smiles and nods, but I can tell she's disappointed at the lack of drama.

'Anyway, we'll be late. Enjoy your breakfast.' I turn to leave without waiting for a response and march back to the car.

'No coffee?' Charlie asks, frowning.

'The line was too big,' I say. 'Let's just go.'

–

We drive to Elaine and Michael's in near silence, me replying every so often to something Charlie says in a non-committal way but I don't dare speak more. Why did Charlie lie to me yesterday? He said he was at the supermarket when I got home to an empty house. He must have been because he came home laden with bags full of our weekly staples. But he never mentioned the woods. He never mentioned meeting a well-dressed man there. Heat pumps across my ears down to my cheeks as I consider the possibilities. It's the second lie Charlie has told me in two days; first he disappeared 'getting petrol' despite the fuel tank being empty afterwards, and now he's been seen somewhere that he had absolutely no reason to be. I sneak a look at my husband from the corner of my eye. He watches the road, his hands in the ten-and-two position as always, totally calm. Or is he? I notice for the first time that his jaw is tensed and a vein marks his forehead like a scar.

I look away. It's too much to think of Charlie like this. Not my Charlie. If there's one thing I can rely on, it's always him.

'Almost there,' he says, breaking my thoughts.

I look up at the street. We're not meeting at the house today. Elaine said it's better if the first meeting takes place outside of their normal family life. I winced at that a bit, as if Issy already has a family and we're coming to take her away from it. But Charlie told me to stop being silly when I mentioned it later, reassuring me that Elaine was just following protocol. She'd done it so many times before, he said, she would know what was best for Issy. He pulled me close and told me that soon, we would know what was best for Issy. For our daughter.

Where's that sense of reassurance now? All Charlie seems to do lately is lie and avoid me. I watch him again, my heart tugging at the frown line marking his brow. This isn't how today was supposed to be.

–

'Morning!' Elaine calls from up the street.

We're waiting by the entrance to the park, hovering so anxiously that I'm surprised no one has called the police about the strange couple by the gates, staring at all the children that pass.

We both wave to Elaine and crane our necks to look behind her where Michael walks hand in hand with…

There she is.

Issy.

Oh my god, she's beautiful. Charlie turns to face me, a smile spreading so wide across his cheeks that my own lips start to curl. I grip his hand and squeeze as we watch the little girl that is to become our daughter toddle up the path. The closer she gets, the more details I drink in. Her hair is so curly! Curlier than it looked in pictures. I heard children's hair gets straighter as they grow up but Issy's has gone the other way. It bounces off her head in ringlets, the blonde curls catching the sunlight as she walks. She's dressed in a blue rain jacket with brown dogs on it. I look up at the sky expecting to see rainclouds but it's the perfect autumn day, and wonder why Elaine has prepared her for the worst in spite of all the evidence. It's only when I see her face that my delight curdles in my stomach.

She looks terrified.

The sight is like an electric shock, a sharp hit to my chest that radiates out, aching across my body. As the three of them get within steps of us, a wild part of me imagines running back to the car; dragging Charlie and simply driving away. All this time, we've dreamed of rescuing Issy but never considered that from her point of view, we will be taking her away from the only home she's ever really known.

'Morning,' Elaine says, her cheeks rosy but her smile tight.

'Hi,' Charlie replies while I stare mutely at little Issy. 'Hello,' he says to her, crouching down to eye-level. She hides behind Elaine's legs but Charlie doesn't react like I would; there's no embarrassment or fuss about the rejection, he simply stays down at her level and says, 'My name's Charlie, and this is Hannah. What's your name?'

The air stills around us as we wait for a reply and just at the moment I'm about to pull Charlie up to break the hope in the air, Issy's face peers out around Elaine's legs.

'Isabella,' she says, almost in a whisper.

I bite down hard on my lip to stop my eyes from clouding; I need to keep it together. The point of today is to ease Issy into us. If I show myself to be an emotional wreck it's not going to be good for anyone.

'Hi Isabella,' Charlie says. 'It's very nice to meet you.' He play-bows from his sitting position and Issy giggles, sliding herself out further from behind Elaine's legs.

He looks up at me, his face so hopeful and joy-filled that it hurts to look at it; this is what my husband deserves. This. When I don't move or speak, he stands up and whispers in my ear to ask Issy about the ducks, like we'd practised.

'Would you like to see the ducks?' I say, my voice cracking in the wrong places and I instantly want to swallow the words. Issy stares up at me, unsure, and for a moment I think she's going to say no but then Elaine steps in.

'You love the ducks, don't you, darling?'

Issy slowly nods, staring at me.

'Well, I think Hannah might have brought some duck food with her, so shall we go and feed them together, eh?'

I feel around in my coat pocket for the promised food, relieved to find it there.

Elaine and Michael don't give Issy too long to decide; they take a hand each and stride off into the park. Charlie and I follow like children.

It doesn't take long to reach the duck pond, thank God – I found it awkward enough just standing next to Issy, not knowing what to do, but walking alongside her is even worse. What do you say to a two-year-old you plan to take home in a few days? I wish I was better prepared for this. All the years I've spent desperately wishing to be a mum haven't taught me a thing about how to actually be one.

Elaine and Michael take a seat on the old wooden bench and Issy hops up with them. There's no room for me and Charlie.

'No sweet pea, you go feed the ducks,' Elaine says, plonking Issy back on the floor. Her big hazel eyes gaze up at Elaine as if she might cry and the tearing across my chest starts again.

'Hey, did you know that ducks actually have *two* stomachs?' Charlie says in his best children's TV presenter voice, kneeling beside Issy. 'Isn't that cool?'

Issy's eyes trail from Elaine to him and the three of us seem to collectively hold our breath as we wait for her reaction.

'I bet we can fill both of those stomachs this morning, what do you think?'

Issy flicks a glance back to Elaine, then to Charlie as if weighing her options, then she takes Charlie's outstretched hand and her gorgeous little face lights up with a smile.

'There's a good girl,' Elaine says, sighing as she sits back on the bench. She gives me a small tight nod, encouraging me to follow Charlie and Issy.

At the water, we both crouch down as the ducks flock to us. Issy laughs in delight and the sound fills me up in places I didn't even know were empty. I watch the ease with which Charlie cajoles her into opening her fists to take the duck feed; he is such a natural father it seems criminal that nature has taken this gift from him for so long. I watch them from behind for a while, afraid that by getting involved I might break the spell, until Issy turns around to face me. She holds her hand out to me and opens it, spilling the duck food on the floor.

Her eyes fill with tears at her mistake.

'Hey, hey, no tears from you,' I say. 'Let's pick this up and feed those duckies, okay?' I scrabble around picking up the duck food, removing bits of gravel from between the pellets. 'Here you go.' I hand her the food and she smiles, tears long gone.

'You,' she says, jamming her hand into mine as she once again opens her fist. This time I'm ready and catch the fallen duck food. 'You,' she says again, pointing at the ducks. I take her little hand in mind and walk towards the pond. I glance up to see Charlie staring at us with so much love and hope that I start to think this really might work out.

The three of us get into a rhythm after that; Charlie hands Issy food, Issy hands it to me, and I chuck it in the water for the ducks. Each time, they flock around us, quacking like mad, and Issy's face lights up as she claps in delight and shouts 'More! More!' at Charlie who happily obeys. I've no idea how long we've been at it by the time the food runs out (I say a silent prayer halfway through that I went so overboard on the amount I bought for today. Charlie had laughed when he saw my little back-pack stuffed full of bags of brown pellets) but I sense that Elaine and Michael are ready to call time on our outing anyway. Once the food is gone, Issy runs back to them and squeezes herself between them on the bench. Charlie takes my hand and holds it tightly, a confirmation that we've done okay.

As we walk back through the park, Michael paces in front of us with Issy on his shoulders while Elaine hangs back with us.

'How was that?' she asks.

Charlie looks at me before replying. I smile.

'Good,' he says. 'She's… She's just lovely, isn't she?' He gazes adoringly at her back as she points at the swans to the side of the park.

'That she is,' Elaine says. 'You did really well.'

'Do you think so?' I ask. 'I wasn't sure if—'

'You were brilliant with her. She'll leave today thinking that you're both fun and kind and that's what today was all about. We're introducing her slowly to the idea that you can be trusted.'

'Will you give her the book tonight?' I ask hopefully.

Elaine nods. 'We'll do it before tea. She's a bit too young to know what's going on, mind. The book is lovely for them older kids but with the littl'uns… I never know.' She frowns and shrugs, her face hardening as if remembering all the other 'littl'uns' who've come and gone from her home over the years.

As we reach the entrance to the park, I start to worry. What if we haven't done enough today to show Issy that we'll be good parents to her? What if I hung back for too long, so worried about being perfect that instead I seemed cold? What if she doesn't like me?

But as we catch up with Michael, he plants Issy back on the floor and she rushes towards me, flinging her arms around my legs.

'Bye bye!' she shouts, letting me go. 'Bye!'

Charlie pulls me close, his arm around my waist. 'Bye, Issy. See you soon.' We both wave as she leaves the park with Elaine and Michael, watching her go.

When they disappear from view, we both let out an enormous breath.

'Jesus Christ,' I say. 'I feel like I just auditioned for the main part in a movie where I don't know the script.'

Charlie laughs. 'You were brilliant, Han. Honestly, you could see how much she likes you.'

'And so were you! You're so natural, I don't know how you do it.'

Charlie shrugs, looking away with a smile. He never takes compliments well but I know this one will mean a lot to him. We walk, hand in hand, out of the park and get into the car.

'I hope she likes the book,' I say as we pull away.

'She will,' Charlie replies. 'But like Elaine said, she's too little to know what it all means, really. Don't worry.'

I look out of the window, worry slowly filling every part of me.

'Charlie... I don't want anything to go wrong.'

'It won't.'

'We can't let anything get in the way of bringing her home...'

Charlie turns to look at me, and for a moment I think I see fear dancing across his features, but then he smiles. 'Nothing is going to stop us from becoming a family, Han. I promise you, I won't let anything stop this.'

Chapter Twenty-Six

Now

Charlie

The drive home goes by in a flash and as Charlie pulls into their drive, he realises that he can barely remember navigating through the lanes at all. His mind has been completely and utterly full of Issy. He is trying to hold on to the feeling of her hand in his, the look in her eyes as he passed her the duck food, the smell of her freshly washed curls. He already loves her. He knows that people always this about their babies, but he had worried whether that instant connection, that immediate love, could ever exist between a child that wasn't biologically your own. There's nothing left to worry about now.

Well, not about Issy, at least.

Hannah is right; nothing must come between them and her, not now. They've been through too much to get so close and have something so horrific fuck it up. Ever since his meeting with Owen yesterday, he's silently raged at this woman, this *Haydee*. How fucking dare she waltz into their lives and try to fuck it up so catastrophically? People were always saying to him and Hannah, 'Oh, you have the worst luck, poor you. I don't know how you do it,' as if they were some sort of special case that no one could identify. When his mum was diagnosed with dementia, word spread through the village like wildfire and people were all too happy to tell Hannah and him how ridiculously unfair their life was. They didn't need telling, of course; they lived it every day. For the last five years, each new year had been remarked with the same phrase: 'Well, it's got to get better this year, right?' and this year it finally had. They've finally found Issy, finally have a real chance of becoming the family they've dreamed of being for so long.

And then this. A dead body. A mysterious woman from Hannah's past set on revenge.

Whenever Charlie thinks about it, he almost laughs. It feels unreal that his wife can be involved in anything like this, more unreal that he himself is. But he has to force himself to admit the truth: they are involved in this and it isn't going to go away on its own. Not since Hannah lied to the police.

'I'm going to head into the office for a few hours,' Hannah says as they walk into the house.

'Really? Do you have to?'

She shrugs, swapping her backpack for her work bag. 'I want to; I've got so many things to tie up before...'

Hannah won't say, 'before she goes on adoption leave,' – as if saying the words will jinx it. They've barely talked about how different their lives will be in a few short days. There was a time when *all* they talked about was what it would be like to finally become parents, to bring a child home and make a family. But now, they skirt around the issue, both too afraid to look the reality in the eye, knowing that their hold on it is so tenuous.

As he kisses her goodbye, he realises that she may also be scared of the future. Hannah loves her job; it's something he loves about her, though he admits he can't fully understand it. She's dedicated to the point of insanity sometimes, and he's been known to drive to the office himself and bring her home when she stays too late. What his wife does matters and he knows that's important. He's never stopped to consider if there's something else driving her compulsion to help abused women, until now.

What happened with Haydee in New York? What does Hannah know? Or, more worryingly, what has Hannah done?

Charlie makes himself a coffee and considers this. He finds it impossible to believe his wife would ever hurt someone, but Owen said that Haydee was back for revenge. He had pushed the man to tell him what he meant, but Owen had clammed up, and told him he was better off not knowing. *The less you know, the safer you'll be* were Owen's exact words and Charlie scoffed at the time, telling Owen this wasn't some sort of fucking film and to cut the bullshit. But the man wouldn't listen; he got in his car and drove away without another word, leaving Charlie with half a story and a whole lot of worry.

When he got home after the meet, there was little time to dissect Owen's warning; Hannah was waiting for him, flapping about the fact they still hadn't finished the book. They spent the evening sticking pictures down, almost wordlessly, both lost in their individual worries.

What can he do about Haydee? Owen's warning that she's dangerous rings in his ears, but how can he do nothing? In four days, Issy will be living here, with them. How can he let that happen with this woman on the loose? When he thinks of her out there, seeking 'revenge' against Hannah as Owen warned him, a violence erupts through his body that he didn't know he was capable of. He's always been horrified by men who hurt women. When Hannah would come home drenched in stories of their violence, he would shake his head in disgust, hold her as she'd cry some nights, wishing the world was a better place. Yet here he is, wishing violence against a woman.

But this woman isn't an innocent victim; she murdered a man. He saw the violence with his own eyes; Jesse's body was laying on the floor, his own blood pooling around him. Charlie didn't know for certain how Jesse had been killed – he didn't stay long enough to inspect the body – but he's heard on the news since that he was stabbed. What sort of woman is capable of that? Jesse was not a small guy, surely he would have fought her off?

Charlie sighs as he reaches the end of his coffee. He feels helpless, lost in a world of too many questions. He's not the sort of man to charge into a situation. If he were he'd simply go to Owen's lodge, bash on the door until he came out then beat him for answers. Charlie would no more do that than he would ask Hannah straight up what's going on. Both approaches are too risky, both leave him to open to hurt. Instead, he turns to the world he knows, the world he is comfortable in, which few people know how to really explore.

Charlie opens his laptop, and begins to search.

–

His first thought is to hack back into The Farm's CCTV system, but he decides against it, knowing the police will have combed through it all already and not found anything of much use – otherwise, surely they'd already be at his door. Plus, though the police are not often the most tech competent, he has to assume they'd have something set up to notice cyber-attacks on The Farm's system at the moment, and the last thing he needs is to be traced for that. He is lucky he covered his digital tracks the night of the murder, though he's sure they've been searching hard for the cause of the missing CCTV. But he can't risk it again.

Owen. That will be his target.

Something is off about the man; Charlie is sure of it. When they met yesterday, he felt an instant dislike for him. He couldn't put his finger on why – perhaps it was the air of wealth and privilege that radiated from him like a cloud of gas. Charlie knows that, on paper, he is the epitome of privilege himself – a white man raised in the Cotswolds. But he went to state school, his mum and dad worked their whole lives – his dad as a farmer and his mum as a nurse – and yet often struggled to pay the bills. Their village wasn't always a place where the rich and famous live. When his parents grew up here, it was just like any other rural village where you knew every single one of your neighbours and were in and out of each other's houses every day. A lot has changed since then and Charlie knows that, as much as he hates to admit it, when his mum passes away and they inherit her house, his and Hannah's lives will be changed.

It's not that he likes to think about that but the adoption process really dug into their finances and it made both of them consider their future in a way they hadn't before. *You don't have to be rich to adopt!* he remembers reading on the adoption website back in the early days. You don't have to be, he'd thought, but surely it helps?

He was worrying about it one day at his mum's, before her dementia really set in, when she started rustling through her post then slapped down a letter from a local estate on the table. The bold black font boasted they had clients willing to pay upwards of £800,00 for a property like hers if she'd consider selling. *Well, at least when I go, you won't have anything to worry about on that front. You'll be a very rich man!* his mum said with a grin.

But no matter how rich he gets, he'll never be like Owen. That kind of wealth just drips off you; the kind that shows you've never had to worry about money a day in your life. That you expect places like The Farm to exist, to cater for your every whim. And the good thing about people like that, Charlie thinks, is that they're often too out of touch with reality to understand just how vulnerable they are.

He sends Owen a text from a fake number. He goes with something simple, something that Owen will click without thinking, he hopes. *Your bar bill has not been paid, please update your room details here to continue use at The Farm.*

He inserts the phishing link, hidden behind a vanity URL and presses send. He waits, panicking for a moment that Owen will have 'people' to deal with this sort of thing and that he'll just forward it across to an assistant. But within ten minutes, Owen clicks the link.

Bingo.

With the malware now safely installed on Owen's phone, Charlie is in and he can see everything.

–

An hour or so later, Charlie paces his kitchen. He found Haydee's number quickly once he was in Owen's device and though he stayed on the man's phone for a short while, there wasn't much of interest there. A ridiculous number of photos and videos of nights out, beautiful women and older men sitting around pools, clubs and on planes. It's a different life. Dodgy browsing history too, which he'd expected, the kind of porn that he always hears about men like that watching on crime shows – young girls, choking, multiple partners – but he tries to tell himself that's none of his business. It's not what he is looking to find. Owen has done lots of online searches for Haydee, too. He's also sent her a lot of messages, ranging from the low key 'we need to talk' to wildly threatening 'if you don't reply I will send someone over and kill you, Haydee. Don't make me.' Again, Charlie tries to reason that Owen is not the bad one here; that he is trying to protect himself from meeting the same fate as Jesse.

To hack into Haydee's phone, Charlie has to be cleverer. He doesn't think she'll fall for an unpaid bill scam like Owen so instead he texts her from Owen's number with a link that, if clicked, will grant Charlie access to everything on her phone.

> Stop ignoring me, or I'll show the police this

He then deletes the message from view so that Owen can't see it, and blocks Haydee's number so that if she tries to reply, Owen will never know.

It takes her longer than Owen, over an hour, before the link is clicked. Charlie jumps up from his desk and screams 'Yes!' when he gets access to her phone, as if this is all some big game that he's winning.

Once he's in, he starts searching through everything he can find but the device is clearly not used that much. There are no photos of friends and family, nothing to show that she is, in fact, a proper person at all. He wonders if this is her real phone or simply one that she used for contacting Jesse and Owen. Charlie has only spoken to Jesse on the Telegram app, and he suspects this is also how Haydee and Jesse communicated – he can't hack into that, so he can't see any chat history. In her iCloud, there are only the messages he's already read from Owen. All of which are unanswered. But it's her browsing history that's sending flickers of fear through his body, confirming Owen's warning that she's seeking revenge against Hannah.

Women's refuge centres near me, she searched a few hours ago.

Then, she found WomenGoFree.

She's been on their website just this morning.

She is looking for Hannah. No, not looking – she's found her. She knows exactly where she is. Hannah is not hard to find; she is not some protected celebrity flying from city to city every week, surrounded by bodyguards and an entourage. His wife is a normal person, and normal people are easy to get close to. Haydee's recent web history shows she knows the exact address of Hannah's work. Has she been there? Has she already contacted Hannah? Is she there now?

He pulls out his phone and rings her.

'Hi, you okay?' Relief floods his body when he hears his wife's voice.

'Yeah, I'm fine. Are you okay?'

She's silent for a second and he panics, but then hears the sound of typing. 'Yeah, just busy. What's up?'

'I… um… I wondered what you wanted for tea?' He shuts his eyes and sighs; he sounds like an idiot.

'I don't know, anything. Can I call you later I'm in the middle—'

'Yep. Bye—'

'Love you—'

'You too.'

He hangs up feeling a mix of relief and anxiety. Part of him feels stupid for imagining that Haydee had already got to Hannah, but then he goes back into her account and reminds himself that this is not a joke. There really is a woman out there who has murdered Jesse and is now clearly looking for his wife.

He thinks of his earlier plan to find out where Haydee is and leak it anonymously to the police. But how can he do that? Issy's face pops into his head again, the recurring background to all his thoughts. If the police question Haydee, whatever Hannah has done must come out. He imagines Andrea, their kind, patient adoption worker sitting on their sofa and telling them they can no longer have Issy. He imagines her telling Elaine and Michael that the adoption has fallen through because the couple is involved in a murder. Jesus Christ. How can he do that? How can he tear apart Issy's life again? How can he and Hannah ever recover?

No.

He isn't going to the police. For whatever reason, it seems like they have no idea that Haydee exists, let alone that she killed Jesse. The only person he can turn to is the person who's as desperate to get rid of this woman as he is.

Owen.

Chapter Twenty-Seven

Then

New York

I don't usually write in this until the evening but today has been so good already even though it's only midday and I won't be able to write tonight so I want to get this down now.

I read back my last entry before starting and I am *so* embarrassing. I actually can't believe that it's me writing these things sometimes when I read them back, I never used to be like this. I've had boyfriends before, but they've never turned me into this. I used to listen to the girls at uni at home crying their eyes out over boys, following them around campus like lost puppies and think they were so pathetic – I wanted to shake them. This one girl, Serena, who was in my music class in the first term, actually dropped out of uni and moved back home just because her boyfriend back there couldn't stand her being away. I thought she was the most pathetic person I'd ever met. But now... now if Jesse asked me to stay in NY, to never go home and instead be with him here forever, I know I'd do it in a second.

Sometimes I think about the fact I'm going to have to leave at the end of the academic year and this horrible panic rips right through me; I can't imagine ever going home properly again. I'm supposed to fly back for Christmas in two weeks but I think I'm just going to stay here. Jesse says New York is amazing over the holidays because everyone else leaves the city and it's only the true New Yorkers who stay. If I don't go home, maybe the two of us will spend Christmas together; we could spend our days wandering through the empty streets, surrounded by the extravagant Christmas lights that deck the entire city. Why would I go back to my parents' falling-down house with no central heating, the walls stinking of days-old booze and gone-off meat? They probably won't even remember it's Christmas.

But anyway, I don't have to think about that right now. It's not Christmas yet and today we have more important things to talk about.

So, yesterday I was obviously being overdramatic when I saw Jesse with Haydee; I'm not even sure I heard what I thought I heard him say to her. I was standing a little bit back and they could have been talking about anything. But I wasn't thinking that when I went down for breakfast this morning. I was waiting in line, standing behind this group of girls who I think do theatre, 'cause they're always dressed in black but with the most 'look at me' hair, coloured to match the rainbow, and they were so loud this morning it was actually hurting my head so I stuck my headphones in and tried to drown them out with The Beatles.

They were mid-chorus when I felt his arms curling around me from behind.

'Morning, gorgeous,' he growled in my ear, plucking one earphone out. I wanted to be annoyed at him but, honestly, my whole body just melted into his. He twirled me around to face him and put the earphone in his ear, 'Help', my favourite Beatles song, blaring out just to us.

God this is going to sound so cheesy, like something out of *High School Musical*, but he started singing along with the chorus in his ridiculously sexy gravelly voice and pulling me into him, singing at me like we were on stage. The whole dining hall were watching us, some of the music students in the corner actually clapping along, and all I could think when he was singing was: *I love you, I love you, I love you.*

Eventually, the song stopped. Everyone in the dining hall clapped and whooped and Jesse took a bow then embraced me again, tilting me backwards for a Hollywood kiss. I was laughing so much that tears were running down my face. The old me would've wanted to shrivel up with embarrassment at a scene like this but with Jesse... I don't know. He just makes everything seem so natural, like of course he's going to serenade me in front of half the school! Of course all our classmates will applaud him instead of booing! Everybody loves Jesse and that means in turn, people also love me. Or at least, they notice me.

I'm not really used to be being noticed; not unless I'm up on stage with my guitar, singing. Even then it's brief, a fleeting recognition that I'm someone worth watching, then the moment I step off the stage the magic is gone. I've genuinely done gigs before where I've stood at the bar after, listening to people talk about how good 'the girl with the guitar' was, with no idea that the girl they're talking about is right beside them. It makes no sense to me; how can I be interesting one moment and invisible the next?

I guess it's a bit like that with Jesse, though. When we're together, people say hi to me. They're so interested in where I'm from, why I came to NY, what it's like in England, but then when he's gone I just fade into the background again. Perhaps I'm just not all that shiny on my own.

But anyway, this isn't the point. The point is that I was wrong about Jesse yesterday. Whatever he was saying to Haydee, it can't have been about me.

After the impromptu dining hall performance, we got bagels thick with cream cheese and coffees to take away and walked across the quad together, hand in hand.

'I missed you last night,' he said.

'Did you?'

''Course. How did the gig go?'

I shrugged, too embarrassed to admit I'd missed it, too busy crying in my room. 'It was okay. It's not as fun playing without you.'

He flashed me a smile and squeezed my hand. 'Nothing is as fun without me.'

My heart clenched at the truth in his words but I batted it away, rolled my eyes and laughed like the cool girl I'm trying so desperately to be.

'Wanna hang out tonight?'

'Sure,' I said, insides still fizzling. 'There's a film showing in the Den—'

He shook his head. 'We got bigger plans than that tonight, babe. Just you wait.'

So I've no idea what we're doing tonight, but I know it's going to be fun. Jesse told me to dress up nice and be prepared to not get home 'til tomorrow. I wonder if he's got a hotel room for the two of us or something. Imagine that! Oh my god, I hope it is. One of those ones you see on TV where they've got floor-to-ceiling glass that looks out over the city and a huge roll-top bath filled with rose petals and bubble bath, a glass of ice-cold champagne placed on the side.

Imagine if that's it?

Anyway, I need to stop writing and pack a bag. I've only got an hour between classes and then he said he'll be here at seven p.m. to pick me up.

God, I am so excited.

Chapter Twenty-Eight

Now

Hannah

'How did it go?' Kate asks the moment I'm through the door. She nods towards the tiny kitchen at the back of the office so we can chat in semi-privacy.

'It went really well,' I say as we reach the kitchen.

Kate flicks on the kettle and starts to make us both a coffee. 'Is that all I get?'

I laugh, a nervous flutter in my stomach as I think about sharing something still so new and raw. 'No, it was great. We fed the ducks. Charlie was brilliant with her. I knew he would be but to see them together… honestly, it just felt…'

Kate places her hand on my arm. 'I bet. I'm so glad, Han. Just think, not long until she's yours for good. Did you talk to her about it?'

I shake my head. 'She's too little to understand. We gave her foster parents the book – you know, the one I was telling you about, with pictures of Charlie and me and her new bedroom.'

'That's so cute. She'll love her room; she'll love living with you.'

Kate pours the boiling water into our cups then tops them up with milk.

'I hope so,' I say as we walk out of the kitchen into the main office. 'How's this morning been?'

Kate sits at her desk and rolls her eyes as I open my laptop. 'Honestly, chaotic as fuck.'

I try not to wince at her casual swearing, glancing at our assistant, Carleigh. She's very young and I do worry that we're a bad influence on her.

'What's happened?' I ask, scrolling through the ridiculous amount of emails that have taken residence in my inbox since last night.

'Oh, you'll be gutted you missed this,' Carleigh says, overhearing our chat. Her eyes are wide and there's a little smile on her face, giving me the feeling I used to get at school when I'd walk into a classroom moments after the joke was made.

'Hardly, Carleigh,' Kate says, suddenly professional. 'It's not something to be excited about.'

Carleigh huffs and turns back to her laptop.

'A woman came in to report an assault—'

'Here? She came in here?'

Kate nods. 'I know. I told her this is only the head office but she wouldn't listen. But you'll never guess who she was ranting about—'

'Who?'

Kate sits back, her eyes now wide. 'Jesse Carter.'

His name sends jolts of pain all through my body. 'What?' I manage.

'I know. She was so upset she basically spat his name out.'

The coffee I've just drunk starts to repeat on me and I have to swallow hard to force it down. 'What did she want? Why did she come here?'

'I've no idea,' Kate says, shrugging. 'I tried to get her into one of the private rooms to talk about it more, offered to call the police for her or one of the actual DV teams but she wouldn't come in. She just kept saying things like, "If this is the PR team why aren't you saying something about men like Jesse fucking Carter? You know what he's done! I wouldn't be here if it wasn't for him…".'

Carleigh can't resist any longer and her chair spins around to face us. 'She was pretty nuts, though, wasn't she? Like, it wasn't a normal woman—'

'Carleigh, you can't say that. Haven't you learned anything from being here? There's no "normal" victim of abuse.'

Carleigh bites her lip and frowns, then looks at me as if I might understand. 'No, I know. I'm not judging her. I'm just telling Hannah, for context. The whole thing was just weird. She seemed manic. Like she really felt Jesse Carter was to blame for men being abusive? I don't know, it was weird.'

'Did you call the police?' I ask.

Kate nods. 'But we didn't really have much to tell them; it's not like we got her name or anything.'

I take small, shallow breaths, telling myself that this cannot be what I think it is. It can't be.

'What did she look like?'

Kate frowns as if trying to remember. 'She was quite small, dark hair, kind of pretty but looked a bit…' She flicks a glance at Carleigh. 'Okay, yes, she did look a bit unhinged. Oh, and she was American.'

I take in a sharp gasp which I try to cover with a cough. It backfires and I end up choking, the panic welling in my chest as I struggle to catch my breath. Kate bashes her fists against my back as tears stream down my face, the air rasping in my throat, desperate to fill my lungs.

Haydee.

That woman sounds just like Haydee.

But it can't be.

Because Haydee's dead.

–

A few hours later, the office has calmed down and everyone is getting on with their work as usual. I've had to sit through an hour-long meeting with the CEO about how to deal with the latest police figures on domestic violence and abuse showing a sharp increase in areas where lower-income households are prevalent. They want me to communicate the strategy for our approach to this but my mind couldn't focus at all. After, the CEO sent me a message on Slack reminding me that I should have brought Kate into the meeting as she would be taking my place in a few days. I bit my lip as I read it; everyone around me is so sure that Issy will be coming home on Monday, that I will be a mother. Everyone except me.

I spoke to Kate a little more about the woman who came here once I'd recovered from my choking fit. She didn't say much; by the sounds of it, after ranting about Jesse she ran out of the office without them being able to get any more information from her. This has never happened before; our office is too rural for someone to accidentally wander in, and all our centres where we have actual trained support staff to deal with victims are clearly signposted on our website. You can probably find the address on Google, but I'm sure it's clear that this location is an office function, made up of PR, marketing and admin; women do not come here for support. Yet this woman did.

Was it because of me? It feels far-fetched yet the only plausible explanation for her visit. Did she, whoever she is, think I would be here? It doesn't make sense, because there are only two people left alive who know what happened to Haydee: me and Owen. And I know Owen would never send a woman in to scare me like that; there would be no benefit to him in doing so. And Owen has always put self-preservation above all else.

Yet there is no-one else who could have done it – surely? And while I don't know why he would want to send someone in to scare me, I don't doubt that he would be capable of it, if it somehow met his ends. I assume he knows where I work, he's the only other person alive who knows what happened to Haydee, and he's currently just a few minutes up the road. He's also the only person I can imagine paying a random woman to come and do this. But the question still remains: why would he? Perhaps he wanted to scare me, remind me of how much I stand to lose if I ever breathe a word about what we did in New York.

But something doesn't sit right. Owen isn't a stupid man; he'll have seen how different my life is now. He'll know there's absolutely no reason for me to ever start talking. Jesse's death hasn't opened anything up for me, it's made me more sure than ever that I'll take the truth behind Haydee's death to my grave.

Suddenly it hits me. What if *Jesse* didn't keep quiet? He could have told someone about what we did before he was killed. The air around me starts to tighten, a cold hand around my neck as I struggle to breathe. He wouldn't. He would never do that to me. He'd never do that to himself.

But then why is some woman in my office, ranting about Jesse? Why is Jesse dead?

Why did I ever let this happen?

Chapter Twenty-Nine

Then

New York

I can't breathe. I don't know what to do. It's been ten hours since Jesse brought me back to my dorm room and I've not moved an inch. I'm just curled up under the covers of my bunk bed like a child, like there's a monster under the bed that can't get me under here. I need to go home. I need to be away from this place, away from Owen, away from Jesse.

But still, the thought of leaving Jesse makes the air in my lungs constrict. How can I do that? How can I leave him?

Shit.

My roommate just came back and asked me what the hell was wrong with me; she pulled back the sheet I've hung from her bunk so that it falls down over my level, closing me off from the world, and looked at me like I was mad.

'Jesse cheat on you or something?' she smirked.

I told her to fuck off and dragged the sheet back down in front of me. She mumbled 'crazy fucking bitch' under her breath and stormed out of the room.

Shit. Shit. Shit.

Owen warned me I couldn't let anyone see me in a state; that I had to act normal. Why can't I do anything right?

It doesn't matter. None of it matters. Jesse said Owen is going to sort it. No one will ever have to know what I've done. I don't know what that means; I can't let myself consider it. Jesse will make it go away. I know that he will protect me. Owen will protect himself; that I can be as sure of as I am of anything.

In two weeks I'll be on the flight back home for Christmas, only this time, I'll stay there. I can't ever be in New York now. I cry harder, aware that this self-pity is disgusting. How could I have done this? I don't even know who I am any more.

Chapter Thirty

THREE DAYS UNTIL ISSY COMES HOME

Now

Charlie

On Friday evening, as he pulls into the busy car park for the pub Owen has suggested, Charlie begins to regret his decision. When he told Hannah he couldn't go to their local tonight, at first she'd just looked confused.

'But we always go to the pub on a Friday,' she said, folding his T-shirts from the laundry basket.

'I know, sorry, but Theo is only back for one night—'

'I didn't even know you still spoke to him.'

Charlie had shrugged and told her he did, sometimes, which was a lie. He hadn't spoken to Theo in about four years since he'd moved to Surrey and started the world's most perfect family with his wife Rachael. Charlie couldn't stand seeing the smug look on his perfectly hand-some face as he posed for another 'super dad' post, a twin on each arm, on Instagram and had muted him years before. They hadn't fallen out, that's not really Charlie's style, but he'd gradually stopped responding to things in the group text and eventually Theo had just faded from his life altogether. It wasn't much of a loss; they'd never really been that close. Theo grew up in the village but had gone off to board in year nine, leaving the motley group of mates from the local comp a little behind. But tonight, he provided the perfect excuse to get out of the village.

Hannah was quiet as Charlie got ready to leave, folding the laundry and putting it away robotically, and he sensed she was upset. As he pulled on his least favourite jumper, not wanting to tar anything he loved with this Owen business, she hugged him from behind.

'Couldn't you just skip it?' she asked, nuzzling into him.

'Han, come on. It's one night.' He shrugged her off, finding himself surprisingly annoyed. He'd found himself wanting to scream at her lately; didn't she know everything he was doing was for her?

'It's our last one,' she said, her voice quiet.

'What?'

She looked up, hurt in her eyes. 'It's the last time it'll be just the two of us,' she said, her voice a mix of hope and hurt. 'Next Friday, we'll be parents.'

He felt a fizzle of excitement which was quickly replaced by another surge of anger. Tonight shouldn't be like this; Hannah was right. It was their last Friday as a couple; they should be celebrating. He imagined them walking into the village pub hand in hand, ordering a bottle of New Zealand sauvignon (Hannah's favourite) and two steaks. That's what tonight should be. A celebration of everything that is coming, a fond farewell to their life as a childless couple without responsibilities. But how can he do that knowing Haydee is out there planning revenge on his wife?

'Sorry darling,' he told her, kissing her on the head. 'There will be plenty of Friday nights when she's here, I promise.'

Hannah hadn't followed him downstairs to stand at the front door and wave him off like she usually would when he went out without her. He saw her silhouette in the bedroom window as he drove away, the feeling of guilt and anger heavy in his stomach.

And now he's here, only thirty minutes away from their village but a pub he's never been to before. Owen suggested it and Charlie is surprised to see it's not a posh gastro pub, the sort the celebrities love around here, but instead a run-down place at the edge of a small town. It even has a kebab van in the car park. A proper drinker's place. He cannot imagine for a minute that Owen has been here before and is glad that for once, Charlie will be more at home than Owen. Though he reminds himself Owen is not the enemy here; they're in this together.

Inside the pub, the atmosphere is rowdy. It's only just gone seven p.m. but it appears many of the men have been here for hours already. There are a lot of builders here, their profession easy to spot with their black workmen's trousers covered in grey and black marks from mud and dust, and their thick, steel-capped boots. A group of them hover at the bar, over-spilling pints being handed out by the bar woman with a smile. Charlie scans the pub for Owen and eventually spots him in the corner by the fruit machine. He can't help but smirk at the sight of him glancing anxiously around the pub, his glass of red wine and smart coat totally out of place. The air is thick with the yeasty smell of years of beer spilled into the carpet and the sound of bellowing laughs and shouts fills the small pub.

'All right?' Charlie says as he sits, faking a casualness he doesn't feel.

Owen simply nods, taking a sip of his wine which leaves blood-like stains on his lips.

'You been here before?'

Owen scoffs.

'What, not up to your standards?'

Owen looks around and crinkles his nose. 'I assumed you wouldn't want to go somewhere people might see us.'

Charlie mumbles that he appreciates that, his feeling of having the upper hand slipping away.

'So, tell me what you found,' Owen says.

A group of young women dressed up like they're in a city centre nightclub, not a rural drinker's pub, slide past their table, laughter ringing out even louder than the builders'. Owen's attention is momentarily lost and Charlie tries not to scowl at the way the man's eyes travel up and down the women's bodies. Hannah would be furious, not just at Owen but at Charlie. What did she always say? 'Men like that only get away with it because so many "nice blokes" sit by and do nothing.' But tonight isn't the night to be the hero. Hannah wouldn't be proud of any of this, and surely his inability to challenge Owen's lecherous looks is the least of that.

'I managed to get into her phone,' Charlie says once the women are far enough away that Owen's gaze has returned to him.

'And? What did you find?'

'She's been looking for Hannah,' Charlie says, the anger flaring up again as he grips his pint, the cold droplets of condensation soaking his fingers. 'She knows where she works. She looked up directions to her office.'

'From where?'

'What?'

'Where were the directions from?' Owen says as if Charlie is stupid.

'Oh, um, I think—' Charlie stumbles, his mind suddenly blank; around Owen, Charlie hears himself become more British, a less charming, more bumbling Hugh Grant.

'Do you have it?'

'What?'

Owen grits his teeth. 'Whatever you found. Do you have it now, on your cell?' He gestures for Charlie to hand over his phone but he shakes his head.

'I can't get to it here, I need to go via my secure VPN, the Wi-Fi...'

Owen frowns, clearly lost by what Hannah would call Charlie's 'tech babble'. For some reason, he is holding out that he does indeed have the address that Haydee was looking for directions from. Something about Owen is putting him on edge tonight; he seems even more abrasive than he did in the woods and for the first time Charlie wonders just what this man plans to do to Haydee if he finds her.

'Well, what do you have?' Owen eventually says.

'I don't know...' Charlie mumbles. 'I know she is looking for Hannah, and she's been obsessively reading articles about Jesse's murder, and doing searches for you—'

'What about me?'

Charlie shrugs. 'Just general Google searches, for your name, looking at the website for The Farm—'

'Jesus Christ, man!' Owen shouts, bashing his fist against the table. Two women a few tables away turn to look at them in alarm. 'Sorry, ladies,' Owen says, his transatlantic drawl turning their frowns into bashful smiles.

'You enjoy your evening.' Unbelievably, Owen actually winks at the women and to Charlie's utter bemusement, this causes more smiles and even a giggle.

Turning back to him, Owen lowers his voice. 'You do understand what's happening right now, don't you? Haydee is planning something – she is dangerous and looking for me *and* your wife. Doesn't that worry you, huh?'

Charlie bites the inside of his cheek. 'Of course it fucking does, why do you think I'm here?'

'Then stop fucking about, man, and tell me where she is.'

Charlie sits back and looks around the pub. The builders at the bar have moved to the pool table and they laugh loudly as one of them takes a shot and misses. The young women have taken a table nearby and watch them with mischievous eyes. No one here looks like they have a care in the world and Charlie thinks how fucking unfair it is that he's here, with this man who he suspects is a total scumbag, instead of in the cosy pub in the village with Hannah. Why is he worrying about the fate of a woman who has already murdered one person, who clearly plans to do something similar to his wife?

He pulls out his phone and slams it against the table. 'She's here,' he says, showing Owen the address saved on his notes app.

Owen keeps his eyes glued to Charlie and for a moment Charlie imagines police rushing in, Owen revealing the wire under his shirt with a smug grin. But what would he be charged for? He's not really done anything wrong, right? His mind goes to the blood-filled hotel room, Jesse's lifeless body. The security cameras he hacked into before he even arrived that night, pre-empting the need to delete evidence of his presence at the scene. He cannot claim he is innocent here. And why should he be? He's sick of being the good guy. Sick of waiting for him and Hannah to finally get all the good things they deserve. Maybe life doesn't work like that after all.

'You're sure?' Owen says, still not looking at the address.

Charlie nods.

'Anyone else know about this?'

'No.'

'Hannah?'

'No.'

Owen nods slowly and finally looks at the address.

'What is it? A hotel?'

'Airbnb,' Charlie says, taking back his phone and bringing up the Airbnb listing, handing it back to Owen. Charlie doesn't need to see the screen to know exactly what Owen's looking at; he's studied the thirteen pictures of the holiday cottage hundreds of times. He knows you walk straight into the hallway from the front door; on one side is the living room and on the other the small galley kitchen where the stairs are. Upstairs is one small double bedroom and a bathroom. That's the entire property; it's not homely or welcoming, it's been done up to look like nobody and anybody could live there. Haydee has rented it for three weeks for £1200 and been there two already. That means whatever she is planning will be over soon.

'Security?'

Charlie shakes his head. 'It's rural, no neighbours for at least a mile.'

'You're sure she's there?'

He shrugs. 'As sure as I can be. The rental isn't in her name, but she's booked it through her email, paid with it from a PayPal on her account.'

'She won't have rented it in her name. She won't want to leave a trace.'

Charlie bristles with the reality of what they're discussing. Haydee rented this house for one purpose: to be close to those she wants to kill. One of them is already dead. The house is only twenty minutes from their own, in a village they've not been to because there's absolutely nothing there – it is barely a village at all, really, more a farm track that you drive through to get elsewhere. The idea of this woman being so close to them kept Charlie up last night and even now he wonders if he has done the right thing coming here tonight and leaving Hannah alone. Suddenly, he is desperate to get home, to leave this rowdy pub and get back to his real life.

'I have the key code,' Charlie tells Owen.

Owen pulls a piece of paper from his pocket and a pen, sliding them over to Charlie. 'Write it down. The address, the key code, anything else I'll need.'

Charlie starts writing, hesitating as he writes the code. 'Need for what?'

Owen cocks his head, one eyebrow raised. 'You really wanna know?'

'Well… I just think… I don't know. What are you going to do?'

Owen sighs and looks around him. Satisfied no one is listening, he leans into Charlie and speaks in a low tone. 'Charlie, do not forget this woman is a murderer. She has already killed Jesse and from what you've told me, Hannah is next on her list. You still have a choice in this. We can go the police, tell them everything. But remember, I'll have to tell them things about Hannah that you're not going to want to hear; things that will change your entire life.'

Charlie hesitates. Is he really the sort of man who will put a woman in danger? Even if that woman is a murderer?

'Couldn't we report it anonymously? I can give them all the evidence I have about Haydee and they won't need to connect—'

Owen laughs. 'Come on, man. You don't think the first thing Haydee will do when they arrest her is to tell them everything Hannah and Jesse did to her? You really want her talking to the police like that? Maybe you'd feel differently if I told you exactly what Hannah—'

'No,' Charlie snaps, his hand up to stop Owen's words. 'I don't need to know.' He writes the key code on the paper, the pen digging in so hard he wonders if the numbers will be pressed into the cheap wooden table below forever.

'Yeah,' Owen says. 'The less you know, the better. Trust me, man. By tomorrow afternoon, all of this will be history. You'll never have to worry about Haydee, or Jesse, or me ever again. I promise.' Owen picks the piece of paper up and slips it into his pocket. 'And by Monday, you'll be the proud father of that little girl. Issy, isn't it?'

Charlie recoils, horrified that Owen knows this about them, hating to hear Issy's name on his lips. Owen smiles.

'How will I know it's done?' Charlie asks, getting up and putting on his coat.

'You don't need to know.'

'What? Of course I bloody do!'

'Charlie, trust me. By tomorrow afternoon, this problem will be gone. You have my word.' Owen nods at him, a small smile creeping on his lips, and Charlie curls his hands into fists. He's not an idiot; he knows Owen is not a trustworthy man, but on this, he does at least believe him. Owen has as much to lose here as Charlie. Without another word, Charlie turns and leaves.

As he pulls away from the pub, the night sky growing darker the further he gets from the town, he allows Owen's warning to sink in. *You don't think the first thing Haydee will do when they arrest her is to tell them everything Hannah and Jesse did to her?* He wonders just how much Hannah has been keeping from him and if he is really strong enough to pretend all of this never happened. Owen is going to get rid of Haydee, of that he's sure. But will that be enough, Charlie wonders? Can they really go on like nothing has happened when each of them is concealing so much from each other?

Hours later, he crawls into bed beside Hannah. Her warm body curls into his. He made himself drive around the country lanes for hours before coming home, desperate to rid his body of the anger it was carrying. In a few days, Issy will be here. That is what he has to focus on. They can repair the cracks in their marriage for her – they have to.

'What time is it?' Hannah murmurs in the darkness as he wraps his arms around her waist.

'Shhh, go back to sleep,' he says.

'I missed you tonight,' she says.

'I missed you too.'

'Don't leave me again.' Her words are uneven, formed in a half-sleep state and he wonders how much of this conversation she'll even remember tomorrow.

'I won't, I promise. Everything is going to be okay now. Go back to sleep.'

Long after the sounds of his wife lightly slumbering, Charlie lies awake staring at the ceiling. He tells himself he's done the right thing by leading Owen to Haydee. What other choice did he have? But as he drifts off, all he can is see Jesse's blood-soaked body lying on the floor and the sharp sense that ever since that day, his moral compass has been off. Perhaps it can never return to centre.

Chapter Thirty-One

TWO DAYS UNTIL ISSY COMES HOME

Now

Hannah

Charlie is on edge and it's starting to completely throw me off. I'm the one who should be a wreck, not him. I've checked my phone obsessively since yesterday, expecting a follow-up from the police or Owen but there's nothing. The silence makes me uneasy and Charlie's bizarre and distant demeanour isn't helping. On top of that, we're desperately trying to put together Issy's room; we only have today and tomorrow until she's here and still the bedroom is unpainted, the bed yet to be put up and the only furniture in her room a sad little wardrobe tucked into the corner. It's hardly a good look – it makes us seem totally unprepared, like we're telling her from day one that we can't be trusted.

But we can.

We can do this.

We're good people. We'll be good parents.

'Charlie, what are you doing down there?' I shout down the stairs, unable to keep the annoyance from my voice any longer.

'I'll be up in a minute,' he shouts back.

'But what are you *doing*?'

This time, he doesn't reply and I huff loudly and stomp back to the bedroom. Despite our dreams of painting the walls with a fairy-tale castle like I'd seen on Instagram, we've settled for baby blue and pink paint instead, with two walls to be painted blue and one pink. I ordered the paint online last night while Charlie was out and it arrived this morning, thank god. If we get the first coat on before lunch, we'll have time to do a second coat by dinner and it'll be dry tomorrow so we can put the rest of the furniture in before Andrea arrives with Issy on Monday. That's the timings in theory, anyway. But with Charlie disappearing every five minutes and looking harried when he is here, I can't see how we're ever going to get this done.

I pad across the sheet-covered floor and lean down to place more FrogTape around the skirting boards. This is the part of painting I hate, the finicky preparation, trying to get the lines straight as your hands shake. Charlie has been useless. Every time he's been in the room he's been glued to his phone or walking around aimlessly with his eyebrows knotted so tightly it's a wonder he hasn't caused permanent lines in his forehead. I listen again for sounds of him coming back upstairs but there's nothing. What is he doing down there?

I keep telling myself that he's worried about Issy coming home. In a normal life, that would be enough of a worry for anyone to cause them to shut down. But that's not how Charlie and I react to stress. Over the years of IVF and adoption, we've been lucky (despite the obvious ill luck that brought us there in the first place) because we've stuck together. So many women I know through IVF forums, podcasts and books blame infertility for the breakdown of their marriages and I was terrified when we first started our process that it would be the same for us, but it was the opposite. Our world became small, just the two of us against everything. No one else knew what we were going through and as such, we closed ranks. We told each other everything, every worry, every unkind thought, everything. Well, about that side of life, anyway. I told myself throughout that the one secret I was keeping from him was irrelevant to our relationship; consoling myself with the fact that it happened before we even met – in a different life. Since the day I met Charlie, I've never kept a single thing from him about my life from that day forward, and I honestly believe that he's never kept anything from me.

Until now, when I have absolutely no idea what's going on with my husband.

There's just no way he can have discovered the truth about me and Jesse, or what happened to Haydee. I'm sure he has thought a lot about my lie to the police when I asked him to be my alibi, and I've no doubt he's unhappy that I never mentioned that I once knew Jesse. But I don't think that's enough to cause his current state. Or maybe it is? Charlie doesn't keep things from me, but he is slow to voice his emotions. If he is upset purely about the alibi lie, he may not want to admit that to me yet with everything focused on Issy right now. I've got to stop obsessing over this; there are so many things to let myself look forward to and yet I'm stuck in the past.

Charlie always says I never let myself enjoy things and he's right. How can I, when I know that someone is dead because of me? Everything I've done since that night has been about balancing the scales. I've spent so long believing I owe the world for my wrongs that part of me even now can't let myself accept that I deserve Issy; that Issy deserves us.

As if sensing I need reassurance, Charlie appears in the doorway, two cups of tea in hand.

'Almost done?' he asks as he hands me one, inspecting the FrogTape.

'Yeah, just the light switches to go.'

Charlie puts his tea on the windowsill and gets down on his hands and knees.

'What are you doing?'

He tuts. 'You haven't got this straight,' he says, pulling off my tape and repositioning it.

'Don't come in and criticise after you've left me on my own most of the morning,' I snap, aggrieved that instead of comfort, he's offering criticism.

Charlie doesn't react but instead pulls another piece of tape up and carefully sticks it back down. I watch him incredulously. What is going through his mind?

'It's just not straight,' he says again.

'Well, if you want something done right, do it yourself. Isn't that what they always say?'

His hand stills for a second as he stops picking at the FrogTape, but he doesn't reply to my jibe. It's like I'm not even here. The gnawing fear that he knows the truth scratches at my scalp. If Charlie does know about Jesse, surely he would have said something to me by now? Plus, how the hell would he have found out? The world that Jesse and I occupied is so far removed from Charlie's that I have felt safe over the years hiding here. Not that my life with Charlie has been about escaping. At first I thought it was, but it didn't take me long to fall so completely in love with him I knew I'd never be able to leave. Or tell him the truth. Because in Charlie's world, bad things happen to bad people, good things to good. There's no room for grey, no room for mistakes.

How could I ever tell him the truth? My biggest fear in all of this has been that he's right. We do get what we deserve. That's why we can't have children; that's why Jesse turned up dead basically on our doorstep the second the universe gave me something good. But all through this Charlie has been the one who hasn't deserved it; there's no world in which that man deserves any of this. So where does that leave us?

'Charlie…' The desire to ask him straight up what the hell is going on has become too strong to ignore. 'I don't know if I'm being crazy here but I feel like you—'

'We need a roller.'

'What?'

He stands up, turning to face me but his eyes don't meet mine. 'For the walls. It'll take too long with brushes. We need a roller.'

'We have one in the shed.'

He shakes his head, still not looking at me. 'I threw it out after we painted the hall.'

'Why would you do that?'

He frowns and sighs. 'It was broken. I'll go and get one.'

'What, now? From where?'

He scratches his beard with both hands, his movements suddenly frantic, so unlike my calm, still husband. I take a step back as he storms past me out of the room. I wait a moment, a little dumbstruck, then walk to the landing.

'I won't be long,' he shouts as he reaches the bottom of the stairs.

'But where are you even going, Charlie?'

234

He shrugs on his jacket and picks up his key. 'Chippy,' he says, referring to the nearest town. 'They'll have one at Gill's. I'll be an hour, max, then we can get on.' He finally looks at me. 'Okay?'

'I'll come with you.'

'No,' he snaps. 'I won't be long. I promise. Just stay here, okay? Don't go out.'

'What are you talking about?'

'Just don't leave the house. Okay?'

His manic energy makes his keys jingle in his hand and I nod uncertainly, utterly at a loss as to what has suddenly made my husband so desperate to flee the house or why he needs me to stay inside it. He turns his back on me and leaves. The front door slams, making me jump, followed by the sound of the lock being turned – trapping me in.

I sit on the top step and listen to his car pull away, the wheels spinning as he careers off up the lane. Did he know I was about to ask him something he didn't want to answer? Is that why he's gone off like this? I tap my fingers against the bannister and tell myself to stop being paranoid. Tensions are high between us, of course they are; we're about to change our entire lives. I've hardly been the best version of myself over the last few days; maybe my anxiety has started to rub off on him.

Locking me in is nothing sinister. He quite often does it absent-mindedly and I have keys, so it's not like I'm actually trapped inside.

I go back into the bedroom and start FrogTaping the light switches as if nothing is wrong. I tell myself that by the time Charlie is back, everything will be ready to paint. If he was here, Charlie would make me finish all the prep before I started painting but he's not, so I do it my way and dip my paintbrush into the gloopy open can of paint. As

I brush the baby blue across the once-white, now greying walls, each stroke covering up what was there before, I convince myself further and further that my worry about Charlie is all in my head. There's no way he knows what's going on. The only person left alive who knows about it is Owen who wants this all kept secret as much if not more than me, and the police clearly have little interest in me as they haven't followed up after my phone call to them on Thursday. And I'm certain now that the woman who came into my work that same day was nothing more than a coincidence. It's not like I'll be there if she comes back either. Yesterday was my last day before adoption leave. It felt surreal that I'd finally reached that point. Sure, I wasn't heading out the door with a belly fit to burst, but I was leaving knowing that when I next came in I'd be a mother.

I *am* going to be a mother.

Nothing bad is happening. Charlie doesn't know a thing.

I finish my section of painting then text him to see if he's got to Chippy yet. It's been twenty minutes and the journey normally takes ten on a good day. I get the instant reply saying his phone is on 'Do Not Disturb' mode for driving. I sigh, decide to wait another five minutes and try again.

The same message comes back. Where is he? Why is he still driving?

I stand up and pace the room, the shed outside catching my eye.

I don't know what makes me do it, but before I know it, I'm padding across the damp garden in a pair of Charlie's too big trainers I've chucked on, battling with the shed door which has expanded in the rain and stuck. Eventually, I jerk it open and take a step back.

The roller, the one we've had for years that Charlie swore he threw out, stands at the back of the shed. Where it's always been.

Chapter Thirty-Two

Now

Charlie

He revs the engine harder, then slams his foot on the brakes as the car skids around the corner of the lane. Opposite, a silver Volvo blares its horn and the man in the driver's seat mouths expletives at Charlie. He raises his hand to apologise but the Volvo driver shakes his head, mouths 'fucking idiot' and drives off, leaving Charlie shaking in his seat. He needs to calm down. He needs to take a second and think this through. What does he think he's doing, speeding around the lanes like some sort of fucking boy racer? He could have got himself killed. He imagines Hannah getting the call from the police to say he's dead, imagines her sinking down the wall as the officers stand in the doorway, her anguished screams ringing in his ears. Would she still get Issy? He shakes his head to rid himself from going down this path. He's not dead. The police aren't going to visit Hannah with the death knock. Issy won't need to find another home. Everything is fine. Or at least it will be if he can just get there now.

He pushes the car back into gear and, when his breathing has returned to normal, follows the single track lane further until Google Maps tells him he has reached his destination. He pulls the car up in a passing place and switches off his engine.

He's here.

Hannah was right; if you want something done right, you have to do it yourself. How had he ever trusted Owen to fix things? It's his family that needs protecting, he needs to sort this himself. The right way. Not by letting some thug like Owen take matters into his own hands.

He tells himself this over and over as he walks up the small, overgrown path to Haydee's Airbnb, a sense of dread building in his stomach with every step. He looks around for Owen's car and spots it partially hidden by overgrown bushes to the side of the cottage. Relief flushes through him as he imagines Owen in the living room with Haydee, calmly telling her to leave him and Hannah alone. He realises quickly how ridiculous this scenario is; Haydee is a murderer, not some defenceless woman Owen can cajole. Charlie can't let himself forget the danger she poses.

He approaches the front of the cottage. A cream-painted stable door is the only thing now separating him from what's next. Should he knock? What is the protocol for confronting a murderer? He suddenly feels foolish, out of his depth. He should have made a plan before he got here, or at least before he got out of the car. The drive over passed in a blur of anger and fear – since he was with Owen yesterday all he's been able to think about is what the man will do to Haydee. He's found himself terrified for the woman, though he knows this is illogical – she is the one who murdered Jesse. She is the one who is stalking his wife, threatening his whole life. But still, deep down, he doesn't trust Owen. He knows the sort of man he is; he's read all the gossip columns online about Jesse and him, the two 'lads' of the celebrity world, sleeping with women so young it should be illegal, then casting them off. If these are the stories that make the papers, he can't bear to imagine what they do behind closed doors.

Charlie may not be the most worldly-wise, but he knows when someone is a good man. And Owen is not one. So why has he put his trust in him until now?

Before he can question himself any further, he moves towards the door, his hand raised to knock but a scream stops him in his tracks.

'Please! Owen! Stop—'

The anguished cry screeches through the door and knocks Charlie off balance. He is forced into action as he bashes on the door.

'Haydee? Open the door. Hello?'

He hears crying, loud wailing sobs, followed by cries of 'Help me, please, help me!'

'I'm calling the police,' he shouts, fumbling for his phone. He types in the number fast – 9 9 9 – then hovers over the call button. 'Haydee?' he calls again. 'Owen?'

Now there is silence.

His whole body turns hot as sweat drips from his brow. What has he done? What has he made happen? He puts the phone back in his pocket and bashes against the door with his fists again, before beginning to kick.

'Let me in!' he screams. 'Owen, I swear to God if you don't let me in—'

The door gives way.

'Owen?' he shouts one more time before stepping into the cottage. There's an eerie silence as he creeps through the small, dark hallway. The house is cold, as though the heating has never been switched on, and the whole place has a feeling of being deeply unloved. *Bloody Airbnb*, he finds himself thinking despite everything, *taking over the area without a care.* He stops after a few steps and tries to bring himself into the present as the sensations of his body start coming back to him. He's sweating, despite the cold, and his heart is racing in his chest; so heavy that it beats through his ears, making it impossible to listen out for Owen. He runs his hand against the bare hallway wall to settle himself. Left or right, he wonders?

He pushes the door handle to his left and steels himself as it opens.

It's empty. A small, newly installed kitchen without any character. He scans the room quickly before shutting the door.

Right it is.

His hand shakes as he grips the door handle. He looks back to the front door. He could just leave. No one would ever need to know he was here. But then he hears it: small, feral cries behind the door. Owen? Without a second thought, he yanks open the door and rushes through.

'Oh my god. Oh – oh – Jesus Christ! Owen?'

The man is face down on the floor. At first, Charlie tells himself he's simply hurt; that the blood pooling around his head isn't that bad and any moment Owen will sit up with a grin, but when he crouches down beside him and puts his hand to Owen's neck, he can't fool himself any more.

Owen is dead.

The room spins as Charlie backs away. This cannot be happening. He tries to focus on Owen's body as his vision sways, still half expecting him at any minute to stand up and tell him he's all right, just a scratch. But of course he doesn't. Owen lies in a pool of his own blood, deadly still. The metallic smell crawls up Charlie's nostrils.

Again, Charlie tries to convince himself that he can simply walk away, get back in his car, drive home and not have to face this but then he hears it for a second time: the soft cries.

He snaps his head up, his eyes finally released from the sight of Owen's body, and looks around the room. Just like the pictures online showed him, the room is sparsely furnished; a claret worn sofa sits one side against the magnolia painted walls in front of a thick black TV. The flagstone floor only enhances the room's harsh, unlived in feeling.

Then he sees her. Curled up in the corner of the room, shaking violently as she cries.

She's so small. That's his first thought. Child-like.

She's covered in blood, that's his second.

She's a murderer, the third.

'Stay there!' he shouts at her huddled form. 'Don't fucking move.'

The words land between them almost comically as the woman looks up at him. Her large green eyes remind him of a deer's, the sort you see dart out in front of your car on the lanes, too late to stop. He holds her stare for a moment before it becomes unbearable.

'Help me, please... help me.' Her voice is soft and shakes as she speaks, the American accent only intensifying the movie-like quality of the scene.

'Haydee?' he asks.

She opens her mouth then closes it again, shrinking back on herself.

'Who are you?' she asks.

Charlie lets his gaze fall back to Owen's body which lies between them. He looks at the blood pooled around his head and wonders how long it will take before the puddle reaches his own feet. He takes a step backwards in anticipation.

'Don't go!' the woman shouts. 'Please—'

'I'm not going anywhere. Not until the police come.'

'No!' she cries, suddenly releasing herself from her balled-up posture and standing, gripping the sideboard behind her. 'Please, please let me explain.' She's crying, tears falling down her pale face.

'I know who you are,' Charlie says.

She cocks her head to the side, as if examining him, then tucks her brown hair behind her ear.

'Haydee,' he says again.

She lowers her eyes and nods.

'You killed Jesse.'

'What? No. No! I didn't!' She rushes towards him but stops when she realises she'll have to step over Owen's body to reach him. He takes another step back and she holds her hands up.

'Is that what… Is that what he told you?' She points to Owen but can't make herself look down at his body.

'You killed him,' Charlie says, now nodding at Owen.

Tears fill her eyes again as she shakes her head. 'No, no, no,' she whimpers.

Charlie erupts. 'He's dead, Haydee! Can't you see that? You can't get out of this! He's fucking *dead*!'

She sobs and reaches out to Charlie, finally making the decision to step over Owen. She grimaces as she does it and Charlie scuttles backwards again, now pressed up against the wall of the room. He looks around for something to defend himself with but the bland living room offers little in the way of weapons.

'Stay back!' he shouts, his hands held up in front of him.

'Please,' Haydee sobs, only inches away from him now. 'Please, you have to listen to me.'

Up close, he sees she is older than she appeared before. Mid-thirties, he would guess. Possibly younger but the lines around her eyes betray a harsh life. She's skinny, the kind of skinny that makes him touch his own ribs in horror; you shouldn't be able to see someone's bones from the outside. How can this woman have murdered both Jesse and Owen? He lowers his hands, feeling faintly ridiculous at the idea that he needs to defend himself from her.

'He attacked me,' she says, breaking his thoughts. 'He was going to kill me. I... I had no choice.'

Charlie imagines what Owen might have come here to do, finally admitting the truth that deep down he always knew. The truth that had made him get in his car and come here today despite wanting to be left out of this whole sordid mess. He knew Owen was never coming to reason with Haydee. There was only ever going to be one end to this. Did he know that when he first gave Owen her address? He can't let himself believe that he knowingly put Haydee in this position but on some level he must have. He is complicit in this. He has blood on his hands.

'You're lying,' he snaps back.

Haydee grabs at her stomach, as if his words have physically wounded her.

'I know what you did to Jesse, Owen told me. I know he was coming here today to get you to stop – to get you to leave us alone—'

'Us? I don't even know who you are!'

'No. But you know Hannah – my wife. Don't you?'

Recognition flickers across her face then she frowns. 'Jesse's Hannah?'

He winces, wants to tell her no, she's not *Jesse's* fucking Hannah, she's his, but knows this will only confuse matters and right now all he needs is to get his head straight.

'But what… Why are you here? What…' Haydee shakes her head, confusion crawling all over her face.

'You know why. You were coming after her—'

'Coming after Hannah?'

'Yes, you killed Jesse and now you want to kill—'

'*Hannah?*' She sounds out the name as if she's never heard it before.

'You looked up her work address,' he says.

The woman stares at him blankly, her skinny frame shaking, dots of Owen's blood spattered across her bony face. She looks so frail and afraid, part of him wants to pull her towards him, sit her down and tell her it's okay. Charlie shakes his head, unable to keep up with these mind games. 'It doesn't even fucking matter now,' he snaps, determined to get back in control. 'I'm calling the police. Owen is dead.'

He takes out his phone and starts to unlock it but she rushes forward and bats it from his hands. It lands with a thud on the hard floor.

'Please, please don't call the police.' Her voice is small again, desperation leaking through her words. 'They won't understand! They won't—'

'What won't they understand? That you murdered two men?'

'I didn't kill Jesse; why do you keep saying that?'

'Because you did! And now you've killed Owen to cover it up.'

She shakes her head. 'No, no, no; you've got it all wrong. It was Owen, Owen killed Jesse.'

245

She looks at him with such sincerity that it knocks the wind from him. 'You're lying. Why would Owen—'

'Because of me. Because of what happened in New York… because…' She waves her hand in front of her as if to conjure the words, tears spilling from her eyes again. 'Jesse thought I was dead,' she whispers. 'Owen told him I was dead. When he realised I wasn't, he wanted to help me but Owen…' She shakes her head. 'Owen could never let it come out.'

'Let what come out?'

'What he did,' she cries. 'How much do you know? About New York?'

Charlie shrugs, feeling completely out of his depth. 'I know enough.'

'You mean you know what *he* told you,' she says, pointing angrily at Owen's body. 'After what they did to me…' She swallows, as if whatever happened is too painful to put into words.

Does she mean Hannah and Jesse? Or Jesse and Owen? Charlie can't bear to ask, seeing the pain that Haydee carries with her even now – surely Hannah, his Hannah, can't have done this to her?

'There was a party… Things got out of hand. I was unconscious; Jesse thought I was dead. He thought they'd killed me… Owen told him I was dead.' She takes in a deep breath and a glob of snot dangles from her nostril, leaving Charlie simultaneously revolted yet more aware than ever of her vulnerability.

'That doesn't make any sense,' he says. 'Why would Owen want Jesse to believe you were dead?'

Haydee sighs as if she can't believe Charlie doesn't see it yet. 'For control. It was all about control. Owen became Jesse's manager after that and the rest, as they say, is history. What better way to tie someone to you forever than making them believe they'd covered up a murder for you?' Haydee shakes her head and wipes her nose with the back of her hand. 'Owen paid me to keep away. To stay dead.' She stares at him, her glare firm and unwavering, as if willing him to believe her.

'So what happened? Why did you come back?' he hears himself ask, but his words sound far away, as if they've been spoken by someone else entirely.

Haydee smirks, the smile ghastly on blood-spattered face. 'The money stopped. Owen didn't want to pay any more. I've spent most of my adult life running away, never setting down any roots, living under a fake name, changing cities every few years to avoid ever being found and what do I get for it?' She shakes her head. 'I should have known he'd do this to me.

'When the money stopped, I contacted Jesse. I thought if he knew the truth, if he knew what Owen had done, he'd help me...' She pauses. 'I'd read about him over the years, of course I had; he was impossible to avoid. Despite his lifestyle, he seemed like a good man. He told *USA Today* that he went to church every Sunday. I thought maybe some of that was about repentance, you know? That he felt bad for what they'd done to me all those years ago.'

The reference to 'they' makes Charlie wince again; where does his wife fit into all of this?

'And he did,' Haydee continues, shrugging sadly. 'Jesse *was* a good man. As soon as I contacted him, he promised to help me. He couldn't believe what Owen had done, he hated him for it.'

Charlie shakes his head. 'I don't understand,' he says. 'You're telling me all this time Jesse thought that he'd killed you?'

She frowns then nods. 'Something like that, yeah...'

Charlie closes his eyes, needing a minute to think. He still doesn't understand what part Hannah might have played in this horrifying story and he's too scared to ask.

'Jesse was going to confront Owen,' Haydee says, so lost in her telling of the story that she seems completely unaware of Charlie's discomfort in hearing it. 'The night that he died. He was going to tell him he knew the truth and he was going to go to the police.' Her tears are back now, flowing freely down her face. 'I should never have let him,' she cries. 'I knew what Owen was capable of; I should have known what he'd do to keep his secret—'

'You really think *Owen* killed Jesse?'

'Yes,' she states clearly, betraying no flicker of doubt. 'I know he did.'

Charlie leans against the wall, the room spinning again as he tries to suck in the air around him. He thinks of all the ways he's helped Owen; how he led him here to Haydee. How could he have been so stupid?

'Please,' Haydee's voice, now strained and childlike, brings him back into the room. 'Please help me. I can't go to jail; I can't—'

'You won't go to jail it was self-defence.'

'How would I prove that? You think they're going to believe me – an ex-junkie who's spent most of her life under false identities? You think anyone is going to want the truth about Owen and Jesse's lies coming to the surface?'

Charlie shakes his head. 'They're famous, they're not untouchable—'

'Do you have any idea how much money is at risk if the Jesse Carter *brand* is ruined? Billions. Fucking billions.' She pulls at her hair as she begins pacing in tiny semi-circles in front of him.

He pauses for a moment, desperate to be able to tell her that nothing bad will happen to her; that bad things happen to bad people and good to good. But what if he's wrong? What if there is no such thing as justice and things just happen, regardless of what you do? Look at him and Hannah. His whole life he has done the right thing, been kind, helpful, selfless, and look where it's got him.

But what's the alternative? Help a woman he barely knows cover up a murder? The idea is inconceivable. He shakes his head and starts to tell her the police will know what to do but as he does, he hears the sound of a car pulling into the lane. Fear clutches him by the throat.

'Stay here,' he snaps.

Her eyes are wide with terror as she looks from him to the body on the floor.

He creeps into the stone hallway, his heart bashing in his chest as he approaches the front door. The swirled glass in the stable door is just big enough to see through, though the outside is distorted like something from a horror movie. He stands to the side of the glass, trying to make sure no one can see him from the other side, and peers out.

A figure moves towards the door.

A figure that, even distorted, Charlie would recognise anywhere.

Chapter Thirty-Three

Now

Hannah

I walk up to the cottage totally unsure of myself. Why would Charlie be here? But the location of his phone on Find My Friends is blinking at this very spot. I passed his car on the lane, leaving mine just behind his on the passing place. At first I couldn't work out where he could have gone but then I spotted the tree-lined lane and followed it to this door. Should I knock? What will I say?

For a moment, I imagine that a woman will answer. *Is my husband here?* I'll ask and her cheeks will colour. She'll be beautiful, of course, and young. He'll appear behind her in the hallway. *Hannah, I'm so sorry*, he'll say, and my world will end. I bite my lip. The whole scenario feels so unlikely. Charlie would never hurt me. Not like that. I'm being ridiculous; there must be a rational explanation. Perhaps he had to take a diversion on the way back from buying the roller we didn't need and his car broke down. This might have been the only house he could find to get help. But why wouldn't he call me? His phone hasn't died; I know this because his location is still flashing even as I look at it now.

Enough.

Just knock.

As I do, the door opens, as if someone was standing there this whole time.

'Hannah.'

I step back as Charlie appears in the doorway.

'What are you doing here?' I ask.

Charlie opens his mouth then shakes his head. 'You need to go.'

'What?'

'Go, Hannah, you need to go. You can't be here.'

Pain radiates through my chest as I picture the mysterious beautiful woman again. Is this really happening?

As I step forward, so does Charlie, his arm pressing against my chest to push me back.

'Charlie!' I shout. 'What the fuck? Get off me!'

'No, Hannah, go, please go. I'm begging you—'

We wrestle on the doorstep but his grip is half-hearted, and I think even now Charlie can't bear to cause me physical pain. I push past him and into the dark hallway. He doesn't follow me but stands in the doorway, shutting the door behind him, as if resolved to his fate.

'Is someone else here?' I snap, quickly followed by, 'Where is she?'

He looks momentarily confused then sighs as if this whole thing is exhausting for him. Pure hatred burns in me then for a second. Who *is* this man?

'In there,' he says, pointing to the door on my right.

I scoff, unable to believe he is giving in so easily. I push the handle down before I can convince myself out of it and fling open the door.

At first, the room appears empty. My eyes roam it hungrily, ready to hurl myself at whoever has taken Charlie from me.

Then I see them.

Bile rises in my throat.

I stumble back out of the door.

I feel Charlie catch me.

'Don't look,' he says, his voice hoarse. 'Please, Han, don't look.'

He pulls me down onto the floor, wrapping his arms around me as I cry, my body shivering at the sight of all that blood. Who is it? I didn't even notice if they were male or female, the visceral shock at seeing a dead body so severe that it's like my eyes shut themselves down before I could make anything out. Charlie holds me for a moment then releases me. I hear him walking back into the room, his footsteps heavy beside me.

'What the... Where is she? Hannah, where is she?'

His voice cracks as he shouts and confusion reigns over me. The body, were they not dead? Has she, whoever she is, escaped in the seconds between me backing out of the room and now? Hope springs through me; perhaps this is not the end of our world; perhaps whatever Charlie did to this woman is fixable. Perhaps she is fine.

I force myself up and back into the room.

My body jolts again at the sight.

The body is there. I don't look directly at it but can see its outline without moving my eyes.

My husband is pacing the room, pulling back the curtains, asking again and again, 'Where is she?' He's lost his mind, I think. The body is here. They're right here.

'Charlie...' I say. 'She... She's there.' I point to the body, unable to look at it.

He snaps around to me, hope realigning his features, but it disappears when he follows where my finger is pointing. He shakes his head. 'No,' he says, his voice desperate. 'Not Owen. Haydee. She's gone.'

I look up to my husband, then back to the body. Only this time I let myself see it. See him.

Owen.

The room spins around me. Owen is dead. Owen is lying dead here in the living room. Whose house are we in? I look around for any signs of personal items – photographs, books, ornaments – but the room is perfectly beige and nondescript. As I do, a second realisation hits me.

Charlie said Haydee.

Haydee.

The name sounds foreign from his lips, a dirty word that doesn't belong between us.

'Charlie…' I say, my voice coming out little more than a whisper.

He flicks his gaze up to me, seeming startled that I'm here.

'Haydee is… Haydee's dead.'

He shakes his head fiercely and pushes past me, out through the door. I follow him into the dark hallway where he looks up and down then paces back up and opens the other door. He marches into the room that I can already see is empty, a small kitchen with nothing on the worktops except for a container of cheap instant coffee. He moves to leave the room but then doubles back on himself, pushing down the door to what looks like the garden. It opens and he jumps back.

'She's gone,' he says. 'She must have… Oh god, *oh god*!'

'Charlie, stop!' I shout, desperate to pull him out of himself. 'What are you talking about? I don't understand.' My hand shakes as it pulls at his jumper.

He snaps around to face me; his face is white. I search his eyes, desperate to understand what is going on while horror stories play out in my mind. Has Charlie killed Owen? The idea is impossible yet my husband is here, alone, with Owen's dead body on the floor next door.

'Charlie,' I say again, softer this time. 'Did you… Did you do something to Owen?'

This finally snaps him from his daze and his eyes grow wide as he steps back from me. 'What? No, no… I didn't— that wasn't— it was her! Haydee was here, she—'

'What are you talking about?' I cry. 'Haydee is dead!'

He shakes his head and grips my hands by the wrists, bringing me so close to him I can smell the coffee on his breath from this morning. Was it really only hours ago that we drank coffee in the kitchen and talked about paint colours? It can't be; how can that world be a part of this one?

'She's not, she's not dead. I saw her. I promise you, she was here.'

'But that doesn't… You're wrong, it can't be her.'

Memories of that night flood in as Charlie pulls me to sit at the pine kitchen table. Even hearing her name slip from Charlie's mouth so easily is bizarre; how can this be happening? How does he even know about her, about Owen? I think of Owen's threat to me; *don't tell anyone and nor will I.* Did he go back on that, somehow getting Charlie involved? At the thought of Owen, a sharp kick hits me in the stomach. Owen is dead. He's lying in the room next door. This feels too unreal. There is too much to battle with in my head as memories of him alive just a few days ago at The Farm collide with memories of him fifteen years ago in New York. Alive. With Haydee.

Suddenly, I need to know for sure that he's dead. I never checked him when I arrived. What if he's just injured? What if Charlie knocked him out and he's lying there, struggling, waiting for help? I dash from the kitchen through the hall back into the living room and gasp as I enter once again to be confronted with the scene. I instantly know that my hope is misplaced. There is too much blood here for Owen to be alive but still, I have to check.

I bend down beside him, far enough away to avoid the pooling blood, the metallic smell assaulting my nostril, and lean across to rest my fingers on his neck.

No pulse.

My stomach tumbles beneath me.

Of course there's no pulse.

Behind me, I hear Charlie enter the room.

'Hannah,' he says, his voice urgent. 'Hannah, look. Please, Han.' He urges me to stand up, to take my fingers from the dead man's neck and I do.

He's holding a note in his shaking hands.

'What—'

'Just read it,' he says, handing it to me.

> *No one ever has to know any of us were ever here.*
> *Just get rid of him, please. I will sort the rest.*
>   *-H*

I read it again, once, twice, three times. But it still makes no sense. H?

'What happened here?' I ask Charlie for what feels like the millionth time.

He shakes his head, tears coming to his eyes and I want more than anything to hug him and take the pain away but he has to go through it, he has to push through and tell me what the fuck is going on.

'He was dead when I got here,' he says. 'I swear. Haydee… She… She said it was self-defence. That he attacked her—'

I shake my head and grip his arm. 'Whoever was here it can't have been Haydee, Haydee's dead; I—'

'She's not,' he says, so sure of himself I feel the urge to slap him. 'Owen told you she was, didn't he? He told Jesse that too but—'

'But what? This doesn't make any sense!'

'Hannah, we don't have time for this now. I'll explain everything but I promise you, Haydee is very much alive. And Owen is very much dead.'

Our eyes fall back to his body lying not six feet away from us. 'What are we going to do?'

–

It didn't take us long to convince each other that the police aren't an option. There is too much to explain, too much at stake.

'We can't get rid of him,' I say, the words falling from my mouth like some bad movie script. Everything has a film-like quality in this room, my words don't feel my own, Owen's body simply a horrifying dummy. I get the terrifying urge to laugh as Charlie walks around his corpse, looking for ideas. This does not feel real.

'We could… leave him here?' Charlie suggests.

I shake my head. 'I touched him. DNA. Didn't you?' As I wait for his response my stomach tightens. Even now, I need to know that my husband is a good man; that his first instinct was to try and save a life even while we discuss how to dispose of the body. He nods and I let out a tight breath of air.

For the first time since I arrived, Charlie stops pacing and stands at the window, drawing the curtains tight. The light from the open door through the hallway is the only thing keeping the room from being plunged into darkness. It is a relief, at first, to have Owen's body slightly clothed in darkness. I watch as Charlie breathes in and out, slowing each time. He transforms in front of my eyes from the manic man I didn't recognise, into the calm, still husband I have always known.

Eventually, he speaks. 'We have to call the police.'

'What? No! No – we can't, we ca—'

'Hannah,' he says, his voice still and hard against my own fluttering words. 'We don't have a choice. What else can we do? We *can't* get rid of his body.'

I shake my head, looking from the body to Charlie in despair. Of course this is what he wants to do. Charlie is good. Charlie always does the right thing. Anger flares up in me then, burning through my veins, touching every part of me.

This isn't fair.

This cannot be happening.

Charlie sighs and nods, his body so firm and still I have the urge to run to him and shake him as if somehow bringing back the frantic man from earlier will break him from this spell of sanity.

'Yes we can,' I say, firmly. 'And that's exactly what we're going to do.'

Charlie looks at me, his eyes burning with pain and I feel my heart break. It's a familiar feeling. I cannot describe how many times a heart can break and yet your body keeps going. I can't describe how many times I have told Charlie

I can't keep going and he's held me up wordlessly, making sure that I can.

I think of the last time our IVF failed, when I saw the blood in my knickers before we even got to test day to see if our transfer had worked. How I stumbled into the living room, eyes blurry with tears, and didn't even have to say a word to Charlie. He held me on the living room floor as I sobbed animalistic cries that I didn't know I was capable of. Charlie held me so tightly that I could let myself collapse. He pulled me up when I couldn't stand, nursed me for days when I couldn't get out of bed. All the time his own heart broken.

I think of how, six months later, he came to me in the morning, a cup of decaf coffee in hand and presented the adoption papers he'd printed out upstairs. The hope that filled his face as I cried, once again, for all our lost babies before and yearning for the idea of one we had yet to meet.

I think of Issy, her beautiful round eyes so full of hope and love when we met in the park on Thursday. In just forty-eight hours she will come home. My earlier worries about the house not being ready for her now feel inane; of course it doesn't matter that the room isn't beautifully painted or that we haven't yet bought her the perfect 'welcome home' present. What matters is that we love her. And my God, we love her. I feel it in the pit of my stomach, this raw, animalistic love that I have for a child who is not yet mine but feels like she always has been. My daughter. Mine.

What would happen to her if we went to the police? Elaine and Michael already have another foster child on the way. She won't be able to stay with them. They would never let her come to us, not if we're wrapped up in a murder investigation. We'd never be able to see her again. So, what then for Issy? Another home. Another process. Another long wait to find the perfect family, meanwhile she grows older, more difficult to place.

She might never get a new family. She might end up staying in foster forever only to be kicked out at eighteen never knowing real love, a real home, a real family.

I picture Haydee when she turned up in New York. Barely eighteen, no family to care for her. Too skinny, too brittle. Marks on her arms where the needles had plunged.

There is no way I will let that happen to Issy. She deserves a better life.

Charlie groans quietly from across the room, shaking his head at my suggestion to get rid of the body. But we must. Charlie has to trust me; he has to let me hold him up for once. This man who has done everything for me, has been through it all, holding me up, never letting me down.

Doing everything right.

I will not let him go to prison.

I will not let them take Issy from us.

I will not let our lives be ruined again because of Jesse *fucking* Carter.

This time, I will be the strong one. Charlie can collapse, I will hold him up.

I can do this for both of us.

I owe him that.

Chapter Thirty-Four

Now

Hannah

I move across the room decisively, as if by doing so the answer to *how* we get rid of the body will jump out at me.

'Han, wait,' Charlie says, his hands up. 'I can't... We can't—'

'We can,' I snap back. 'We have to.'

He shakes his head. 'I can tell the police the truth. I can tell them that Haydee killed him. It wasn't me, we haven't done anything wrong.'

The hope that swims in his eyes is heart-breaking and enraging at the same time. He doesn't get it. Even now, Charlie believes in the simple facts of right and wrong. He doesn't understand how, even with the best intentions, people can be dragged into things that are wrong believing them to be right, and how the police don't care about any of that.

'But I have,' I say, my voice so small I wonder if he'll hear it at all. 'I *have* done something wrong.'

He sighs. The hope drains from his face and he nods slowly, as if he knew this was coming. 'You can tell me, Han. Tell me how you're involved in this, please.'

I shake my head, but I'm resigned to my fate. I knew this day would come. You can't run forever. Isn't that what I told Jesse so many times over text message straight after it happened, before he blocked me, desperate to get him to come back to me? I grimace at the memory, the desperation and horror I felt at the time as much to do with Jesse leaving me as what we'd done.

I move closer to my husband, stepping over Owen's dead body, not letting myself look down at him or the blood congealing on the chipped flagstone floor.

'I met Jesse at uni in New York,' I start. 'Like I told you.'

Charlie nods and it feels important to me that he knows my whole story wasn't a lie.

'But he wasn't just some classmate, like I said, he was…' I pause, unable to describe what Jesse was to me. 'He was everything.' Tears pool in my eyes and I can't look at Charlie any more, knowing his heart will be breaking into pieces so small we may never put them back together. 'You know what it was like for me at home. I had no real friends, my parents didn't pay any attention to me and I was lonely, so lonely. I got to New York and I thought I would fit in straight away, make loads of friends, become a bloody pop star or something and finally be the person I was meant to be.' I shake my head at my own childish naivety. 'But it didn't feel like that when I got there. I felt the same stupid, awkward me, always on the edge of friendships, never quite fitting in anywhere. But then, one day, Jesse started talking to me. We were going to the same concert – Laura Marling.'

I flick a look up at Charlie whose brow is furrowed. He may not even have heard of Laura Marling. Though she was once my favourite singer in the whole world, I've not listened to her since New York.

There was a period when it felt like you couldn't turn on Radio One without hearing one of her songs; I had to switch off every time she came on. Her haunting voice took me back to New York in an instant. 'We started going out,' I say, aware that Charlie doesn't need the intimate details of the relationship. 'Almost immediately after I met him, we became a couple. I was obsessed,' I say, my cheeks colouring. 'He was nothing like anyone I'd met before and he had all these music connections. He promised he'd help me record an EP and get it to all the big labels.' I shake my head, embarrassed at my own naivety. How many young women have fallen for this line? Got swept up in the proximity of fame? I sound so shallow and I know Charlie won't understand how this was such a big factor in everything that came next because Charlie has never known me as the girl whose whole life revolved around music. 'It was all I wanted, back then, to be a musician—'

'I know.'

'What? I've never spoken to you about—'

'Come on, Han. You think I don't hear you singing when you think my headphones are in? You think I didn't see the way you'd watch the singers in the pub on Friday night when we first met? You'd tear up sometimes, and I'd see the longing in your eyes. I always wondered why you'd never sing, why you stopped playing...'

I bite my lip, looking down at the blood-speckled floor. Of course Charlie knew. It had been a few years since New York when we met but everything I'd lost was still bubbling at the surface, my desires squashed down by necessity – not disinterest, like I told everyone when, overnight, I refused to sing again and sold my guitars. Even now, my hands form the shapes when I hear certain songs, the long soft pads of my fingers desperate to feel the frets beneath them again.

'Well… anyway, I don't know. I guess I lost myself to Jesse. Looking back on it, it was never a healthy relationship. He always felt as if he was about to slip from my grip, always kept me just that bit distant so that whenever he showed me attention, I jumped. It was pathetic really, how I hung off him.'

'What happened with Haydee?' Charlie asks. His tone is level but I can tell there's annoyance there. He wants me to get to the heart of it; he doesn't need to hear about my desperation for another man. But it's all part of it, that's what I need him to understand. That what happened happened because I wasn't myself.

'Being with Jesse was like a drug. I'd do anything for another hit. I know that sounds insane, trust me, I've thought about this a lot. It's the only way I can explain what happened… that I was under the influence of him.'

'Han… Please.'

'There was a party,' I say, my voice trembling now as we get nearer to the truth. 'Owen was there. Owen was always there. He didn't really like me – or he liked me too much, I could never tell. He was always making seedy remarks about Jesse and me. We often shared an apartment in the city on the weekend, one of Jesse's dad's, and Owen had the room next door. He'd… He'd listen to us. Then the next morning when Jesse would go and get coffee Owen would sit across the table from me and mimic my sounds.' My cheeks burn with the humiliation of it, hearing myself through Owen's mouth, like a wannabe porn star. So desperate, so dripping with longing. 'I would tell Jesse about it after, but he'd laugh it off like it was nothing—'

'Hannah, please, please just get to—'

'I am, I am. Sorry. There's just so much…' Speaking about it has made all sorts of emotions come up but the one I feel most strongly is shame. Even before Haydee, I was always so ashamed of myself around Jesse. My eagerness, my desperation. Owen saw it all and never tired of reflecting it back to me. It was why I couldn't stand to look at him.

'Haydee was seeing Owen,' I say and Charlie frowns, as if he wasn't expecting this. 'But she liked Jesse. It was obvious. Owen knew it too; he was never the main attraction. He didn't look like he does – did – now. He was just some scrappy kid hanging off Jesse's coattails who no one really liked but everyone had to tolerate because for some reason, Jesse liked him.' I take a breath, surprised at the spite I still feel for Owen.

'But Jesse wanted a party, so he had one. It was at his dad's apartment, even though a few weeks before we'd had a party there and his dad had… His dad beat the crap out of him the next day. Right in front of me.' I pause for a second, remembering Jesse cowering behind the expensive black velvet couch as his dad beat his fists down on him, calling him a *useless son of a bitch*. He didn't care that I was watching in horror from the doorway, clutching at my body in a bra and thong like something from a film. He smiled at me as he left. *Do yourself a favour, darling, and get yourself a real man.* His eyes roamed my half naked body and I felt physically sick; Jesse's blood was still on his hands, smearing the door handle as he turned it to leave. Jesse was curled in the corner, sobs shaking his body. When I tried to hug him, he pushed me away so hard I bashed my head against the wall and yelped in shock. *I'm sorry*, he said, grabbing at me, *I'm so sorry Han, I love you, I love you, I love you.* He kissed the back of my head and we cried together.

'Hannah,' Charlie snaps. 'The party.'

'Sorry… Yes, Jesse threw a party and I went. We'd argued the day before; I was jealous that he was always doing things with Haydee and Owen. I wanted to see him more and…' I wave my hand, realising this is irrelevant, that I have to keep going or we'll never get to the truth. 'I got pretty wasted. Everyone did. There were a lot of people there, too many even for his dad's massive apartment. There were drugs. A lot of drugs. I had never done any before New York but since meeting Jesse I'd started doing them a lot, cocaine mostly. But that night, I don't even know.'

I look up at Charlie, whose face is grey. He looks at me like he doesn't know me and in a way, I suppose he doesn't. Not this version of me. The worst drug Charlie has ever done is a bit of weed smoked at the back of the pub on his sixteenth birthday in the village. We laughed about it over the years, how tame we both are.

What a lie that was.

'I don't remember that much. I know Owen got everyone out eventually. It must have been four, five in the morning by this point. It was dark but the sun was starting to come up. I remember that because his dad's bedroom had a view over the skyline and I saw a glimmer of orange peeping over the buildings as they undressed me—'

'What? Who undressed you?'

Things get blurry here. Everything is a flash of colours and textures. The feeling of my silk slip dress being pulled over my head, staying over my face for a second too long and feeling like I was going to suffocate. The hands on my legs, spreading them apart. Haydee's laughter. Owen's voice. Jesse's voice. More laughter. The feeling of Haydee's breast in my hand. I'd never touched another girl before. *Smile, girls*, Owen's voice directing us. The flash of a camera phone. Then, nothing. Black.

Just black.

'All of them,' I say, a whisper. 'I don't know how it happened. It never made any sense to me after, I wasn't... I wasn't like that and I hated Owen and Haydee but somehow we were all in bed together. The four of us.'

Charlie's eyes widen as shame trickles through my veins, as if this is the worst thing about that night.

'Did they force you?' he demands, colour rising in his cheeks.

I shake my head. 'No. They wouldn't have needed to. If Jesse wanted to do something...' I don't need to finish my sentence. Charlie must know by now that I did whatever Jesse wanted. His little puppy. A rag doll in his arms.

'What happened to Haydee?' Charlie asks, back on track, forcing us toward this train wreck that I'm desperate to look away from.

'I woke up on the floor,' I say, remembering the feeling of the thick carpet on my face, drool around my mouth. 'The sun was almost up by then so the room was lit. I could barely lift my head, the banging behind my eyes was so severe I thought I was having a stroke but then I heard voices. Panicked voices.'

Jesse and Owen were whispering at each other, but so loudly they may as well have been screaming. *What the fuck are we going to do?* Jesse was saying, over and over, his whispers becoming louder and more desperate. I tried to lift my head but the pounding was getting worse by the second and I winced at the sight of the sun. *I'll sort it*, Owen eventually said, the whisper gone, his low voice uncharacteristically certain – more like Jesse's than his own. *Just get her out of here.*

'Jesse walked across the room and lifted me up under my arms. It hurt; I remember asking him to stop, to leave me on the floor but he pulled harder and that's when I opened my eyes properly. I saw Haydee face down on the bed. Her naked body turned over, so small. She had a red handprint on her bum. I always remember that. It was so red and I gasped at it, looking between Owen and Jesse, wondering whose hand had hurt her like that.

'"What did you do?" I screeched at them, breaking free from Jesse's grip as I walked over to the bed. I turned her over, but she was cold. I didn't… I thought she was just sleeping, crying maybe, her face turned away from them both at what they'd done to her. But then I saw the finger marks around her neck.' The words spill up through me and I think I'm going to be sick, remembering the mottled bruising on her thin white neck. 'I shouted again, "What did you do?" But this time, Owen came at me, pushing me back on the bed so I was lying next to her. "We didn't do anything," he spat at me. "This was all you."'

Tears are pouring down my face now as I recall the moment I realised what he meant. Me? I had done this to her? I held my hands up to the light.

'He told me I had strangled her,' I say, my words now barely a whisper. 'He had it all on his phone. He said I didn't stop even when she asked me to. He said I killed her.' Air whooshes out of me at this admission as I double over, letting the sobs take over my body. 'I don't know why I did it. I hated her,' I admit, the words

267

finally released. 'I wrote that in my diary over and over but still, it never made sense that I could do something like that. I don't know what happened. I couldn't remember anything – I still can't remember anything. But it was the drugs, whatever I'd taken had made me…'

In a second, Charlie is by my side, holding me up and for a moment the world resumes its natural order. I am the mess and Charlie is my saviour.

'You didn't kill her, Han. She didn't die.'

'What?'

Charlie brushes the hair from my face and tips my chin to him. 'Owen told you she was dead, but she wasn't.'

'But I felt her, she was cold. She was dead… She was—'

'I don't know what you felt, Han. But I promise you, you never killed anyone. Haydee is very much alive. I saw her today. In this room. I promise you, she was here.'

'But that doesn't make any sense.' I wriggle out of his grip and try to order my thoughts. I felt her neck, didn't I? I checked for a pulse. Surely I checked for a pulse. But as I play the scene again, I can't be sure. All I know is I turned her over and she was cold. They told me she was dead. So I believed them.

'What happened after, Han?'

I shake my head, now fuzzy with the idea that Haydee is alive. 'Jesse forced me out of the room. I grabbed some clothes from his bedroom and we went into the street. He called me a cab back to school, made me promise to not breathe a word of this to anyone. He said he'd call me that night. I told him we needed to go to the police but he made me promise I wouldn't. "You'll go to jail, Han," he told me. "I'll never see you again. Is that what you want? To spend the rest of your life stuck in some American prison, never even being allowed visitors?" I was terrified. I knew I should tell the truth but he said he would sort everything, that no one ever needed to know and he was going to keep me safe.'

Charlie reaches for me again and I let him take my hand.

'You must hate me.'

He shakes his head. 'I could never hate you, Han. I love you. No matter what.' He looks up at me sadly, tears threatening to fall, but then sniffs and nods, as if that's enough of that. 'Did you come back to the UK? Did Jesse tell you what they did with her?'

I shake my head. 'I came back a week later. I already had a flight booked for Christmas. Jesse never spoke to me again. Owen turned up at my dorm room the next day and told me if I ever told anyone about what happened he'd make sure I got the electric chair. He had it on video, he said. Me choking a girl to death, smacked off my face. He said he'd show it to the judge and they'd make sure I got the death penalty.' Sick laughter bubbles up in me at hearing these words, so out of tune with the rest of my life. 'I don't know if they even have capital punishment in New York—'

'They don't.'

'No, well. I was scared enough to never say anything to anyone. I came back here, finished my degree – just about – and then got the job at WomenGoFree and met you. It didn't make up for what I'd done... Of course it didn't but I wanted—'

'To make amends,' Charlie finishes for me, as if my actions make sense. 'And you never spoke to Jesse again?' The way he says it, with such hope, makes me want to crawl inside him and stay there forever.

269

'Never,' I say. 'If Haydee wasn't dead then he lied to me—'

'He didn't know.'

'What?'

Charlie puffs out his cheeks and scratches the back of his head. 'Haydee said that Owen paid her to "stay dead" and told Jesse she'd died that night.'

'But why—'

'To control Jesse.' Charlie shrugs, as if this makes no sense to him either.

'So Haydee didn't… I didn't—'

'No, Han. You didn't kill anyone.'

The words take a second to land but when they do, they overpower me and I fall to the floor. I am not a murderer. I am not guilty. Whatever I did that night, Haydee survived.

Chapter Thirty-Five

Now

Charlie

Hannah is on the floor, her body convulsing as she sobs. Owen's body lies next to her, his spilled blood dangerously close to her jeans, looking more lifeless than ever. Charlie should hold her; he knows he should but he finds himself rooted to the spot. All this time, Hannah has held this in. Their whole life together has been built on a lie. He shakes his head. That's not true. He can't let it be true. He loves Hannah. More importantly he *knows* Hannah. The story she told shocked him to his core; he finds it near impossible to imagine Hannah, *his* Hannah, doing the things she described. But then, he thinks, aren't we all capable of doing things we never thought possible? What about his own actions over the past week? Fleeing a crime scene. Hacking into strangers' phones to track them down. Assisting a murder. And now, contemplating covering one up.

He knows Hannah is right. They can't walk away from this unscathed if Owen's body is discovered. They have to get rid of him.

'Han,' he says. 'Get up, you have to get up.' He tugs at her arm, pulling her up roughly. As he grips her thin arm he realises this is what Jesse must have done the morning he thought Haydee was dead. He loosens his grip and wraps his arms around her waist instead, breathing in the familiar scent of the vanilla and sandalwood perfume he buys her every year. 'Come on, darling. We have to do this. Come on.'

With that, the sobbing stops and she sniffs loudly before wiping her face. She nods, as if the spell is broken and she's ready to work. He's seen this side of her many times before; bold, decisive. He knows she thinks that he is the strong one, the one who has held them up through years of failure and heartbreak, but it's always been her. Yes, she falls apart. She cries, sometimes for days, refusing to get out of bed. But when she decides enough is enough, she shows a steely determination that he has always admired.

'Does anyone know you're here?' she asks him now after a few deep breaths and he shakes his head resolutely. 'Has anyone ever seen you and Owen together?'

'At the pub, last night possibly—'

She reels back, hurt in her eyes. 'You went to the *pub* with him?'

He shakes his head again. 'Not our pub, another one. Not in the village – Jesus! We went to one in Moreton. It was just locals. I didn't see anyone I recognised, no one paid us any attention.'

'You're sure?'

He nods. 'Absolutely.'

Hannah looks at Owen's body. 'We need to get rid of his car. It must be a rental.'

Charlie has visions of walking into the rental car office dressed as Owen, returning the keys as if nothing has happened. The vision breaks up as soon as it comes; he could never do that. It's too big a risk.

'We could burn it?' Hannah suggests, still staring at Owen. 'Put his body inside and… Burn it?'

He grimaces, unable to believe these words are coming out of his wife's mouth but he finds himself nodding, telling her yes, that's probably the best thing to do. She walks forward and kneels by Owen's body, carefully avoiding the blood, and reaches into his jeans pockets. She feels around.

'Empty,' she says, turning back to him, her face white. 'No phone, no keys.'

He frowns. 'Try the other pockets.'

She turns Owen over, the squelch of the blood under his dented head forcing bile to rise in Charlie's throat but he manages to hold it in and looks away while it settles.

'Nothing.'

'But that doesn't make sense, he drove here, I saw his car…'

Hannah jumps up and runs out of the room, and he hears the sound of the front door swinging open. Within a few seconds, she's back. 'The car's gone.'

'What?'

'Haydee was here? You said she was here before?'

He nods.

'She must have taken it.'

Their gazes fall back to Owen.

'What did the note say?' Hannah asks. Charlie picks up the note from the coffee table where he left it and reads it back.

'*I'll take care of everything else,*' Hannah reads. 'Perhaps she meant his car and phone?'

Charlie hears a strange laugh chortle from his throat. 'How kind,' he says. 'How kind of her.'

Hannah shrugs, seemingly unbothered by this turn of events, and leaves the room once more. Alone with Owen, Charlie once again feels like the very idea of them disposing of his body is totally preposterous. They are two normal people. How can they consider doing this? But the alternative is even more impossible. He waits, uselessly, until Hannah comes back into the room.

'The garden,' she says, slightly out of breath. 'Did you see the garden?'

He shakes his head and frowns, wondering if his wife has totally lost her mind. Does she really want to talk about the garden right now?

'It's huge. Goes down to a wooded area. We could...' She drifts off and he suddenly realises what she means.

'*Bury* him?' Charlie splutters. 'You want us to *bury* him?'

Her eyes shine as she nods. 'No one will ever look, will they? Why would you dig up a garden like this?' She leaves the room and this time he follows her, through the hallway into the kitchen then out of the back door.

She's right; the garden is enormous. The top half is manicured, with a weathered teak garden table and chairs on the patio near the door and a stone path that winds down to the garden shed. But after that, there is basically a whole other garden. A compost pile covered in junk, presumably from when they renovated the house to turn it into a holiday let; old pine chairs hacked to pieces, a dark oak dresser covered in paint, even an avocado bath suite. You would never know it was here if you were a guest; the shed hides the pile of rubbish and beyond that there's a wooded area, just like Hannah said.

'What if they decide to renovate the garden?' Charlie asks Hannah.

She shrugs. 'They won't. Surely they'd have done it by now? The rest of the house is finished, isn't it? They must have decided to just do this part of the garden and leave the rest as it is.'

'But they might,' he says, unsure.

She sighs and throws her hands up. 'What do you want me to say, Charlie? They might dig the garden, yes, they might. But if they do, what will they find that can connect us to him? We've never stayed in this house; god knows how many people have. How would they tie it back to us?'

'DNA,' he says, but he sounds as unsure as he feels.

'Only if they had our DNA to begin with,' she snaps back. 'And they don't have mine; do they have yours?'

He shakes his head. Of course they don't; he's not a criminal.

'Plus, if they do ever find him, it'll be near impossible to know who was staying in the house when it happened. Won't it? It's not like they date bodies to the day and I bet this place is filled with different people every week.'

Charlie stares at his wife as if she is a stranger. Is this information she's garnered from the many thrillers she buries her head in each night, their pages filled with murderous intent? Or is it something more sinister? He shakes the thought. This is Hannah. His Hannah. She's always been good in a crisis and that's all she's doing now.

'Okay,' he finally says.

Her shoulders move down half an inch and she tells him to look in the shed for a shovel.

Once again, he swallows down bile.

–

An hour later and they are almost done with the hole. *The grave.* Sweat drips from his forehead down into his eyes and it stings. He slams his foot down on the shovel once more and throws the dirt over his shoulder. The ground was hard at first, resistant, but the further down they went, the easier it became. His head barely reaches the top of the hole now they've dug down so deep, though Hannah stopped digging a while ago, both terrified they'd somehow dig so far down that they'd get stuck down there together forever. It was a horrible image, the two of them trapped in the dirt, unable to climb out to safety. He imagines Owen's body resting here forever, never to be found, soil clogging his nostrils, worms curling through his mouth. He stops himself. He knows he can't let these thoughts take hold or they will suffocate him.

'I think that's enough,' Hannah says from the top of the hole. Her face is smudged with dirt and he wishes more than anything he could tell her to go home and wash up, to leave this to him, but he knows it's not possible. He can't do it alone.

She holds her hand out to him and they quickly realise she won't be able to pull him up. Hannah disappears for a moment then returns with a step ladder she must have found in the shed.

'Tie something to it,' he says before she passes it down. 'Otherwise we'll not be able to get it back up.' She disappears again, but doesn't come back with rope – that would be too easy. Instead, she's taken off her jumper and tied one arm around the top of the step ladder. She lowers it down slowly, checking that the jumper will reach all the way to bottom of the pit.

It does; he tightens the knot before he steps on the ladder and climbs out of the hole. *The grave.*

Hannah pulls the step ladder up behind him and they both breathe a sigh of relief as they stand at the side of the hole together.

'How will we move him?' Hannah asks in a small, childlike voice. Charlie has already had time to consider this. While he was digging, the repetitive motion aching his body, he has run through the whole thing. They will wrap him in a bedsheet from the cottage, lower him down, then take the bedsheet out. They will have to find a place to dump the bloodied sheet. It will be evidence and some part of his brain knows that the less evidence they bury with him, the better. Again, he wonders how either of them have retained any of this knowledge and how much they *don't* know; how much they are missing that could tie them to this forever.

'Go in the house and find a bedsheet. There must be a laundry cupboard somewhere,' Charlie tells her, sounding more authoritative than he feels. He glances around the garden, looking up to the skyline as if in fear of being overlooked, though there are no other houses to be seen. The cottage is a mile or so from any other houses; he'd noted that the first time he'd looked up the address on Google Maps and again when driving here today, as if he knew that the isolated location would serve them well.

They are safe. For the moment, they are safe.

He follows Hannah inside, leaving her to go upstairs while he returns to Owen. The smell of the blood – or the body, he can't tell – is souring and he tries to breathe through his mouth to stop the foul odour clawing at his nostrils.

'Found one,' Hannah says from the doorway. He turns to look at her, thinking of all the times she's held a sheet out to him at home. He'd usually take it from her and

277

make the bed. Like normal people. Now he reaches to take the sheet from her and can barely believe he is about to wrap a body in it. The sheet is not fitted, he notices with relief, just a big, plain white sheet. He wonders about the person who owns this house, if they could ever imagine what would one day happen in their living room. He thinks of this as he bends down and begins to wrap Owen's cold, heavy body in the sheet. The blood seeps through from the flagstone floor. Charlie thinks how lucky they are that the room is not carpeted. Blood would be hard to remove from carpet. These thoughts flit through his head as he turns the body, wrapping it further in the sheet. What can they use on the floor? There will be bleach in the house. There must be. Or will they use cleaners? Some holiday lets use cleaners. Haydee's booking said she wasn't due to check out for another week when he last looked, but what if she changed her plans since then? A panic seizes him as he imagines the cleaner's key turning in the door, finding him and Hannah here, blood on their hands. His movements speed up and he looks down at the body, wrapped from head to toe like a mummy.

'You take his legs,' he tells Hannah.

She opens her mouth for a second as if to argue but then nods.

Together, they lift the body.

–

After, Charlie stamps on the ground to cover the hole. The grave. His efforts are wasted; the land surrounding where they have buried him is a wreck. No one would notice a mound in the ground, even a human-shaped one. But still, they do everything they can to cover their tracks. Hannah went back into the house a while ago while he shovelled dirt onto the body, to clean up, she said, but he thinks she couldn't stand the sight of the body disappearing beneath the soil. Too morbid.

He takes the sheet and puts it in an old burnt-out bin the owners must use for bonfires. After a brief trip to the kitchen to find a lighter, he comes back and sets it alight, along with some garden waste. He watches as the flames take hold. It doesn't take long for the sheet to disappear to the ashes. He throws a watering can of water over the top of the bonfire to stop the smoke then walks back to the house, careful to remove his mud-encrusted shoes before walking in.

Hannah is on her hands and knees in the living room.

The blood is gone. He wonders how she got rid of it all so quickly, but he supposes that after the sheet mopped up the pool around Owen's head, there might not have been as much as he imagined.

'What if they bring in one of those blue light things?' she asks, her eyes round and terrified.

Charlie shrugs. 'I don't know, Han. Remember, there's no reason to think Owen was ever here.'

She nods, then scrubs at the spotless floor again.

'Come on,' he tells her, pulling her up. 'We need to go.'

'Just one more spot—'

'Han, there's nothing there. Come on.' He pulls her to her feet and takes the bottle of bleach from her then walks into the kitchen and puts it in the cupboard under the sink. Like nothing happened.

By now, it is nearing five p.m. and the sunlight is starting to wane. It occurs to him for the first time that someone may have seen their cars parked in the passing place. A flicker of fear itches at his neck but he keeps it from Hannah, no need to panic her further.

'We should be seen somewhere,' he tells her instead.

'What?'

'Before we go home. We should go somewhere public. So that if anyone… if anything happens, we'll have an account of where we were, that we were having a normal Saturday. Acting normal.'

'I can't see anyone, Charlie. Look at me!' Hannah points to herself as if she is soaked in blood, her guilt colouring her clothing. The shocking truth is that Hannah looks fine. The dirt from her face has been smudged off, whether through sweat or washing her face he doesn't know, but other than the terrified look in her eyes, his wife is unchanged. To the outside world, they are the same people they've always been.

Charlie knows he is not the same. His clothes are filthy and he reeks of sweat. But he has another top in his car along with a pair of wellies he can easily put on, to make his dirty jeans appear like they've been stomping through the woods on a pleasant weekend walk.

'Trust me, Han, we need to do this.'

It takes them another ten minutes to leave the house. The usual panic you feel at leaving a holiday home is intensified a thousand times over as they walk around the house again and again desperately checking they've left nothing behind. Nothing except a body.

In this time, they have decided that Hannah will stop at the cafe on the way home, knowing that someone from the village will be in there to chat. She'll tell them how they have spent the day doing Issy's room, that Charlie is making a last-minute run to the big Marks in Chippy to stock the fridge before her arrival. He will go into the shop and buy everything that a little girl could want. He will make sure to smile at the shop assistant and tell her they're preparing for their little girl to come home, to make sure he is remembered. As if an alibi this late in the day will save them. But they hold onto their plan, so sure that they can get away with this. That they deserve to.

As they pull out from the house, neither of them lets themselves believe they have covered up a murder. They tell themselves that they have saved Haydee from a lifetime in prison; saved her from something she doesn't deserve after everything she has been through. It was self-defence. There was nothing else they could have done.

Chapter Thirty-Six

ONE DAY UNTIL ISSY COMES HOME

Now

Hannah

The FrogTape won't stick down. I press it hard with the pad of my thumb but it sticks to that instead and rips away when I move.

'Fucking thing!' I scream, launching the roll across the room.

'Han.' Charlie appears behind me, his hand on my shoulder. 'It's okay.'

Tension vibrates through me as I concentrate on breathing in for six, hold it for seven, let it out for eight. And again.

It's barely eight a.m. on Sunday morning but I've been in here an hour already. How could I sleep after what we've done? Will I ever sleep soundly again? When we got home yesterday, separately, we relayed our stories to each other like criminals. I'd been to the coffee shop, where I'd seen plenty of the villagers including, of course, Olivia, who I am beginning to suspect must be rather miserable at home to spend all her waking hours at the cafe with various friends. Charlie went to Marks where he bored a shop attendant half to death with stories of prepping for Issy. No one suspects a thing.

I shocked myself by how normally I acted at the cafe. I thought everyone would know; that they'd be able to smell the iron scent of decay from Owen's blood which must be buried in my skin despite the way I'd scrubbed at the sink. But no one said a thing. Just the normal chat. As if nothing had happened.

It should have been a relief; that I could slip back into normal life so easily, that my guilt wasn't written all over my face. It was the same way I felt returning from New York. Back then I curled up in my childhood bedroom after dinner with my parents and wept because they had no idea their daughter was a murderer. Only, I wasn't, was I?

Whenever I think of Haydee, a burst of rage overtakes my body. How could Owen do that to me, to Jesse? I don't understand the full story yet, I know that. Charlie and I have barely spoken since we got home. He made cheese on toast for us both then ran me a bath, either to force me into relaxing or to get me out of the way. This morning, I got out of bed while he was still asleep and it seems he's now up.

He walks into the spare room, Issy's room, with his head down.

'Why were you even there?' I finally ask. Last night, in the early hours the question shocked me awake but as I watched Charlie sleeping, his brow furrowed even in his dreams, I couldn't bring myself to wake him to ask. Now, I bring his chin up to face me and look me in the eye.

He rubs his face with his hands and when he takes them away I see the impact of yesterday on him. His eyes are red raw; dark heavy bags cling to his skin. He looks a mess.

'It's such a long story—'

'We have time.'

He nods, knowing this is inevitable. 'It started with Jesse.'

Charlie tells me everything then. How he intercepted a letter meant for me from Jesse a month ago and faked texts from me in attempt to break up whatever was happening before it took hold. I wonder for a moment what would have happened if I'd received the letter instead. Would I have replied? Would I have met Jesse in another circumstance? Would he still be alive? But these questions are pointless. I know what it's like to torture yourself with what-ifs and I can't do it again. I think of the emails Jesse sent me that landed in the bad place. So many near misses have happened along the way to bring us to this conclusion. Was Jesse going to tell me the truth about Haydee? My heart aches for him at knowing how his world would have been ripped apart when he realised what Owen had done to him. But so little of the story makes sense to me. If he was coming to the UK to tell me the truth about Haydee, why did he bring Owen? How was Jesse still with him after knowing what he'd done? My thoughts race on as Charlie continues his story.

He tells me how he tracked down Haydee for Owen, believing her a dangerous murderer who was now looking for me. Owen had convinced him she wanted revenge for what we did, and wasn't going to stop at killing Jesse. I was next, he said, he really believed I was next. So he led Owen straight to Haydee's door. He winces as he tells me this, and I pull him into a hug, trying with everything I have to reassure him that he is not responsible for what happened. He could never have known Owen would attack her.

But, could he? I have always thought Charlie to be good, properly no-grey-areas good. But he is not stupid, not by any means. What did he expect when he led Owen to Haydee? He must have known something bad would happen.

'I did,' he says, and I realise I have spoken my thoughts out loud. 'It's why I went to the cottage yesterday. I couldn't bear the idea of him hurting her, or her hurting him, or anything terrible happening because of me. I thought I could get there in time and stop it... Whatever it was.'

'I don't understand how you even found her,' I say.

Charlie presses the palm of his hands against his eyes, leaving red marks on his delicate skin. 'I was there the night Jesse died,' he says, and my heart stops.

The confession winds me for a second. 'Did you—'

'No! God, Hannah. No, I didn't have anything to do with his death.' The colour drains from his face as his eyes grow huge. 'You believe me, don't you?'

I do. I think I do. I know I do, but my hands shake as I pick up the FrogTape once more and recommence my task. I place it around the light switch, sticking it down and ripping it back up when my shaking hands can't get it straight. Again, I try, and again.

'Han.' Charlie's breath is on my neck. He sweeps my hair so it falls over my shoulder and kisses me softly. 'I'm sorry,' he says. 'I'm so sorry.'

He turns me around to him and presses me against the wall. Our lips meet instinctively and suddenly my body is on fire. I want my husband in a way that I haven't for years, in the way I used to before sex became timed and medical.

An hour or so later, we're still lying with our clothes piled around us on the spare bedroom floor.

'This is Issy's room!' I suddenly shout, grabbing my T-shirt and shoving it over my head.

'I don't think she'll mind,' Charlie laughs. 'Seriously, Han, it's fine.'

But I'm too busy shoving my clothes back on like a disgraced teenager to take any solace from his words.

'What if the room smells of—'

'Han!' Charlie's up now and he grabs me roughly by the arm. 'Stop, seriously. I promise you, we will not be the first parents to have sex in their child's bedroom.' He smiles, a red tint marking his cheeks as the words leave his lips. Parents. We are parents.

I smile, allowing his certainty to pass through me.

'You really think she's going to be here tomorrow?' I ask tentatively.

He nods as he pulls on his joggers. 'I know she is.' He picks up the FrogTape and finishes putting it around the light switch in one easy movement. His hands don't shake, he doesn't hesitate, he just gets it done.

—

Later that day, we've painted the whole room and we wait for it to fully dry before applying the second coat. We're in the kitchen now, making lunch after a morning of hard work. We haven't discussed what Charlie told me yet, but I know it's coming.

'What happened when you…' I don't need to finish my question for Charlie to know our interrupted conversation is now ready to resume.

He dips his teabag into his tea, in and out, and discards it on the side.

'He was already dead,' Charlie says, his tone so deadpan I feel myself wince.

I nod, as if this information isn't ripping out my heart and sticking it back inside me, raw and bleeding. Charlie saw Jesse's dead body. Jesse is dead. It hits me again, like a train. It has been almost a week since I learned the news but it's like it's been suppressed amongst everything else. Or perhaps I am now allowing myself to feel the grief I didn't feel entitled to before when I associated Jesse with the worst thing I ever did. But now, Jesse is not a conspirator in the murder I committed, he is a victim of Owen's. We are all victims of Owen's.

My thoughts turn to Haydee, that poor frail girl who just wanted to be loved. I hated her so much back then, so jealous of her 2000s heroin-chic look which I could never attain, I realise now, not because I was lazy but because I was healthy; I was doing the occasional line of coke to impress my boyfriend, not snorting it repeatedly off the back of filthy toilets before waking up in different beds every few weeks with nowhere to call home. My parents may be difficult, but they were safe. My life was safe. Before I met Jesse I'd never touched anything more than weed. A few weeks with him turned me into someone I didn't recognise and I wonder who the Jesse figure was for Haydee, and if she had ever been lucky enough to know a comfortable happy life before drugs at all.

'Was Owen…' I don't know how to finish the question.

'Was Owen what?'

'I don't know… was he… there?'

Charlie looks at me like I'm insane and I suppose that I am. 'I told you I didn't know Owen had killed Jesse until Haydee told me, why would he be there?'

I shrug, unsure of myself. 'I don't know. I just thought…'

'Do you not believe me?'

'Of course I believe you.'

And I do. There have been so many lies throughout this whole mess but I know now that Charlie is telling the truth. He has stumbled into this trying desperately to protect me, that's his only crime. Being stupid enough to love me so much that he'll risk everything for me.

'No one was there,' he says gruffly. 'Jesse was lying on the floor in the middle of the room, bleeding. A lot. I ran away, okay? I was terrified. I thought if I told anyone it would make me look guilty – and even if it didn't, it would bring the police to our door and how could I do that to you? To Issy?' Tears pool in his eyes and I see my own guilt and terror reflected back at me. All week, Charlie and I have been plagued by the same fears.

I pull him to me and we cry together again, so horrified by the mess we have made of all of this.

'How could you not tell me?' I ask and he replies with a silent shake of his head. I dip my face away from his as I think of all the things I've not told him either and the familiar creep of shame prickles at the back of my neck, but Charlie's soft touch brushes it away.

'No more secrets,' he says. 'If anything good has come out of this, it has to be that. It's you and me in this together now, Han. We both know everything. We can never tell anyone else. No matter what happens with us—'

'What do you mean?'

Charlie's eyes grow fierce and I fear for a moment that he is going to tell me that he's leaving, that this is too much, that after everything it's over.

'I'm not going anywhere,' he says, as if reading my mind. 'Not now, not ever.'

I believe him. I believe in what he's done for me. For our family.

We go back upstairs and walk into Issy's room hand in hand.

'We did the right thing, didn't we?' I ask as we take in what is now undeniably a little girl's bedroom. 'You're sure there was no other—'

He silences me with a tight squeeze of my hand. 'We did the right thing. Owen was a murderer. Haydee was… Haydee was innocent. There was no way we could have told the police what she did, even if it wouldn't have put us in danger.'

I nod, and I want to believe that our motives were so pure. We were protecting Haydee. A woman whose life stopped at eighteen when I strangled her, not to death, but to the death of the life she knew. Her whole life after that night was spent running away, living off Owen's dirty money. That's no life. For Charlie, I think it is as simple as doing the right thing by her. But for me, the motive is much less pure.

We were covering our backs. Ensuring that no one ever finds out about the twisted person I became with Jesse and Owen. That person is not someone you would ever trust with a child. I'm not that person any more; if I want to be a mother, I can't be.

And it's the only thing in the whole world I want. Nothing can take it away from me now.

Chapter Thirty-Seven

THE DAY ISSY COMES HOME

Now

Hannah

They're here. They're actually here.

We hear the sound of tyres on the road before we can see the car. We've been standing anxiously in the bay window of the living room overlooking the street for an hour, coffee cups long cold in our hands as we wait.

'Is it them?' Charlie asks as I crane my neck to spot the car.

A fizz of something – terror, excitement – flutters in my chest as I see the dark blue of Andrea's Toyota.

'Yes,' I tell Charlie, though he can now also see the car and squeezes my hand tightly.

Andrea pulls up to the curb and is joined within seconds by Michael's battered Corsa. Issy will have travelled with them and I strain to see in the back of their car for her blonde head but Charlie pulls me away from the window before I spot her.

'Come on,' he says, dragging me to the front door. 'You don't want Issy to catch you watching her from the window like a nutcase.' He laughs but it sticks in his throat, the sound raw and hungry and wild.

Neither of us have slept very much. How could we, after what we've done? I dreamed of burying Owen alive, hearing his cries only once we'd dumped the last shovel of soil on top of him. I woke drenched in sweat to find Charlie out of bed already. In the kitchen, he sat at the table with a cold cup of tea in front of him, head in his hands. *He was definitely dead, wasn't he? We did bury...* He looked up at me with his eyes black. *He was definitely dead.* I nodded and went back to bed but it was hours before Charlie followed me up. We must have had two, three hours of rest at most and yet we're still bouncing around this morning like excited puppies. How can we not? The moment is here; Issy is coming.

There must be something sick inside of me to take joy in this, knowing what we've done to get it, but part of me feels righteous in my glee. Five years it has taken us to get here. Five years of hope. Five years of pain, of waiting, of disappointment, of heartbreak. That kind of longing, that kind of despair, it breaks something inside of you. Perhaps it's why burying Owen felt like the only way forward. Would a person without a hole inside them so readily have dug a grave? How can we know? All I know is that we were broken, and we have done this. But now Issy is here.

Now we are whole. Now things will be better.

–

'Shall I pop the kettle on?' Andrea says once we are all seated in the living room, Charlie and I staring at Issy hungrily as she plays on the floor between us and Michael and Elaine.

'Yes, if you could, that would be great, thank you,' Charlie replies as I continue staring.

Issy is captivated by a picture book she's brought with her. It's the kind that has fuzzy material inside. A woolly sheep is currently being prodded by her pudgy fingers.

'Sheep!' she squeals, holding the book up to Elaine.

Elaine smiles and tells her yes, good girl, it is a sheep. I glance at Charlie, a smile curling at my lips. She knows animals. Of course she knows animals. I think of the informational videos I've watched on YouTube late at night about early years child development. I hear the confident American woman's voice advising that children should be able to name animals and follow two-step instructions such as 'take off your socks and give them to me' by twenty-four months. I have the bizarre urge to utter this sentence just like the woman on the video did, so sure that her daughter would obey. But I won't. I'm scared to even speak to Issy, let alone give her a command, in case she ignores me entirely.

Andrea walks back in the room with two cups of tea and I tear my eyes away from Issy to get up and help her bring the other mugs in.

In the kitchen, she places a firm hand on my shoulder. 'Are you okay, Hannah?'

My eyes dart to my hands, as if the mud from the grave is still encrusted in my fingernails, but my hands are clean. There is not a speck of dirt on me. Nothing.

'Only, it's okay not to be,' Andrea continues. 'It's a lot to take in. It's normal if you're feeling apprehensive—'

'No,' I interrupt. 'I'm not. Not at all. There's nothing more I want than for Issy to be here.' I smile, too wide, and see Andrea recoil away from me briefly before she resumes her normal blank expression. How many times has she done this, I wonder? How many times has she dropped a child off with a new family, simply hoping for the best? Probably a hundred times at least. To her, today is another day at work. But for us, it is everything. It is the beginning of a life we have dreamed about for years, a life that has been waiting for us, putting everything else on hold. And now it's here. And I wish more than anything that I could scrub clean the memory of this weekend so that it would not seep into today.

How did I cope after New York? I force myself to think back on those early days when I arrived home, the memory of that night still half blank and blurry, with only Owen and Jesse's words the morning after the evidence of my crime. It wasn't until I started my first job working with victims of domestic violence and abuse that I felt I could look myself in the mirror again. As if I had somehow balanced the scales – not equally; nothing I did would ever right the wrong I believed I had committed against Haydee, but I knew that falling apart would solve nothing and instead dedicated myself to helping other women.

That's what I have to do here. There is a little girl in the other room desperate to be loved, to be mothered. I can do that. If there is one thing I am sure of it's that I can give Issy all the love in the world. We both can.

I pick up the cups decisively and march back into the living room. Once I've handed them to Elaine and Michael, I sit down on the floor next to Issy.

'What's this one?' I ask, stroking the black and white felt of the book.

She looks up at me, slightly shocked, as if she might decide I'm not safe to talk to, but then looks at Elaine who nods kindly, before turning back to me.

'Cow!' she squeals, jabbing her fists into the felt along-side mine.

'That's right. And what sound does a cow make?'

She opens her mouth as if she is going to do it then frowns and looks around at Elaine again. Before Elaine can get involved though, Charlie jumps up from the sofa and throws himself down beside us.

'Mooooo!' he bellows. 'Moooo!'

There is a second when I think we've got it wrong, we have been too much and Issy will run and hide but then she smiles, so wide we see her tonsils. She tips her head back and copies Charlie. 'Mooo!' she howls, before falling to the ground in a fit of a giggles.

Charlie looks over her to me, nodding slightly, which I return.

It's okay, the nod says, everything is going to be okay.

–

Hours later, everyone is gone but the house feels full. Issy is here. Issy has stayed with us.

The goodbyes were painful; Issy's whole body shook with excruciating sobs as Michael and Elaine drove away but Andrea stayed with us for a while to help calm her down. She sat Issy on her knee and told her the story she's been telling her all week, about how Charlie and I are her new mummy and daddy and we love her very much. She cried harder at that, saying she wanted Elaine and Michael (or, as she calls them, 'Lainey and My-my') and the rejection hurt like nothing I've experienced before. Of course I know she is just a child crying for the only safe parent figures she's ever known, but I wished it hadn't had to be like this. Eventually, Andrea calmed her down and chose that moment to leave.

It feels so strange to be alone with Issy, to have her in our home unsupervised. It's time for her nap soon – Elaine was very keen to impress this upon me as she left, as if I might force Issy to stay up all day and night if she didn't make sure I knew. I can't imagine how it feels for Elaine to drive away from Issy today, leaving her with two people who, despite the formal processes, are basically strangers. Guilt gnaws at me as I imagine the utter horror Elaine would feel if she knew what we did just two days ago. But no, we are not going to think of that today. Today is about Issy.

I walk back into Issy's bedroom where she is sitting on the bed with Charlie. He is attempting to read her a book but she's more interested in the puppy patterns on the sheets we bought her. They're Cath Kidston which was a bit of a splurge but when I saw them online I couldn't resist; the baby-blue fabric is dotted with every kind of puppy you can imagine, with the names of each breed beneath. I take a seat by Issy on the bed and read her a few.

'Dachshund,' I say pointing to one, 'or you can say "sausage dog".' This gleans a smile and she strokes the puppy on the duvet.

'Sausage dog,' she says in a small voice.

'Sweetie, I think it's time for your nap,' I say, trying to make my voice as reassuring and motherly as I can as I rub her back gently.

As if on cue, Issy opens her mouth wide in a comical yawn. I pull the covers back on her bed and she gets in without a word.

'I'll come wake you up soon, okay?' I wait for the moment when she kicks and screams, tells me she wants to go home or that she needs Elaine but she just stares up at me with her big doe eyes and nods.

Charlie tugs me out of the room gently, his hand on my back guiding me away.

We've done it, I think. She's here. We've done it.

Everything is going to be okay.

Chapter Thirty-Eight

Now

Charlie

Their daughter is asleep upstairs.

He says it to himself again and again, unable to believe the deliciousness of the words on his lips. Watching Hannah put Issy down for her nap will go down in his memory as one of the greatest sights he has ever seen. When will all of this fade, he wonders? When will he join the legion of parents who seem to do nothing except moan about their children? He hopes never, but he isn't that naive. He can't imagine a time when being a father will feel anything except an absolute miracle. Perhaps it always will to him. God knows he's worked so much harder to make it happen than most.

Downstairs, he makes them both coffee as Issy sleeps. Hannah is giddy in a way he hasn't seen her before. She's so happy she can barely sit still but it's undercut with fear, he can see that. She's asked three times already if she should go and check on Issy and it's only been twenty minutes since they left her. Each time he's told his wife, no, let her sleep and each time she's nodded before chewing on her lip. The worry seems to come in waves. Right now it's abated and her face is brimming with joy. He wishes he could find a way to keep only this emotion in her, to banish the terror that any minute they will lose this happiness, that in some way they don't deserve it.

'Han,' he says, placing the coffee in front of her. 'It's okay.'

She looks up, tears already brimming in her eyes and nods. 'I know.'

'She's here, nothing is going to happen.'

'Don't say that,' Hannah snaps. 'You'll—'

'I can't "jinx" it, Han,' Charlie sighs.

Hannah's cheeks colour, aware of the childishness of her superstitions. 'But how do you know no one will find out about him?' she says, seeming to have lost the ability or willingness to say Owen's name since Issy arrived.

Charlie breathes in deeply and tries to sound as convincing as he can. 'No one is going to find his body. And if they do, there's nothing to tie him to us. Right?'

She nods; they have been through this dance so many times since Saturday.

'Hannah,' he says, now kneeling in front of her and taking her hands in his. 'We did the right thing. You know we did. Owen was a murderer. He killed Jesse and would have killed Haydee too if she hadn't stopped him. We saved Haydee from a life in prison. You know what we did was right; she didn't deserve that.'

Hannah nods. He's realised she needs to hear this speech often. At the moment, at least a few times a day.

He's willing to give it to her as often as she needs it. Maybe this will become a ritual that lasts with them a lifetime; maybe he'll never stop telling her these facts.

What they did was right.

They both need to hear it.

And if occasionally Charlie remembers a different version of the night Jesse died – a version where the man gargled in pain on the floor a name that Charlie could have sworn in the moment was *Hannah*, not *Haydee*, and instead of helping the dying man, calling an ambulance while there was still a chance for him to live, Charlie shut the door and let him die alone – he tells himself that the mind can play all kinds of tricks. He tells himself that he is a good man. He always does the right thing.

And when he can't tell himself that – when he's sure that horrifying version of the night is the truth – he tells himself that sometimes perhaps the right thing is people getting what they deserve.

It works both ways.

Chapter Thirty-Nine

One week later

Now

Hannah

Issy chatters away as I clear up the dishes from breakfast; muesli and coffee for me, strawberry yoghurt and juice for Issy. We've settled into a routine remarkably quickly and I have to remind myself as I rinse her sippy cup that she's only been here a week. Seven days. But seven days of Issy is like a lifetime; she's soaked in like an expensive moisturiser making me feel like she's the only thing my skin has ever needed.

Charlie is out buying more milk. His mad dash to the shop on Saturday yielded extravagant items that were more like something you'd buy for a child's birthday party rather than feeding them for the week, unsurprising really given the circumstances of the day, and we haven't had chance to do a proper shop since. Our first week together has passed quickly, like something out of a dream. We took Issy to see Charlie's mum, her grandma, and I thought Charlie might burst with happiness. It was one of Diane's good days, as though the dementia had given her a brief pass for that day to not only allow her to make new memories, but to relive the old ones. She spoke of Charlie at Issy's age as if the memories of her son as a boy had never been missing at all, just waiting for an appropriate time to come out. Issy adores her, and keeps asking every day since when she can go and see 'Ganma' again.

We haven't heard anything from or about Haydee since. Charlie has kept an eye on communication to their phones; Haydee has had none which seems ominous but Charlie thinks the phone he hacked was probably a burner. Owen had a lot in the first few days. Messages from journalists asking about Jesse. The police repeatedly reminding him he needs to contact them to be interviewed. None of the messages have been returned and they've since stopped coming; Charlie says this is a sign the phone has been disconnected.

I won't go so far as to say we feel safe now but I do feel somewhere near at peace with what we did. Charlie has taken to repeating like a mantra that *we did what we had to*; that we did *the right thing*, that Owen was a murderer and Haydee a victim that we saved. Each night he repeats it as we get into bed. He doesn't need a response, he just needs to say the words, to have them heard.

It's very hard to believe that it wasn't the right thing now that we have Issy. She is so happy, so utterly loved and wanted in this house it feels absurd to imagine we could have done anything different, anything that would have threatened the life we now share. I do still dream about Owen; I still hear his screams as we shovel dirt into his open mouth and he begs us to stop. He's always alive, always begging for his life. But it wasn't us who took it. We just cleaned things up. That's the mantra I tell myself. We are not guilty. We did nothing wrong.

301

'Mumma!' Issy yells from her high chair, and my heart fills. She has just started calling me this in the last day or so and each time she says it I feel like I'm shedding my old skin and being remade into something good.

'Yes, darling?' I say, turning around to face her. The morning sunlight spills across the kitchen from the front door. We've learned that Issy doesn't like to be sat with her back to the door and so positioned her high chair side on with a sight line down the hall from the front door through to the back.

'Look!' she says, pointing at the door. 'Look!' Her chubby face beams so wide I can barely force myself to turn away to follow where she is pointing.

I briefly see a person's outline through the glass in the front door and register a flicker of annoyance before turning back to my daughter. My *daughter*. The word is still utterly delicious every time I think it, let alone say it. We're still in the 'trying it out' phase. Charlie and I will say it to each other around the house, testing it out, hoping to be brave enough to announce it to the world any day. We've been able to keep things just between the three of us for the last week, only venturing out into the world to visit his mum. We've let our phones ring out, our texts go ignored. It has been wonderful, a total retreat from the world. As if on cue, at that moment two things happen: my phone rings and the door knocks again – the outside world suddenly desperate to get in.

I check Issy is safely strapped into her high chair and pick up my phone from the worktop as I walk to the front door. Kate has called. Again. She's been phoning on and off for days but I've been resolute in my silence. I love her but I can't let her in just yet. There's no way she won't mention work and I don't want that world colliding with this. As I push down the handle of the front door, a text comes in.

> Han, please ring me ASAP. We really need to talk.

I frown – the tone isn't like Kate at all – but before I have a chance to think about it any more, the door is open and the air is knocked out of me in one foul swoop.

Police.

Police on my doorstep.

They're in plain clothes, but the ID cards flipped open to show their credentials tell me everything I need to know. I'm sure plain clothes officers are worse than uniform – more serious – this fact is dragged from the back of my mind somewhere and hits me with a jolt.

'Good morning. Mrs Wilson?' the younger female officer says. Her face is obscured momentarily by the sun and she holds up the hand that doesn't have her ID badge flipped open to shield her eyes; I take the millisecond to rearrange my expression from one of terror to something approaching normality.

'Yes?' I manage, my voice small.

'May we come in, please?' The sun fades and her face comes into view. She's pretty, despite the lack of make-up and hair pulled back into a tight bun at the nape of her neck. Around my age, possibly younger. A man stands by her side in silence. He looks harsher; a large nose looms in the middle of his craggy face and I catch his eye for a second too long. I avoid his glare and make a show of studying their ID cards as if I suspect they might be frauds, blood pumping in my ears with a ferocity that threatens to deafen me.

'Mrs Wilson, are you okay?' The female officer speaks again and I'm forced to nod quickly and open the door wider to let them through.

As I guide them through to the kitchen, my footsteps drag. Is this the last time I will ever walk freely in my own home?

Issy kicks and chirps in her high chair as we enter the room, delighted to see more people. I watch her face as they sit at the table. No, this is not delight. She wriggles, her face turning puce as she eyes the officers. She looks from them to me, and begins to cry.

Of course, I realise, Issy has seen police before. When her birth mother overdosed and left Issy to cry out in anguish alone while her body slowly decayed, it was officers who came to Issy's rescue. She will have been picked up by someone just like these two, held against their rough nylon uniforms, sirens perhaps blaring in the distance as she cried, her mother's body carted away like rubbish.

What have I done?

How could I bring her home, knowing that this was a possibility? That once again, she could be forced to watch as her mother is taken away and never returned home to her?

'My husband is on his way home,' I blurt, wanting to buy myself some time. Charlie will know what to do. I am useless without him.

The female officer exchanges a concerned look with the other before wiping it from her face and looking back to me.

I pick Issy up from her high chair and pull her into my chest. 'It's okay, sweetie,' I tell her as she cries, more softly now that she's in my arms. 'It's okay.' I turn her away from the officers so that I'm facing them and she is tucked safely into the nook of my neck, facing the front door as she likes to.

'We're sorry to come unannounced,' the female officer begins. 'We have tried to contact you over the last few days on the phone but it looks like you've had your hands full.' She smiles and a moment of hope bubbles in me.

I think of the missed calls on my phone, withheld numbers that I've assumed were spam. All the time that has been the police. But why would they wait? If they had found Owen's body and traced it to us, why would they give us a few days to get away?

'I'm going to pop her down in the other room,' I tell them before carrying Issy into the living room where I switch on the TV and start another episode of *In The Night Garden*, her favourite. She's placated now as I place her safely into her playpen and tell her I'll be back in a minute. As I leave the room, I regret the choice immediately. If I am to be taken from Issy any moment, I should have kept her with me until the very last second, breathing in her indescribable scent of warm skin and love. But no. She does not need to see what is about to happen. She deserves to be cocooned from that. At least this time I, as her mother, have a choice over what horrors my daughter is subjected to.

'I'm just making some tea,' the officer says when I come back into the kitchen and find her flicking on the kettle with the assurance of someone who has done this in strangers' homes many times before. 'I'm DC Arlam, this is my colleague DC Stanton.' She smiles and nods towards the cupboard above her head as if asking me if that's where the mugs live. I nod back and get three teabags from the cupboard next to her. I pass them to her and she pops them into the mugs just as the kettle boils.

'Milk?' she asks and I nod, mutely. 'Sugar?' I shake my head and she smiles again. 'He has two, despite me telling him it'll rot his teeth. Do you have—' I reach behind her for the sugar pot and slide it over.

When the drinks are made, we carry them to the kitchen table and sit back down with DC Stanton who allows me a moment of hope when I realise he's staring out at the garden in the manner of someone who is utterly disinterested in what's going on around him. This does not feel like a man who has come to arrest me. But why else would they be here?

'Mrs Wilson—'

'Hannah,' I say.

'Hannah, we've been trying to contact you for a few days as I said—'

'We've just brought our daughter home,' I say, eyes flicking to the door as if I'll be able to see around corners and into the living room where she watches TV. 'One week ago.'

DC Arlam arches a perfectly shaped eyebrow and I watch the confusion on her face, as she tries to work out my words.

'She's adopted,' I finally supply.

The confusion clears and DC Arlam smiles. 'Oh, how lovely. No wonder you've been avoiding calls,' she says. 'I imagine this week has been rather special.'

I nod, but all I can think is how hollow that sounds compared to the feelings that have anchored themselves to my chest this week. It is more than special. This last week with Issy has been *everything*.

306

'What is…' I stop, unable to bring myself to ask why they're here, because once I know I can never unknow and god, I wish more than anything I could take us back to ten minutes ago when I was in the kitchen with my daughter surrounded by a bubble of happiness. Outside, the skylark that has taken residence in our garden sings away; he's barely stopped the last few days as if he is watching over Issy – her welcoming brigade that hovers nearby to keep her safe. But this morning his song feels like a warning, like he was telling us to get out of the house before this could happen, before these people came to take me away.

'Have you spoken with anyone from your work recently, Hannah?'

I blink. 'My work?' I ask, trying to understand the connection. 'No, I've been on adoption leave…'

'Of course,' DC Arlam smiles. 'Well, I'm afraid this might be a bit of a shock—'

'What's happened? Is Kate okay?'

'Yes, yes,' she says quickly, before taking a sip of her tea. 'Everyone's fine.'

The skylark's still going, his notes becoming higher and higher, closer together, like the drumroll to the officer's words.

'Late last week, a package was sent to your work. Addressed to you.'

I crease my brow in confusion. 'A package?'

'Yes, it was sent to you but as you said, you haven't been in work so your colleague, Kate Lawrence, opened it.'

I nod, desperate for them to get on with it while also dreading what comes next. Is it evidence of what we did to Owen? Did someone see us burying his body and record it? Send it to my work to… To what? Perhaps it was from

Haydee; Charlie said she knew where I worked. Is she blackmailing us?

'Are you okay, Hannah?' DC Stanton asks and I nod firmly, trying out a smile as if this is all fine.

'What was in the package?' I manage to say before taking a sip of my tea to bring some moisture to my throat. It tastes burnt, like the hot water scalded the bag for too long.

'Did you know Jesse Carter?' DC Arlam asks and at that moment, no tea in the world could save my sandpaper throat. The officers look at me and I nod. 'You spoke with my colleagues a few weeks ago, didn't you? You said' – she gets out her pocket notepad and flicks through – 'that you met Jesse as a student in New York.'

The skylark is silent and I think good, good for him fleeing the scene before things get ugly. In the living room, Issy cries loudly, one single sharp word: 'Mama!' and I jump up.

'I'm sorry,' I say, 'I have to…'

I rush from the room, no longer caring what happens in the kitchen; my sole focus on getting to my daughter when she needs me. She's standing up in her playpen, face puce as she cries for me.

'What's wrong, darling?' I ask, scooping her up and checking her body for signs of pain.

'Mama!' she says again, calmer this time, and nuzzles her face into my neck. I soon realise her only source of discomfort was me being out of the room. My heart thuds in my chest against hers. I imagine this could be our last moment together so I cherish it; bury my face into her mop of curly hair and breathe it in. She smells of strawberry, the scent of the gentle shampoo Charlie rubbed into her curls last night as she giggled in the water.

'Everything okay?' The voice comes from the doorway and I bury my face deeper, not ready to face the officers again. Issy's body stiffens in my arms and I hate myself then for bringing these people to her door once again.

'Fine,' I eventually say, breaking the spell between Issy and me as I turn to face DC Arlam. She is standing in the doorway, looking almost gooey-eyed at Issy.

'Shall we?' she asks, gesturing back to the kitchen.

Issy burrows down into my chest, turning her face away from the officer and I nod, then drag my feet across the living room carpet, to the hallway, through to the kitchen with Issy heavy in my arms. Each step takes me closer to the inevitable. To the end.

Chapter Forty

Now

Hannah

I keep Issy in my arms as we sit back down. She's unhappy being near the officers but I can't bear to leave her in the living room alone again and I'm not sure I could have prised her out of my arms if I tried. Her pudgy fingers grip onto the neck of my jumper tightly as I take in deep breaths to try and fill my lungs with the air they're so desperately craving.

'So,' DC Stanton booms, 'where were we?'

DC Arlam takes this as the cue to produce her notebook again, a tight smile on her face as she asks, 'So, you knew Jesse Carter?'

A tight nod.

'But you hadn't seen him since you left New York...' She flicks through the pages of the notebook. 'Fifteen years ago?'

Another nod. 'Yes, that's what I told the officers the other day.'

'Yes, yes,' she replies. 'We're just double-checking. So you'd not had any contact with Jesse Carter since you were students? He hadn't got back in touch while he was staying at The Farm?'

I shake my head, the email that landed in the bad place threatening to topple me.

'I told the other officers that he had been emailing me,' I say, trying hard to remember my exact words from before, 'but that I hadn't received them due to a spam filter we have in place at work.'

DC Arlam nods while looking at her notepad as if my statement now matches what she expected.

DC Stanton shifts in his seat, looking at Issy before staring at me. 'Were you aware of an assault that took place in December 2007?'

My throat is so dry I can barely croak a reply. 'No,' I say.

'Yes, between Jesse Carter and, we believe, Owen Peters—'

'No.'

But he's not finished, 'And a young woman.'

Haydee.

Blood rushes to my face, sweat itches at my scalp. They know. They know everything.

I shake my head. 'No,' I say again. Issy starts to cry, lightly at first then, when I fail to comfort her, loudly and all at once. Angry, feral cries that force me from my chair. 'It's okay, darling, it's okay.' I rock her back and forth, though she's too old to be treated like this, no longer a baby but not yet quite a child, somewhere in the middle, somewhere vulnerable and uncontrollable. She clamps her arms around my neck and sobs into my jumper, her tears sinking through into my skin. She knows, I think, she knows that I am about to be ripped from her, just like her real mother was. How cruel, how utterly selfish and vile I have been to think this was the best path forward for her.

I whisper, 'I'm sorry,' and rock her until her cries begin to subside and my cooing becomes a slow patterned song, uttered under my breath so that only Issy can hear. *I'm sorry* I say, again and again until it no longer sounds like words.

The officers have become blurry figures in the background while we continue this dance. I'm aware that I should be acknowledging them, allowing them to speak, but the longer I lose myself in Issy, the harder it is to return to the world.

'Mrs Wilson?' DC Stanton's blunt tone eventually forces me out of my dream-like state. I open my eyes and look at them. Their faces are impatient but not concerned. How long was I whispering to Issy? It felt like hours but I realise from the looks on their faces that it cannot have been more than seconds. How strange time is to work so independently of us.

'Sorry,' I say. I sit back down, Issy still clung around my neck. 'What were you saying?' My voice sounds almost normal.

'The package that was sent to you at work last week,' DC Arlam says. 'It contained a video.' The statement is hard, definite, objectively factual in a way that none of our words so far have been.

'A video?' My mind pictures a video cassette tape, as if is twenty years ago. But they did say a package. Was there CCTV outside the Airbnb? We saw no cameras, we checked. But there must have been. Someone has captured us on film and sent that to my work. Perhaps Haydee herself as her final revenge. There is no other explanation.

Something like calm washes over me; the truth is here, someone has seen us, everything is over. In the face of it,

I'm no longer terrified. It's like I've lost all feeling except for the reassuring thud, thud, thud of Issy's heart against mine.

'Yes,' DC Stanton cuts in. 'A video of an assault. It would be more accurate to call it a—' He eyes Issy before lowering his voice. 'Rape.'

Oh.

Not this, then. Not the murder.

The rape.

Rape. Why had I never thought of what happened to Haydee like this before? Despite knowing how it ended, I'd always pictured her enjoying the night with Owen and Jesse, though I never pictured her enjoying my part. But her with the two of them; I imagined all sorts of things. But no, she must have been unconscious. The thought hits me like a slap. They had sex with her while she was unconscious? Worse... I strangled her while she was unconscious?

'Do you have any idea why this video would have been sent to you?' DC Arlam asks, and I notice her voice is soft, kind. Not the tone you would use for a... what am I? I am not a killer; that I can be sure of, as Haydee is alive. But I am nothing good and yet the officers talk to me as if I am.

'That's...' I struggle for the words. 'That's awful... I... Who was on the video?' I ask.

The officers look between themselves as if deciding whether to divulge this and I think they are acting because surely they have discussed this already? Their hesitation is merely theatrics.

'We believe the video shows Jesse Carter, Owen Peters, and an unidentified woman.'

The world shifts again. Am I the unidentified woman, or is Haydee? If it were me, surely she would be questioning me over that? It starts to burn between my legs. Was I raped? God, this is unbearable. I jiggle Issy on my lap as she twists my hair around her fingers, catching it every now and again, the pain reminding me to breathe.

'Do you know Owen Peters, Mrs Wilson?' DC Stanton asks.

Do I, not did I. They do not know Owen is dead. I pat Issy's back and glance at my fingernails, expecting them to still be filthy with the mud from Owen's grave but they are clean, manicured, innocent.

'A bit,' I say. 'Back in New York. Not well.'

'Do you have any idea why this tape would have been sent to you?'

I open my mouth. I am not in the tape. I am sure of this now. The officers are looking at me like I am on the edge of this, whatever this is, not slap bang in the middle. 'No,' I say. 'I'm sorry... I don't...'

DC Arlam narrows her eyes as she watches me. 'Do you often get things like this sent to your work?'

I shake my head again. 'No, never. We don't really deal with the public—' I correct myself. 'I mean, with the victims. We're behind the scenes.'

'Your colleague, Kate Lawrence, mentioned that a woman did come into the office recently to report an assault and kept mentioning Jesse Carter?'

I had forgotten this. How had I forgotten? It must have been Haydee. Kate has seen Haydee. Haydee has been in my world. I am connected to Haydee, therefore connected to Owen, and they will use that one day to connect it all when they find his body.

'Hannah?'

'Sorry, yes, I think Kate mentioned that but I wasn't there so...'

'You didn't see this woman?'

'No, I was out, meeting...' I look down at the bundle of child in my arms, still twisting my hair, looking up at me as if I am the only person in the world. 'We had an adoption meeting that morning.'

DC Arlam smiles and looks at Issy. I should put her down, I know I should but I can't bear to. Perhaps she won't understand our conversation; perhaps it's fine to keep her here until the last moment.

'Do you have any idea who that woman might have been?' DC Stanton cuts in, his tone impatient. 'Your colleague believes the woman in the video and the woman who came into your office that day are one and the same.'

Are they asking me because they know I was there that night? I must be in the video, after all, though they've not said it yet. Are they waiting for me to lie? I shake my head. 'I'm sorry, no. I haven't seen either so I'm not sure how I can help...'

DC Arlam puts her notepad on the coffee table between us and flicks through the pages until she comes to two blurry photographs. 'These stills have been pulled from the video. The quality is poor, as you'll see, camera phones were not high quality back then.'

The room spins before I train my eyes to the pictures, evidence of that night now staring at me from my kitchen table in my safe house in the Cotswolds with my daughter on my lap. There was never going to be an escape from this, was there? But I force my eyes to look, to keep up the pretence that I am a normal person, helping the police, nothing more.

It's not me.

I am not there.

Instead, I see the distant yet totally familiar shape of Jesse's naked body next to Haydee's small frame, and Owen too. Would I recognise them just from this image though if I hadn't seen this scene in my nightmares a thousand times? The lines of their forms are indistinct, their faces barely recognisable. But I know them.

'God this is awful,' I say, looking away. 'But I'm sorry, no. I don't know this woman.'

DC Arlam sighs. 'It was a long shot,' she says. 'Your colleague Kate opened the video and watched it in full before passing it to us; it's really quite disturbing so you're lucky to have missed out on that.'

I say nothing, still so unsure whether they have seen my own naked form on the tape. 'Did they send a note… anything with the video?'

The officers look between themselves as if deciding whether to tell me. 'There was a note,' DC Stanton says. 'Addressed to you. It said "Everyone should know what happened. Even you."'

I frown, the words painful to hear. 'Even me?'

They nod. 'It's why we hoped you'd have some answers for us about this. It feels like this was sent to you in a personal capacity, rather than a professional.'

They don't know. They have no idea. Outside, the skylark sings again. 'I'm sorry,' I say, my voice level in a way I thought it might never be again. 'I really have no idea why someone would send me this. Perhaps they wanted to get media attention for the crime… to make Jesse Carter pay for what he did.'

Something flickers in DC Arlam's eyes and I realise this is already the motive they have been working with; that I was never front and centre in this crime.

'We do need to warn you to be careful,' DC Stanton says, standing. 'We have reason to believe whoever sent this tape is also involved in the murder of Jesse Carter.'

'Involved how?'

He holds my gaze. 'We're not able to disclose that.'

'You think the person who sent the tape... killed Jesse Carter?'

The officers say nothing but they do not have to.

They know it to be true.

But Owen killed Jesse, that's what Haydee said.

Owen killed Jesse and Haydee killed Owen in self-defence.

But what if...

Haydee killed Jesse?

And then killed Owen to cover it up?

Oh god. That would mean...

The sound of the front door opening drains every last drop of blood from my skin.

'Hannah?' Charlie's worried voice shouts from the hall. He appears in the doorway red-faced, his eyes wide and fearful as he takes in the officers.

'Dada!' Issy cries in my arms and despite everything else around us, a smile lights up Charlie's face as he steps forward and takes her from me. My arms feel empty without her, bereft, as they fall back into my lap. Charlie stands in front of me, bouncing Issy on his hip like she loves, her face now lit up with joy while my husband's has grown pale. His eyes flit between the officers and me as if he can will them to disappear on his own.

'Mr Wilson,' DC Stanton says, standing.

'What's going on?' Charlie snaps and I beg him silently to calm down before he raises any more suspicion. He glances back at me and I smile tightly, hoping to communicate to him that everything is fine.

'It's something to do with work,' I start to say at the time as DC Stanton begins to talk.

'I'm afraid your wife was sent a rather distressing video in the post at work.'

Charlie frowns then looks at me, unsure. 'But she's not at—'

'It was addressed to me but Kate opened it,' I supply.

'We just needed to ask her some questions about it,' DC Arlam says now, standing. 'But I think we've got everything we need, right?'

DC Stanton takes another look at me, then Charlie, as if debating.

'Go away!' Issy suddenly shouts from Charlie's arms, her face screwed up in frustration. 'Go 'way!'

'Hey, hey,' Charlie says, turning her to face him. 'There's no need for that.' But our daughter is inconsolable, tears falling down her plump red cheeks as if this is suddenly all too much.

DC Stanton chuckles, a deep throaty sound, while DC Arlam smiles uncomfortably. 'I think we'll take that as our cue to leave.'

'I'll take her out,' Charlie says to me before leaving the room with Issy still in his arms. His footsteps bash against the stairs as I hear him walking her into her room, her cries decreasing with every step.

'Sorry about that,' I say. 'She's still settling in… It's all new.'

'Of course,' DC Arlam says. 'Don't worry at all. Like I said, we have everything we need and we'll be in touch if anything else comes up.'

'What will happen now?' I say.

She shrugs. 'Depends where the investigation takes us.' As if seeing the fear in my eyes she adds, 'I'm sure it won't bring us back here, don't worry.' She pats my arm and nods towards the door for me to lead them out. As we walk down the hallway, my heart grows heavier, head buzzing with this the possibilities of this new information. Haydee could be guilty. Owen could be innocent, of murder at least. I could remain on the periphery, out of shot, barely involved at all.

'We'll call if we need to follow anything up,' DC Arlam says, the other side of the door now.

I nod, saying goodbye before shutting the door. Through the glass, I watch their figures growing smaller as they retreat and I don't look away until the sight of the unmarked black car blurs and fades to nothing in the distance.

'Han,' Charlie calls from the top of the stairs. His face is white, his eyes wide. I thank god that he wasn't here throughout the questioning. There is no way Charlie could have hidden his guilt. 'What the fuck?'

'Shh,' I snap.

He shakes his head. 'She's down for a nap.'

'But it's not time!'

He runs down the stairs and when he reaches the bottom says, 'Do you really think that matters right now? Tell me what happened. What's going on?'

We walk into the kitchen, shutting the door behind us to prevent any stray words making their way up the stairs and creeping into Issy's room.

I flick on the kettle while Charlie hovers beside me getting out two mugs and placing a teabag in each.

'Kate was sent a tape—'

'I thought you said it was sent to you?'

I sigh loudly. 'Yes, it was, but Kate opened it—'

'What was on it?' Fear dances in his wide eyes.

'Not us,' I say, quickly. 'It was the video of that night…'

He frowns. The kettle clicks, steam escaping from the top. I pour boiling water onto our teabags and watch as the colour turns brown.

'The night in New York?'

I nod. We take our mugs to sit at the kitchen table.

'So they saw…'

I shake my head. 'I don't think I was on it,' I say, the words falling out with a mix of ecstasy and horror. 'They didn't seem to recognise me, anyway…'

Charlie screws up his face and takes a sip of his tea, instantly regretting it as he clicks his tongue against the roof of his mouth. Too hot.

'I don't understand.'

'No, nor do I.'

'Did Kate watch it?' he asks.

I nod.

'You need to talk to her.'

'What?'

'Find out what was in the video. Perhaps the police weren't telling you the whole truth. Perhaps they did see you on that tape and were coming here to see if you'd lie about it.'

The thought churns my stomach and I grip my hands around the mug, scalding my fingers. Why had I not thought of that? If they knew I was on the tape, I've just put myself top of their list of suspects having lied about it. But how can I phone Kate if she has seen me on the video? I think of her incessant calls over the last few days, the text message she sent me earlier saying to call her. Shame prickles my skin.

'Han,' Charlie says, peeling my fingers from around the mug and lacing them with his. 'Call her.'

Chapter Forty-One

Now

Hannah

I can't bear Charlie to watch me as I do it, can't bear for him to hear Kate's description of what she saw. Though I've told him what I did to Haydee, the idea of him hearing someone else potentially narrate it is too horrifying. So I go into the living room and leave Charlie sitting at the table, my tea abandoned.

The line rings once, then again. For a moment I think she won't answer and I can go back into the kitchen, finish my tea, pretend this isn't happening. But then...

'Hannah!'

'Kate, hi,' I say, pacing circles in the living room.

'Oh my god, I've been trying to get hold of you for days. Are you okay? Is Issy—'

'Everything's fine,' I say, though this feels like a lie.

'Oh, good. Good...' Her voice trails off, losing its urgency.

'The police came over—'

'Oh! I wanted to speak to you before, but I couldn't... well, you know. Are you okay? What did they say?'

I listen carefully for traces of disgust in her tone but the sounds of the office in the background distract me. It's busy; voices talk over each other in a wall of noise.

'Are you at work?'

'Yeah,' she says. 'Mad day. I'll go in the other room.' The sound of the phone pressing against her hand as I imagine her cupping it to walk across the office fills the line and I wait, counting the steps it will take her to get there, my heart beating in time with her footsteps. 'You there?'

'Yeah.'

'God,' she breathes heavily down the line. 'Honestly, it has been the most insane few days. Did they tell you? About the video?'

'Yes...'

'Oh Han, it was awful. I just couldn't believe it when I saw...' Her voice trails off and I'm desperate for her to speak again, to tell me what she saw but my mouth is so dry I can't imagine it ever forming the words. 'It was addressed to you; did they say?'

I manage to squeeze out a strangled reply. 'Yes, they said.'

'I've been opening all your post. I have to, in case something gets missed, right?'

'Yeah, of course,' I tell her again, hearing the panic in her words as if she's done something wrong. 'Did you... Did you watch it?'

She sighs and I imagine her sitting in the small office on the blue spin-around chair that we desperately need to replace, the seat lowering ever so slightly with every movement. 'Yeah,' she says eventually. 'It was... It was awful, Han.'

'What happened? On the video, what did you see?'

'It was him, Jesse Carter. And Owen Peters – I barely recognised Owen at first, he's changed a lot since then. The video is shit quality too, must be years and years old.'

She pauses as if waiting for my reaction but my throat has dried up again and all I can give is a grunted 'mmm' to get her back on track. 'They were... I don't know, at first it looked like it was a threesome – the two of them and this girl. She looks young, but then so do they. But then... the longer it went on, the more I realised something wasn't right. Her body kind of slumps when they move her about and then... God, Han, I can't even say it.'

'What? What happened?'

'Jesse Carter, he... He strangled her.'

I grip the windowsill as the phone slides from my hand.

'Hannah?' Charlie runs in, holding me up under my arms and retrieving the phone from the floor.

I press my fingers to his lips and shake my head, trying to signal that Kate is still on the other end. I grab the phone from his hand and press it back to my ear.

'Sorry,' I say. 'I was walking down the stairs and I... I tripped.'

'Shit, are you okay?'

'Yeah, fine, fine. Sorry, things here are a bit...'

'I haven't even asked about Issy! Sorry, Han. The video it just really—'

'Are you sure that's what happened?' I ask.

She pauses. Charlie watches me but I push him away so that he can't hear her on the other side. Upstairs, there's a bang and both our eyes flit to the ceiling as if we'll be able to see Issy through it. 'Go,' I mouth at Charlie, desperate for some space to hear Kate's words. Once he leaves the room, I ask again.

'You said *Jesse* strangled this girl? Are you sure?'

'Yes,' Kate says warily. 'Why wouldn't I be sure? What did the police say?'

'Was anyone else with them on the video? You said it was Jesse, Owen and a girl. Was there anyone else?'

She sighs again and I imagine her rubbing the spot between her eyebrows like she does when she's stressed. 'There was someone else in the room, I told the police that. But she wasn't... You couldn't really see her. She was slumped in the corner. I think passed out. At least, I hope passed out.'

The wind again is knocked out of me.

The night comes back to me in fragments like it always does. The smell of the fresh sheets on Jesse's bed; Owen's whiskey-stained breath, sweet sticky sweat on Haydee's body. The carpet pressed into my cheek. The blackness. Owen's face in mine, telling me what I'd done.

He was lying. They both were. I didn't do it.

I was passed out on the floor.

It wasn't my hands around Haydee's neck but Jesse's.

'What happened then?' I manage to croak. 'After he strangled...'

'I think they realised then that she wasn't okay,' Kate says, her voice low as if she can barely utter the words. 'It was hard to see exactly but they try and wake her up... I don't know. Owen realised the camera was still on not long after that and it gets switched off.'

'Wow,' I mutter, unable to find the words.

'Yeah...'

'I don't know what to say.'

'The girl from the tape,' Kate says, her voice back to full force. 'I think she was the one who came into the office the other day. You know the one I mentioned?'

I close my eyes, feeling it all coming full circle. 'Are you sure?'

'Well, no,' she admits. 'The video isn't great so it's hard to be certain. But it makes sense, doesn't it? If they did something to that girl and she somehow had evidence of it, wouldn't she want everyone to know? So he didn't go down in history as pop royalty?' The venom is back in her voice and I'm reminded of the day we found out Jesse had died, the argument in the office that now feels a million years ago.

'Why do you think it was sent to you?' she asks, bringing me back to the present.

'I don't… I really don't know.'

Charlie appears back in the room, a look of concern on his face and I wave him away.

'I'm sorry, I've got to go. Issy…'

'Of course,' she says. 'Is she okay? Settling in?'

I tell her everything is great but the smile that usually accompanies talk of Issy won't appear and a deep thread of terror is running through me.

'The police told us to be careful,' Kate adds. 'I don't want to worry you because there's really no reason to worry – it's not like you're a target – but the police said that they think the same person who sent you the video killed Jesse.'

'They said that?'

'Well, not exactly,' Kate admits. 'They said they were linked, but we all know what that means, don't we? I wouldn't blame her,' she carries on. 'If it is the woman from the tape, I wouldn't blame her if she killed him. Men like that never pay, do they?'

I say nothing, unable to form a response that will keep Kate happy and not kill me. Instead, I tell her I'll bring Issy into the office soon to meet everyone and ring off, then fall onto the sofa and bury my face in the pillows.

'Han? Han, what is it? What's happened?' Charlie says, shaking my shoulders and forcing me to turn my face to him. I expect to find I'm crying but my face is resolutely dry.

'It wasn't me,' I say.

He frowns and tilts his head, unsure of my meaning.

'I didn't strangle Haydee, it wasn't me.'

He nods, as if he always knew this, as if he knew I couldn't possibly be capable of such an act.

'Kate watched the video. I was… I was passed out in the corner.'

'Did she—'

'No,' I rush to correct him. 'She didn't know it was me. You can't see, apparently. But it wasn't me, it was Jesse. Jesse strangled her. It wasn't me.' I feel it then, the relief and horror pouring through me in equal measure. All these years, I did nothing. All this time, I was innocent. Haydee was alive and I was innocent.

'We could have told the police,' I say, the realisation dawning on me. 'I wasn't involved; we didn't have to… We could have told them everything.' The words come out as choked sobs, hitting Charlie hard in the chest.

'No,' he says, gripping me by the shoulders. 'No Han, we couldn't. It was too late for that. You'd lied to the police; I'd hacked into Owen's phone. There was no way we were getting out of this unscathed if we'd told the truth.' He stares into my eyes, desperate to make me see things the way he does, desperate for me not to unravel. 'We can't take it back now. We just have to stick to the plan. Remember, we did what we had to do. Owen murdered Jesse. He would have murdered Haydee. We had no choice.'

I chew my lip.

This is the moment I should tell Charlie the truth. I should tell him that there's a chance Haydee was lying to him; that she murdered Jesse in cold blood and likely did the same to Owen. But what then? How will my husband, my kind, honest, 'always do the right thing' husband, cope with that truth? Either way, Owen is dead and we buried his body. Owen is not innocent in all of this. He engineered every moment of pain; forced Haydee to live a false life; forced Jesse into unknowingly depending on him forever, and left me believing I was a murderer – all to give him what he wanted. He may not have murdered Jesse, he may not have tried to murder Haydee, but he deserves what he got.

'Yes,' I tell Charlie. 'You're right. I know you're right. And this is fine. The police don't know I was on the video; there's no way to tell it's me. And now they know that Jesse and Owen had an enemy, an enemy who is not us. Who is nothing to do with us. There's nothing to link us to Haydee, even if they do find out it's her in the video.'

Charlie nods, moving his hands from my shoulders down my arms, his grip loosening, becoming more comforting.

'We did the right thing,' he says again.

I nod, biting my lip to stop the tears spilling from my eyes. Upstairs, Issy cries for me. The pull of her in need of me is so strong it's like my body reacts before my brain and I get up, leaving Charlie alone in the room. Before I shut the door, he calls for me.

'Han,' he says and I turn to face him. 'I love you.'

I smile, the feeling bittersweet on my lips. 'I love you too.'

As I walk up the stairs towards my daughter, the decision solidifies in my mind. Charlie does not need to know that Haydee killed Jesse. Charlie never needs to know that we are complicit in murder. An accidental killing in self-defence he can live with. But he cannot become the villain of the story. I will not put that on him.

In Issy's room, I lean into her cot and pull her out, the weight of her firm against me.

'Mama,' she chirps, the words still so fresh and unusual on her red lips.

'It's okay,' I tell her. 'Mummy's here, and I'm not going anywhere. Never, ever, ever.'

Chapter Forty-Two

One Year Later

Hannah

'Fruit Shoot!' Issy calls from the back seat, her voice a sing-song melody that I will never tire of hearing.

'In a sec, darling,' I say, checking my mirrors before indicating left to turn down the small lane. I switch up the car speaker, letting Issy's current favourite song fill the car, the sunshine melody overridden by her attempts to sing along. She shouts, 'You, you!' telling me she wants me to join in and I do, my voice filling the car in a way that I once thought it could never do again. Whenever Charlie hears me sing now, it feels like something in us both is healing.

Issy has turned into such a happy little girl, too. Everyone says it, as if they are surprised by the fact. I suppose in some ways, they should be. Issy had little chance of turning out this way if you take into account how her life began. Looking at her now, you would never suspect the darkness from which she took her first tentative steps into the world. I smile back at her in the rearview mirror, my heart full to bursting with the happiness of her.

Winding down the narrow lanes, the song comes to a stop and Issy shouts 'Again, again!' from the back but this time I tell her no. It's good to have boundaries, Charlie keeps telling me as I give in to her every whim. Now that I'm back at work three days a week, she's started nursery and is proving rather a handful there, though the staff seem to adore her despite her increasing demands for attention, toys, food, whatever she so desires. So I'm trying to be better, to occasionally say no – when the stakes are low enough, anyway. Issy sticks her lips out in a pout, locking eyes with me in the rear-view mirror but I shake my head and say no again and to my surprise she rearranges her face back to neutral and picks up her doll to play with instead. As I turn up the radio, she talks to her beloved Clare Bear, moving her worn arms and legs about in animation.

'…*Today marks one year since the death of superstar Jesse Carter…*' The radio newsreader's voice wafts into the car and I grip the steering wheel tighter. I knew it was today, of course I knew, but hearing it spoken about so publicly makes the hairs on the back of my neck stand up.

> '…Jesse's death remains a mystery, with no arrests or charges ever made but investigations continue. His manager and long-time best friend, Owen Peters, went missing shortly after the death. Investigators say they are treating the disappearance as linked but are not looking for any suspects…'

Though I know this line well, having heard it multiple times over the last twelve months, there is still a sense of relief in the last line. *They are not looking for any suspects.*

> '…Fans have posted hundreds of memorial videos and pictures over the last few days

from outside Carter's home in New York but the site has also seen protests from women's groups amidst rumours of a video tape reportedly showing both Jesse Carter and Owen Peters engaging in sexual assault...'

I switch the radio off, not wanting the vile words to infect Issy's ears, but as I glance in the mirror once more I see I needn't have bothered as she's consumed with Clare Bear.

The video never became officially public here in the UK but I know it was shared on news sites in the US – their reporting laws are much less stringent than ours – after it was 'leaked' from an unknown source. I have wondered many times if Kate is responsible for this, after she realised that the police in the UK were not interested in pursuing the line of enquiry as the crime happened in the US and one suspect was dead, the other missing. If she did leak the tape, I have to admit I'm grateful because it helped us. Once news of a verified sexual assault hit the mainstream media in the US, Owen's disappearance appeared completely natural. He was a man running from a crime. Nothing more to see here.

I can't say we've properly relaxed since the day Jesse died, but the tight grip that's been held on my chest is loosening day by day. We've taken small steps throughout the year to distance ourselves from Jesse Carter. We both came off social media completely after finding it impossible to not be plagued with news stories about his death and various allegations of sexual assault that followed it from anonymous women across the world. It's been easy, in a way, to disappear from normal life for the last twelve months; it's what everyone has expected from us – to give our whole selves to Issy and no one else. Least of all the murder of a disgraced celebrity. Today, we are taking one step closer to breaking the chain between us all.

I scour the trees, looking for the break in the foliage that shows me I have to turn left, then spot it. The driveway is basically hidden from view now, the trees overgrown since we bought the place and they stopped accepting guests. As we drive through the gap, Issy shouts 'Adventure! Adventure!' from the back seat.

Charlie is already here; he'd left the house by seven thirty this morning to pick up the keys from the estate agent and left me and Issy to burrow down in bed. The sleepy state didn't last long before she was bored and wanted her breakfast, but still we've somehow managed to be three hours behind Charlie and it is now half past ten. As I stop the car and get out to free Issy from her car seat, I take a moment to breathe in the September air, listening to the skylarks singing above me, not another sound to be heard.

It's not the first time I've been here since that day, we came for a viewing with the eager estate agent a few months ago, but this is the first time I've allowed myself to feel the memories from before. I plonk Issy down on the drive and she runs towards the door squealing for Charlie.

He appears at the front door, his grey hoody mucky already, and smiles as he picks up our giggling daughter. This scene could not be more different to the one I faced that night one year ago when I crept up the driveway convinced Charlie was cheating on me or worse. Now, as I walk through the door, stepping into the dark hallway, the memories flood in. Charlie and Issy turn left for the kitchen but I press the handle down on the door to the right, the living room, where Owen died. I push open the door and hold my breath, but the room before me is not like that day. The flooring is halfway demolished already – Charlie's morning project – and light spills in through the dusty windows. The room is empty. No sign of Owen. No sign of a murder.

'No, Issy! Wait!' Charlie calls from behind me and I spin around, lifting Issy from the floor before she steps on a nail. Charlie runs in behind her, his face red and terrified at the thought of her being in pain but his shoulders drop when he sees her in my arms. 'Sorry,' he says, 'I had my back turned to get her a Fruit Shoot.'

'Fruit Shoot!' she yells, wriggling in my arms to be put down. We walk out of the living room and into the kitchen, shutting the door behind us to stop Issy exploring again.

'You did that quickly,' I say to Charlie once he's settled Issy with a drink.

He nods. 'I just wanted to start getting it out… Before we do anything else.'

I smile back at him, the unspoken words falling between us.

Two things happened at once six months ago that we couldn't deny the symmetry of. Charlie's mum died suddenly, after a fall at home. It was awful, the grief so raw and painful I wondered if we'd ever get through it, but we did. Issy made us. We can't fall apart when we have her. She needs us.

Then, this house came up for sale. The house where Owen died.

With Diane's death came a lot of money. She'd always told us we'd be rich when she was gone and she was right; her house sold for close to one million which is totally ridiculous given she bought it on a nurse's and farmer's wage. But its proximity to The Farm and obvious curb appeal in such a sought-after village meant the Londoners flocked to it and it was sold within days. When we went into the estate agents to sign the papers, I noticed with horror the familiar cottage in their window. I tugged on Charlie's sleeve, urging him to turn back and look at the 'For Sale' notice and understand what it meant. We'd been so sure the garden would not be dug up as the owners had done their renovations already to let it out through Airbnb, but suddenly our certainty felt stupid and naïve. A new owner might easily want to renovate the garden. I knew we had to buy it.

Charlie made the offer the same day we agreed the sale of his mum's house. We paid £100k over the asking price to secure it, but with the money from Diane's cottage, it was easily within our reach. If anyone asks why the sudden purchase, we tell them we'd been looking for suitable holiday homes in the area to bring in extra income now that I'm working part-time and this one was perfect.

In truth, the only perfect thing about it is that if we are the owners, no one can dig up the garden but us. Stepping into the garden now, I feel a sense of peace with what we've done. It's better to have Owen nearby, where we can watch over his grave. Ever since that night, I've been plagued with dreams of someone digging up his body without us even knowing. We've not talked about exactly what we'll do with the garden, with his grave, now that we own the land but knowing that it's ours is enough for now.

'When do the first guests arrive?' I ask Charlie while Issy runs around us in circles, delighting in a private game neither of us know the rules of.

'Not until next month,' he says, and I nod. I knew this, but hearing it confirmed helps. 'We've got loads of time to do it up.'

The cottage is in a fine state really, there's no need for work but I think our compulsion to rip everything out and re-paint, re-plaster and re-tile comes from the need to cover up what this house contains, as if by leaving things as they are, Owen's blood might start to seep from the floorboards.

Charlie and I will do most of the work ourselves; he's taken a leave of absence from work and is looking forward to getting his hands dirty after so long behind a screen.

'What first?' I ask.

'Cleaning,' he says, laughing as he brushes the dust and dirt from his hoody.

—

A few hours later, we're tired and hungry. Issy has been brilliant while I've scrubbed every last inch of the empty kitchen, playing with Clare Bear and making up songs to keep me going, but now it's time to leave. Charlie locks up the house while I wait on the drive, staring at the back gate leading to the garden. Even now, part of me does not believe that Owen is lying there beneath the soil, but I know he is. We put him there ourselves.

Still, he is safe. We are safe.

As I drive away from the cottage, following Charlie's car down the winding lanes, a trickle of guilt starts to eat away at me.

I never told Charlie the truth. He still believes the story that Haydee told him; that Jesse wanted the truth to come out and Owen killed him to shut him up, then tried to kill her too.

The longer I've had to think about it, the more I realise how totally untrue this ever was. Haydee probably did go to Jesse, like she said, to expose the truth but he wouldn't have reacted kindly like she said; he wouldn't have been open to ruining his entire career, his entire life, in order to bring her justice. That wasn't the kind of man he was. He was the kind of man who would let his teenage girlfriend believe she was responsible for a crime that he himself committed. Anything to avoid the blame. That's who Jesse was.

I wonder, often, how it happened. Whether Haydee went to Jesse's cabin that night expecting him to be kind, to do to the right thing, and instead he refused her request or worse – laughed at her. Told her no one would ever believe her. Did she lash out? Slice his throat in a moment of rage? Or was it planned? Did she follow him to the UK knowing he was looking for me and kill him before he got the chance to give me his side of the story?

I'll never know the truth, not in full. I'll never know how much Haydee acted in self-defence, but I do know that she used us just like everyone else did. She needed Charlie to believe she was a victim to help her cover up her crime. Charlie needed to believe that he was saving her. He still does. He couldn't live in this grey like I can.

And I can. For twelve months, I've lived like this.

There have been moments of stress, of anxiety and guilt so horrifying that I thought I couldn't keep going, but mostly, I'm fine.

No, I'm happy.

As I pull up to our front door, I let out a breath. I am happy. Issy snoozes gently behind me, her head lolling on her car seat. I wait five, ten minutes, allowing her to sleep before I pick up her heavy body and carry her into the house. Her head thuds lightly against my chest and I know in this moment that we've done the right thing. There was no other way out of this if we wanted Issy, and my god, Issy is all we've ever wanted.

'Hannah,' Charlie calls from the living room.

'Wait a sec,' I shout back, walking up the stairs. I carry Issy into her room and place her gently down on the bed, amazed to see that her sleep has not been disrupted as she nuzzles down into the pillow. I kiss her on the head before walking out, pulling the door softly behind me.

'Hannah!' Charlie shouts again, this time more urgently.

'What?' I say, entering the living room. He has the television on pause, the sight of the woman on screen unfamiliar yet horrifying – my heart lurches in recognition before my mind can place the woman's features. I walk closer to the screen, her face growing huge as I step forward. Charlie presses rewind, then play.

She fills the screen. Her face morphs from unfamiliar to shockingly known, but rounder, healthier, less emaciated. Pretty. Made up.

The shot pans out to show a man seated opposite her. He wears a bright blue suit and is handsome in the way that all American TV stars are. I recognise but can't name him. Some TV chat show host who flickers up occasionally when a big star has done something terrible and interviews them about it afterwards.

Seeing him with her turns my stomach, then he speaks.

'I'm here with Haydee Miller who claims that she was sexually assaulted and left for dead by Jesse Carter and Owen Peters.'

Sick rises in my throat as I grip the sofa.

The presenter keeps talking as Charlie appears beside me, his hand holding on to mine so tightly that I think he might break it.

'Viewers may remember this clip that circulated last year and I warn you, viewer discretion is advised as these are some disturbing scenes.'

The all-too-familiar clip plays. I see my body curled in the corner, barely visible from the crop but still my heart pangs knowing that it's me, that I am on screen in millions of homes across the UK.

The screen clips back to the studio where Haydee wipes a solitary tear from her cheek. Why is she doing this? Why is she risking everything by raking it up? I turn to look at Charlie. The colour has drained from his cheeks completely; he looks like a condemned man. The American presenter asks Haydee the question on mine and everyone else's lips. Why now?

'I've wanted to tell my story for a long time,' she says in a small but assured voice. 'While Jesse was alive, I was too scared to. But now, he's gone and everyone should know what happened to me. There are two people responsible for this: Jesse Carter and Owen Peters. The whole world should know who those men were. Too long, women have hidden in the shadows, terrified to voice the abuse we suffered. As if somehow we deserved it. Today, I'm speaking out. Today I'm finally ready to tell my story.'

She holds her stare on the camera, her head tilting to one side and for a moment I think she is talking directly to me. Telling me that everything is going to be okay. She won't include me; I am the curled up figure in the corner of the room. I am nothing.

The sound of the post falling through the letterbox feels so loud that I jump apart from Charlie, expecting the worst. He shakes his head and goes out to fetch it. We are both wordless as the TV drones on in the background, cutting back to the main UK studio where four women discuss the clip on their chat show.

'Hannah,' Charlie says, handing me a thin envelope with my name handwritten on the front. I rip it open hungrily, as if I know what it will contain.

Holding it in shaking hands, I read the words.

Your secrets died with them. I promise.

I fall to the floor, the letter flying out beside me as Charlie grabs it.

He reads the words aloud, his voice breaking up.

We huddle against the sofa, breathing our sobs into each other, our grip on the world, on this life we've built, feeling as paper thin as ever.

–

Later that night, we put Issy to bed together. She's been fed and bathed and cuddled and now all she wants is sleep. We've heard nothing more about Haydee but I imagine over the coming weeks she will invade our lives regularly. I want to be furious with her for being so careless. How can she go on television talking about what they did to her when she knows she is responsible for their deaths? How can she stand that level of scrutiny? But part of me admires her; her willingness to be seen, to have her suffering recognised, even if it means facing what she's done.

But no, Haydee is many things but she is not a martyr. If she thought there was any chance that going public with her abuse would implicate her in the murders, she'd never do it.

I know that for certain because Haydee is like me; she is a survivor.

As I pull the door closed on Issy's bedroom, I tell myself and Charlie that everything will be fine. We can survive this.

We have to.

Those men have ruined enough of my life; they are not coming for the rest. I don't know what will happen now, neither of us do, but I think for the first time that, despite the extraordinary circumstances, we are no different to any other parents. No one knows what is coming. No one knows for sure that their family is safe. No one knows if their children will stay with them forever. None of us know the future. This is part of being parents; the uncertainty, the guilt, the constant worry. This is the price we must pay to have everything we always wanted.

I can learn to live with that.

Epilogue

Haydee

She cuts the call and looks at herself in the mirror. The make-up from yesterday's television interview is still heavy on her skin; she hadn't wanted to wipe it off. She'd wanted to keep the feel of the occasion for as long as she could but now it feels clown-like and grotesque.

'Who was that?' David says, slumping next to her on the bed.

They're still in the hotel room paid for by the studio. It's one of the nicest she's stayed in, even considering the nights spent with drunken bankers and businessmen when she was younger and more beautiful. She runs her hands over the soft cotton sheets, already desperate to keep the memory on her skin.

She doesn't think she's beautiful any more. She felt it, yesterday – or at least, something approaching it. But today she's tired. Today she looks at herself in the mirror and sees every inch of her thirty-five years etched into the crinkles of her skin. Every second of her ugly life reflected back at her.

'It was the producer from *The Daily Angels*,' she says to David.

'What did they want? Offering more money, I hope.' He flicks on the TV to a car chase scene that plays out dramatically on the huge flat screen across from the bed.

'No, that's not what they said.' She gets up and opens the mini-bar fridge, looking longingly at the small bottle of champagne. Will the producers cover their bar bill, she wonders? Fuck it, she needs a drink, a proper drink. It might be her last decent one for a while.

After she's downed a glass, the dry bubbles tickling her nose, she tells David the news. 'They've cancelled my next appearance,' she says.

'What?' he snaps, flicking off the TV.

'The show,' she says, shrugging. 'They don't want me on tomorrow any more.'

'They'd better be fucking joking.' His fat red nostrils flare and she inwardly recoils. 'Do they want us to tell the whole world how they're shunning America's favourite "victim"?' He makes air-quotes around the word and sneers. 'Ring them back. Now. You tell them—'

'I'm not telling them anything,' she says. 'There's no point. They have someone else.'

'What?'

She sighs and picks up her phone, googling the name she's just learned. *Sophie O'Connor.* Even her name sounds purer than Haydee's. The first result that comes up is a story that reflects much of what the producer told Haydee just now.

> Brave victim speaks out against Jesse Carter.
> 'Jesse stole my virginity days before my sweet sixteenth.'

Haydee clicks the girl's – now young woman's – photo and feels herself age further. She is young, probably twenty-one or so now, and impossibly innocent-looking. Blue eyes, blonde hair, tiny waist and clear skin. She is

America's perfect girl next door. Haydee scrolls further and eventually sees a mention of herself as the 'first victim to speak out', but already her picture is small in comparison, the words about her assault now just a few lines in the middle of Sophie's account of her own ordeal. Haydee hands the phone to David and watches him read, his cheeks growing redder as he takes in the words.

She wishes he weren't here. She's been wishing that a lot lately. When they met two years ago, she thought she'd never tire of his musty wood-smoke smell and funny British accent. But now it sets her teeth on edge.

They'd met in Vegas – isn't that where all the great love stories start? He was on a 'lads' weekend' he told her, though she never met any of the other 'lads'. She thought he was rich; he'd just had a big win and treated her like a queen that first weekend, lavishing her with expensive dinners, dancing all night, and sleeping in a huge king-size bed in his hotel suite during the day. She thought she loved him; so much so that when he asked her to come back to London with him that same weekend, she packed up her meagre possessions and went without question. There was nothing keeping her in Vegas. She'd been there for a year or so picking up bits of work here and there – none of them requiring ID. That was the problem with living off Owen's money; it took everything else away. How can you make a life for yourself when you don't even have a real name? David offered her a way out; the chance of a real life. Finally.

But London wasn't what she imagined. David, or 'Dave' as his friends back home called him (she can't bring herself to), wasn't some big-time banker as she'd been led to believe but worked in the call centre for a high street bank and had a serious gambling addiction. The night she met him was the last time she's ever seen him win.

'What the fuck are we going to do, then?' he says to her now, grabbing the bottle of champagne from the side and swigging it from the neck. The bubbles escape from the rim, sticking the black hairs on the back of his hand to his freckled skin.

She shrugs again, too tired to worry about this now; too resigned to convince him to feel the same. 'There's nothing we can do,' she says. 'It's over. It was good while it lasted and now it's over.'

It had been good – despite how they'd got here. For the last few weeks they'd lived the life she'd dreamed of. The amount people would pay for her 'story' was ridiculous to her still, and sitting in studios being dolled up and asked to cry on cue suited her perfectly. She should have been an actress, she realises now. This is the life she was meant to have. But she'd had too many disappointments to contend with in her life to let this one cut her deeply. Nothing lasts forever, not for people like her. There's always a younger, prettier girl in the wings waiting to come out. Today, that girl is Sophie. Sophie is what a victim should look like. Haydee is not. She's always known this.

But David can't let it go so easily. 'No,' he says, slamming the bottle on the table, letting the last bubbles escape again and pour down the side, staining the plush cream carpet. 'We didn't come this far to have some stupid little tart take everything from us. We didn't—'

'*We* didn't do shit!' she cries. '*I* did everything! So I say when it's over.'

He's on her then like a flash, holding her by the throat up against the wall. She sees the anger in his eyes, the same anger she saw in Jesse's the night she killed him; the same she saw in Owen's before he took his last breath.

She'd never wanted to kill Jesse. She never thought she was capable of it. Jesse was an accident.

When David found out about her deal with Owen, he got greedy and made her ask for more. But the gamble didn't pay off and Owen cut her off completely – all too aware of her desperation. But David couldn't let it go. He told her to go to Jesse; he had more to lose than Owen. And of course she did. Like a good little lapdog, she contacted Jesse and he agreed to meet her and give her enough money to start over again in return for her continued silence. She thought maybe he felt sorry for her. She felt sorry for him sometimes; he thought he'd killed her, after all. They were both victims of Owen's, in a way.

But he didn't feel sorry for her. From what she could tell, Jesse Carter barely felt anything at all.

He laughed at her. When she asked him for the money he'd promised, he laughed. *You think I'm going to give a single dollar to a slut like you? Go on, tell the world 'your story'. See if anyone believes an old junkie bitch.* She saw red. She didn't mean to kill him. But she's not sorry that she did.

With Owen, it was different. He gave her no choice. It was kill or be killed – she knew that from the moment he bowled through her door, that wicked wolf-like sneer on his face – and she wasn't going to wait for him to strike before she did. Someone might say that's not really self-defence, but what do they know? If she's learned anything over the years, it's that you can't wait for a man to show his true colours; you have to act first. It's the only way to survive.

Charlie arriving and covering up for her had been a total fluke. When she heard a man bashing on the door moments after she'd delivered the fatal blow to Owen's head with the iron fire rod, she panicked. But then she realised she could play the victim; she'd have to. That Charlie was the type of man who wanted to believe in the innocence of women was a stroke of the sort of luck that Haydee thought was reserved for other people. But it worked. For once, the universe brought her exactly what she needed.

Once Owen and Jesse were both gone and it seemed that the police didn't suspect them at all (or, more likely, had given up the pretence of caring about a dead celeb when he turned out to be a total scumbag) David came up with the new plan. They flew back to the States and contacted every media outlet they could find over the coming months. The media lapped it up, of course they did. She sold her story first on an exclusive basis to one of the more right-wing news stations, allowing them to broadcast it on the one-year anniversary of his death for maximum impact. They paid her well, extremely well. She had evidence, after all: she had stolen Owen's phone containing the video. Haydee could be presented as a helpless victim, forced into a life of crime and prostitution after Jesse Carter and Owen Peters took away her humanity.

But Haydee is still human. She's not just a victim; a body that was once used and discarded. That's what no one seems to understand. It's what she's let herself forget for too long.

David doesn't know she sent the video to Hannah, or the note telling her she was safe. She finds it hard to believe their lives have remained connected in the way they have.

347

The day she went looking for help to leave David, she hadn't meant to turn up at Hannah's office. She had no idea Hannah even worked there until Charlie told her. She'd simply googled 'domestic abuse help' the morning after David had drunkenly smacked her in the face a little too hard when she said she wanted to go back to the US and get away from him and Jesse's death. It's the only time she's ever considered looking for help but when she got there she felt dirty, exposed, not the right type of victim and the way the women in the office looked at her made her sure she'd never seek help like that again.

How funny, she realised after, that she could have come face to face with Hannah that day. Maybe Owen would still be alive if she had. Instead, the first time she saw the woman again was after Owen was lying dead on the floor and Haydee was hidden outside the cottage listening after David went to dispose of the car. Haydee's anger grew as she heard Hannah say she believed she'd killed her. How Jesse and Owen had spun it like that. Haydee hasn't stopped thinking about her since. She'd been so jealous of Hannah back then; the perfect, talented Brit who could afford that stupid expensive school with Jesse. Haydee and Owen were the outsiders, the token poor kids that tagged along. Hannah was everything Haydee could never be and she'd carried that resentment with her over the years; the idea that Hannah had carried on her life unscathed by Jesse and Owen. But hearing her with her husband, Haydee realised that Hannah had in some ways been as trapped by those men as she had. Haydee wanted to set her free. She wanted to do a good thing for someone, for once.

'It's not fucking fair,' David says now, letting his grip on her neck loosen as she falls to the floor. 'You deserve to get something for what they did to you.' His little piggy eyes narrow at her, waiting for her to join him in the righteous indignation but this time, she finds she can't. He paces the room, hands scratching at his balding head. He snaps around suddenly. 'What about that bloke?'

Once the air is back in her lungs she rubs her throat and in a scratchy voice manages to ask, 'What bloke?'

'The one that… you know.' David mimes shovelling and Haydee frowns. How is she with this man who can let himself profit from a murder but can't bring himself to say the words? 'He must have some money.'

Haydee takes a step back.

'We should write to him,' David says, warming to the idea, his little pig eyes lighting up at the prospect of another gamble. Another hit. Another big win. 'Tell him we've got evidence of him… you know.' He mimics shovelling again. 'He'll pay us off.'

Haydee nods, slowly, her hands still at her bruised neck.

It would work.

She knows it would.

Though she only met Charlie for a few minutes, she could tell just how far he was willing to go to keep Hannah safe. He buried a body for her, for Christ's sake. How easy it would be to blackmail him; she could be set for life once again. He probably deserves it, she thinks. Somewhere in his life he probably got a bit too handsy with a girl, he probably broke someone's heart, raised his hand to a lover when she wouldn't do what he wanted. They all have. Haven't they?

But she thinks of Charlie's face again, of the words she heard him exchange with Hannah while Haydee hid outside, listening, and finds she doesn't want to believe he is like the others.

'Come on,' David nudges her. 'Pack your shit up. We need to go somewhere to send an email to him. I saw an internet café down the street.' He starts grabbing their things from around the room and shoving them into the case. She watches as he grabs the beautiful white and yellow dress she was given to wear on her last television appearance, the one that made her feel like an innocent virgin, and balls it in his fat fists, the grease from the potato chips he ate earlier marking the delicate silk fabric.

Something in her snaps then.

This man will not stop taking from her.

None of them ever do.

She knew that the night she killed Jesse, reconfirmed it when she watched Owen die. These men never stop, unless you stop them.

She eyes the anti-depressants her doctor prescribed her when she saw him last, complaining of an inability to sleep. It wouldn't take many; a few crushed into the expensive champagne he loves so much and that would be it. There would be one less violent man in the world and she would be free. Surely she deserves that, after everything?

'Sure, babe, whatever you want,' she tells him, slipping the pill-pack into her dressing gown pocket. 'But first, let's have one last drink.'

A letter from Sophie

Dear reader,

Thank you so much for picking up and reading *If They Knew*. This is my third book but the one that I've put the most of myself into. Like Hannah, I once dreamed of becoming a musician; I briefly went to an elite liberal arts college in New York; I now live in the Cotswolds and, sadly, the last few years of my life have been consumed with trying and failing to have children. Anyone who has been through infertility and loss will understand the feelings of guilt and shame that come with it. The question you ask repeatedly is: 'What did I do to deserve this?' That question plagues you deep into the night when another friend texts, 'We have some baby news!' and you have to pretend that their joy doesn't rip something deep inside you. It's there when you see a gaggle of mothers pushing prams around the park, laughing with lattes in hand as you walk alone. It's the cruel jibe that laughs when the line on the pregnancy test never turns positive, or does then disappears so quickly days or weeks later that you start to wonder if it ever happened at all. When those moments turn into weeks and weeks turn into months then years, you really do start to believe that you're being punished.

That feeling is what sparked the beginnings of *If They Knew*. Then, when my husband and I were filling in IVF paperwork, I came to a question: *Have you ever been charged with a crime?* Luckily, I have not (nor have I committed one – well other than the occasional fake ID and underage drinking, of course). But I thought – what if I had? And what if I'd never been caught for it? That kind of guilt would eat you up at the best of times but when your body is betraying you so badly I can see how easy it would be to spiral into chaos. Everyone I know who has been in Charlie and Hannah's position has admitted to acting in ways that are so far out of character they barely recognise themselves. This was something I wanted to explore – albeit in a rather unique set of circumstances – how far would someone go in their quest to be parents?

If you're going through something similar (not the dead pop star ex-boyfriend up the road, that's a whole other problem) I will tell you this with certainty: you did not do anything to deserve this. The world doesn't work like that. If it did, it would not be so easy for men like Jesse and Owen to live without repercussion; to damage lives and move on as if women are mere footnotes in their story to be deleted and discarded without care. It is deeply satisfying to write books where these men do not always win.

Whether this story resonated with you on a personal level or not, I do hope you have enjoyed it. Books have been my escape and comfort for most of my life and more so than ever in the last few years. If this book provided you with even a moment of temporary relief, then my job is done.

Again, thank you so much for reading. I would love for you to leave a review on Amazon, Kobo, Apple and Goodreads if you enjoyed the book; I read all my reviews and appreciate every single one. If you enjoyed *If They Knew*, you may also enjoy my previous books, *All My Lies*, and *Keep Them Close*. To keep up with my writing life, do connect with me on Twitter @sophielflynn and Instagram @sophieflynnauthor.

Sophie x

Acknowledgments

Wow. My third book! It was only last year that I wrote the acknowledgments for *All My Lies*, my debut, so I can't quite believe I'm now doing this for a third time. It is a true honour but it does get trickier to know who to thank and in what order…

I will start with my fantastic publishing team at Hera. My editor, Keshini, your thoughtful and intelligent edits make me a better writer and I'm so glad to have the chance to work with you (and that you always push me for just one more twist!). My copyeditor, Jennie, thank goodness for your eagle eyes spotting all my mistakes. My proof reader, Jennifer, for forever correcting my inability to use commas correctly. Rose Cooper, who designed this fantastic cover. Thanhmai and the sales team at Canelo for getting my books into shops and the hands of readers. Elinor for your excellent publicity work making sure people know my books exist. And the rest of the team at Hera – thank you all. You are the best.

My agent, Kate Nash, and her wonderful team – namely Amy Gilroy and Bethany Lucas – for going above and beyond. The bookshops of the Cotswolds are all the better for your efforts, of course! Thank you.

My author friends – you know who you are, you've been in every book so far. You are wonderful and I'd never get through this without you.

Janelle, Pearl, Verity – you've been there from the start and will never not be in my acknowledgments.

Everyone needs a work friend like Kate and I'm so lucky to have many friends beside me at Jericho Writers. A few extra special mentions: Rachael, you are actually my life saviour and I would be lost without you, thank you for everything. Anna – for blowing up balloons, hosting events where you big me up, and making me laugh every day even when I want to cry (especially then). If you have to have a day job while writing, have one at Jericho Writers so you can meet these brilliant people.

A huge thanks to my former colleague in cyber security, Russ, who never asked 'why' when I DM'd him one night asking how to hack into other people's phones and CCTV and instead gave me detailed instructions (which, in hindsight, perhaps was a little worrying, Russ). Any mistakes on that process, however, are mine alone!

Thank you to the kind people online who responded to my call for help researching the adoption process. Again, any mistakes in the process are mine.

Thank you to the fantastic book bloggers who have been such a massive support online. Particularly Vik (@littlemissbooklover87) who never fails to review my books with such kindness and excitement that it makes all the long hours writing feel worthwhile.

My wonderful family. My sister, Rosie, who is always my first reader. Mum, I hope this one didn't make you cry too much and I'm sorry if it did. Dad – my biggest promoter – you've been officially promoted to Regional Sales Rep. Nicky, who'll always give me an honest review – you'll be glad to see I left your life alone and stole from my own this time!

To my utterly gorgeous-in-every-way nieces, Hibiki and Hikali. You made it incredibly difficult to work on this book in Spain because all I wanted to do was play with you – but thank you for your eagle eyed proofreading over my shoulder. But no, Hibiki, you are still not old enough to read this book – even if you are 'ten with a reading age of sixteen'! To the rest of my Dales family, you're wonderful in every way. Thank you. Jill, I hope that you aren't crying right now. Or you, Dan.

Tom, this is – in many ways – our story and I'm very grateful for you letting me share it with the world. We'll bring home our own Issy one day, I promise.

And finally, to you, dear reader. I will be forever grateful and amazed that you've picked up this book! Thank you, thank you, thank you. Please keep reading my books and telling anyone who will listen about them; I really want to do this forever.